ONE BAL . JRN

DAVID J. GATWARD

WEIRDSTONE PUBLISHING

One Bad Turn
By
David J. Gatward

Grimm: nickname for a dour and forbidding individual, from Old High German grim [meaning] 'stern', 'severe'. From a Germanic personal name, Grima, [meaning] 'mask'.
(*www.ancestory.co.uk*)

CHAPTER ONE

SHE ARRIVED HOME TO AN EMPTY HOUSE, CARRYING A broken heart, and bruises inside and out. The house felt like she had walked into a church looking for sanctuary. This was her place of rest, of healing, and she needed it again. Her bank account was full, though. Because she'd worked damned hard to make sure she'd never be broke again. As for her heart and the bruises? Well, that just served her right, didn't it? She'd trusted someone, let down the drawbridge in that impenetrable wall she'd built around herself, and the man she'd let in, once he'd seen the truth of what was inside, had ransacked the place.

A couple of years ago, she'd done everything she could to rewrite her story and escape a living hell. She'd left behind very little but also so much, and would never go back. Where she was now, it was a new beginning and it still could be. He just wasn't going to be a part of it. She still had her new home, new life, new name. She was still safe. She'd made sure of that.

The only thing which hadn't changed was her profession. Before that moment, when against all the advice she'd been given, she had disappeared into the night, her existence had been only pain. She'd been used. Someone's abused pet, always coming back for more no matter how bad it was, in the hope of some scraps thrown to the floor. Now, though? Now she was in control. Strong, too, and she wasn't going to let a little knock set her back. This was her life and she was doing it all for herself.

She understood that learning the truth behind who she was, what she did and had done to survive, was going to be difficult to take in and to accept. But she'd trusted him enough to risk it all and he had thrown it back in her face. And for what? Lying back and thinking of England? Not always, no. Sometimes she thought about other things too, such as what was going on in her favourite television soap opera, what she was going to have for dinner, or the fact that her life now was worlds apart from what it had been. Never once though, over the course of her time with clients, had she ever thought of Queen and country.

The past few days had been a romantic break, something she had never done in her life before. And maybe that had weakened her. There had been some shopping, a lovely hotel, delicious food, romance, even a walk in a park, hand-in-hand. But then, when she'd told him, when she had finally opened up fully like he'd begged her to, it had all gone so wrong. She had seen a side of him then that she'd never suspected. One she never wanted to see again, and neither would she, that was for sure.

For a moment she just stood there drinking in the house, letting it heal her with its cool darkness. It was the cutest and cosiest little cottage she had ever set her eyes on. A dream house. And it was hers. It had only taken a year to save up enough for the deposit.

With its slate roof, walls thick enough to stop a volley of cannonballs, wood-burning stove, and tiny cottage garden, she had snapped the place up a year ago before she'd even viewed it in person. The tiny one-bedroom place she'd had before had been a great halfway house. She'd been able to put up with the damp, the dripping taps, the odd smell, because it had enabled her to set herself up, establish the 'new her', save enough to end up here. And she was daring to think that life, at last, was good after all.

Dropping her leather suitcase in the hall and kicking it under the stairs, her anger and sadness sending it further than she'd meant to, she slipped off her shoes and headed straight upstairs to the bathroom, taking with her a couple of bags of the shopping she'd brought back from the break.

The bathroom, like the rest of the house, was small, but she'd certainly made good use of the space. The roll top bath was divine, but the showerhead hanging above it was the clincher. So large was it that when the water was on, standing under it was akin to stepping outside into a rainstorm. Best of all, there wasn't even a hideous shower curtain to deal with because she'd made sure that the bathroom was also a wet room. Any water that splashed over the side simply drained off down a flower-shaped brass outlet in the centre of the floor.

Stripped off, clothes dumped on the floor for the moment, she turned on the shower and placed a bottle of some rather expensive and exclusive shower gel within reach. The hot water hit the cool air of the house and steamed immediately. She breathed it in, willing the moisture to clean her from the inside out. Then she stepped up over the edge of the bath and disappeared into blissful oblivion, easing her fingers through her long, black hair as the water rained down.

Standing there as the almost-too-hot shower drummed into her flesh, she did her best to wash away what had happened. The shock of how their argument had turned physical made her flinch as she gently washed over the bruises. A cry caught in her throat but she refused to let it take her. She'd been through too much to give what had happened control. Never again.

She had expected some form of response, yes, because that was understandable. But she'd hoped her explanation, her history, it would all have eased it a little. And it wasn't like she was going to do it forever, was it? That had never been the plan. The work helped her get out from where she had been before, enabled her to put some money away, and then she'd move on. And soon. But he obviously hadn't wanted to wait, instead, lashing out at her with words and a slap that had stung all the way through to her still-broken soul.

Personally, she wasn't disgusted by why she did. Quite the opposite really; she'd chosen the work during a period of her life when things were desperate, and she needed some extra money. The big difference now, though, was the clientele. Years ago, it had been backseat punters and alleyway humpers, anything for some money just to get by, to buy food, to have enough for the next fix. Life had been risky, dangerous, and she'd lost count of the times she'd ended evenings on the job bruised and bleeding. Then she'd been rescued, except it had all been a lie, and somehow life had become even worse.

It was one thing to pick and choose what you wanted from the trash, and another thing entirely to be force-fed the worst just one person would ever provide. The abuse, the beatings, the prisoner-like life had taken its toll, and in the end, pushed her far enough to turn on her rescuer-turned-personal-twenty-four-hour-nightmare. Did she worry about it? Not anymore, because there was nothing to worry about. And those times, they were just memories now, locked away in a box she'd never open ever again. Sometimes though, she wondered about the legal side of things, grey as they were, and the social side, too, how it would affect her future.

Her last client, seen a few days before the now-broken romantic break, had been, like most of those she now met with, male, mid-forties, and earning well. And by well, he was a seven-figure man to whom money just wasn't an issue. Which helped in being able to afford her seeing as she wasn't exactly cheap, not anymore. She wouldn't have gone ahead with the arrangement otherwise. He was a businessman, of what exactly she didn't know, but he had given her his name, his telephone number. Something to do with business consultancy. Just a simple website, but enough to go ahead with the meeting. If she knew who the clients were, what they did, a little about their background, there was less chance of things going wrong. Obviously, bad things happened, horror stories did their rounds. But she was careful and, so far, nothing had ever gone wrong.

Lost to a world of hot water, her eyes closed to the pleasure and pain threshold of her senses pushed almost to their limit, the pain of the slap and the other bruises easing, she reached for the shower gel. It wasn't there. Her heart stopped. She opened her eyes, the water blinding her, streaming down her face. Where was it? Where the hell was it? Panicked now, adrenaline dumping into her system, she felt around with her hands to no avail. All she could think was that someone was here, someone was in her house, they'd found her-they'd found her-they'd found her-they'd found her ...

Deep breaths.

She closed her eyes, forced herself to calm, to get her thoughts in order, take control again.

Her vision cleared. She saw the bottle of shower gel standing on the floor.

She laughed, heard the scars of her own shattered nerves splintering a little as she wondered at the odds of the bottle being knocked off only to land on its bottom on the floor and just far enough to be out of sight.

She grabbed the bottle, stood up again, and was soon cocooned in a thick lather that smelled of high Alpine meadows.

Deep breaths once again, calm descending.

Was it her name? she wondered then. Was that what had made him flip? That he'd known her as one thing only to find out it was something else? And he hadn't even believed her when she'd told him her real name, had he? Just called her a liar, yelled at her, screamed.

Showered, she shook herself free of those moments and stepped out, wrapping herself in a luxuriously thick dressing gown the colour of a clear midnight sky resting over the sea. She trotted from the bathroom and across the landing, past the doors to her bedroom and the spare, and back downstairs. Her heart had calmed a little now and she forced the dark thoughts away.

Downstairs she thrust her clothes from the evening into the washing machine then turned to her fridge and heaved on the handle to open the hefty door. Light poured out and with it came the welcoming cool air which promised something delicious. And there it was, a bottle of expensive champagne and a platter of smoked salmon she'd prepared earlier for just this moment. She didn't always eat like this, and a few years ago, she'd never eaten like this in her life. The thrill was still there and she guessed it always would be.

Her phone buzzed. She ignored it. Tonight was her time alone and nothing was going to interrupt her. There was nothing he could say now. She wouldn't let him. She had already moved on because she knew how to survive.

From the kitchen, she walked through to the lounge, jumping between the thick rugs like stepping-stones on the flagstone floor. That it had been a hot day didn't stop her from quickly setting a match to the logs sitting in the stove. She'd pre-laid it before heading out earlier. Then, with the fire alive and dancing behind the glass of the stove door, she rested the champagne and salmon on a coffee table, grabbed the remote control for the television, and dropped herself down into the embrace of her armchair.

Bliss!

A while later, with the salmon gone and the champagne threatening to follow suit, she knew it was probably a good idea to head to bed. She just didn't want to. The shower had certainly added to that, and the champagne had been that one final thing that had made everything perfect. But she was still resisting. So back to the kitchen she went, finishing her champagne on the way, to make herself the kind of snack no one would ever believe that she liked: a peanut butter and raspberry jam sandwich. She had lived on them once: cheap and full of energy and always delicious. And while she was at it, why not wash it down with a little more champagne?

Sandwich made, and now with another freshly opened bottle of chilled champagne in her hand, she couldn't help but dance a little as she slipped back through her cottage and into her lounge. Which was when something crashed into the side of her head with such violence that her legs could do nothing to stop her from slamming into the ground.

What had happened was so immediate and unexpected that she didn't even scream. She just lay on the floor of her lounge, pain stabbing lightning forks through her body. She tried to push herself up from the floor but the angry edge of a shoe's heel in the small of her back pushed her back down.

'Ollie?'

No answer came, just more pressure from the heel as it ground into her and made her cry out.

'You need to get out!' she yelled. 'It's over! You had your chance, you blew it!'

Still nothing.

She saw her phone, grabbed it, hit an emergency number she'd set up in the hope she'd never have to use it. Then a hand snatched it up and killed the call.

The heel in her back lifted and she pushed herself up so that she was sitting on the floor, facing away from her attacker. She rubbed her head, turned around. Her hand came away wet and red. The pain began then, cracking her skull.

She couldn't make out who the figure was now in front of her. She assumed it was Ollie, but she couldn't be sure. And that only made her more worried. Whoever it was, he was standing in shadow, his head hidden in darkness deep inside a hood. Then he moved and hands were around her neck, squeezing tight. The world around her faded, turning black.

When she woke up she was tied to a chair in the kitchen. A blindfold was tight around her eyes.

'Ollie? What are you doing? Whatever it is, you have to stop. This makes no sense!'

A laugh then, cold and crackled, the sound of paper scrunched before it's set on fire.

'What do you want? Is it money? I can give you money. Just let me go and I'll give you whatever you want.'

Silence was her answer, thick with someone else's sweat, the violence and rage leaching from their skin.

She was panicking now. Her heart rate was through the roof, her breaths short and sharp.

'Please ... There must be something we can do. Just talk to me—'

A hand was around her throat before she could finish speaking. Then a bright burning pain seared into her skull and she screamed and screamed, the pain burning deeper.

'My ... my ear ...? You've cut off ... my ear!'

She screamed as the pain reached its crescendo and then kept building. Every synapse in her brain sparked with panic and it burned through her like acid.

She sensed a body lean in close then smelled mint from the gum her attacker was chewing. It was mixed with the stale smell of cigarettes.

'No one's coming to help.'

The voice was gruff, filled with malice. It could've been Ollie's, could've been anyone's. All she could hear now was her own panic, her racing heart, her breathing.

The deafening crack of a gunshot blasted the moment to pieces. More pain slammed into her as her foot exploded. But she couldn't scream, her attacker's hand now clamped hard over her mouth. Terror and hopelessness crashed into each other, shattering. Tears streamed down her face.

The weight of her attacker lifted. She breathed, leaned forward, gagged and spat and vomited.

She grabbed at the very thinnest of last straws.

'There's a box,' she said, sitting up, spit and blood and what she'd only just eaten dribbling from her mouth. 'In the kitchen. Underneath the sink. Money. Cash. Down payment on the rest. Whatever it is, you name it, I'll pay it. Please...'

She heard a zip yanked open then a mean, gloved hand gripped her mouth and forced her lips apart.

She screamed, but the sound was a choked gurgle. Then a powder fell, filling her mouth, her nose, her eyes with a taste and smell and sensation she recognised all too well. And soon, nothing mattered. Nothing mattered at all.

And it never would again.

CHAPTER TWO

The shout was more than enough to wake Matt from his slumber, but the quick, sharp punch to his arm that followed didn't give him any choice in the matter.

Heart thumping, and groggy from a much-needed evening nap on the sofa in front of the fire, Matt stared bleary-eyed at his wife of forever and more.

'What was that for?'

'Your phone,' said Joan, jabbing a finger at the coffee table in front of them.

'What phone?'

Matt then noticed the sharp trill attacking the air like a murderous drill.

'Oh, right, that phone...'

'I'd have answered it myself, but it's not exactly easy to lean forward in my current state, now, is it?'

Matt reached out to silence the bane of his life, his gaze resting just long enough on Joan for his heart to sing. Even with the annoyance in her eyes and the frown on her face, he found her a joy to behold. That she was now barely days away from giving birth to their first child just made her even more beautiful, not that she believed him when he said so. Yes, he was a soppy old goat, but he didn't care. When you were the luckiest man alive, soppy wasn't the half of it.

'Are you going to answer it, then, or just stare at me like the living dead?'

Matt grabbed his phone, but as he went to answer, the caller got in first.

'It's me!'

The voice belonged to Police Constable Jadyn Okri, an officer who made up for his lack of experience with the energy and enthusiasm of an adrenaline junkie throwing themselves from a plane.

'Officer Okri?'

'You said I should call if—'

'Didn't think you were on duty,' Matt said, concerned.

After the rough time Jadyn had a while back, Matt and the rest of the team were still keeping an eye on the young police constable, just in case. After several weeks off, and regular counselling sessions, which were still ongoing, Jadyn had only returned to work a week ago. He seemed to be doing okay, though Matt was fairly sure that the constable's sharing of his therapy sessions with the whole team, almost word-for-word, wasn't entirely necessary.

'I swapped with Jen,' Jadyn replied. 'She was feeling a bit rough today, remember?'

Matt did, but still ...

'Anyway, I had a few things to do,' Jadyn continued, 'so being in the office made sense. You know how it is.'

'I do,' Matt said, impressed with Jadyn's care for his fellow officer, but concerned nonetheless. 'You're supposed

to run any changes in your duties by me, Harry, or Gordy.
You know that.'

'I do, yes,' Jadyn said. 'I thought I had. Sorry. I won't do it
again.'

The line was silent for a moment.

'Okay, well, as you've called me, you may as well get to
the point of why,' Matt said, sitting up. As he did so, he
noticed that the light from the window was now the gloopy
grey of the evening being chased by the thick darkness of
night.

'You said I should call you if anything important
happened,' Jadyn said. 'So that's what I'm doing, what with
the boss being away and all. And I thought it best to give you
a call before I headed over. To the important thing that's
happened, I mean.'

'What important thing? Heading over where? Here?'

Matt stared out through the window, half expecting to
see Jadyn pulling up outside.

'I mean, it's probably just a nosy neighbour thing,' Jadyn
said, clearly ignoring Matt's questions, 'but thought I'd best
let you know, just in case. I mean, that's what you asked me
to do, isn't it, to let you know? If something was happening, I
mean. Or had happened. I'm not just calling you because
nothing's happened. That would be a bit weird, wouldn't it?'

Much like this phone call, Matt thought.

'Just in case of what?' he asked. 'What are you talking
about? What's happened? What nosy neighbour? And you're
rambling, Constable, so just get to the point so I can get back
to my evening.'

Matt saw a look of stark worry and confusion spark in
Joan's eyes on hearing not just his words but the tone of his
voice.

'Mr Whaley, the one who just called it in,' Jadyn said.

'Called what in?'

'The milk bottles.'

Matt wanted to scream.

'Milk bottles? What milk bottles, Jadyn? Get to the point, lad, come on!'

Working hard to resist the urge to reach down the phone line and throttle Jadyn, Matt glanced over at Joan. Shaking his head, he mouthed, 'Sorry about this, Love.'

Joan just smiled back at him and sunk back deeper into the sofa, her hands resting on her large belly.

'The milk bottles that he's seen piling up outside his neighbour's house,' Jadyn explained. 'Well, I say neighbour, but he's said the house isn't exactly next door, just down the lane a bit, I think. But it's technically next door because it's the next house down, if that makes sense? And he's not seen her, for like a week, or a few days anyway, I'm not really sure. And those milk bottles had him thinking, about where she was, so he called it in. So, that's where I'm heading once I've finished telling you where it is I'm going and why I'm going there.'

'Stop!' Matt said, raising his voice as he heaved himself to his feet and rubbed the weariness from his tired eyes. 'Just stop rambling, Jadyn, please, and start from the beginning. Maybe then this'll make some sense.'

'What, you mean start from the beginning, like once upon a time?'

'No, I do not mean like once upon a bloody time at all!' Matt said.

'I'm joking,' said Jadyn, and Matt heard a laugh just creasing the edges of his words.

Taking a slow, deep breath, Matt asked, 'So, what is it

that's actually happened, then? What and where are you going to be on your way over to? Do we know anything about this neighbour—Mr Whaley, you said, right?'

'He lives over Reeth way,' Jadyn said. 'In Swaledale.'

'I know where Reeth is,' Matt said. 'Get to the point, lad, if there is one.'

'Well, Mr Whaley called in all worried about his neighbour,' Jadyn said.

'And that's why you've called me, yes, I've got that bit.'

'Exactly,' said Jadyn. 'Because of the milk bottles.'

Matt rubbed his eyes once again, the weariness not so much refusing to shift as nailing itself firmly to the floor. But he knew what Jadyn was getting at.

'A concerned neighbour then,' Matt said. 'I think I understand now.'

'He said that he's knocked on the door a few times, banged on the window as well, but nothing,' said Jadyn. 'It's like she's vanished.'

'I doubt very much that she has,' said Matt.

'Would be weird if she had though, wouldn't it? You know, like one minute she's there, living her life, saying hello to Mr Whaley in the morning, fetching her milk from the door. And the next, *poof!*'

In his mind's eye, Matt could see Jadyn miming a mini explosion with his hands.

'Well, thanks for letting me know all of that,' he said. 'But remind me tomorrow to have a little chat with you about what I mean by important.'

'This isn't important, then?'

'Not really, no!' Matt said. Then he softened his tone and added, 'Well, no, that's not what I meant. You've done as instructed, so well done on that. But right now, I think you're on top of it, aren't you? More than capable of handling it I should say. So, you don't need me. Not yet, anyway.'

'I just thought—'

'You did, and that's fair enough,' said Matt, cutting Jadyn off. 'Like I said, well done. I'm very impressed with you following what I said to the very letter. All credit to you on that front. But now, if you don't mind, I'm going to get back to what I was doing and leave the rest of the evening in your very capable hands.'

'Capable hands?' said Jadyn. 'Well, if you're sure about that.'

'I am,' said Matt.

Call over, Matt placed the phone back on the coffee table and slumped back down beside Joan.

'All sorted?'

'Nowt to sort,' Matt said. 'Someone's called in concerned about a neighbour. He's got it all in hand.'

'That was Jadyn, then, yes?' asked Joan. 'How's he doing now after everything?'

Matt heard the change in his wife's tone.

'Why do you ask?'

'Because he's been on the phone to you a few times since he came back to work,' Joan said. 'And he wasn't like this before what happened to him, was he?'

'No, you're right, he wasn't,' Matt said. 'And he's not supposed to be on duty tonight either. Apparently he swapped with Jen because she wasn't feeling too great. Which is commendable, but also a bit of a worry.'

'You think he's afraid to go home?'

'Perhaps,' Matt said. 'But what happened to him, well, it wasn't at home, was it?'

'Doubt that really matters under the circumstances. It's

not that simple. What he experienced, it's going to be with him for a good while, that's for sure. And it'll rear its ugly head in ways no one can expect, least of all Jadyn.'

Matt leaned back into the sofa, sinking deep.

'You sound just like Harry.'

'He knows what he's talking about, then,' Joan said.

'When it comes to PTSD, yes, better than most.'

Matt put his arm around his wife, hugging her close.

'How are you feeling?'

'Enormous,' Joan said, drumming her fingers on her belly.

'Not long to go now, though.'

'It's taken long enough for us to get here, so a bit longer won't make any difference, will it?' said Joan. Then she winked and added, 'Could come any time, though. Nervous?'

'Of course not!'

'Liar!'

Joan laughed and poked Matt in the arm.

'Okay, so I am, but I'm excited as well,' Matt said. 'We're going to be parents, Joan! You and me, a proper mum and dad! Can you believe it?'

'We are that and yes I can.' Joan leaned her head on her husband's shoulder. 'Never doubted it for a moment.'

It didn't take long for either of them to fall asleep, cuddled up together and blanketed in their mutual affection, helped on by the warmth of the fire burning softly in the grate.

CHAPTER THREE

WITH THE CALL TO DETECTIVE SERGEANT DINSDALE finished, Jadyn wasted no time in shutting up shop at the Hawes office, jogging down the short lane to the marketplace, to then hop into his vehicle. He was happy to admit to himself that he was rather excited to be heading over to Reeth, on his own, to investigate something.

So what, if it was just someone worrying too much about the whereabouts of their neighbour? That didn't matter. A call had come in, he'd checked in with the DS as instructed, and he was now on his way over to check it out in one of the team's incident response vehicles. Brilliant! Also, there was the slight matter of his head, or to be more specific, what was in it.

After what had happened to him, the assault, even though it was only a couple of months ago, his physical recovery had been swift. Jadyn put that down to a healthy diet punctuated by gorging on pizza. He still had bruises, though most had faded to nothing now, but the marks on his neck from the rope, they would take a while. And that was the problem, right there. Not the damage on the outside, which had been caused by the attack—the punches and kicks and the rope—but the haunting echo of it all deep inside. The flashbacks. The memories that would hammer into him at any moment of the day or night, gut-punching him out of the blue. Those were the killers. And sometimes he just needed a distraction to take his mind off it all, to break the repetition of those memories constantly playing out behind everything.

Jadyn sucked in a deep breath through his nose, breathed out, shook his head in some futile act to dislodge those awful memories, if only for a while, then turned the ignition key and headed off to Swaledale.

With a choice of two routes, Jadyn could either head straight over the Buttertubs Pass at this end of the dale and down through Swaledale, or take a drive along the main road to Bainbridge, through to Askrigg, and then up over the top and down into Reeth. He decided to head to Bainbridge, not because it shaved a whole five minutes off the journey, but more because he found the Buttertubs Pass at night to be just a little bit sketchy.

He knew it was safe—in winter it could be downright treacherous—but at the same time, racing along the pass, the side of the road just disappearing into a yawning chasm of darkness and rock, set his nerves on edge. And he could do without that right now for sure. He wasn't sleeping brilliantly as it was. Forcing himself to have nightmares about plunging off a precipice to die in a violent and probably very explosive car crash wasn't going to help any. The night-time terrors he was having to deal with, which clawed at him in the dark, waking him in a sweat, his voice screaming to a strangled choke, were more than enough to be going on with, that was for sure.

Sweeping through the valley, Jadyn was struck by just how lucky he was to be doing this job in a place such as Wensleydale. He'd grown up in Bradford, but he didn't miss it. The people perhaps, yes, old friends, and his family very much so, but Bradford itself not a bit of it. This had surprised him somewhat because, like everyone he'd grown up with, he'd enjoyed the city life. That place, it was home.

Moving away, though, well that had changed him. He'd tried to explain this to his friends, those for whom Wensleydale was a backwater, so rural and remote that to live and work there was tantamount to social-life suicide. To them, it was the English version of Redneck Central, everyone rolling around in Land Rovers, waving shotguns in the air, and drinking warm beer. Which, to some degree, was fairly accurate, Jadyn thought to himself with a smile.

'So, what are the clubs like? The bars? What do you do at the weekend?'

It was a question Jadyn had batted away too many times and his answers had become more and more ludicrous over time. 'Go down the pub for a couple of beers and a game of darts' or 'Head out for a walk' had very soon turned into 'Wear flat caps', 'eat cheese', and 'wrestle sheep.'

The road out of the back of Askrigg was steep, a thin line of grey thread left loose to hang down the side of the great moor-blanketed mounds of the fells. The land around him was black against a dark sky lit by a bright moon and a splattering of stars. Glancing out of his window, Jadyn thought how the moors seemed impenetrable, as though to venture into them now would be to lose himself to the wildness of it and never return. This only made him even happier that he hadn't taken the Buttertubs Pass, because staring down into the seemingly bottomless chasm that yawned along its side was enough to give anyone vertigo.

Breaching the top of the hill, Jadyn headed down now into Swaledale. He laughed, wondering what his friends back in Bradford would think of the place if they thought Wensleydale was remote. This was a valley that still breathed with an old breath, the scars of its mining history still clear to see if you fancied a walk. The valley bottom, eerily clear under the milky moon, was a cross-stitch pattern of walls and meadows. The houses of the villages here huddled together to fend off the storms which so often danced along its slopes.

When Jadyn eventually drove into Reeth it was as though he was rolling onto a film set. That villages like this existed at all was a wonder to him, with its large green surrounded by the dwellings and lives of the folk who lived and worked in the place.

After a few wrong turns, which in a place the size of Reeth was impressive to achieve, Jadyn at last came to the house of Mr Whaley. It was a detached property, though not large. At its front was a thin area of gravel kept away from the pavement by iron railings. Down the side of the house he saw the rear end of a small car.

Parking up, Jadyn climbed out of his vehicle and approached the door. He raised a hand to knock and the door opened before he had a chance to do so, blinding Jadyn for a moment with the light from inside.

'How do,' said the silhouette in the doorway, a warm, yellow light streaming out from the house behind him.

'Police Constable Okri,' Jadyn said.

'Are you, now?'

'Yes. Yes, I am,' Jadyn said, not really sure how else to reply.

'And you're here on my doorstep, aren't you?'

'Mr Whaley?' Jadyn said. 'You called about your neighbour?'

'I did that,' Mr Whaley replied. 'And I don't need you to be reminding me about it, either. I know what's going on. Still got all my marbles, I have, like.'

The silhouette lifted a hand and tapped the side of its head.

'Perhaps I could come in for a moment?' Jadyn asked.

'And why would you be wanting to do that, now?'

Jadyn was beginning to wonder if the journey had been a wasted one, though any journey in the Dales was never truly wasted, not with roads and views like he'd enjoyed on the way over.

'It's about your neighbour, like I said,' Jadyn attempted to explain. 'I'm here in response to your report about where they are or, to be more specific, where they aren't. I understand that you're concerned as to their whereabouts.'

'I am that,' the silhouette said. 'Best you come in so that we can have a talk about it, don't you think? Better than standing out here getting all brass monkey about it.'

The silhouette stepped back into the light and at last, Jadyn was able to see Mr Whaley clearly. At a guess, Jadyn had him at getting on for at least eighty years old and he was wearing not only a fine set of fading striped pyjamas but also a green dressing gown, a woolly hat, and Wellington boots. His accent was so thick Jadyn wondered if the man had even ventured beyond Swaledale itself. It was a voice from the past, preserved in documentaries, old movies, and period dramas.

'Head on through to that door at the end of the hall,' Mr Whaley said. 'That's the kitchen. I'll put a brew on if you fancy.'

Jadyn stepped into the house. He was immediately hit by the warmth of the place and the smell of an open fire. This struck him as a little odd. Summer was here and although the Dales were rarely swelteringly hot, the past few days had certainly been warm. Then, when he came into the kitchen, he found the explanation.

'You don't have a cooker,' Jadyn said, glancing around.

The kitchen had the usual suspects of wall cupboards and cabinets, a small dining room table and chairs, a sink. But, to Jadyn's disbelief, he didn't see a cooker anywhere. The walls were bare except for the occasional picture of a Dales view. On a sideboard against the wall, he saw a framed black and white photo of a man and a woman.

'Are you blind, lad?' Mr Whaley said. 'Over there in the wall, you see it? Of course you see it. It's hard to miss. I can see it and I'm eighty-six!'

Jadyn stared. What he saw was not an oven. Not by any stretch of the imagination. He'd seen Agas and such like in houses across the Dales, but this certainly looked more primitive. It was a cast-iron stove, the kind of thing he'd only ever seen in history books and museums. Flames were visible through a glass window set in the front. To one side of this was a door, which he assumed to be the oven. And on the top rested two large chrome lids. A high-backed wooden chair sat to each side of the stove, worn shiny and smooth with years of use.

'Wife died a few years back,' Mr Whaley said, the statement seemingly connected to nothing they'd spoken about.

'Oh, I'm sorry,' he replied, glancing over at the photograph.

'Only me left, you see,' Mr Whaley continued, filling up a kettle. He then lifted one of the chrome lids on top of the stove and set the kettle down on a hotplate.

'And you actually cook on it?' Jadyn asked.

'On it and in it,' Mr Whaley said, and opened the small iron door to the side of the fire with a flourish. 'See? Perfect for a good bit of meat is that. It's not just a cooker now, neither. It's a lovely warm place to sit down and just be. And this is where I live now, really. Don't need the rest of the house unless I have visitors. And I don't have visitors. Nice and cosy, isn't it? Tea?'

Jadyn gave a nod of agreement and was soon holding a mug of tea and staring at a plate of cake.

'Sit yourself down and grab yourself a slice,' Mr Whaley said. 'You're making me feel tired just staring at you.'

Jadyn made to sit at the small dining table.

'No, not there, get yourself down here by the fire with me, lad. Much more comfortable.'

Jadyn parked himself in one of the chairs by the stove. He took some of the cake, had a nibble. It was good, probably from Cockett's, he thought.

'Right, then,' Mr Whaley said, staring at Jadyn over the top of his mug. 'You're not local, are you?'

Jadyn sighed.

'Why do you say that?'

'Your voice,' Mr Whaley said. 'Always been good with accents, you see. Can't place that one, though.'

'Bradford.'

'Never been.'

'You should, it's not a bad place.'

'Don't really need to travel anywhere when I live here, do I? Now, how's about you remind me why it is you're here again.'

'Your call about your neighbour,' Jadyn said.

'Oh, yes, of course. Melissa! Lovely lass, she is. Always happy to have a chat with an old goat like me, and that doesn't half cheer you up, that's for sure.'

'Do you know her full name?' Jadyn asked.

'You know, I don't,' Mr Whaley said. 'Always known her as Melissa. She tried to get me to call her Mel, but that just didn't sit right. Too familiar, if you know what I mean. Yes, too familiar.'

'Do you have her phone number?'

'And why would I be needing that, now? She's just down the road a way, isn't she? If I needed something, not that I can imagine what that would be, I'd just pop round. No point giving her a call. Anyway, I don't have a phone.'

Jadyn wasn't sure he'd heard right.

'But you called us,' said Jadyn. 'About your neighbour. About Melissa. That's why I'm here.'

'I called from the telephone box in the village,' Mr Whaley said. 'Never been one for the phone. We had one when the wife was still here, but no bugger ever called to speak to me and I never had the urge to call anyone myself. So, when she, well, you know, I had it disconnected. Last thing I needed was folk bothering me. Like my peace and my quiet, I do. And it's not like there's anyone out there who'd be calling me. Not now.'

Jadyn, taking another bite of the cake, took his pen and notepad out and stared at the paper for a moment, digesting what Mr Whaley had just said.

'Do you have a photo?'

'Of Melissa?'

'Yes.'

'Of course I don't!' Mr Whaley's voice was all shock and indignation. 'What kind of pervert do you think I am?'

'I don't think you're any kind of pervert!' Jadyn said, stumbling over his words. 'That's not what I meant at all!'

Mr Whaley was still talking.

'I don't go around taking photos of women, lad!'

'I wasn't implying ...'

'I should bloody well hope not!'

Jadyn took a deep breath to try and compose himself.

'Don't have a camera anyway, so I couldn't, even if I wanted to. Which I don't. So I didn't. Or haven't.'

'Can you give me a description of her?' Jadyn asked, moving on from trying to understand what Mr Whaley had just said.

'She's the most beautiful woman I've ever seen,' Mr Whaley said, face deadly serious. 'Apart from my dead wife, obviously. And I've seen Marilyn Monroe.'

'Blonde, then?'

'Of course she wasn't blonde!'

'But you said Marilyn Monroe ...'

'I know what I said! I can hear myself speak, can't I? Melissa's tall. Long dark hair, expensive clothes, dangerous shoes.'

'Dangerous?'

'God knows how she walked on them, especially across cobbles. Asking for trouble.'

Jadyn decided to move on as Mr Whaley then proceeded to walk across the floor on tiptoe. Jadyn assumed it was the old man's impression of someone walking in high heels. Instead, it looked more like someone stumbling home from the pub four sheets to the wind, as his dad would've said.

'When was the last time that you saw her?'

'That'll be over a week ago anyway, for sure. I was just popping out to head down to the Black Bull, like I do every evening,' Mr Whaley said. 'Like to go there for a pint or two, and a pickled egg. Can't beat a pickled egg. I make my own, true enough, but you can't beat sitting in a pub and having one in a packet of salt and vinegar crisps and washed down with a pint, now, can you? You want to try one?'

'What, you mean like now?' Jadyn said, his mouth still full of cake, crumbs jumping from his mouth as he spoke.

'Good lad!' Mr Whaley said, leaning over to clap Jadyn hard on the knee with a hefty hand. Then, seemingly from thin air, he revealed a jar filled with brown liquid and strange floating globes. 'Here you go!'

From the jar, Mr Whaley pulled out a pickled egg jabbed onto the end of a fork, the white colour gone and now a faded, almost antique, brown. The reek of vinegar was enough to make Jadyn squint.

'See what you think of that, then!' Mr Whaley said, encouraging Jadyn to eat the egg with a big grin, wide eyes, and a flick of a finger. 'Go on, get it down you!'

Jadyn didn't give himself time to think, and before he knew what he was doing he was biting into the egg. His teeth cut through the rubbery surface and vinegar exploded in his mouth to mix violently with the cake still occupying it. But if it was a fight between which taste would win out, the cake didn't stand a chance, as behind the vinegar swept the eggy yolk, the soft yellow charging after the harder white to mix it up with a few sultanas and cherries on Jadyn's appalled tongue.

'Well?' Mr Whaley said.

'I'm ... I'm not sure, if I'm being honest,' Jadyn said, doing his best to swallow the disgusting mulch in his mouth. He grabbed his tea, took a swig, but that only turned what he was trying to eat into some kind of slurry. He swallowed, somehow managed to hold it down, took another swig.

'Can't say I've ever had one with cake myself,' Mr Whaley said. 'But well done you for trying that combination. Judging by the look on your face it's one I'll be avoiding. Curiosity killed that cat, and all that, didn't it?'

Jadyn had to wonder then why Mr Whaley had even offered him the egg.

'So, just to confirm,' Jadyn said, the vinegary taste of the pickled egg still stabbing him behind the eyes, like it was now somehow lodged forever in his brain, 'you've not seen your neighbour, Melissa, for a week, correct?'

'That's it, that's what I said. She was heading off and I've not seen her since. Usually, I see her driving off here, there, and everywhere. She's got a boyfriend, I think. Only seen him a couple of times. Military type I would guess.'

'Why?'

'On account of him walking around wearing all that camouflage. And his short hair. Her car's still there, mind. Which is a bit strange, isn't it? What with the milk piling up as well.'

'If her car's there, did you see her when she returned, then?' Jadyn asked.

Mr Whaley gave a nod.

'She pulled up as I was heading out. Rushed in, she did. So we didn't stop for a chat. She was dressed all, well, you know ...'

Jadyn saw Mr Whaley's expression change to something

that made him look like he was trying to consume the recently suggested combination of tea, cake, and a pickled egg.

'I'm not sure that I do,' Jadyn said.

'Well, you know, *fancy*,' Mr Whaley said, leaning forward, voice a shade quieter.

Jadyn still wasn't really sure what the old man was getting at and decided to move on.

'Is there anything else you can tell me?'

'Not that I can think of, no,' Mr Whaley said. 'That was definitely the last time I saw her. I think I heard a car later on in the evening, very late on actually because I was back here in my bed, but her car was there in the morning, so there's that, isn't there?'

'Do you know what time that was?'

'Like I said, it was late.'

'Can you be more specific?'

'No.'

Jadyn stood up.

'Well, I'd best head around to the house and have a look around.'

'I'm sure I'm just worrying over nowt,' Mr Whaley said, 'but she's a lovely lass, and I'd hate to think of anything terrible happening to her. And things do happen, don't they? Awful things. To people. All the time.'

Jadyn didn't know how to respond so just walked back through the house.

At the door, Jadyn was about to leave, when Mr Whaley held him back for a moment to hand him something.

'Here,' he said, handing the constable a jar. 'See what you think of these. Different recipe. There are chillies in there, too. They'll put hairs on your chest, they will. I gave some to old Charlie the other night and he nigh on melted right there in front of me, grabbing for his pint, spilling it, grabbing for mine, then running to the bar and screaming, *"Milk! Yoghurt! Anything, please! God help me!"* Never laughed so much in my life!'

Jadyn lifted the jar and saw the brown shapes of eggs floating in even darker brown vinegar. They looked more like a bizarre laboratory sample preserved in formaldehyde than something he was being asked to consume.

'Thank you,' Jadyn said, with a shake of the jar. After Mr Whaley's description, he was pretty sure he'd never be opening it.

'It's been a pleasure,' Mr Whaley said. 'Right grand, like. Now, you will pop in, won't you, to let me know if you find out where she's gone?'

'Of course,' Jadyn said. 'Not a problem at all.'

With a wave goodbye, he left Mr Whaley in his doorway. As the door closed behind him he was fairly sure he heard the old man laughing to himself about something. Jadyn had a fairly good idea as to what. He'd certainly never be eating a pickled egg with cake again, that was for sure.

Jadyn headed down the road a few paces till he was outside Melissa's front door.

'Right then,' he muttered to himself, and walked up to the house and knocked.

CHAPTER FOUR

HARRY TOOK UP THE GLASS IN FRONT OF HIM AND swiftly sunk the remaining half-pint of beer held inside it. Above him, the sun blasted down a torrent of heat, and he almost wished they'd decided to sit inside the pub instead of out in the beer garden.

'Thirsty, then?'

'A little.'

'I'll order another.'

'My round.'

Harry stood, picked up the two empty glasses from the table, and made to head back into the pub to the bar. Behind him, Detective Chief Inspector Robbie Kett, a man Harry had met while working on a particularly grisly case a few years ago, and who he'd helped out from time to time was dealing with a newcomer to the table. And they were getting just a little bit shouty and poking Kett with a sharp finger.

'Need a hand?' Harry asked, stopping midway to the front door of the pub.

Kett was one of the few people he could call a friend who

wasn't either an old mate from the Paras, none of whom he'd seen in a good few years, or one of the team from up in Hawes. Everyone he'd worked with in Bristol had been little more than colleagues. Losing touch with them had been as easy as it had been unemotional.

The detective didn't answer, only rolled his eyes. Then the sharp finger turned into a clawed hand and grabbed hold of his trousers to give his leg a shake.

'Daddy, Alice keeps saying that I can't be a unicorn and I can, look!'

The four-year-old girl in front of Kett lifted her other hand and glued it to her forehead. Clasped in her white-knuckled hands was a long, black and clearly very grubby poker.

Kett dodged out of the way just in time as the poker thrust up and towards his face, narrowly missing the head of her younger sister Moira, who was sitting on his knee.

"No!" yelled Moira.

'Dear God, Evie, what the—'

'It's my unicorn horn!'

'You nearly knocked Moira's head off!'

Moira giggled. 'I wanna be a unicorn!'

'Do you like it?' Evie asked. 'It's really long and I can poke things with it. I found it over there. It's my special unicorn horn and I'm going to do magic with it.'

Evie swept around with the hand holding the poker to point over at a fire pit in the centre of the beer garden. It narrowly missed the ankles of a man wearing a sharp suit and the kind of face Harry never trusted, all fake smiles, designer stubble and eyes hidden behind expensive sunglasses. A thick black mark from the poker now stood proud on the girl's forehead.

'Kids want anything?' Harry asked.

'Crisps,' Kett replied. 'Lots of crisps. By which I mean, all of the crisps. And just get them water to drink. They're bouncy enough as it is without more sugar in them.'

Harry left Kett and his daughters to it and was soon inside the pub whereupon he ordered two beers, a jug of water and three small tumblers, and all of the crisps.

'How do you mean, all of the crisps?' the young man behind the bar asked.

'Couple of bags of each should do I think,' Harry said.

'You sure about that?'

Harry's lack of response was enough to have the man shuffle off to get on with the order. When he returned, Harry was staring back over at Kett. The detective was now dealing with three children instead of two, his eldest having joined him.

The barman asked if there was anything else. When Harry turned back around to see the crisp packet version of Everest teetering on top of a tray in front of him, he said no, paid, and headed back outside to join Kett and his daughters.

'Here we go!' he said, placing the tray on the table. He looked at the oldest of the children, an eight-year-old called Alice who had perched herself on his stool. She stared at him with an unnerving intensity.

'Crisps,' Harry said. 'Help yourself.'

'What flavour?'

'All of the flavours, I think,' Harry said, sitting down on another stool pulled from an empty table. He then read through some of the crisp packets. 'Salt and vinegar, cheese and onion, chorizo I think that is, beef and mustard...'

Before he'd finished, Alice was already tearing open a packet.

'They're chilli flavour,' Harry said.

'I know,' Alice replied. 'My favourite.'

'You sure about that?'

Alice didn't answer, she just ducked beneath the table and proceeded to crunch her crisps while sitting on the floor.

'That normal?' asked Harry, handing a pint over to Kett.

'For this family, yes.'

'What about Evie?'

'I want Monster Munch,' Evie said, and Harry noticed how she was no longer holding the poker. The large black mark on her forehead remained though.

'Looks like they didn't have Monster Munch,' Harry said.

'That's not fair!'

'You've got that right.' Harry threw over a packet of salt and vinegar. 'Try these instead.'

'No.'

Kett laughed.

'Welcome to my life. What do you think?'

'Busy,' Harry said, wiping away the froth from a slurp of beer. 'How do you get anything done?'

'I don't,' Kett said.

'Ah.'

Kett opened a packet of cheese and onion for Moira. Harry watched as he attempted to help her eat but she was having none of it. She stuffed a chubby hand into the packet then into her mouth, crisps going everywhere, her eyes wide with delight.

Alice's hand reached up and over to the pile of crisps and took another packet.

'You finished those other ones already?' Harry asked.

Alice opened the crisps, stuffed in a mouthful, her unblinking eyes still on Harry.

'Anyway, they keep me sane,' Kett said. 'A little bit of normality in our lives. We all need it, don't we?'

Evie was thumping a fist down on a packet of salt and vinegar. Harry was about to warn her it would pop if she kept on doing that when it did. Crisps exploded across the table.

'Evie!' Kett sighed. 'What did you do that for?'

'I'm a unicorn!' Evie said, reaching for some of the loose crisps and pushing them into her mouth. 'I can do anything I want to!'

'Maybe I need to be a unicorn,' Harry said. 'It would certainly help right now.'

'You've not got the face for it,' Kett said.

'That's mean, Daddy,' said Evie.

'He's got a point, don't you think?' Harry said with a wink.

Evie almost smiled back, then asked, 'Why do you look like that?'

'Had a fight with a gorilla,' Harry said.

Evie gasped.

'Really?'

Harry gave a very serious nod, said nothing.

Evie almost smiled, then frowned.

A few minutes later, and with most of the crisp packets opened and the table covered in a crunchy layer of detritus, Evie hopped off her stool and ran off. Alice clambered out from under the table and chased her.

'Don't annoy anyone!' Kett shouted, watching them dance off across the beer garden to a small slide and set of swings.

'You're a lucky man,' Harry said.

'I'm a tired man, is what I am,' Kett fired back.

On his lap, Moira, the youngest at two-years old, was crunching crisps in her fist and scattering them. He wasn't about to question it though; the kid was quiet.

Harry took another slurp of beer. Surprised to find an unopened packet of crisps, he tucked in.

'So, apart from the five-star fare you're currently enjoying,' Kett said, 'and the exceptional company of course, what other reason do you have for trundling all the way down to Norfolk from Wensleydale?'

Harry gave a non-committal shrug.

'Oh, well, you know...'

'Life's good up there, right? I mean, it must be. It's a beautiful part of the world. Hardly somewhere anyone would want to leave, even if they had to.'

'I needed a break,' Harry said. 'You know, I don't think I've had an actual holiday in over two years?'

'If this is what you class as a holiday then things are worse than I thought,' Kett said. 'And I heard about your trip to Scotland a few weeks back.'

'That doesn't count either,' said Harry. 'Flying up to the Highlands to meet a gruff DCI whose own investigation has resulted in the solving of one of your own, isn't exactly two weeks in Benidorm.'

'Missing child, wasn't it?'

'It was,' Harry said. Sometimes he forgot how busy he was. And what had happened in the Dales with Jadyn, well that investigation had overshadowed some of the other cases he had been involved with.

'Who was the DCI on the other end, then?'

'Logan,' Harry said. 'We didn't exactly have much to say to each other. But he did a bloody good job, I'll give him that.'

Kett raised his glass.

'I'll toast that,' he said.

Harry chinked his glass against Kett's and said, 'A change of scenery is good. Helps you think.'

'Ah,' said Kett.

Harry raised an eyebrow and stared hard at Kett from beneath it.

'Ah? What do you mean by, Ah?'

'You said *think*,' Kett said. 'People don't go on holiday to think. They go away to relax and unwind and to forget. Usually with lots of alcohol.'

'I'm not good at any of those,' said Harry.

'You do surprise me.'

Harry leaned back, stared up at the sky, then came back to the table.

'Something's come up,' he said. 'Firbank's been in touch.'

'Your old DSup?'

Harry gave a nod.

Alice Firbank was his old Detective Superintendent from when he'd been working down south in Bristol.

'Called me a couple of weeks ago.'

'What about?' Kett asked as Moira grabbed one of his fingers and started to chew. "Youch, Moira! Go play with your sisters."

He lifted her off his lap and she bolted into the garden.

'A job,' Harry said, watching her go. 'Back down south.'

CHAPTER FIVE

THE SOUND OF HIS KNUCKLES AGAINST THE WOODEN door was cold and empty, echoing back at Jadyn as though he had knocked against the boarded-up entrance of a tomb. But this was just a house. A quiet house, soaked in darkness, and the windows said nothing about what was inside.

Jadyn tried again, harder this time, because that first knock had suffered from a little too much politeness. It had been the kind of knock used in the hope of not actually waking anyone up.

'Hello? Melissa, this is Police Constable Jadyn Okri. I need you to come to the door, please, if you can.'

Nothing. Just an eerie silence. And it was deafening, Jadyn thought.

Standing back from the door, he spotted the collection of milk bottles, and looked up at the house. There was a small gate to the right of the house, he noticed, and as he stared at it, he found himself rubbing his chin thoughtfully and stopped immediately. He was hardly some great detective now, was he? So, no point pretending to be one.

So, what did he know so far? Melissa had last been seen a week ago by Mr Whaley. He also claimed to have heard her drive off later that same night.

At this thought, Jadyn turned back to the road to have a look at the car parked outside the house. It was a white Porsche. Well, Jadyn thought, whoever Melissa is and whatever she does, it clearly pays well enough.

Wandering over to the car, he had a quick scout around it, peering in through the windows, but not close enough to touch. It wasn't just the fingerprints he was concerned about, but the car alarm. He'd had run-ins with some really sensitive ones that would scream at you if you so much as blinked in their direction.

With the car giving nothing away, Jadyn went back to the house, and after a moment of deep and purposeful consideration, he clenched his fist and battered it hard enough against the door to sting.

'Melissa? This is Police Constable Okri!' His voice was raised now. A clear shout, made all the louder by the quiet night gathering around him. 'I'm just here to check that everything's okay. If you could come to the door that would be very much appreciated, thank you.'

Again, no answer, no response. It was as though the house had simply consumed his knock and his voice, sucking them down to nothing.

Jadyn turned from the door, moving to the right to have a look through the window. Which wasn't very easy because the curtains were pulled. When he walked to the other side of the door he found the curtains there to be drawn across the window as well, whatever was inside was hidden from the peering eyes of the outside world by the thickest curtains.

With no other options open, Jadyn moved to the small

gate at the side of the house, found that it was open, and pushed on through. He walked down the side of the house, the darkness ink-black. At the rear of the property he walked into a small yard, garden just beyond disappearing into shadow. Nothing special that he could see with his torch, but pretty all the same in its simplicity, he thought.

Turning to face the back of the house, Jadyn once again saw that no lights were on, no sign that anyone was home. The car out front and Mr Whaley's words suggested that really there ought to be, he thought, so he walked up to the backdoor and gave it a hard thump with the heel of his left hand.

More silence. Only this time Jadyn felt as though the shadow-clad shapes in the garden were crouched behind him and staring expectantly, creeping closer. He swept the beam of his torch around, momentarily acutely aware of his isolation. The light cut a wound through the black, dragging parts of the garden into the light only to then have them disappear once again into it like vessels sinking in the blackest of seas.

His hand tight on his torch, Jadyn peered in through the windows, these uncovered, unlike those round the front of the house. He saw nothing that would give him any hint as to where Melissa was, just a kitchen, a dining room. Except that in the kitchen he noticed an empty bottle of champagne alongside what looked to him like packaging for food.

Something about this was wrong. Jadyn knew that in his gut. The house was too quiet, too still. It was not the silence associated with a building vacated for a reason, but the stifling hush of walls hiding something. Though what, exactly, he hadn't the faintest idea. His heartbeat was up and he rubbed his hands together, his palms clammy. *Calm down, just calm down.* But it wasn't that easy, even with the breathing technique the counsellor had shown him. He tried it, focused on his heart rate, didn't want that racing away, spiking his adrenaline.

Walking quickly back around to the front of the house, trying to ignore the creeping sensation that something in the garden was now following him, Jadyn made his way once again to the front door. There would be no harm in giving it one more go, he thought, so without hesitation he knocked once again. This time, though, there was no ignoring him, the heel of his hand thumping at the door hard enough to rattle the hinges.

'Melissa? Melissa, if you're home, if you can hear me, then give me a sign, make a sound, anything, okay? I need to know that you're alright!'

Shaking his head and wondering what else he could do, other than head back to the office and crack on with filing a missing person report, Jadyn reached for the doorknob and gave it a twist.

The door opened, just enough.

'Bloody hell!' Jadyn muttered, admonishing himself for not trying that at the very beginning and assuming that the door was locked.

Torch on, Jadyn pushed the door to swing fully open. He brought the beam of his torch up and swept it into the space beyond. He saw a hallway leading to the rear of the house, stairs a few steps away, to the left a closed door.

Jadyn stepped in over the threshold, purpose in his stride. Everything was fine, he said to himself, as he took a moment to listen to the house. Nothing to worry about at all. Around him, the quiet of the night was almost deafening, Jadyn thought, so thick was it around him, closing in, pressing against him, a blanket.

Breathe ...

'Melissa, I've just entered the house,' Jadyn called out. 'Please don't be alarmed. My name is Jadyn Okri and I'm a police officer.'

He heard a quiver in his voice, just on the edge of his words.

The door clunked shut behind him.

'Shit...'

Jadyn gasped, dropped his torch, snatched it up again almost too desperate to have it in his hand. He could hear his blood thumping through his ears, his heart racing. The darkness here, it reminded him of a barn, oily mean voices, a pure fear as sharp as lightning. Maybe I shouldn't have come into the house, he thought. But there was no one else here, was there? It was just him and all he was doing was checking out a supposedly empty house. He was fine.

A memory then, of a barn, voices, something over his head, a foul stench, pain, and a fear that had him crippled.

Come on, just hold it together...

A door to his right was open and Jadyn stepped into it to find himself in the kitchen, the one he'd peered into from the rear of the house. It was a large room and looked to him like two rooms knocked into one. Expensively furnished too, he thought, with one of those fridge-freezers that look big enough to walk in. The torch beam picked out the champagne bottle, the food packaging. But other than that, the room was a cold place, devoid of life, and looked as though no one had been in it for days. Though one thing struck him as odd: the dining table was clearly one made for four chairs, yet he saw only three.

Back out into the hall, Jadyn gave a shout once again, but there was no answer. He hadn't expected there to be one, but he just thought it made sense to make his presence known.

Jadyn walked over to the door opposite. It was as he leaned himself into it, his fingers clasping the handle, that he noticed scratch marks on the floor. Something had been dragged out of the kitchen. The missing chair, he thought. But why? Then came the smell. Walking into the house he'd not noticed it at all, probably because the breeze from outside had followed him in. But now, as the days' old seal on the door broke with his gentle force, something mired in a sweet foulness crawled its way out. Curiosity numbing the cautious part of his brain, he opened the door.

Jadyn coughed, gagged, wanted to turn and run. The fear inside him was a barbed thing now, twisting faster and faster, pain shooting through his system. The stink in the room was threatening to make his eyes bleed and his first thought was to flee, to just get the hell out, because whatever caused it, wherever it was coming from, he was pretty bloody sure that he didn't want to see it. And the images now coming at him thick and fast were filling his mind, proving harder to ignore, his palms no longer just clammy but itching with prickly heat. But he was a police constable and this was his job, so it wasn't as though he had much choice. He could give Matt a call, but if the stench turned out to be nothing then he'd never live it down. No, he had to push on, deeper into the room, investigate.

Pull yourself together...

So, covering his mouth and nose with the sleeve of his jacket, that's exactly what he did.

Stepping beyond the door and into the room fully, Jadyn saw how the thick curtains, which draped all the way to the floor, let not a single thin shard of light in from the night outside. No moonlight, no streetlight, the room was bare of intrusion from any light at all. The scratch marks from the kitchen continued on the floor in a ragged arc.

Slowly, Jadyn cast his light, following the scratches, the end of the beam bringing into stark, full-colour relief, a room as simple as it was expensive. Not just the wallpaper or the curtains either, but the television on the wall, the wood-burning stove, the art on the walls.

A thrumming sound, coming from his right, an area of the room he'd yet to peer into. No, it wasn't a thrumming, more a vibration, Jadyn thought, and he continued to swing his light beam around, cutting across the walls, a sofa, until it came to rest on ...

Jadyn gagged, tasted vomit blasting its way into the back of his throat, managed to keep his lips shut as he bolted, then threw up outside, barely making it out of the door. He retched, couldn't stop, the stink in his nose and the taste in his mouth overwhelming him as what he'd just seen, the horror of it, danced across his mind, a movie he didn't want to watch but couldn't stop. But something else was having its mean way with him now and he was no longer at a house in Reeth, but in a barn, a rope around his neck, laughter in his ears, pain everywhere, so much pain. Then the rope pulled, his feet left the ground, and his mind was blasted into a thou-sand pieces of hell.

Jadyn reached for his phone, hit dial, his breath coming hard and fast.

Matt answered.

'Officer Okri,' the DS said, but before he had a chance to say anything more, Jadyn shot a reply down the line with a sharp, desperate, panicked bark.

'There's a body!'

CHAPTER SIX

Driving into Reeth, Matt wondered why it was that so many call-outs seemed to happen at night. He'd been having such a lovely evening lazing around on the sofa with Joan, making the most of the fact that they probably wouldn't be doing anything like it again for quite some time once the baby arrived.

With the way Jadyn had sounded, though, he'd had no option but to get shifting. Whatever the lad had discovered, it had sent him into a spin. Matt hadn't heard all that the constable had said, mainly due to the retching, but he'd caught a few snippets, which had been more than enough. Something about flies, a body covered in white flour, and pickled eggs.

Ahead, the bright moon had lit the village up like a celestial floodlight. The green, surrounded by the staring windows of houses and hotels—and one of Matt's favourite pubs on earth, The Black Bull—had an otherworldly quality to it. The green at Bainbridge always seemed brighter somehow, he thought, more modern, despite the stocks in the centre.

At Reeth, though, the green seemed to be trapped in another time. Here, he could imagine a horse and cart trundling through, whereas in Bainbridge only the modern motor vehicle belonged. Walking through the place was a journey that followed the whispers and memories of ghosts. Matt had certainly felt the hairs on the back of his neck stand up more than once or twice when walking through Reeth's lanes.

Leaving the green behind and ignoring the urge to head to the Black Bull, a huge task in itself, Matt slipped down a small road and soon saw Jadyn's vehicle. The police constable was standing beside it and gave a wave. Matt could see that Jadyn looked shaken, his face wide-eyed and serious. And he was fidgeting, pulling at his fingers, rubbing his palms.

'Evening Constable,' Matt said, climbing out. 'So, you're having an interesting night, then, by the sounds of it. How are you doing?'

He wasn't about to say anything about Jadyn's behaviour, not yet anyway. But he was definitely not himself.

Jadyn stepped away from his vehicle, his movements nervy and sharp. He kept glancing back at a house just along from where he was parked as though he was concerned that he was being watched.

'The call came in from the neighbour, Mr Whaley,' Jadyn said. Then he pointed to the other house, the one he couldn't seem to stop himself looking at. 'He lives in this house here, but it's the one down there where I found the, er, well ...'

'What did Mr Whaley have to say?' Matt asked.

'He seems to know her well enough,' Jadyn said. 'She moved in about a year ago. Says they were on good speaking terms. You know, a hello and a natter in the morning, that kind of thing.'

'And that's it?'

Jadyn shook his head.

'Got a description as well.' He opened his notebook. Matt saw that the constable's hands were shaking as he read out the description.

'Dangerous shoes?' Matt asked. 'You sure about that?'

'I think he meant high heels,' Jadyn said. Matt noticed that the constable's voice was strained a little, stress pulling at it. 'He did an impression of walking on them, all wobbly legs. And he was very keen to point out that she was, and I quote, *the most beautiful woman I've ever seen, and I've seen Marilyn Monroe.*'

'That's quite a reference,' Matt said. 'Who mentions Marilyn Monroe nowadays? And she was blonde.'

'Actually, she was naturally brown,' Jadyn pointed out. 'The blonde was all hair dye.'

'That's a strange fact to be carrying around with you.'

'Googled it while I waited. Keep my mind off what happened... no, I mean, what I saw, in the house.'

Matt noticed Jadyn's slight change of direction, like he'd caught himself partway to saying something else.

'I'm guessing Mr Whaley is of a certain age, then,' Matt said. 'If he's mentioning Monroe.'

'Eighty-six, he said.'

'That's some age. Good for him. It must be like every day is a welcome surprise.'

'He doesn't have a cooker,' Jadyn said.

'What?'

'A cooker,' Jadyn repeated. 'He doesn't have one. Can

you believe that? Well, he does, but not electric or gas. It's this wood-fired thing.'

'Like an Aga, you mean?'

'I know what an Aga is,' said Jadyn. 'But this one you can actually see the fire. And I thought Aga's were oil?'

'How relevant is this to why you've called me over?' Matt asked, aware then that Jadyn was focusing on a random detail.

'Not at all,' Jadyn said.

'Best we get on then, don't you think?' Matt said, wondering then if perhaps Jadyn was just stalling. Which was a worry in itself. 'If I need to talk to Mr Whaley I'll pop round later.'

'He's proper Yorkshire, if you know what I mean,' Jadyn said, 'Accent thicker than a slab of Wensleydale cheese.'

'That one your own?' Matt asked.

'It is.'

'I think I'll borrow it. But moving on; you had your chat, then what?'

Jadyn pointed at the other house again. 'I headed over. There were no lights on, the place was quiet. I knocked at the door but there was no answer.'

'Is that when you saw the body?'

Jadyn shook his head, the movement slow, haunted.

'I knocked a few more times, had a scout around the back, saw nothing, so went round and knocked at the door again. Then I gave the doorknob a twist and—'

Matt folded his arms and stared hard.

'You mean you didn't try opening the door to begin with?'

'No,' Jadyn said. 'I just assumed ...'

'Never assume,' said Matt. 'Lesson learned, yes?'

'Yes, Sarge.'

'So, the door opened and in you went. And you saw?'

Jadyn went to speak but stalled, his words dead in his throat.

Matt saw worry writing itself across Jadyn's face. He was wringing his hands again, shuffling his feet.

'Jadyn, are you alright?' he asked.

'What? Yes, I mean, no, actually, not really.'

Matt kept quiet, just waited for him to explain.

'It's going to sound daft, I know,' Jadyn said, 'but that house, the darkness, the smell of it, it took me back to what happened, in the barn, like. You know, back to what happened, when I was ...' Jadyn's voice broke. He took a breath. 'It wasn't the same or anything, but for some reason, that's all I could think of. I ... I had to get out. I threw up.'

Matt thought back to what Jadyn had gone through a couple of months back, how he'd been snatched off the streets of Leyburn, tied and hooded and taken to a remote barn. He'd been beaten, strung up with a rope around his neck, left for dead. That he was doing so well at all was a credit to the kind of person he was.

'It doesn't sound daft at all,' said Matt. 'It doesn't take much to trigger a memory. You can't go second-guessing this stuff, you know that.'

'I think it was the darkness mainly,' Jadyn said. 'Other stuff too, maybe. I'm alright. Honestly, I am. It just took me by surprise, that's all, seeing that body. With the smell, it was so claustrophobic and then all I could think of was that hood they put over my head, you know? The smell of it, how it tasted. Everything.'

Matt rested a firm hand on Jadyn's shoulder. The

constable shuddered, flinching almost at being touched. Matt gave the shoulder a squeeze.

'Don't expect too much,' he said. 'You're doing well. Better than well, if I'm honest. The whole team's here for you. You know that.'

'I do,' Jadyn said. 'But it really set me off, you know? Wasn't expecting it. Caught me off guard.'

The constable shuddered again and shook his head.

'Look, you don't have to go into the house again,' said Matt. 'I'm good to go in on my own, no bother at all. I'll just pop my head around the door, have a nosy and—'

'No, I'll come,' Jadyn said, a deep breath sucked in and exhaled with purpose. 'I can't hide away, can I? I need to face things, deal with what happened.'

'Only if you're sure. There's no rush on any of that. It'll take time. Months. Maybe longer.'

'I'm sure.'

'Well then,' said Matt, reaching into his car to grab a torch. 'After you ...'

When they came to the door, Matt caught a distant scent on the dark, dank air slopping out through the door. He reached into a pocket to pull out a small, plastic tub, unscrewed the top, then held the tub out for Jadyn.

'Vapour Rub,' Matt said. 'I always carry it. Dab some under your nose. It'll make your eyes water, but it'll at least go some way to masking the stink inside.'

'I keep meaning to get myself a pot,' said Jadyn, dipping his finger into the goo.

Matt closed the lid and handed the pot over.

'You don't need to,' he said. 'You can have this one. I've a few laying around.'

Jadyn pocketed the pot.

'I'll go first,' Matt said. 'And before you complain, no, it's not because I don't think you'll cope with it. It's because I'm the senior officer here so I need to assess what we've got and then decide on what we do next.'

'Fine by me,' Jadyn said.

Matt stepped forward and over the threshold into the house and as he did so, the smell he'd noted outside grew so thick so quickly that he gagged. The air wasn't so much tainted as permanently stained, the stink dancing in it so fetid that Matt wondered if the best thing to do once they were done would be to demolish the house. It was the kind of smell so richly foul that it would have already slipped itself deep into the fabric of the building and there would be no getting rid of it no matter how deep the clean. And on those hotter days of summer, the heat would call it out again to tease the air with the everlasting memory of death. He saw scratch marks on the floor, from the kitchen, across the hall, and through another door.

'That's the kitchen,' Jadyn said, pointing right.

'Yes, but the smell's coming from in there,' Matt said, and armed with his torch made his way left through an open door, behind which shadows waited.

The room was a tomb, that was Matt's first thought, and he hesitated before going any further, almost afraid of disturbing the dead. The floor-length curtains kept out any chance of light from outside seeping in. He focused on the bright white, distorted circle of his torchlight as it crept and crawled across the surfaces in front of him, looking for signs of what had gone on in this room before they had entered it. He saw the scratch marks and followed them. Then, as a magnet pulls iron filings to it, the torch beam was dragged onward to rest at last on the body.

'Sweet Jesus ...'

'You could say that,' said Jadyn.

Matt had seen some things in his time, not only on the force, but as a member of the Swaledale Mountain Rescue Team, but this ... this was something beyond anything he'd ever witnessed. It was a scene so traumatic and wrong that there was almost a theatrical air to it, Matt thought, like it had been staged.

'The flies have cleared a little, so that's something,' said Jadyn.

'Yeah, but it's not much though, is it?' said Matt.

'No, it's not,' Jadyn agreed.

'You okay?'

'So far,' Jadyn said.

'If you need to leave ...'

'I don't. I'm good.'

Matt was standing just beyond the door. There was no way that he was going any further. Whatever had happened here was no accident, of that he was damned sure. So, that meant it would be a call through to Forensics.

'Jadyn?'

'Yes, Sarge?'

'Would you mind giving Gordy a call? Harry's away so we're going to need her over ASAP.'

'What about Forensics?'

'I'll do that in a minute,' Matt said.

Jadyn left the room.

Alone now, Matt focused on what was in front of him. The body, which right now he assumed belonged to Melissa, though it was hard to tell from the state it was in, was sitting in a kitchen chair. Behind it, an armchair had been pushed out of the way. An expensive one, too, Matt thought, by the looks of it, all gold velvet and scatter cushions.

The body's head was snapped back, the side of it a mess of blood. He spotted a clean hole in the forehead. Judging by the gore on the wall, now dried and black and feeding a colony of maggots, the contents of the skull had been forcibly ejected most likely by a bullet or two.

The face and the top half of the body were covered in a white powder partially turned into a crust by dark blood. It gave the scene a distinctly other-worldly feel, Matt thought, the contours of the body like a snow-covered wilderness. The arms were tied back behind the chair, the ankles to the front legs. Matt spotted a champagne flute on its side, a bottle, a few plates home to rotting food and the things which fed on it.

A sound behind him interrupted his thoughts and Matt looked to see Jadyn standing in the doorway.

'The DI's on her way,' he said.

'What did you tell her?'

'Enough,' said Jadyn. 'You want me to call Forensics?'

Matt gave a nod.

Jadyn pulled out his phone and made the call.

CHAPTER SEVEN

'A job?'

'It's not a job, it's an "initiative,"' Harry said, unable to stop himself from throwing air quotes around the word.

'Oh God,' said Kett.

'Oh God, indeed,' Harry sighed.

'Well go on, then. Don't leave me hanging.'

'Why are you hanging, Daddy?'

The question was from Evie who had returned to the table from the play equipment in the corner of the beer garden.

'It's a turn of phrase,' Kett said.

'What is?'

'What I said.'

'Yes, but why are you hanging when you're sitting? That doesn't make sense.'

Kett glanced over to Harry, rolled his eyes, but beneath the frustration a smile glimmered.

'Here,' the DCI said, and handed his daughter a packet

of cheese and onion crisps. 'Why don't you go and share these with Alice?'

'She doesn't want to play with me,' Evie said, and Harry saw the girl's face fall then, the deepest of sorrows in her eyes as they filled up. 'She never wants to play with me anymore.'

HARRY SPOTTED one of the bar staff collecting glasses on a nearby table and caught her eye. When she came over he pulled out his wallet.

'Is there any chance that this fine establishment also sells that special kind of chocolate?'

'Special kind?'

'Yes,' Harry said with a wink. 'You know, that chocolate that only we adults know about and only give to children on very, very special occasions. Like now.'

'But now isn't special,' Evie said.

Harry leaned over to Evie and whispered, 'You mean your dad hasn't told you, then?'

Evie shook her head, intrigue already pushing away her sadness.

'Maybe he doesn't know.'

'Know what?'

'That today is Evie Day.'

'Evie Day?'

'Yes,' said Harry. 'I think your dad was probably too busy to remember, but I did, so you know what that means, don't you?'

'What?'

'Chocolate!'

Evie's eyes lit up and Harry turned to the girl holding the tray of empty beer glasses, handed her a tenner, and said,

'Spend all of this on chocolate and put whatever change there is in the tips jar.'

The girl gave a nod, a bright smile, and headed off into the pub. She returned barely a minute later, her hand filled with chocolate bars. Harry handed one of the bars to Evie.

'This is to share now,' he said. 'You can share, can't you?'

Evie's nod wasn't exactly convincing.

'I hope you can,' Harry said, 'because sharing is what Evie Day is all about. And if you share well, you know what you get?'

Evie shook her head.

'More chocolate!'

Kett laughed.

'I can share better than anyone ever!' Evie said, then she was gone.

'I'm impressed,' said Kett. 'For someone who doesn't have kids, you certainly know how to manage them.'

'Like I said, you're a lucky man,' said Harry, but as the words fell, so did Kett's face. 'How's it all going? How are you all getting on?'

He'd never asked Kett much about it, but he knew enough to understand that Kett and his family had been through hell after his wife Billie had been kidnapped.

Kett shook his head.

'Good days, bad days,' he said. 'And something tells me it's not over yet.'

'If you ever need help with anything,' Harry said.

'Yeah, I know,' said Kett, taking a swig from his pint glass. 'How are you with a hammer?'

'Fixing stuff?'

'Breaking stuff.'

Harry laughed.

'The initiative?'

'What is "the initiative" exactly?' Kett asked, changing the subject.

'Setting up a new station where I grew up,' Harry said. 'I think someone, somewhere in government wants to do something to show that, despite all the cuts and the loss of numbers, the government is doing something.'

'It's always doing something,' Kett said. 'It's just that usually none of it's any good. So, what will the job involve?'

'I'm guessing a lot of bollocks and nonsense,' Harry said.

'You'll be getting that in writing, yes?'

'Obviously.'

Kett leaned back a little and stared over at Harry, arms folded.

'Job description?'

'There isn't one, not yet, anyway,' said Harry. 'Apparently, that would be down to the person who took up the position. And it won't start till later in the year. But my old DSup, she wants me to consider it.'

'This the same old DSup who sent you north for being a royal pain in the arse?'

'Of course.'

'Glutton for punishment, is she?'

'Undoubtedly.'

'She must've given you some idea, though,' Kett asked. 'Setting up a new office, well, that's a bit open-ended, isn't it?'

Moira, who had fallen asleep on her dad's lap, woke with a start, punching him in the nose, her fist close to forcing its way into a nostril.

'Ow! Moo-moo, what are you doing?'

She glowered at him, then climbed off his knee in search of her sisters.

'It's going to be everything and anything involved in setting the office up,' Harry said. 'And I don't just mean recruitment, because there's no actual office, not yet, anyway.'

'Let me guess,' said Kett. 'Local community currently has access to a desk in the library, right?'

'On the nail,' said Harry. 'Bloody useless.'

'Could be a good move though,' said Kett.

'It could be, yes,' said Harry. 'She said if I make a success of it, next thing I know I could be a Detective Superintendent myself.'

'So, what's the problem?' asked Kett.

'Me,' Harry said. 'That's the problem.'

'In what way?'

'In every bloody way!'

Harry noticed a tugging at his sleeve and looked down to see Evie.

'Did you share?'

Evie nodded furiously.

'So, more chocolate, then?'

More nodding.

Harry obliged and as Evie ran off back towards her sisters, excitement in every step.

Kett said, 'You don't want the job, then?'

'I didn't say that.'

'Well, you've not said much.'

Harry's voice grumbled in his throat.

'I know it makes sense, career-wise,' he said eventually, picking up his pint then placing it back down again without a sip taken. 'But, the thing is, up north?'

'It's not so grim?'

Harry laughed.

'It's not,' he said. 'I didn't want to go right at the beginning, but it gets under your skin. The team, well, they're like nothing I've worked with before. For a start, they actually like each other and there's no stabbing each other in the back, either, no career idiots trying to trip you up.'

'What else?'

'The beer's good,' Harry said. 'The Dales themselves, they're beautiful. You ever been? You should. Come up and stay if you want. Ben's not around much as he's more often than not round at Liz's. She's one of the PCSOs on the team. Been seeing each other for a while now.'

'Ben's happy up there as well, then?'

'He's got a job, settled into actually being himself,' Harry said. Kett didn't know much about Ben, so it was good of him to ask. 'The difference is amazing. And I know it's hard to believe, what with me having a face like this, but I've been seeing someone for a while now, too. I've even got a dog!'

It was this last nugget of information that hit home more than anything and Kett, who had been partway through another slug of beer, spluttered.

'A dog?'

'Exactly!' Harry said. 'The hell is wrong with me?'

Kett shook his head, rested his beer back on the table, stared over at Harry.

'I think there's clearly a very big problem here and you're just not seeing it.'

'I'm not?' Harry said. 'What is it, then? What am I not seeing?'

'You're happy,' Kett said.

'What?'

Kett shook his head, his smile working loose enough to become a laugh.

'You're happy!' he said again.

'What's that got to do with anything?'

'It's got everything to do with everything!' Kett said.

Harry wasn't sure what to say next. Kett had a point. Looking over everything, perhaps the man was right. He was so unused to being happy and content that he was immediately seeing it as a problem, a barrier.

'You've a choice,' Kett said, and lifted a clenched hand, thumb extended. 'One, you take the job, and two'—he extended his index finger—'you don't. You can do as many SWAT analyses as you want, look at it from every angle, but what it boils down to, more than anything else, is where you think you'll be the happiest. And as soft as that may sound to hardened coppers like us, that's just the way it is. Where will you be happy, Harry? That's what you've got to ask yourself. But I think you already know the answer.'

'I do?'

Kett sighed.

'Go home, Harry,' he said.

'Train's booked the day after tomorrow,' said Harry.

'Exactly.'

CHAPTER EIGHT

'Harry won't be sorry he's missing this,' said Gordy.

'Well, I've not told him yet,' said Matt.

Gordy laughed and Matt heard an echo of the Highlands in the sound. She'd headed over as soon as she'd received Jadyn's call and arrived before the scene of crime team, who had yet to arrive.

'Very sensible,' she said. 'We can handle this. He's on leave. Best to leave him well alone. Calling him now would be like taking a stick to poke a sleeping bear.'

'You know what he's doing, though, don't you?' Matt said. 'Visiting another DCI. I mean, who does that and calls it leave?'

'People like Harry,' Gordy said.

'I don't understand it. Well, I do, but you've got to be able to leave your job, otherwise it takes over, doesn't it?'

'It does,' said Gordy. 'But sometimes, that's all there is. It's a survival thing. Harry was in the Paras then the police. And being a Para isn't something you leave in the barracks. That's with you. It's with him, still, all these years later; the soldier he was, he still is, if you see what I mean.'

'Old habits?'

'I suppose so, yes,' said Gordy. 'Harry is what he is. Though, I think he's changed in ways that have shocked him, more so maybe, than anyone else.'

Matt smiled, nodded.

'You wouldn't be talking about Grace and that daft dog now, would you?'

'Not only that,' said Gordy. 'He's changed in himself.'

'You think so?'

Gordy raised an eyebrow. 'I know so.'

'Yeah, you're right, he has,' agreed Matt. 'He's sort of the same but different, if that makes any sense.'

'It does.'

A sound caught Matt's attention as bright lights swept round and down the lane towards them.

'Well, here they are,' Matt said, as a cold shiver from standing out in the late evening for so long chased down his spine.

Two large, white vans pulled up behind Gordy's vehicle. Doors opened to spill figures into the darkness. One broke away and walked towards them.

'DI Haig and DS Dinsdale,' said Pathologist Rebecca Sowerby. 'Ambulance is on its way, too.'

'Evening,' Matt said. 'Though it's nearly morning, isn't it?'

'Grimm around?'

'This time, no,' Gordy said.

'Ill?'

Matt laughed.

'Harry ill? I'm not sure he knows what that word even means.'

'He's on leave,' Gordy said.

'I'm surprised he knows what that word means either,' said Sowerby. 'So, what have we got? Your constable left a bit of a garbled message with us. Milk bottles and dangerous shoes were mentioned.'

'At least he didn't get as far as the pickled eggs,' said Matt. 'You were lucky.'

Behind Sowerby, her team unpacked their kit, pulled on PPE. One of them, fully dressed now in paper white, came over, carrying a camera and flash.

'Okay to head in?' he asked, glancing at Sowerby who in turn looked at Matt.

'Make yourself right at home,' Matt said.

The photographer gave a nod then left them for the house and his details were taken by Jadyn who was now working as the Scene Guard.

'You know, I've no idea of that man's name,' Matt said. 'Seen him enough times, but never been introduced.'

'That surprises me,' said Sowerby. 'His name is Simon Parks, Si for short. And he's usually the one doing the introducing. Very chatty, if you know what I mean.'

'Oh, I know exactly what you mean,' Gordy said, remembering speaking to him outside the church in Askrigg the previous year. Inside, the body of the world-famous singer, Gareth Jones had been found hanging from a bell rope. 'A little too enthusiastic about the subject matter if you ask me.'

'Enthusiastic?' Sowerby said. 'Well, better that than someone who doesn't give a damn. Back to what we've got in there, then,' Sowerby said looking at Matt. 'You mentioned pickled eggs.'

Matt quickly ran through what Sowerby and her team were going to find inside.

'Well, that certainly sounds both interesting and horrific,' she said.

'There are some things you can never unsee,' said Matt, and then he jabbed a hard finger towards the house. 'And that in there? It's right up there, believe me.'

'Has my mum turned up yet?' Sowerby asked.

'That's a point, she hasn't,' Matt said, glancing then at the road expectantly. 'Jadyn?'

'Yes, Sarge?'

'Any news from the district surgeon?'

Jadyn shook his head.

'Said she'd be over right away.'

'Well, she's clearly not, is she?'

There was nothing Jadyn could say to that.

Matt rubbed his chin.

'I'll give her a call,' he said, then looked to Sowerby. 'I know procedure is that she confirms death before you folk head in, but in this case, I think we can bypass that, don't you? Margaret's the punctual type so this isn't exactly in character.'

Sowerby went to answer as a moan from the house cut through and Matt glanced over to see Simon standing at the door. He was steadying himself against the wall.

Matt called over. 'If you're done in there, then you need to leave the crime scene.'

'Just a minute,' Simon replied, raising a hand.

'No "just" anything,' Matt said. 'Get yourself out and over here, now!'

Simon pushed himself away from the house and started to walk, except the walk soon become a jog and a few seconds later the sound of retching from behind a car further down the street was heard.

'Well, I don't think I've ever seen that happen before,' Sowerby said. 'Prides himself on his cast-iron constitution.'

Simon approached them, wiping his mouth.

'Sorry about that,' he said. 'It's just, well, while I was in there, something sort of burst, if you know what I mean.'

Sowerby held up a hand to stop the man from speaking, but he ignored it.

'Not sure what it was, but there was this soft popping sound, then this oozy mass spilled out.'

'Simon ...'

'That was bad, but the smell that came after it? Like being hit in the face by a burst bag of God knows what. Reminded me of—'

'Simon!'

Simon stopped speaking.

'Oh, right, yes. Sorry.'

As Simon headed off, Sowerby said, 'Well, best we get on with what we're doing then.'

'I'll give your mum a call now,' Matt said.

'She's fine, I'm sure. Probably just got herself trapped in a pair of Wellies or something.'

Left alone with Gordy, Matt punched a call through to the district surgeon. The phone rang then went through to voicemail.

'No answer?' said Gordy.

Matt shook his head.

'It's not like her at all. She should've been here half an hour ago, stomping through the place, bellowing about goodness knows what.'

'Give it a few minutes,' Gordy said.

Matt wasn't so sure.

'You don't need me right now, do you?' he asked.

'Everything's in hand,' Gordy said. 'The SOC team will do their thing, everything's quiet.'

'Then if it's all the same with you, I think I'd rather head on over and be shouted at by Margaret for making a fuss over nothing, than stand here wondering if something bad has happened to her.'

'Watch as you're driving over,' said Gordy. 'I've seen that woman behind the wheel and she seems to regard all road signs as little more than polite suggestions rather than the actual law.'

Matt laughed and headed off towards his car. Jadyn's voice caught him sharp.

'What is it, Constable?'

'Just wondering where you're going, that's all,' Jadyn said. 'It's not Joan, is it? Is she—'

'No, she's not giving birth,' Matt said, then explained where he was heading.

'I can do that,' Jadyn said. 'It's no bother.'

'No, you stay here,' said Matt. 'Scene Guard is an important job.'

'Is it?'

'Of course!' said Matt, patting Jadyn encouragingly on the shoulder. 'In fact, if you really think about it, you're basically the one who's in charge.'

And with Jadyn's face beaming at him as those words bounced around in his mind, Matt headed off into the night.

CHAPTER NINE

Inside the house, Rebecca Sowerby was spending yet another night staring at yet another body. In the back of her mind was a seed of concern for her mum, but that was understandable. Best to ignore it and crack on, she thought. It wasn't as though worrying was going to make any difference. She'd call her when she was done.

With a path of raised tiles laid across the floor, from the front door and through to various parts of the house, she was now standing in what was clearly the lounge. This was a nice room she thought. Or it had been until what she was now staring at had taken place. It was better than nice, actually; it was plush, expensive, a haven. Not huge, but a good enough size for a little party, a few drinks, that kind of thing. Or just an evening on your own with an open fire, a bottle of wine, some good cheese, and just to finish things off, a good book.

The walls were plain white except for over the wood-burning stove to her left where bare brick stood out in stark, rustic contrast to the rest. A few paintings were hung—colourful splashes of goodness knew what. Rebecca had no idea what any of them were meant to be other than expensive. Yes, this was a room she could like. Shame about the body really and everything that came with it like a collection of the world's most gruesome fashion accessories.

From where she was standing, dressed all over in the white paper suit of her trade, the smell was the first thing to note. The vapour rub under her nose, which was itself covered with a face mask, was fighting a losing battle. The miasma was a thing both sickly sweet and noxious, like someone had sprayed the sharpest of vinegars in the air, soaking the place with enough of it to make your eyes water.

Beyond that, there were the liquids, the fluids the body can't help but gift to the world around it when it starts to decompose. And under the bright lights stationed in the room, Rebecca was drawn to their colours, a swirling, glistening trail of reds and blacks and greys.

Next was Mother Nature herself, or at the very least her hungry minions, because the human body, left alone for a few days to rot, was an all-you-can-eat, all-day buffet bar for flies, but also for rats. Rebecca had heard somewhere that if you stood in a populated area, you were never more than six feet away from a rat. Whether it was true or not, she didn't know, but right now she doubted it was even that far. The body, a swollen, distended and crippled zeppelin of dead flesh, had been gnawed. The eyes had been the first thing to go, of that she had no doubt, the glistening, liquid-filled globes most likely quite the delicacy. Everything else had been chewed, the milky glow of bone shining in places through glistening, weeping flesh.

If there was one thing that never ceased to amaze her, it was how a person could go from alive to dead and it just didn't seem to matter. A person was a library of memories and dreams and experiences, an impossibly vast collection of all the things a life involved. Death swept that away with its cold, swift fire. No fanfare. No trumpets. Just death. She wasn't one for deep philosophical discussions. However, to be so close to death, and so often, to be up close and intimate with those who had passed, often in the worst of circumstances, she just couldn't see how this was all there was. There was too much to what made up everything a human was, for something to not go on after.

Rebecca shook her head to dislodge these thoughts. They were morose and depressing. Reflecting on the deeper philosophical ideas of what came after only sent her into some deep, existential panic. She was alive and she had a job to do. And she was pretty sure no one did it as well as she.

Moving closer to the body, she saw now the wounds which had undoubtedly killed the victim. A bullet wound to the forehead and the gore on the wall behind. At first glance, and in the odd light of the room, she'd taken it to be another piece of inexplicable wall art. But there were other wounds, too, and they hadn't been fatal. They had, however, been inflicted violently and she was damned sure the victim had been made to suffer. The one on the side of the head, the mess that had once been an ear, stared back at her, daring her to imagine what it had been like to experience.

The wrists were tied together behind the chair, and although the hands had been chewed she could still see that some of the fingers were missing, snipped off and on the floor she guessed, though they would be long gone and in the belly of a rat. The ankles were also tied to the chair. The face was swollen but not just because of decomposition. It had been beaten, with exactly what she didn't know, but perhaps she'd have a better idea about that once the body was cleaned up and laid out in front of her on a stainless-steel slab in what passed as her office, though there was a definite lack of executive toys. Not even a decent desk.

Something wasn't right about the body, though, but what was it? She edged closer, peering in, making sure she wasn't in the way of any light bathing what she was trying to look at. Then she heard footsteps and turned around to see two other people all in white PPE.

'You done?' she asked.

'We are. How's things in here?'

'Grubby,' Rebecca said. She pointed at the body. 'Does this look right to you?'

'I'm assuming you mean apart from all the blood and decay.'

'Just doesn't look right to me,' Rebecca said. 'How she's sitting or something. I'm not sure.'

The two figures moved closer to the body.

'Looks like she's been propped up,' one of them said.

'That's exactly it,' said Rebecca. 'Like her body had been leant against something. '

'A cushion I'd guess,' said the other.

Rebecca edged closer to the body and reached out.

'We'll do that,' said one of the others and both of them stepped forward.

Carefully, they took hold of the body and leaned it forward.

A faint click sounded.

'Shit ...'

OUTSIDE, and having waved Detective Sergeant Dinsdale off, Jadyn had made his way back over to the crime scene.

'You look ... smug,' Gordy said. 'Anything I should know about?'

'Sarge says I'm in charge,' Jadyn said, very aware of the grin on his face. Then he realised that his mood wasn't being reciprocated and had to work hard to look serious. 'Well, no, I mean, what he actually said was ...'

'Not that, I'm assuming,' said Gordy. 'Me, detective inspector; you, police constable, remember?'

Jadyn was now very aware that he'd said too much, letting his mouth run off with itself before he'd had a chance to think about what he was saying and who he was saying it to.

'I'd best get back to what I was on with.'

'That's probably for the best,' said Gordy, unable to hide her smile. 'The SOC team are now all in the house.'

'Rather them than me,' Jadyn said, remembering what he'd seen in the place.

'Really that bad?'

'Worse.'

'Well, they'll be out soon enough I should think, so get yourself over there to tick them off as they come out.'

Jadyn started to walk back over to the house. As he did, he saw a car driving slowly down the road, the figure inside staring. He saw short hair and was pretty sure that the driver was wearing combat fatigues. Jadyn waved at the car to catch the driver's attention, but whoever it was accelerated away. Then an explosion ripped through the house as though the place had taken a direct hit from a surface-to-air missile.

Every window on the ground floor burst, sending a violent hail of glass out into the world with enough speed to lacerate flesh. The concussion from the explosion swept on, winding people, knocking them off their feet, setting off car alarms. The night came alive with the sound of dogs barking. Flames and dust and muck and brick chased after the glass, swift pyroclastic clouds made from the remains of everything that had been inside the house where the explosion had occurred. But other things were in those clouds: nails and bolts and knots of scrap metal turned into killers in the blink of an eye.

Jadyn, caught by the blast as he had started to make his way up to the front door, flew through the air, a puppet with its strings cut. One minute he was on his feet, the next thing he was freefalling at speed to slam into the side of his vehicle. He didn't hear the impact, only felt it, a hammer blow that seemed to vibrate from his skull right down to his toes. Then he was tumbling, his movement a thing over which he had no control, and he came to a rest on the far side of the car, away from the house.

Silence. That's what Jadyn noticed then. Except it was the kind of silence that was more than an absence of sound. Instead, it was as though some sounds had been permanently deleted and all that remained was a huge space where they should have been, and in their place, the howl of dogs and the scream of car alarms desperately trying to fill it.

For a moment, Jadyn didn't move. Not that he couldn't, he just wasn't sure if he should even attempt it. What if something was broken; a wrist, a leg, his neck? He flexed his fingers on one hand then the other. Well, they're okay, he thought, and moved on, flexing muscles, slowly checking himself over, squeezing his eyes shut to focus, to not miss a pain, a hint that something, somewhere, was wrong. But nothing was, and groggy as a drunk after a three-night bender, he carefully sat up and then with deliberate slow-ness, climbed to his feet.

The house stared back at him. It was a wounded thing now, with torn curtains flapping through broken-teeth windows, tasteless serpent tongues flicking uselessly at the air. The front door was open, broken, hanging by one hinge. A faint orange light could be seen, a fire taking hold. A thought struck him so cold and hard and angry that he jolted: *There are people in there* ... And he was moving, stumbling, using his car to help keep him on his feet.

'Stop!'

The shout was loud and sharp enough to have him pull up fast and Jadyn turned to see the detective inspector staring at him. Her face was cut, blood running down her cheek, she was covered in dust, and she was holding her arm funny, Jadyn thought, like she was stopping it from dropping off.

'There are people in there!' Jadyn said. 'The SOC team! Sowerby!'

'I know!' Gordy said. 'But you can't just go rushing in! That was an explosion! None of us know what's happened. So don't you dare move!'

A movement caught Jadyn's eye. From the house, a figure emerged only to stumble and drop to its knees.

Jadyn heard the wail of a siren, saw an ambulance turn into the end of the lane. He looked at Gordy. She stared back.

'Go!' she said, a phone now up against her ear.

And Jadyn ran.

CHAPTER TEN

FOLLOWING A TAKEAWAY CURRY, WHICH HAD VERY nearly taken his head off, and just enough beer to make the edges of his vision go fuzzy, Harry had headed off to get his head down. It had been good to talk to Kett, and what he'd said had made sense, but Harry still wasn't sure. He knew as well as anyone that opportunities didn't just fall into your lap on a daily basis. So, when they did, it was usually a good idea to take full advantage of them.

Lying on his bed, unable to muster the energy to get undressed or turn out the bedside light, Harry checked his phone. Nothing from the Dales, so that was something, just a missed call from a number he didn't recognise. A scam call, no doubt, he thought, some company trying to sell him the easy way to make his fortune through bitcoin or some such bollocks.

Placing his phone on the floor, Harry stared up at the ceiling, thinking back over the past twelve months. They'd flown by, that was for sure. Life in the Dales had changed him, though a part of him worried that it had made him a bit soft. Somewhere, deep down, he missed that harder edge of himself, and how he'd been able to use it more before heading north.

Not that life had been dull by any means since arriving in Wensleydale, the exact opposite actually, but he wasn't exactly cracking skulls like he used to. But did that really matter? He wasn't a young man anymore, but he wasn't old, either. Was that the problem then? Was he feeling old? Perhaps.

Life in the Paras had been lived at breakneck speed. It had been exciting and terrifying in equal measure. Joining the Police Force hadn't given him much of a change in pace, either. There was more paperwork, that was true, but some of the things he'd done, the crimes he'd investigated, and the criminals he'd had to deal with, it had been a new kind of war and he'd relished being in the thick of it. So, where was he now? And did it really matter if that life had now gone? He wasn't used to thinking so deeply and it was making his head hurt.

A knock at the door jarred his thoughts. He was almost thankful for the interruption.

'I'm still awake,' Harry said, sitting up with a yawn.

The door opened and where he'd been expecting to see Kett a smaller figure stood.

'Evie?'

She walked over to Harry and stood beside his bed.

'You okay? I'll go get your dad.'

Evie started to sob.

'What's up, kiddo?' he asked.

'I did something bad,' she said, and before Harry could do anything about it, she fell forward, burying her head in the mattress.

Harry sat up, reached down, and lifted Evie up onto his lap. She wrapped her arms around his neck and wet his skin with warm tears, her sobs setting a gentle rhythm to the moment.

'It'll be okay,' Harry said, not really sure what to say. 'It can't have been that bad?'

Evie sat back, wiped her eyes.

'I didn't share,' she said. 'I ate all the chocolate myself.'

'Oh,' said Harry. 'Right...'

'You said it was Evie Day, not Moira Day or Stupid Alice Day. So I ate it, and I feel bad.'

'Well, I guess you're technically right about that,' he said.

A larger shadow appeared in the door.

'Nightmare?' Kett asked through a yawn.

'Misunderstanding,' said Harry. 'You're a good lass, Evie, and don't think otherwise. Next time, you'll share, won't you?'

'I will,' she said, rubbing her eyes as Kett picked her up. 'Thanks Uncle Harry.'

'Uncle Harry,' said Kett approvingly, giving Harry a smile.

Lost to the darkness and his thoughts a weariness came over him. He was also far too full, that was true enough, but he was also at a fork in the road of his life that he'd never expected, perhaps never even wanted. So, which way to go, Harry? he thought.

Harry closed his eyes and at last gave in to the evening's food and drink, happy to let them work together to send him to sleep.

A trill rent the air, shattering the silence with the violence of smashed glass.

Harry sat up, grabbed his phone. His watch told him that

he'd been asleep a couple of hours, the morning now drifting on towards two. A call at this time was never a good sign.

'Grimm,' Harry said, rubbing his eyes, yawning.

'Harry, it's Gordy.'

'Bollocks ...'

'You know, I thought you might say that,' said the DI.

Harry could hear the stress in her voice and behind it nothing short of chaos—a chorus of shouting and clattering that took him straight back to the battlefield.

'What the hell's going on?'

'Not enough time to tell you right now,' Gordy said, a gasp of pain stabbing her words. 'I just think ... you need to get back here ... as soon as you can.'

'You're hurt? Where are you? Gordy, you need to tell me what's happened! Is Matt there? Where's the rest of the team?'

Gordy's answer was a strangled, pained cry.

'I'm on my way!' Harry said, already out of bed, still in his clothes, adrenaline racing through him like electricity. 'I'll be there as soon as I can. Have someone keep me updated on what's going on. I need the details.'

No answer.

'Gordy?'

Still nothing, just the sound of something having gone terribly wrong.

'Boss?'

'Jadyn?'

The police constable's voice cut through the melee. He was out of breath.

'There's been an explosion,' Jadyn said.

'An explosion? What the hell are you talking about? What's happened to DI Haig? Is she alright?'

'She's okay,' Jadyn said. 'Dizzy spell, I think. Handed me the phone so she could throw up.'

Harry heard Gordy admonish Jadyn for handing over too much unnecessary information.

'You said there's been an explosion? Where?'

'In Reeth,' Jadyn said. 'Crime scene just went up. Never seen anything like it. People are hurt, Boss. I need to go. I've called Jen, Liz, and Jim.'

'Is Matt there?'

'No.'

'Why the bloody hell not?'

'The district surgeon didn't turn up so he's away checking up on her.'

'Oh, right,' Harry said. 'Look, I'm heading back now. Keep me updated, okay? Send me what details you can, as soon as you can.'

'I will,' Jadyn said.

Harry killed the call.

Kett was at the door.

'Shit storms have a habit of always rolling in when you're away, have you noticed that?'

Harry stared at his phone, still trying to work out just what the hell was going on at the other end.

'I don't know what's going on, but it sounds bad,' he said. 'Something about an explosion at a crime scene. Sounds like my DI copped it a bit, too.'

'You need to be heading off, then.'

'I do.'

Kett checked his watch.

'There's a train just before six.'

'That's four hours away!'

'I could see if the pool car's available?' Kett said.

Harry noticed a smile creep across Kett's face.

'Why is it that I already don't like the sound of that?'

Kett held up a hand to shush Harry while he tapped in a text. An answer came back a beat later.

'I'll be honest with you, pool car is a grand term. It belonged to one of the team, needed to sell it, and well, he just couldn't.'

'Couldn't? How is it possible to be unable to sell a car?'

Kett's smile grew.

'You'll find out for yourself in, oooh, about twenty minutes I should say, when it gets dropped round.'

When those twenty minutes had passed, and Harry had been given a moment to take in the rich visual splendour of the pool car, he walked over to Kett and shook his hand.

'Thanks for everything,' he said. 'Except this.'

'My pleasure,' Kett said. 'You drive safely now, and take care of Gerald.'

'Gerald? Who the hell is—'

Harry stopped. Looked at the car, then back at Kett.

'You named it, then.'

'We had a lottery. Everyone put their suggestions into a bag, the winner was pulled out and here we are. Gerald!'

Harry opened the driver's door and squeezed himself into the front seat. His face was so close to the steering wheel he could bite it.

'You ever seen that movie, The Incredibles?' asked Kett.

Harry shook his head.

Kett laughed.

'There's this scene where the dad squeezes into their family car. What I've just witnessed? Funnier.'

Harry gave up trying to get comfortable, hoofing the seat back with a violent shove.

'Just out of interest, what is this?' he asked. Then he added, 'Beyond purple, I mean.'

'It's a Perodua Kenari,' said Kett.

'That's easy for you to say.'

'I'm not sure that it was. Anyway, it should get you back to the Dales. It may not look like much, but it's reliable.'

'Is it now?' Harry asked.

'I'll be honest, I've not a clue,' said Kett. 'I'm just trying to make you feel better.'

Harry slammed the door, started the engine, then opened the window with the aid of the world's most uninspiring switch—which was quite the achievement, he thought—to give himself some arm room.

'It isn't working.'

'Safe journey,' Kett said, handing Harry a flask of coffee. 'And I hope everything's okay when you get back. Even though I know that it bloody well isn't.'

Harry gave a farewell nod, somehow managed to find first, and headed off on his journey.

CHAPTER ELEVEN

As journeys went, Harry had definitely had worse. But comparing a ride across the desert in the back of a Warrior infantry fighting vehicle, while the locals took pot-shots at you with AK47s and RPGs, with driving across the country on motorways in the Perodua seemed a mite unfair. After all, the Warrior was certainly faster and more comfortable and had been daubed in a colour that didn't make you want to empty your stomach as soon as you set eyes on it.

Harry had pulled over at the first service station to load up on supplies. Kett's coffee could only do so much. What he needed was energy drinks, chocolate, mountains of crisps, and some cheese and onion sandwiches. Stocked up, he'd continued on his way, making as much use as he could of the early hours and the empty roads, gradually becoming more hyper as he fuelled himself on caffeine, sugar, and taurine, whatever the hell that was.

The car stereo was woefully inadequate. If Harry accelerated, and in the Perodua acceleration was a relative term, then a buzzing sound would cut through whatever was coming out of the speakers, which wasn't much, even at full volume. Reception seemed to vary as to which direction Harry turned the steering wheel. No matter what he did to tune it in, the radio seemed to insist on only ever giving him local radio. The car was blessed with a CD player, but with a choice between Tex Ritter's Greatest Hits, 70s Love Songs, and a boxset of television themes, he stuck with the radio.

A call came in a couple of hours into the journey.

'Harry, it's Matt.'

'What's happening? Jadyn said you were over at Margaret's.'

A pause from Matt had Harry even more concerned than he already was.

'Matt?'

'Yes, sorry,' Matt said. 'Rough night. Margaret's fine. What do you know so far?'

'Bugger all,' Harry said. 'All I got from Jadyn was that there'd been an explosion. In Reeth, of all places.'

'Well, all of that's correct,' Matt said.

Harry could hear the weariness in the man's voice.

'An explosion in Reeth? What was it, dodgy gas heating? What about casualties?'

'Jadyn was over checking up on a possible missing person,' said Matt. 'You know, one of those calls from a concerned neighbour. Didn't think there was much in it so figured he would be able to handle it. Managed to find himself face-to-face with the resident who'd been dead a week. Young woman, too, though we're still trying to pull together details on the deceased seeing as there's not much of her left. Sorry, that came out too harsh, but you know what I mean.'

'But what's a MISPER or any of that got to do with an

explosion?' Harry asked. 'And what about the district surgeon? Is Margaret alright?'

'She's okay,' Matt said. 'Took a tumble on the stairs. I found her in her hallway and called an ambulance. The paramedics have had a busy night in Wensleydale that's for sure.'

'She's okay, then?'

'She's in hospital is all I know at the moment. Once she was sorted, I was back over to this. To the explosion.' A breath. 'Harry ... it's bad.'

Harry felt sorry for any medical staff having to deal with Margaret.

'Who was the victim?'

'The woman in the house? As yet, we don't know,' Matt said.

Harry picked up on the odd way Matt answered. Were there other victims then? What the hell had happened?

'All we've got right now are rough details,' Matt continued. 'Like I said, a young woman, mid-twenties. We only know she was called Melissa because that's what her neighbour told us.'

'No ID, then?' Harry asked. 'Nothing in the house?'

'If there was, then finding it isn't going to be easy, seeing as the place just got blown to pieces,' said Matt. 'Have to hope that the next SOC team find something in what they'd already taken from the house.'

'I'm not liking the sound of this,' Harry said. 'And what do you mean, the next SOC team?'

'There's nowt to like,' Matt said, ignoring Harry's question. 'The photographer had been in and then the pathologist and the rest of the SOC team were doing what they do. They were finishing up when it happened, when the place just went up. I've never seen anything like this in my life, Boss. Never.'

'Houses don't just explode,' Harry said. 'You said the SOC team were in there when it happened ...'

'I did. They were, and ...'

'And what?'

Matt's answer wasn't forthcoming.

'Matt?'

'We've got two dead at the scene,' Matt said. 'Caught in the blast. Plenty of others are walking wounded.'

Harry couldn't speak. Thankfully, Matt kept talking.

'Sowerby's in a bad way, Boss. The explosion took her out of the window. The two who were killed, they were with her when it went up. Looks like their bodies—' another breath '—well, they shielded her, a little anyway. Enough that she's still very much alive.'

'Where is she?'

'Hospital,' Matt said. 'The ambulance was already here, what with the victim to pick up, so they were able to get to her and the others sharpish. Air ambulance was called in, got her off good and quick.'

'How bad?'

'How the hell should I know?'

Matt's tone took Harry by surprise, but he let it pass. From what he was hearing, the DS had every right to be knackered and on edge.

'They rushed her off,' Matt continued, his voice calmer. 'Jadyn and Gordy helped, as did anyone who wasn't caught up in it too badly. Had to keep the locals back, though. Then the fire brigade arrived because the place was burning.'

The more Matt told him, the more Harry was worried about what he was returning to.

'So we've a body count of three, then,' Harry said.

'Like I said, it's bad,' Matt said.

'Bad? It's an absolute bloody mess by the sound of it,' said Harry. 'How are you holding up?'

'Barely, but I'm alright. Have to be, don't I?'

'Have you any idea what caused the explosion? Anything at all? I know it's too early, but are you sure it wasn't gas? I've seen it happen. An open oven and a careless match will take a house apart like you wouldn't believe.'

'There was no smell of gas when Jadyn and I went in, you know, before the explosion,' Matt said. 'The only smell was that of the victim. For the house to go up like that, we'd have smelled it for sure.'

'Right,' Harry said, unable to mask the worry in his voice.

For a moment or two, neither man said a word.

'So, where are we with it all now?' Harry eventually asked.

'I've got Jim, Liz, and Jen over,' Matt said. 'They're just keeping folk away from the place for now. It's all cordoned off. The fire brigade are still on with the house. Once they've said it's safe we'll be able to have a look around. Well, not us, but the new SOC team. Gordy's at the hospital.'

'What? She's injured, too? How bad?'

'Just a few cuts and bruises but they're just checking her over to make sure.'

'Not much we can do then for now,' Harry said. 'You didn't mention Jadyn.'

'I sent him home,' Matt said. 'He shouldn't have been on duty anyway. Swapped with Jen without passing it by me first. I'll be having a quiet word with her about it later on.'

'Well, if he's been up all night, he'll be knackered.'

'It's not just that,' Matt said. 'He was first on the scene. Don't think he was prepared for what he found.'

'No one ever is.'

'No, that's not what I mean,' said Matt. 'He was on edge when I arrived. He'd been sick. Said it had reminded him of what happened on that case with Bill Dinsdale.'

Harry understood then what Matt was really trying to say: PTSD. And if there was something Harry really did know about better than most, it was that.

'When's he next in?'

'Tomorrow. And he said he saw a car slow down outside the house just before it went up.'

'That's a bit suspicious, isn't it?'

'Neighbour told him that she had a boyfriend. Military, we think. And Jadyn's pretty sure that whoever was in that car was wearing combat fatigues.'

'Anything on the car or whoever was driving?'

'Nothing,' Matt said.

'Not really a surprise considering what happened.'

'But we'll follow it up tomorrow for sure.'

'Make sure Jadyn sees me first thing,' Harry said. 'Sounds like I need to have a little talk with our police constable.'

'How long now till you arrive?' Matt asked.

Harry stared out through the windscreen as though the dawn breaking over the road in front of him would give him an exact answer.

'Two to three hours at the most,' Harry said.

'Let me know an arrival time and I'll head over to the station to pick you up,' Matt said.

'No need, I'm driving,' replied Harry.

'But you took the train to Norfolk.'

'I made other arrangements,' said Harry.

At this, Matt laughed.

'Ah, the perks of the job, eh? Just flash that shiny DCI badge around and you get handed—'

'Anyway,' Harry said, not wanting to go any further with that line of enquiry, 'I'd best get on and leave you to it.'

'I'll text you the address,' Matt said.

Conversation over, Harry was half tempted to lob his phone out of his window. Nothing that he'd been told by the DS had made his day any better. An explosion, the body in the house and two others dead, numerous injuries, someone suspicious driving past just as the house went boom, Jadyn … It was a lot to take in and the sound of it all buzzing around his head was too much. Three deaths? The press was going to love this, he thought. He reached for the Tex Ritter CD, pushed it into the stereo, and found himself listening to *High Noon*. Thoughts of Gary Cooper facing a lone gang of killers, though hardly relevant, didn't exactly improve his mood.

CHAPTER TWELVE

When, just under three hours later, Harry finally arrived in Reeth in Swaledale, he wasn't entirely sure that the copious number of energy drinks he'd consumed on the way had been such a good idea.

On the plus side, they had kept him awake and alert, and he had arrived safely without any mishaps. He had, at times, been sorely tempted to slam the Perodua into a brick wall, a tree, anything to take away the pain of driving it, but the important thing was, that he hadn't.

The downside, however, was that Harry was pretty sure, thanks to all the caffeine, that he could now hear time. It was a thin, whining sound in the middle of his brain and it wasn't doing his mood any good at all. It reminded him of a dentist's drill burrowing into his skull. This, and the fact that he was both horribly awake and ferociously tired at the same time, meant that when he saw who, or to be more accurate *what*, was waiting for him outside the house, his notoriously low patience threshold was practically non-existent.

Harry brought the car to a halt, bouncing the front

offside wheel into the kerb. Heaving himself out of the vehicle, he walked straight over to the waiting crowd of reporters. They were all armed with an eclectic array of mobile phones, cameras, notepads, and bad fashion choices.

'Right then,' Harry said, 'I'm Detective Chief Inspector Grimm. Now, before any of you go asking any questions, I think the best thing that you can all do is to sod off for now. I've more important things to be getting on with. Thanks for your time though. Really.'

A ripple of gasps and sharp intakes of breath jostled with nervous laughter.

No one moved.

'As you can all clearly see, this is a crime scene,' Harry said. 'We have a job to do. And, unlike yours, it's an important one. If and when we have something to say to you lot, I'll make sure that you're first to know.'

A hand shot up, a voice barked out.

'Mr Grimm—'

'Weren't you listening?' Harry asked. 'Which part of what I just said wasn't entirely clear? Was it the *sod off* bit? I don't see how it could've been. I didn't exactly whisper it now, did I? Whispering isn't really in my skill set. Shouting is. Bellowing, even. Do I need to demonstrate? I'd be more than happy to, but it might be a good idea to step back a ways.'

More voices called out:

'But what actually happened?'

'Can you confirm that a body was found in the building?'

'Do you know who the victim is?'

'Is it correct that there are two other casualties?'

Harry ignored the questions and pushed his way through the gaggle of press until he came to the cordon tape surrounding what was left of the house. On the other side was a face he recognised, eyes wide, lips pursed. Beyond her, the rest of the team, though he saw that both Jadyn and Gordy were missing. Jadyn he'd not expected to see until tomorrow, but Gordy's absence was a concern.

'Detective Constable Blades,' Harry said.

'Good to see you, Boss,' Jen said, lifting the tape for Harry to duck under. 'Sorry about all of this. How was the journey?'

'The bit in the car was just about bearable,' Harry said. 'However, the walk at the end of it through this lot is enough to make me want to go and change my clothes and have a damn good shower, preferably in hot bleach.'

'We've not spoken to them, in case you were wondering. They just turned up.'

'I wasn't,' Grimm winked. 'This lot can sniff out the whiff of a hint of a rumour of a story in their sleep.'

'DCI Grimm!' yet another voice called from the crowd on the other side of the tape. 'Can you tell us what caused the explosion? The public has a right to know!'

'Excuse me,' Harry said to Jen, and he whipped around to push himself up against the tape and into the crowd of reporters just enough to have them stumble back a little, a bear bristling with rage and threatening to break out of its cage.

'The public what now?' he growled, his voice growing louder as he spoke, a rumbling storm hammering down on anyone unfortunate enough to be in front of him.

'They have a right to know what happened, Detective. Or are you withholding information? Not sure how people would see that, are you?'

Harry could see now that the question was from Richard

Askew, a journalist he'd had a few conversations with before. None of them good.

'Why don't you step forward a moment?' Harry asked, and he raised a curled finger to beckon Askew forward.

The journalist approached, bravely at first, like he'd just won a major prize, looking around as though expecting applause. As he drew closer to Harry the confidence on his face started to crumble under Grimm's furnace-like stare.

'See that house behind us?' Harry asked.

'Yes, of course I do,' Askew said. 'What kind of question is that?'

'Now that you ask, it was a rhetorical question,' Harry said. 'Surely you know what those are? I speak, you listen, it's quite simple.'

'Yes, of course I know. And that's not what I meant.'

Harry ignored him.

'Now, that house, as you'll see, is no longer a house, is it?' he said. 'And do you know what a house is?' Harry held up a hand to stop the man from answering. 'It's a home, isn't it? And people live in homes. It's their place of comfort and safety. But this one? Well, it's no longer that, is it? You know what that means, don't you? Events like this, it's not about the building, it's about the lives of the people who lived there, their family, their friends, the people who turned up in the middle of the night to deal with this, everyone who will, from this day forward, be working every hour God sends, and more besides, to get to the bottom of what happened. So, you tell me, does the public have a right to know any of that? Or is it—and forgive me if I'm overstepping the mark here—just you and yours encouraging little more than rabid gossip-mongering? Well?'

Askew did a good impression of a goldfish.

'That's what I thought,' Harry said, and with nothing else to add, turned back to Jen who had now been joined by the rest of the team. As he went to speak, something caught his eye and he dropped down to a crouch. There, in the grass at his feet, he saw something shiny and picked it up.

'What is it?' Jim asked.

Harry peered at the thing between his fingers.

'A ball bearing,' he said.

'What's that doing here, then?'

'That's what I'm asking myself right now,' Harry said. 'Matt mentioned something on the phone, about the boyfriend?'

'Well, we don't know if she definitely had one,' Jim said. 'But according to Jadyn, the neighbour had seen someone around.'

'Military bloke, right?'

'Yes,' Jim said.

A shout came over from the journalists.

'Have you found something, Detective? Can you tell us what it is? Is it important?'

Harry didn't answer. Dropping the small metal ball into a pocket, he turned to Jim.

'PCSO Metcalf?' he said, his voice very loud and very clear so that everyone within earshot heard him.

'Yes, Boss?'

'I want you to keep this lot behind that cordon. Any of them so much as attempt to put a toe across it, you have my permission to fetch that dog of yours and set him on them.'

Harry saw a ripple of disbelief make its way through the reporters strong enough to have them all step back a little.

'You mean Fly,' Jim said. 'That dog?'

'That exact dog,' Harry said. 'Viscous little bugger as we

all know. How you keep him under control is anyone's guess. But it's a good job you do, that's for sure.'

'We're still talking about Fly, aren't we?' Jim said.

'We are indeed,' said Harry. 'Right, the rest of you, follow me.'

Leaving Jim with the reporters, Harry led the others away and over towards the house. He made sure they weren't too close to the building, however, the walls of the place not looking all that stable. Smoke still drifted from the shattered remains. Broken glass littered the grass in front of it like frost. And the air was still rich with the pungent tang of fire.

'Right then—' Harry said, but Matt's hand was in the air. 'You do know you can just go to the toilet if you need to, don't you?' Harry said.

'It's Swift,' Matt said. 'He's on his way.'

Harry was actually warmed by this news, which was a rare experience indeed. Usually, having to prep himself for a meeting, no matter how short, with Detective Superintendent Graham Swift was enough to give him the worst case of stomach acid. But over the past few months, their relationship had thawed just enough to make things workable.

'You're smiling,' Matt said.

'Of course I am,' said Harry. 'He can deal with the press. He'll love that.'

'Good point.'

Harry glanced behind the team to the house, but his first thought was for Gordy.

'Any news on Detective Inspector Haig?'

'She's been patched up and sent home,' Matt said. 'She did her best to convince me that the best place for her was here, but I wasn't having it.'

'And you being her subordinate, she took that well, I'm

sure.'

'Sometimes, folk just need to be told,' Matt said. 'Us lot, we're like family, aren't we? Not just a team. And as you know, we look after each other, it's what we do.'

'True enough. When will she be back on duty?'

'I've said to see how she feels tomorrow.'

'And Constable Okri?'

'He'll be in tomorrow, too,' Matt said. 'He got thrown about a bit by the blast, but he's been checked over and he's fine. Tough lad, that one.'

'Fire service?'

'You just missed them,' said Liz. 'They're sending someone over later to check up on the place. Advised us to keep well away from the building until they've had time to properly assess how safe it is. And from here, it doesn't look safe at all, does it?'

'No, it doesn't,' said Harry. 'Which has me worried that cordon tape isn't going to keep people back.'

'Already thought of that,' said Jen. 'Once we're done, Jim's going to head home and fetch some sheep pens. We'll put those up as a temporary barrier. Not perfect, but more sturdy.'

'Sheep pens?' Harry said. 'You can't be serious! You mean we, the police, have nothing more suitable to hand? Some proper decent barriers? Surely!'

'You'd think, wouldn't you?' Liz said. 'Could probably get some from Harrogate.'

Harry shook his head, rolled his eyes.

'No, sheep fencing will do, I'm sure. What else?'

Matt said, 'Obviously the photos won't be in till later today. And we've not had much from the SOC team yet. Not really a surprise with two of them d—'

Matt's voice broke with the weight of what he had been going to say.

'What about Sowerby?'

'Not really sure,' Matt said, rubbing tiredness from his eyes. 'Like I said to you when you were driving, it looks like the two from the SOC team took most of the blast, shielding her just enough. I'll call the hospital in a bit to find out more if I can.'

'That's going to be a lot for her to take in,' Harry said. 'We've had nothing else from them, then?'

'No,' Matt said. 'We've been told another team is being scrambled to come out and see what else they can find. But that's being coordinated with the fire service so we can be sure no one's in danger. Oh, and Bomb Disposal are on their way.'

At this, Harry did a double-take.

'What? Why wasn't I told earlier?'

'We only just found out ourselves,' said Matt. 'That news came from Swift.'

'But Bomb Disposal?' said Harry. 'Who the hell said this was a bomb?'

'It was something Sowerby said, when she was taken away in the ambulance,' Matt explained.

'What did she say?'

'She was in the room with the body. She was examining it and she saw something stuffed behind it. Two of her colleagues came in and they went to check it, and ...'

'And what?'

'She heard something click.'

Harry's blood ran cold and in his pocket his fingers clasped around that small, metal ball.

CHAPTER THIRTEEN

'And when were you told this?'

'We weren't, Swift was,' said Matt with a weary shrug. 'He heard about what happened to the SOC team, called the hospital, and one of the team told him.'

'But a click could be anything, couldn't it?' Harry said. 'A click doesn't automatically mean that this was a bomb. This is Swaledale! Why would there be a bomb in a house in a village in Swaledale? Just doesn't make sense at all!'

'Best we're sure though, don't you think?' said Jen.

'Of course it's best we're bloody sure!'

Harry took a deep breath.

'Sorry about that,' he said. 'Didn't mean to raise my voice.'

'You do it better than most,' Jen said. 'We're used to it.'

'So, we've got the bomb disposal unit coming over. Brilliant. Absolutely tremendous.'

Harry shook his head. Everything he was seeing and hearing about what had happened here in the quiet village of Reeth was getting progressively worse. And now the bomb squad had been called. It was the last thing he needed. One of the last things, anyway. The list of last things he needed that he carried around in his head seemed to get longer with each day.

'You don't sound best chuffed,' Liz said.

'I'm not,' replied Harry. 'Have you worked with them before, any of you?'

Everyone shrugged, shook their heads.

'Well, I'm just hoping that whoever they send up here is better than who I had to put up with down south.'

'Put up with?' said Matt. 'How do you mean?'

'I'm being unfair,' Harry said. 'It wasn't the whole unit, just the commanding officer. Proper career soldier, which I have no problem with at all, but the way he went about it? That, very much so. Did everything like he was still running a fire team on patrol, always shouting, loved a good salute. Terrible man.'

Harry then noticed the hint of a smirk on Liz's face.

'Something funny?'

The smirk spread to Jen and Matt.

'At least we don't have to salute,' Jen said.

'And what's that supposed to mean?'

'Don't worry about it, Boss,' Matt said. 'I'm sure it'll be fine when they turn up. Like Jen said, best to be sure.'

'And on that, when exactly are they turning up, then?'

'We've been told sometime later this morning.'

'Good,' said Harry. 'The sooner we can get cracking the better. Once they and the fire service have done their thing and made the house safe, we need the SOC team in there sharpish. The longer we wait the more chance there is of evidence being ruined.'

'It isn't already?' asked Liz.

'Forensics can find something in the worst of places,' Harry said. 'But the weather could put an end to any hope of us getting anything more out of there if it starts raining.'

'But the forecast is fine,' said Matt. 'Sunny all day.'

Harry laughed, though there was little joy in it.

'I've lived here long enough to know that the weather forecast is little more than gazing into a crystal ball while keeping your fingers crossed. Now, is there anything else? What about the neighbour, has anyone had a chat with him other than Jadyn?'

'He's already been out and about,' said Matt. 'Bought us all mugs of tea and some cake.'

'For breakfast?'

'You shouldn't limit cake to being just a snack or a treat. It's properly versatile.' Matt leaned in as though he was about to share the most precious of secrets. 'You ever had it fried?'

'What?'

'Fried,' Matt said.

'No, I heard what you said, I just can't believe that it's actually what you said. Who in their right mind ever fries cake?'

'It's wonderful,' Matt said. 'Fried fruit cake and a bit of bacon. Sets you well for the day, that does.'

'Nice with an egg, too,' Liz added.

'Oh, bloody hell, yes,' said Matt. 'Can't beat it.'

Harry held up a hand.

'Enough!'

For a moment, no one spoke. Probably all thinking about fried cake, Harry thought in disbelief.

'So, my understanding of what we have so far is, and to be brutally to the point here, not one sodding thing of any bloody use to anyone at all.'

'You've definitely summed it up succinctly there,' Matt said. 'Not sure we can add much more.'

'But we need to, and fast,' Harry said. 'I'm not going to have us all sitting on our arses waiting for the forensics report or the bomb disposal unit or anything else. We've got three dead, numerous people injured, and if there's nowt else for us to be going on with, then we're all going to have to walk the streets, aren't we? And we do have something, although it's not much: the boyfriend. Detective Sergeant, what do we have on him? Anything?'

'According to Mr Whaley, he's seen a man with the victim a number of times. Military by the sound of it, but as to a description, he can't give us anything beyond him having short hair. No details on the car either.'

'Which is no description at all,' Harry said. 'Someone local might be able to tell us more, and that's what we need to find out. Not least, because Jadyn may well have spotted this same individual driving past just before the explosion. And speaking from experience, my gut tells me the car will be something fast. Army lads have bugger all to spend their money on, living in barracks and being away a lot. So they blow what they do have on their motors.'

'We can divide it up,' suggested Jen. 'Reeth's fairly small. If we each take a few streets and go knocking on doors, then we should get around the place today easily.'

'By lunch, if we get to it now,' said Liz.

'What are we asking?' said Matt.

'Front and centre, up there with seeing if we can track down this army lad, is we need to find out as much as we can about the victim,' Harry said. 'What do we have so far? I'm assuming only what Jadyn managed to find out?'

Matt pulled out his notebook and read through the

description given by Mr Whaley. 'And we know that her first name was Melissa. It's not much.'

'It's enough to be starting with,' said Harry. 'She lived here long enough for people to know her, right? So let's find out what we can. We need to cover all the local pubs, restaurants, shops, anywhere she'd be likely to visit. She doesn't sound like the kind of person people would forget, either, not from that description, scant as it is on detail. Knock on doors, ask questions, let's see if we can't build a picture of who she was, what she did, why she lived in Reeth, anything.'

'Sounds like a plan,' said Jen. 'Give me a minute and I'll divide the place up and give us each a sector to cover.'

'Good,' Harry said as the sound of a car approaching caught his attention. He didn't look round to see who it was. He knew. 'Swift?'

'You must be psychic.'

'Right, then, best you lot crack on with what we've just talked about. I'll join you in a bit. Jim can stay and keep his eyes on the press. I think the threat of Fly had the desired effect.'

'Yeah, they don't want to be licked to death, now, do they?' said Jen.

Harry turned from the team to see Swift ducking under the cordon tape. Harry met him halfway.

'Morning, sir.'

'Grimm.'

'This is one of those occasions where my name matches the situation,' Harry said.

'So I've heard.'

'What do you know so far?'

'Enough to have me here,' Swift said. 'Unidentified body, two dead on the SOC team, injuries ...'

'I'd have called later. I was on my way back from Norfolk so wanted to just get here and assess the situation first before I did.'

'And how was Norfolk?'

'Flat,' Harry said.

Swift made to walk towards the house.

'Best we stay back,' said Harry. 'Fire service is sending someone out to assess how stable the place is. Once that's done another SOC team will be sent out to see if they can recover anything. And there's Bomb Disposal as well.'

'From this?'

'Have to try, Sir.'

'Anything on the victim?'

Harry nodded over at the rest of the team who were making their way under the cordon tape to head off around the village.

'We don't know much yet. Female, mid-twenties possibly, first name only. So they're heading off to knock on doors, find out as much as they can from the local community. Hopefully we'll be able to build some kind of picture then of who she was. Bomb Disposal is on their way as well, like I said. Trouble is, from what I understand, the body was near the explosion which means—'

'There's not much of it left.'

'Exactly.'

'Do you think it could've been a bomb?'

'In Swaledale?' Harry said. 'In Reeth? It doesn't make sense. I just don't see how.'

Trouble was, deep down, and thinking about what he'd heard, it was hard to see that it could be anything else. And then there was the ball bearing he'd found earlier. But that couldn't be what he thought it was, could it?

102 DAVID J. GATWARD

'Doesn't mean it didn't happen.'

'I've dealt with bombs,' Harry said. 'Not just in theatre when I was in the Paras either. Down south, we had more than our fair share of prank calls, true, but a number of times we had the real deal. Most of those were terror-related.'

'Most?'

'It doesn't take much to find out how to make a bomb,' said Harry. 'Worse still, it's horrifying what criminals are getting their hands on now. They treat the dark web like a 24/7 supermarket. Military-grade stuff. Kit I've only ever used professionally. Found this one bloke in a flat with an RPG. It was so old if he'd have used it then he'd have probably blown himself to pieces, but there it was, just sitting next to his television.'

'The world's a dangerous place, Grimm. Three murders in a place like Reeth is evidence of that.'

'It is.'

Swift turned from the house and stared at the reporters.

'How long have they been here?'

'Too long,' Harry said. 'I've already said my bit.'

'And how did that go? I'm going to assume terribly.'

'As expected,' said Harry. 'They're still here.'

Swift rubbed his chin.

'Well, it looks like you have everything in hand,' he said. 'What say I deal with the press and leave you and the team to get on with as much as you can.'

'That would be very helpful, Sir,' said Harry, impressed with Swift's offer.

'And it might be a good idea to find out who owns that car there,' Swift said. 'If we have the bomb squad turning up, they'll want the space.'

Harry looked to where Swift was pointing and saw a white Porsche. Nice car, he thought.

'I'll have a word with the team,' Harry said.

Swift gave a nod and then, neatening up his hair with his fingers, he made his way over to Jim and the small crowd he was still holding at bay.

Harry looked again at the Porsche then waved Matt over.

'We need to get this moved if we can. Must've been a royal pain in the arse for the fire service having it parked right there.'

'I'm afraid we can't move it,' Matt said.

'What? Why?'

'It's the victim's car. SOC team were supposed to take it away, but obviously things kind of got out of hand and this was forgotten.'

Harry jumped at this.

'So no one's had a look inside yet? Has anyone done a follow up on the numberplate to find out her details?'

'All of that's been sent through,' Matt said. 'As for getting inside, no one can. No keys.'

Harry shook his head.

'Not going to be an easy one, is it?' said Matt.

'No,' Harry agreed. 'It isn't. But we should get something on the car pretty soon.' Then he looked up the street and saw the next house along from where they were standing. 'That's this Mr Whaley's place, right?'

'It is,' Matt said.

'Time I went to introduce myself I think.'

CHAPTER FOURTEEN

At the door to the house, Harry gave a swift, hard knock against the wood. A shuffling sound answered it. The door slid open to reveal an old man who, to Harry's eye, appeared to have walked straight out of an early episode of Last of the Summer Wine. Right down to the flat cap.

'How do,' the man said.

'Mr Whaley?' Harry said. 'I'm Detective Chief Inspector Harry Grimm.'

'That you are,' Mr Whaley replied.

'I understand that it was you who called in about your missing neighbour?'

'I did, yes,' Mr Whaley said. 'Spoke to your young constable about it.' He leaned then out of his door for a look at what was going on. 'Terrible what happened. Just terrible. But it's like I said to that constable, terrible things happen to people, don't they? Terrible, awful things.'

'Mind if I come in?' Harry said.

Mr Whaley smiled broadly, showing teeth in surprisingly good order, Harry thought.

'Of course,' he said and stepped back. 'In you come then.'

Harry stepped into the house.

'Just along there,' Mr Whaley said, directing Harry along the hall.

Harry walked on and found himself in a kitchen.

'Sit yourself down,' Mr Whaley said, gesturing over towards two chairs either side of what Harry assumed to be the oven, a fire burning behind glass. 'Your constable certainly found it warm there I think.'

Harry made his way over and sat down.

'Tea?'

'No,' Harry said. 'I won't be staying long. Just thought I'd introduce myself, see if there's any other information you can provide about Melissa.'

Mr Whaley came over and sat opposite Harry. For a moment neither man spoke and Harry quickly became aware that he was being stared at.

'You're not from round here, are you?' Mr Whaley said.

'No,' Harry said with a laugh. 'What gave it away?'

'That accent, it's more Somerset than Yorkshire, I'm thinking. I'm good with accents, see.'

'Moved up here last year,' Harry said, impressed. 'Just to step in for a while, that kind of thing.'

'Must be very different up here to life down that way.'

'You could say that, yes,' said Harry. 'You ever been down there yourself?'

Mr Whaley leaned forward, grabbed a poker, opened the door to the fire and jabbed the metal spike in hard. Then he lobbed in another log. When he spoke next he was still holding the poker, only it was pointing at Harry rather than the stove.

'I like it up here, it's quieter,' he said. 'Than other places, if you know what I mean.'

'It is that,' Harry said. 'Bristol certainly isn't.'

'You must miss it, though.'

'Used to think that I did. I'm not so sure now.'

Mr Whaley tapped Harry on his knee with the end of the poker, leaving behind a grubby smudge.

'You going soft, then, is that it?' he said.

Mr Whaley was clearly not one for holding back on speaking his mind, Harry thought, a little amused.

'Maybe I am,' Harry said. 'But life's busy up here, too.'

Mr Whaley rested the poker back against the wall and sat back.

'You sound like that bloke in that movie, what was it now? Oh yes, Local Hero.'

'Can't say I've seen it.'

'What? It's a classic. Some oil executive heads off to persuade this village, by which I mean bribe them, that having a new oil refinery there is a great idea.'

'And what happens?'

'The place, the people, it changes him,' Mr Whaley said. 'I won't tell you how it ends, because that's not fair now, is it? But I can see that this place, the Dales, it's changed you, hasn't it?'

'You're a little too wise, I think,' Harry said.

Mr Whaley laughed and asked, 'So, how can I help, Detective?'

'Well, I know that you spoke with Constable Okri,' Harry said.

'Told him all I could as well.'

'I just wondered if there was anything else that you might not have mentioned?'

'Like what?'

'I honestly don't know,' said Harry. 'Anything, really. Might seem unimportant to you, but to us, even the smallest of details can make a difference. You mentioned a boyfriend as well, I believe?'

Mr Whaley looked thoughtful for a moment. While the man was quiet, Harry glanced around the room. He spotted a black and white photo in a frame of a younger man and woman.

'Is it just you, then?' Harry asked.

'It is,' Mr Whaley replied. 'Just me. No bad thing, really. Happy with my own company.'

'That I can understand.'

'No one to get in the way or to always have to think of something to talk to them about.'

'I've just found myself with a dog,' said Harry, not really sure why he offered this information.

'Damned foolish thing to do,' Mr Whaley said. 'Getting a dog. But each to their own.'

Mr Whaley said nothing more for a moment. He didn't mention the woman and Harry decided it wasn't his place to pry. There was enough tragedy in the day as it was. The last thing he was going to do was risk wading through even more, particularly if it had been laid to rest long ago.

'So, have you thought of anything else?' Harry asked. 'About Melissa, or this boyfriend? You've said he was military. Was there anything else, perhaps details about his car? Details, no matter how small, are always useful.'

'You know, I have remembered something,' Mr Whaley answered, and again that poker was in his hand.

'Anything that might help we'd be grateful of.'

The old man leaned forwards.

'Look, now I didn't mention this to your constable, because to be honest, I didn't actually think of it then. But you being here, with that accent of yours? Well, that's jogged my memory you see. Got the old mush in my skull stirring a little.'

'Anything you say is confidential,' Harry said. 'You have my word. Do you have the boyfriend's name?'

It was a shot to nothing, but Harry could never quite quash the hope that one day, someone would give him a piece of information so useful and key to a case that he'd solve it in hours.

'Good at keeping secrets, are you?'

'What?'

'I suppose you have to be, don't you? Things you've had to deal with in your job. Can't be easy.'

'No, it's not,' said Harry. 'You were going to say something, about Melissa, maybe?'

'Oh, yes,' said Mr Whaley. 'Now what was it? Oh, yes, that was it, and you'd reminded me of it, hadn't you? Just a moment ago. Actually, no, when you turned up on my doorstep it was.'

'Really? And what was it?'

'Your accent,' Mr Whaley. 'Like I said, I'm good with accents, you see. Said that to your young officer, too.'

'What about my accent?'

'Same as hers, it is,' Mr Whaley said. 'Like you've both come here to advertise the joys of drinking cider.'

Well, that was something, anyway, Harry thought. Probably not much, but you never knew just where a tidbit like that would lead. Though more often than not it was nowhere at all.

Mr Whaley stood up.

'I've things to be doing,' he said, clapping his hands together as though his day was just packed and he didn't want to be wasting time just sitting and talking. 'Places to go, people to see, that kind of thing.'

'That makes two of us,' said Harry, rising to his feet. 'Many thanks for your time, Mr Whaley.'

'No, thank you for coming around, Harry,' Mr Whaley said. 'It's been a pleasure.'

Harry laughed.

'Something funny?' Mr Whaley said, sounding confused.

'Most people I meet don't generally use my first name,' Harry said.

'No point in being all formal now, is there?' Mr Whaley said. 'Not now you've been in my house and sat in my kitchen.'

'No, I suppose not,' Harry said.

At the front door, Mr Whaley leaned past Harry and opened it for him.

'You take care now,' he said. 'And I dare say I'll be seeing you again soon enough.'

'Well, if I've any more questions, I'll certainly be around.'

Outside, and with the door now closed behind him, Harry looked over to see Detective Superintendent Swift fully engaged with the press. Between them, he saw Jen. He wasn't really sure what he'd gained from speaking with Mr Whaley, but that point about the accent was certainly something to bear in mind. So he made his way over to Jen and stored that detail away in the hope that it would be useful later. He also tucked away the movie *Local Hero*; it might be something good to watch with Grace one evening.

CHAPTER FIFTEEN

'ALL OKAY, THEN?' JEN ASKED WHEN HARRY CAME AND stood beside her.

'Just had a chat with old Mr Whaley,' Harry said. 'And I think we could all do with a quick meeting over in Hawes before tomorrow. Reckon you'll all be done in time to get back for four?'

'No bother at all,' said Jen. 'Hopefully, we'll have a little bit more to be going on with by then as well.'

Harry watched Jen jog away, her pace effortless and smooth. It reminded him that a couple of weeks had now gone by since his last run. Whereas Jen was a very keen runner capable of doing ultras that took in the most mountainous of terrain, Harry wasn't. He battled with running but still kept at it because sometimes it was a wonderful thing. And right now he rather fancied just heading out to the Roman road above Hawes, parking just beyond Burtersett to then head up to Beggarman's Lane, then back down again. The fresh air, the exertion, would do him good.

His phone buzzed. When he saw who it was, he answered as quickly as he could.

'Grace.'

'Rumour has it you're back early.'

'I am,' Harry said. 'I meant to give you a call on the way, send you a text anyway, but it was early and I needed to get here as soon as I could and you know how it is and—'

A laugh down the line.

'You're rambling.'

'I never ramble. I'm succinct.'

Another laugh.

'How's Smudge?'

'That's the only reason you called?'

'I didn't call, you did.'

'But you wanted me to. I could feel it.'

'What? What are you talking about? I'm too tired to keep up.'

'Smudge is fine,' Grace said, and Harry heard something attack her phone. 'I think she can hear your voice. She's missed you.'

'Of course she hasn't.'

'I know you don't want to admit it, but she's only got eyes for you. You'll just have to accept that. What's pulled you back here early then?'

Harry knew he couldn't say too much. Though with the press here he had a feeling that the news of the explosion would rip through the Dales like wildfire before the day was out.

'Something over in Swaledale,' he said.

'The explosion?'

Harry couldn't believe it.

'You've heard, then?'

'It's all anyone's talking about,' said Grace. 'Any idea what caused it? Was anyone hurt?'

'Gordy's still at the hospital,' Harry said.

'Was there anyone in the house? I didn't realise the team got caught in it, too.'

'Jadyn and Gordy were here when it happened,' Harry explained. 'They're okay. I'll be checking up on them later, but they've today off anyway.'

'The others?'

'They're fine,' Harry said, then decided to change the subject and not mention what had happened to the SOC team. 'Have you ever fried cake?'

'What?'

'Cake,' Harry said. 'Have you ever fried it? Matt mentioned something about having it for breakfast with bacon.'

'You mean you've never had it?'

'Why would I have?' Harry asked. 'No one fries cake! It's not a thing!'

'It's a great way to use up stale cake is what it is,' said Grace. 'I'll have to make it for you sometime.'

'No you bloody well won't,' Harry said. 'I'm quite sure I can survive without it.'

'I'll make it with bacon and egg. And on the subject of food, you got any plans for tea?'

'You mean dinner?'

'I know what I mean,' Grace said.

'No, I haven't,' said Harry. 'Haven't heard from Ben either, so I've no idea what he's up to.'

'As I'll be coming over with Smudge, we can cook some-thing up together. Nowt posh, just mince and spaghetti or something. Bottle of wine, maybe.'

'Sounds grand,' Harry said.

'Just let me know when you'll be back and I'll head over.'

'Thanks, Grace,' Harry said. 'See you later.'

Grace's reply was drowned out by the bark of a dog. Harry was pleased no one saw the smile on his face because of it. But the vehicle he saw driving towards him quickly killed it. The shadow it cast and the rattle from its diesel engine had the gathered journalists moving quickly out of the way as it pulled up behind the Porsche. A man in combat fatigues leapt out of the passenger door.

'We need this car shifting. Now.'

'I'm DCI Harry Grimm,' Harry said, marching over to meet the officer.

'We can't have this here,' the officer said. 'Need to put in a safe perimeter. Whose is it?'

'Belongs to the first victim,' Harry said. 'The woman who lived here.'

'First victim? How many are there?'

'Three,' Harry said and explained about the SOC team casualties. 'So we've no key to move it. It'll have to stay put for now.'

'Not good enough.'

'You'll have to work around it.'

'Clearly.'

Harry had never been the world's biggest fan of officers. They were an important and necessary part of the army structure, he understood that. What he didn't understand was how normal people entered Sandhurst Military Training Academy only to leave nine months later as arrogant bastards. The place trained them well, there was no doubt about it. The job was to deliver soldiers who could give orders under astonishing stress, make the kind of decisions that lives depended on, but did that really mean the officer also had to be a bit of a dick?

They weren't all like that, for sure, and Harry knew he was being unfair, but there were certainly enough of them about for it to be noticeable. And all of those traits, they never left them, even when they transferred to civilian life. Of course, he'd met some good officers, followed them into battle, saved the life of one or two as well, but it was impossible to forget the arseholes.

The officer had still not introduced himself. Instead, he was already directing his small team to unload their equipment and get suited and booted for the task in front of them.

'If there's anything I can do to help.'

'There isn't,' the officer said. 'Actually, no, there is. You're a Bobby, right? So, can you shift this lot back, please? There's a good chap.'

Harry ignored the 'Bobby' comment.

'Shouldn't you wait for the fire service?' he asked. 'I was told they were heading over to double-check that the building was safe.'

'Already been in touch,' the officer said. 'Calculated risk. They're on their way, but we need to get in there if there's a bomb.'

'I doubt there is now,' Harry said. 'I think the damage is already done.'

'But there might be.'

'Look at the place,' said Harry.

'That's not how bombs work. You can't just blow up a bomb by blowing up another bomb near it.'

'That's not what I was suggesting,' Harry said. 'I've seen this kind of damage before.'

'Yes, but it's a lot different in real life,' the officer said. 'This isn't the movies.'

Harry had now had enough. He was tired, people were dead, nothing made sense. He didn't need some officer with a rod up his arse covering him in hot sarcasm.

'I found this,' he said, pulling the ball bearing from his pocket.

The silver ball rolled around in the palm of Harry's hand.

The officer glanced down.

'And what of it?'

'We both know what this is, don't we?'

The officer said nothing.

'My thinking is that this is a ball bearing from a Claymore,' Harry said. 'And that's an anti-personnel mine, in case you'd forgotten.'

'Of course, I've not forgotten. I just think you're jumping to conclusions, Detective, that's all. And how can you be sure?' The officer looked at the ball bearing again then back to Harry, a frown etched into his brow. 'And how would you even know, anyway?'

'Ex-Para,' Harry said, 'that's how. My face isn't like this because I'm really into body modification and fancy myself as the new Freddy Kruger. Had a run-in with an IED in theatre. And even with a face like this, I was one of the lucky ones, as I'm sure you know.'

Harry gave the officer a moment to think on what he'd just said.

'I don't think there's another bomb. I think that for whoever set this, one was probably enough. Explosions don't always cause a fire by default, but if this went off in a room where a fire was already burning in the grate, then it would spread quickly.'

'Perhaps.'

'And just so we know where we are,' Harry continued, 'you may be OC of your little troop here, but this is my crime scene and you report to me. Are we clear?'

The officer raised his hand to salute but caught himself.

Harry almost smiled.

'I'll leave you to be getting on with it all then.'

'Yes,' the officer said. 'We'll be as quick as we can.'

'I'm sure you will.'

Harry left the bomb disposal team to their work. The ball bearing hadn't really got him thinking until he'd seen them turn up. The look in the officer's eye had then simply confirmed what, at first, he'd thought to be impossible. And the whole thing had him very worried. The only people he had ever dealt with who had the kind of darknet access to get their hands on ordnance like a Claymore were very bad indeed. And if they were here in the Dales that meant a storm was coming. And no one was in any way prepared for it.

CHAPTER SIXTEEN

LATE AFTERNOON CAME ROUND QUICKLY. MATT, JEN, and Liz had cracked on with not only knocking on doors in Reeth, but going further afield as well, along to Grinton to the east and Gunnerside to the west. With the bomb disposal unit arriving, and Swift on-site, Jim headed back to the family farm and returned in his Land Rover with a trailer of sheep pens.

The bomb disposal team had, by then, been joined by someone from the fire service. And, after what seemed a good amount of time simply standing around and rubbing their chins in thoughtful fashion, they agreed that the house was bomb free and safe enough to walk in. But that would have to wait until tomorrow because it had taken that long to get a new SOC team to send out. It wasn't that there weren't enough staff, just that they were busy on other jobs. Harry had been given confirmation that someone was going through everything that was found at the site and that a report would be to him as soon as possible.

'And what exactly do you mean by soon?'

'Well, soon. You know, quickly.'

'Tomorrow? The day after? Next week? Soon can mean a lot of things to a lot of people.'

'Exactly. Soon.'

Whoever was on the other end of the call was not making friends easily, Harry thought.

'And you can't be any clearer than that?'

'No.'

'Right, well, thanks for whatever this was.'

'Not a problem.'

Call over, Harry waited by the bomb disposal unit's vehicle as the officer wandered over.

'All done?' Harry asked.

'We are, yes,' the officer said. His tone had warmed a little after Harry's revelation about his own military past. 'You're good to go now.'

'No bomb, then.'

'No. I'll get my report to you first thing tomorrow. That suit?'

'Very much so,' Harry said, relieved to not hear the word *soon* again.

The officer made to walk past Harry and stopped mid-step.

'Why did you leave?' he asked. 'The Paras, I mean. Why leave and end up doing this?'

'Long story,' Harry said.

'The IED?'

'Partly,' said Harry. 'These scars aren't just on the outside, if you know what I mean.'

'I do,' the officer said. He reached into his pocket and held something out for Harry to see.

'Found this,' he said. 'I know we're not supposed to pick

stuff up from a crime scene but one of my team grabbed it. New, you see, not as experienced. Sorry about that.'

In the palm of the officer's hand was a car key. The fob was a little melted, but it was still very much a key.

'Where was it?' Harry asked.

'In the house,' the officer said. 'Kitchen, I think. I don't remember exactly. Too busy making sure another Claymore wasn't buried under the rubble.'

Harry could see that the melted fob had once contained a button. No way that was ever working again.

'It's a Porsche fob, I think,' the officer said. 'I know it's a bit melted, but you can just about make out the logo.'

Harry turned the key over. He was right.

'My guess, it's for that one over there,' the officer said. 'Shame we didn't have it when we arrived.'

Harry stared at the key, then at the Porsche. When he turned to thank the officer, the man was already in the van. With a wave, they headed off.

Key in hand, Harry walked over to the car.

'You not leaving then?'

It was Matt and he was jogging over to catch up.

'In a minute,' Harry said.

'The others are on their way,' Matt said. 'They'll have the tea brewed by the time we get back for sure.'

Harry lifted the key.

'You think it's for that, do you?' Matt asked.

'Only one way to find out.'

Harry pressed the button. He expected it not to work. It surprised him. The Porsche gave a sharp double beep and flashed its lights.

'Well, bugger me,' Matt said. 'Where did you find that, then?'

'Bomb Disposal did,' said Harry. 'In the house somewhere.'

Harry reached for the car door, stopped, looked at Matt.

'You got any gloves to hand?'

'Sure thing,' Matt said, and he trotted over to his vehicle, returning a moment later with a pair each.

'Shouldn't we be leaving this to Forensics?' Matt asked.

'We've lost enough time as it is,' Harry said. 'We'll do a quick search, that's all. See if we can find anything that'll help.'

'If you're sure.'

'I'm never anything else.'

'No, you're not,' said Matt. 'And it's a little terrifying.'

Harry walked round to the driver's side, opened the door. Matt leaned in, careful to not topple onto the seat.

Harry adjusted the seat to give him more space to work in.

'Like I said, a quick search,' Harry said, checking the pockets in the door. 'A receipt, a note, anything that might be of use.'

Matt dropped open the glove box.

'Anything?' Harry asked.

Matt shuffled through the contents.

'Vehicle manual, a packet of mints, a notebook, and a catalogue of sex toys.'

'Funny time to be making jokes,' Harry said.

'No joke,' Matt said. 'Look.'

Harry turned to see Matt holding a thin, glossy brochure. The cover was subtle; matte black and soft to the touch, with nothing more than an embossed heart showing. Inside, though, things got a little more interesting.

'Why would someone have that in their car?' Matt asked.

Harry shrugged.

'Bag it,' he said, ducking down for a look under the seats. 'Bag everything.'

'I think I've got something.'

Harry looked up.

'What?'

Matt handed Harry the notebook.

'This isn't a notebook, it's a diary,' Harry said, flicking through.

'I know,' said Matt. 'There are names, phone numbers, and addresses on certain days.'

Harry found the date that was the last time the victim had been seen.

'Look,' he said, holding the diary up.

'I see it,' said Matt. 'Want me to call it?'

'Rude not to.'

Matt punched in the number. There was no answer.

'Well, it's something,' Harry said. 'Anything else?'

Matt shook his head.

'Good,' said Harry. 'Because I don't know about you, but I'm gasping for a mug of tea.'

Matt laughed.

'Your own mother wouldn't recognise you,' he said.

'How do you mean?'

'You've changed, Harry.'

'Not too much, I hope.'

'No,' Matt said. 'But just enough I think. Just enough.'

Harry and Matt made to leave when Harry stopped and looked back at the car.

'What is it?' Matt asked.

'We didn't check the boot.'

'It's a Porsche,' said Matt. 'They don't have one. Well, not one big enough to carry anything other than your toothbrush.'

Harry opened the car again, popped the bonnet, and stared at the space inside. Matt joined him.

'You know,' Matt said, 'that's bigger than I thought. And yes, I know that came out wrong.'

Harry reached in under the bonnet and heaved out a black rucksack and a small, pale blue suitcase, which was about the size of hand luggage he would take on a flight.

'Here,' he said, handing the flight case over to Matt.

Matt took it and opened it.

'Dear God!'

Harry, who was about to open the rucksack, looked over at the DS.

'What is it?'

Matt turned the opened flight case around so that Harry could have a good look at the contents.

'Maybe she was in sales after all,' Harry said, thinking back to the recently found catalogue.

'What, so she has the catalogue with her and does door-to-door with a bag of samples?'

The contents of the flight case were intimate in nature, that was for sure, some considerably more so than others. There were also what looked like lengths of satin, some of the tiniest lace underwear Harry had ever seen, and if he wasn't mistaken, a small leather whip. There was also a tube of lube and a packet of condoms.

I don't think we need to go rummaging around in there, do you?' Harry said and turned back to the rucksack he was holding. The weight of the thing had taken him a little by surprise.

'You sure you want to open that?' Matt asked. 'After

what I just found I'd be cautious if I were you. Who knows what else she was hauling around with her?'

Harry ignored Matt and unclipped the bag, yanking it open.

'Well?' Matt asked.

'Clothes,' said Harry, reaching inside, as an odd familiarity at what he was seeing buzzed his brain. 'Warm jacket, down by the looks of things, jeans, T-shirts, underwear. There's other stuff, too; pouches of food, first aid.' He pulled out a small cardboard box. 'And these are water purification tablets.'

Harry then started to remove the items carefully, placing them on the driver's seat of the car. And the more he removed, the more that sense of déjà vu grew inside him.

'Are you looking for something specific?' Matt asked.

'This isn't just a bag packed for a few days away,' Harry said.

'No?'

Harry looked at Matt, shook his head.

'It's a grab-bag,' he said.

Matt's face scrunched up with confusion.

'What's one of those when it's at home, then?'

'They're only ever used in an emergency,' Harry said. 'Everything turns to shit, you grab this and run. Look...'

He held out a few more of the things he'd found inside.

'Cash, high-energy food, toiletries, clothes. There's even a sleeping bag.'

'You sound like you've seen something like this before,' Matt said.

'I have,' said Harry. 'I've got one myself.'

· · ·

BACK AT THE OFFICE, the team were gathered around, all of them nursing a mug of tea. Harry had already finished his and rather fancied another. But he wanted to get on, mainly because he was looking forward to seeing Grace and Smudge and having a catch-up with Ben.

'We'll have a proper meeting tomorrow morning,' he said. 'So let's just get through the main details as quickly as we can, get everyone home for a rest, then we'll be fresh for whatever comes in from Forensics.'

Matt ran through the day's events from his notes.

'Can't say we've got much to be going on with from our door-to-door,' he said. 'Melissa, still no surname as yet—'

'Nothing on the car, then?' Harry asked.

'Still waiting to hear,' said Jim. 'I've handed over the details.'

'Well, chase that tomorrow,' Harry said. 'I'm assuming someone has contacted the families of the two SOC team members?'

'Gordy was on that even as she was taken to hospital,' Matt said. 'She's been in touch with another team to visit them and will relay all information as and when.'

'Anything else on the first victim?' Harry asked.

'From what we've gathered from the folk we spoke to, everyone seemed to think she was friendly enough, but that she generally kept herself to herself,' said Jen. 'They saw her around a bit, in the shops, driving that Porsche of hers. But no one seemed to know her socially, if you know what I mean. It looks like she was known well enough to wish a good morning to and that was about it.'

'Except with her neighbour,' Harry said.

'Seems that way, yes. He knew her better than most. Not that that's saying much.'

'He did mention her accent to me, though,' Harry said. 'Same as mine apparently.'

'So she's from down south, then?' Matt said.

'That covers a multitude of sins,' Harry replied. 'If she sounded like me, then she's from Somerset or Bristol way, I should think. Though most people seem to think that an accent like mine is how everyone talks in the southwest.'

Liz then mentioned what she'd found out from the village store in Reeth. 'Like Jen said, she seemed to be friendly but private. The owner mentioned how sometimes she would come in and really splash out on food and booze.'

'Splash out? In what way?'

'Champagne, smoked salmon, that kind of thing.'

'And they remember that?'

'They said it had become more regular. At first, it was rare, then it was once a month, but recently it was every couple of weeks.'

'She had more money, then?'

'Maybe,' Liz said.

'Anything else?'

'Just the diary we found,' said Matt, 'and that grab bag of clothes and whatnot, and the, er, you know, the ...'

'The catalogue and flight case full of sex toys,' Harry said.

'Yes, that.'

Jen laughed.

'Nowt to be embarrassed about,' she said.

'I'm not embarrassed.'

'You're blushing.'

'My tea's too hot.'

'So, why would she be carrying all of that, then?' Liz asked.

'I can think of two reasons,' said Harry. 'One innocent, the other not so much.'

'How do you mean?'

'Well,' Harry explained, 'it's either for personal use, or they're tools of the trade, if you know what I mean.'

'Bit of a jump to make, isn't it?' Jen asked. Harry could hear the irritation in her voice. 'That she's either got a healthy sex life or is a prostitute.'

'Or she's a sales rep,' Matt said.

This was a conversation that Harry knew could soon go very, very wrong indeed.

'None of this is a judgement,' he said. 'This isn't a moral crusade or anything like that. We're not judging the victim here, remember that. We are looking at evidence and trying to work out what it could point at, that's all and that's enough. What I'm doing is putting forward possible answers to the questions we're posed by what we find. And we either explore them or we don't. I'd prefer to explore them, wouldn't you?'

Harry knew that his tone was hard, but he had a point to make. He'd worked with teams before where judging the character of a victim or witness had ended up messing things up for the investigation. He wasn't about to let that happen here.

'Still, though,' said Jen, 'why would you think that?'

'Because I've dealt with backstreet prostitutes, pimps, and some very highly paid escorts in my time,' said Harry. 'And ignoring the grab-bag, a high-end sports car and a flight case full of sex toys—the same type offered in the brochure we found in the glove compartment—are part of the uniform. And before you say anything, I also agree that this could be innocent, that she's just got a very healthy appetite, perhaps is even part of the swinging scene, and we will explore that too if we need to. Clear?'

Jen nodded.

'The diary Matt found had telephone numbers and addresses written in certain days going back over the past year,' Harry said. 'I've tried the number written against the date when she was last seen, but not had an answer as yet. No voicemail either.'

'Where's the address?' Liz asked.

Harry looked over to Matt.

'Ambleside,' the DS said.

'The Lake District?' said Liz.

'Can't say that I know of any other Ambleside,' said Harry. 'Never been myself, but it looks like I might have to take a trip there tomorrow. And someone can crack on with checking out those other numbers, too, see if we can't find someone who knows something about the victim.'

'Mind if I come along?' Jen asked.

'This isn't a jolly,' Harry said.

'I know,' Jen said. 'But Matt needs to stay here, doesn't he, what with Joan about to pop? And with Gordy not here yet, I'm the only other detective.' She smiled then and added, 'Obviously, if there's a bit of time spare, there's a couple of shops I could do with popping into as well.'

'You did hear what I just said, didn't you?' Harry asked. 'This isn't an opportunity to max out your credit cards.'

Jen gave a nod.

'Of course I did, but actually, the shops might do you some good as well.'

'Shops never do me good,' said Harry. 'Ever.'

'There's a running shop and a swimming shop,' Jen explained. 'You need new trainers.'

'Do I, now? And that's your professional opinion, is it?'

'Yes, it is,' said Jen. 'You've knackered yours and you can't just keep thumping around in them with the sole half off.'

'I glued that back on the other day,' Harry said. 'Anyway, why would I want to visit a swimming shop?'

'To buy a wetsuit,' said Jen.

Her tone, Harry noted, was as though what she had said was a given, the kind of thing which just made sense to anyone hearing it, a stated fact.

'I think we both know that isn't going to happen,' Harry said. Then before Jen could say anything else he asked, 'What about this mysterious boyfriend and/or the individual Jadyn saw outside the house?'

'One of the bar staff at the Black Bull was able to confirm that the deceased was seen in there with a man matching the description we already have,' said Jim

'Anything else?'

'Yes,' Matt said, 'the car. And it sounds like a motor that Jen would get excited about.'

'You're not wrong there,' said Jen. 'Subaru Impreza. In blue, as well. Nice.'

'We've narrowed it down, then,' Harry said. 'Shouldn't be too hard to find if one of us has a drive around Catterick. It's not like we're going to find ourselves searching through hundreds of those, is it? My guess is just a handful.'

Harry was very aware of the time and that he wanted everyone fresh tomorrow for another long day. He asked if there was any other business, keen to finish the meeting and get on with the evening ahead. One which he hoped would involve a natter, a soppy dog, some good food and wine, and the company of Grace.

'Just the Gala, I think,' said Jim.

Harry turned his attention to the PCSO who was sitting to his left, his dog, Fly, asleep on his back under his seat.

'The what now?'

'Hawes Gala,' Jim said. 'Don't you remember it from last year?'

'No, I don't,' Harry replied. 'And I can feel myself regretting asking this already, but what is it?'

'Fancy dress parade, rides for the kids, stalls, tombola, food, beer tent, animal vegetable competition,' Jim said. 'It's brilliant!'

A murmur of agreement rippled through the room, but Harry hadn't got beyond the last thing Jim had mentioned.

'Animal vegetable competition?'

'You get a few vegetables together,' Jim explained, 'and make them look like an animal.'

'Of course you do,' Harry said. 'And I'm wondering now if you didn't quite understand what I meant by any other business, because I'm not seeing how this is relevant.'

'We'll have a presence there,' Matt said. 'It's good PR, isn't it?'

'And we'll need to be in the parade,' said Liz. 'We were too busy last year to come up with anything, but I reckon we should give it a go this year for sure.'

'Fancy dress, you mean?' Harry said. 'The police, as in us, in fancy dress, in a fancy dress parade.'

Liz gave an enthusiastic nod.

'You'll love it!'

'I absolutely bloody well will not,' Harry said. 'And there's no way that any of you are having me dress up as anything, so don't go getting any grand ideas.'

Harry noticed a sly smile then between Liz and Jen. He decided to ignore it.

'Well, I think that's about it,' he said, closing the meeting down before anyone could say anything else. 'See you all tomorrow, nine AM sharp.'

Arriving home, Harry was barely in the door when a bundle of furry energy hammered into him, all paws and tongue.

'Told you she'd missed you,' Grace said.

Harry reached down and picked up Smudge. The dog saw this as an excuse to really go for it, wriggling in his arms and attacking his ear with her tongue.

'I've hardly been away.'

Grace laughed.

'Try telling her that.'

Harry enjoyed a little kiss from Grace, and placed Smudge down on the floor. The dog raced off only to return a few seconds later with a furry duck in its mouth.

'And just what the hell is that?'

'That,' Grace said, 'was a present from your dear brother.'

'Ben bought her that?'

'He's softer with her than you are,' Grace said.

Ben poked his head around the end of the hall.

'I am not.'

Harry pushed on into the house, Smudge working to trip him as he went. He slumped down on the sofa in the lounge. The yawn that slipped from him then was loud and long.

'Dear God!' Grace said. 'Who makes that kind of sound when they yawn?'

'He does,' said Ben.

'It was just a yawn,' said Harry.

'No, that was the yawn to end all yawns,' said Grace. 'I'm surprised there's any oxygen left in the room after that.'

Harry was aware then just how tired he was. He'd been up since the early hours, driven back from Norfolk, been out all day at a crime scene, dealt with the press, the team, the DSup, Bomb Disposal, and even been threatened with fancy dress. And tomorrow was looking to be a day no shorter or less full. Smudge leapt up beside him and leaned in, licking his ear once again.

'So, what shall we do for dinner, then?' he asked.

'Tonight's on me,' Ben said.

'Look, you don't have to cook,' Harry said. 'How about I treat us all to a takeout?'

'No need,' Ben said. 'Look.'

With a flourish, he presented a large, white paper bag.

'And what's in there?'

'Steak pie from the bakery at Cockett's. Can't beat them.'

'And this,' Grace said, holding a bottle of red wine.

'You know what?' Harry said. 'This isn't a bad place to come home to.'

'I'll pour you a glass then, shall I?'

Harry knew he didn't need to say yes.

CHAPTER SEVENTEEN

WITH THE STEAK PIE AND THE WINE INSIDE HIM, BOTH of which had been tasty, though the pie had definitely had the edge on the wine, Harry didn't have much to offer for the rest of the evening. He'd then spent the time dozing and then occasionally waking himself up on the sofa with a snort and a mumbled apology to both Grace and Ben. Smudge spent the evening lying at his feet like she was afraid he was going to leave her again.

When morning came round, Grace was off early to work, so he forced himself out of bed as well. Not that he felt like getting up, but Smudge was insistent that a walk was on the cards, so after breakfast Harry was outside and tramping fields.

The day was starting off with the softest blanket of fog, barely even knee-high, resting on the fields. It seemed to just lay there, Harry thought, asleep almost. Ahead of him, Smudge was bounding about, bouncing up through the pale white tufts, then running back to him full of the boundless joy in life only a dog can ever possess.

The sky was bright, promising a hot day ahead. Though Harry knew that a hot day in the Dales usually brought with it a cool and refreshing breeze. He was weary but being out was doing him good. Not just because the air was cool and fresh still, laced with a metallic tang of damp in the air, but also because to be in the presence of Smudge was better than any pick-me-up.

The dog was a joy, and though he would be very unlikely to ever admit it in public, he rather liked having her around, daft mutt that she was. But he just couldn't help himself. He'd started off their relationship doing his best to be a firm and stern owner, yet the creature's longing eyes had quickly pulled him in. Was he too soft? Yes, probably. Did he care? Not in the slightest. Smudge was a mad, furry, energetic bundle of I-love-you and Harry had a sneaking suspicion that she could bring a smile to his face on even the darkest of days. And though he'd had plenty of those in his life, he had no doubt that there were a few still to go through ahead of him.

Walk done and at the office for eight, with Smudge snuggled up in the corner on her bed, Harry was just putting the kettle on when Matt arrived. Smudge was up and over to him before he'd taken a step into the room.

'Morning,' said Harry. 'Tea?'

'You manage to get some rest?' Matt asked. 'You looked knackered when you headed off yesterday. As for tea, yes. Hardly need to ask, now, do you?'

Harry set to making a couple of mugs, popping tea bags into hot water to allow them to steep for a few minutes, before adding milk.

'It was a long day,' said Harry. 'How's Joan?'

'Could be any minute.'

'Looking forward to it?'

'Yes, and also no,' Matt said. 'I don't mean I'm not looking forward to it, just that, well, it's a big change, isn't it?'

'You'll be fine. You both will.'

'Not like we've any choice in the matter.'

'There is that.'

Harry removed the teabags, poured the milk, glanced at his watch. Jadyn was already fifteen minutes late.

'Jadyn should be here,' he said.

'I know,' said Matt. 'That's why I came in a bit early, just to, you know, add a bit of support, like.'

'I'll give him another five, then I'm calling,' said Harry.

The office phone burst into life. Matt answered.

'Jadyn,' he mouthed to Harry. 'You okay, lad?' he said down the phone.

After a short conversation, he put the phone down.

'Well?' Harry said.

'Says he's feeling rough,' said Matt. 'He did get thrown about a bit over in Reeth. He was signed off as all okay and good to go by the doc, but it could be that.'

Harry wasn't so sure.

'What did he say exactly?'

'Not much,' said Matt.

'Feeling sick, right?' Harry said. 'Did he mention aches and pains, sweating?'

'All of that, actually,' said Matt. 'Needs the day off. You moonlighting as a doctor now?'

Harry shook his head.

'PTSD symptoms,' he said. 'All of them.'

'Personal experience, I'm guessing.'

'That, and what I've seen it do to friends. He's been going to his counselling sessions, hasn't he?'

'As far as I'm aware,' Matt said.

'I need you to check up on that,' Harry said. 'And we'll give him today. There's always a chance it's genuinely a twenty-four-hour bug. But...'

Harry shook his head, looked at Matt.

'It isn't, is it?' Matt said.

'I very much doubt it,' said Harry. 'I'll maybe give him a call later.'

The office door opened and in walked Jim, Liz, and Jen, with Fly racing through their legs to dash over to Smudge.

'Morning, all,' Harry said.

Jim placed a tin over by the kettle.

'Dad made some biscuits,' he said. 'Not exactly sure why. Mostly all he can make is a lot of noise with a hammer while he swears at a tractor. My parents have always been very traditional, if you know what I mean, Mum on with the cooking, Dad doing all the DIY stuff. They share the farm work, like, but then Dad just went and baked this lot up last night.'

Matt was already over to the tin and had it open. He gave them a sniff.

'Bloody well done him, I say,' he said. 'What are they?'

'Shortbread,' said Jim.

Matt took one and bit into it.

'Biscuits for breakfast?' Harry said.

'Of course not!' Matt said. 'I've had breakfast. This is ...' He looked at his watch '... as I thought, yes, this is eight-forty-fives.'

'That's not even a thing.'

'It is now.'

Matt grinned, took another biscuit.

'How's Steve?' Harry asked, as Jen went over to the board and gave it a wipe.

'Big, hungry, and a bit of a softy,' she replied. 'When I'm home he'll insist on lying on the sofa with me. And by on the sofa, I mean on me. He's not exactly light either.'

'I hope you've not said that to his face,' said Liz. 'You'll give him a complex.'

'He's a lizard, Liz!' Harry said.

'Lizards have feelings, too.'

Harry sat back and let everyone get on with settling themselves in for the day ahead. After what had happened over in Reeth, there was certainly plenty to be going on with.

When nine o'clock came round, Harry stood up and went over to the board. Jen moved to stand on the other side, ready to add things to it as they talked through what had happened so far.

'Not yet,' Harry said. 'Let's just have a little chat first, okay?'

A frown on Jen's face let him know that she'd heard a tone in his voice she wasn't sure of.

With the rest of the team sitting down, Harry said, 'First things first, do we have any news on Detective Inspector Haig?'

'She'll be in later today,' Matt said. 'I spoke with Anna and she said that Gordy's fine and would be here now if she wasn't being forced to take it easy.'

'I can't imagine Gordy being forced to do anything,' said Jim.

'I'm sure Anna can be very persuasive,' said Liz. 'Have you ever spoken to her? She's one of those people who, before you know where you are, you're telling her your life story, just opening up about things. It's weird.'

'It's the training,' Matt said. 'She's a vicar.'

'Yes, but they're not all like that, are they?' said Liz. 'Some are absolutely bloody hopeless, all wet and insipid and useless.'

'And some aren't,' said Matt. 'She's a good lass, is Anna. Good for Gordy, too, I think.'

'Right then,' Harry said, 'before we get on with the situation over in Reeth, I just want to have a word about Jadyn. A confidential one, too, if you know what I mean.'

The team all nodded, almost as one.

'We all know what that lad went through a while back,' Harry said. 'Horrific experience, and I think we're all impressed how he's dealt with it. He's tough, I'll give him that, but tough isn't always a good thing.'

'How do you mean?' Jim asked. 'I've always thought that was a bit of a strength myself, being able to just crack on with things.'

'It can be,' said Harry, 'but if someone's gone through something like what Jadyn did, then toughing it out is more often than not the worst approach there can be.'

'He's seemed okay, though,' said Liz. 'Ben's been out for a couple of drinks with him. Said he seemed good.'

'I'm not saying he isn't,' said Harry. 'But I also think we need to keep an eye on him, and I'd appreciate it if that's what we all did. I don't mean we all suffocate him with constant worrying, but we just need to keep an eye, that's all.'

'There's more going on here, isn't there?' Jen said.

Harry gave a slow, thoughtful nod. He pointed at his face.

'When this happened, I didn't exactly bounce back,' he said. 'Took months, probably years to get over it, not sure you ever do, not something as traumatic as that. I still get flashbacks, wake up in a sweat. Sometimes I'm just an irritable old bastard and it's because I've had a bad night of it, not enough sleep. I never went down the alcohol route to cope with it, just threw myself into work.'

'You're talking about PTSD,' Liz said.

'I am,' said Harry. 'And post-traumatic stress disorder is very, very real, believe me. It can and has ruined lives, including those of a couple of friends of mine.'

'You think it's that bad with Jadyn, then?' Jim asked.

'I don't know,' Harry said. 'I just think that for now, the best thing we can all do is keep an eye on him, like I said. Don't make it too obvious, though. I hope that makes sense.'

'Did something happen, then?' Liz asked.

'Over in Reeth,' Matt said. 'When he found the body. It didn't stop him getting on with the job, I'll give him that.'

The room fell quiet for a moment. Then Smudge barked.

'Bloody hell, dog!' Harry said with a start. 'What was that for?'

As if in answer, there was a knock at the door.

Matt went over and opened it to find Anna standing there.

'Hope I'm not interrupting,' she said.

'Not at all,' Harry said. 'Everything okay with Gordy?'

Anna smiled awkwardly.

'Could we have a quick word?'

'Of course,' Harry said. 'Matt? You okay to run through things about Reeth?'

'No bother,' Matt said. 'I'll send Jim on with some water. Anna, you want tea or coffee as well? Oh, we've got some biscuits too, if you want. Homemade by Jim's dad.'

'Just water is fine,' Anna said. 'I won't be long.'

Harry stepped out of the office and led Anna down a

short hall to the interview room, closing the door behind him. He gestured to the small table and chairs in the middle of the room.

'So then,' he said, 'how can I help? Is Gordy okay? I've been told she'll be in later.'

'She will,' Anna said. 'She's not a fan of being told what to do, but I can be pretty firm if I want to be.'

Harry smiled.

'Oh, I'm sure.'

'No, this isn't about Gordy at all,' Anna said. 'It's actually about you.'

Harry's eyes widened.

'Me? I'm not sure—'

'Well, not you specifically,' Anna said, 'but the team.'

'I'm not sure I understand,' Harry said.

There was a knock at the door and Jim entered.

'Here's your water,' he said, then poured two glasses from a jug.

When Jim left them alone again Anna leaned forward.

'I've been thinking about this for a while,' she said, 'and if I'm overstepping the mark, just tell me and I'll bugger off, okay?'

'I'll bear that in mind.'

'Good.'

'So, what's this actually about then?' Harry asked. 'You said the team?'

'I'd like to offer my services,' Anna said.

'I don't think we need a vicar,' Harry said. 'Though there's a few things I should probably have taken to confession years ago.'

'I'm not Catholic,' Anna said. 'Church of England, remember? We're more tea and cake and a good jumble sale than confession and liturgy. Though we do have liturgy, just not as much. At least, I don't think we do.' Anna stopped talking, smiled. 'Sorry, I'm rambling.'

'A little.'

'What I meant is, and like I said, tell me to mind my own business, but I've been wondering, do you have anyone to just talk to?'

'I talk to Grace,' Harry said.

'No, that's not what I mean. And I don't mean some kind of intense counselling session either. Though, I am a trained and qualified counsellor, so I do actually know what I'm talking about.'

'Unlike me right now,' Harry said. 'Because I'm lost, Anna.'

'After what happened in Reeth, and looking back over some of the cases you've all had to deal with, I just thought that maybe you could all do with an impartial ear. Someone who you can just talk stuff through with, nothing official as such, no agenda, just a safe place for a confidential natter.'

Harry sat back.

'It's a good idea,' he said. 'But I'll need to give it a bit of thought and chat with the team about it. I can't just okay it here and now.'

'Wasn't expecting you to,' said Anna.

'Though there is something you could help with...'

'What?'

'Officer Okri,' Harry said. 'Jadyn.'

'The young lad from Bradford?'

'Yes,' said Harry. 'You know about what happened a while back?'

'Absolutely,' Anna said. 'Horrendous. Hard to believe anything like that could happen in the Dales.'

'I'm afraid that wherever you go, and no matter how beautiful a place may be, if you look deep enough, you'll always find a little bit of rot setting in.'

'What's the problem, then?' Anna asked.

'My guess is PTSD,' said Harry. 'He's been having counselling, but I'm wondering if he's the kind of person who is just very adept at masking a problem.'

'You think that's what he's doing?'

'According to DS Dinsdale, something happened over in Reeth.'

'He was the one who found the body?'

'Yes,' said Harry. 'PTSD is a bastard. It'll hang around invisible in the background then swoop in out of nowhere to smash you in the bollocks.'

'You've a way with words, I'll give you that,' Anna said.

'He's had yesterday off and he called in sick today.'

'I can drop by if you want,' Anna said. 'I'm allowed to do that because of this.'

She pointed at the white dog collar around her neck.

'I'd appreciate that.'

'I won't mention you either,' Anna said. 'Word gets around a local community and it's my job to listen when it does.'

Harry gave a nod of thanks. Anna stood up. Harry followed suit.

'Thanks for coming over,' Harry said as he led Anna out of the interview room and to the front door.

'It's really not a problem at all,' Anna said. 'In fact, it's the exact opposite. It's my job.'

After giving Anna Jadyn's address and seeing her off, Harry walked back into the office.

'Right then,' he said, clapping his hands together loudly. 'Where were we?'

Matt was just putting the phone back down.

'What is it?' Harry said.

'It's Sowerby,' Matt said. 'She's been rushed back into surgery.'

CHAPTER EIGHTEEN

Rebecca Sowerby wasn't a member of his immediate team and yet this news crashed into Harry like a wrecking ball. They'd all had a rough time of it lately. And now this. Harry needed more details.

'So, what do we know?' he asked.

'Nothing,' Matt replied.

'What do you mean, nothing? There has to be something, anything!'

'It was Margaret who called us.'

'But she's in the hospital as well, right?'

'Exactly,' Matt said. 'Divisional surgeon with a broken leg kept in for observation. Good luck to anyone trying to stop her moving about to find out what's going on with her daughter.'

'And even Margaret couldn't tell us anything?'

Matt shook his head.

'All she knew was that Rebecca was back into theatre. Maybe there was more, but obviously, she's pretty stressed and upset right now.'

'I bet she bloody is,' Harry said.

He rubbed his eyes hard enough to push sparks into his brain.

'Well, there's nothing we can do about any of that right now,' Harry said at last.

'She said something else though,' Matt said. 'About what happened, at the house.'

'She wasn't there,' Harry said. 'How can she know anything?'

'Sowerby,' Matt said. 'She's been in and out of consciousness, but she spoke with her mum.'

'And?'

'And there was a white powder on the body,' Matt said. 'Jadyn and I saw it, too. All over the place, like someone had just cut open a bag of flour and emptied it on the poor lass.'

'I'm assuming then that whatever it was, it certainly wasn't flour,' said Harry.

'No,' Matt said. 'You wouldn't want to be making a loaf of bread with this, that's for sure.'

'So, what was it?'

'Sowerby says it was cocaine. Obviously that'll have to be confirmed, but I'd doubt she'd say that if she wasn't sure.'

The word sat heavy in the room, echoing in their minds.

'Cocaine?' said Jim. 'I know there are drugs all over the place, like, we all do, but cocaine? In the Dales? Really? I can't believe it.'

'It's everywhere,' Harry said. 'Not just cocaine, but drugs in general. And if that stuff is turned into crack, then ...'

'It's bad, then, is it?' Liz asked.

'You've no idea,' Harry said. 'But I have.' He turned back to Matt. 'And you said it was all over the victim's body?'

'Absolutely,' said Matt. 'She was covered in the stuff.'

'Doesn't make sense. No one wastes cocaine. Last I heard a gram of the stuff had a street value of thirty to forty quid. Crack, which if you can believe it, is an even more addictive version of cocaine, is twenty quid for a rock. A kilo of the stuff is forty grand's worth.'

'So why cover a body in it, then?' Jim asked. 'That doesn't make any sense. Why waste that kind of money?'

'Cocaine in the Dales doesn't make any sense, full stop,' said Matt. 'Nearest thing we have to a drug problem is the few who smoke stuff they shouldn't down by Gayle Beck and the fact that we all probably drink more tea every year per person than anyone anywhere else on the planet.'

Harry sat himself back on a table, the board at his side.

'Right,' he said. 'As far as Sowerby and her mother are concerned, they're both in the right place. And I'm sure Margaret will keep us up to date with what's going on. We've got the body in the house and the two members of the SOC team dead in the explosion. So, what we need to do is the only thing we can do, and that's find the bastard responsible! Agreed?'

No one answered. They didn't need to.

'Jen?'

The detective constable was on her feet and at the other side of the board without a word, pen poised.

'From the top,' Harry said. 'Other than a body covered in cocaine and an explosion causing two more deaths, what do we have?'

'No photographs, not yet anyway,' Matt said.

'What?'

'Everything's all caught up with the team getting hit by

the explosion, Sowerby still being in hospital. I think it's messed up the system a bit.'

Harry didn't want to be this stressed or angry so early in the day.

'Get that crime scene photographer's number and call him as soon as we're done. I don't want excuses from him, I want his job done.'

'Understood,' Matt said.

'As to the explosion,' Harry said. 'I can give us a bit on that.'

'The bomb disposal team sent their report in, then, have they?' Matt asked.

'Not yet,' Harry said. 'But I found this at the site.' He pulled out an evidence bag and held it out for everyone to see.

'What is it?' Liz asked.

'This is a ball bearing,' Harry said. 'It was a lucky find considering how it got there in the first place.'

'I'm not following you,' said Matt.

'I've seen these before,' Harry said. 'As had the bomb disposal team. And that confirmed it for me.'

'Confirmed what exactly?'

'That this here is a ball bearing from a Claymore.'

'A sword?' said Jim. 'Why would a sword have a ball bearing?'

Harry shook his head.

'It wouldn't. I'm referring to the anti-personnel mine named after the well-known Scottish sword. Contains a layer of C-4 explosive set behind about seven-hundred of these steel balls, which are all secured in resin. When detonated, by remote control or by booby-trap, these little buggers are sent out at a speed of around twelve hundred metres per second. Has a range of about one hundred metres and sprays the balls out in a sixty-degree arc.'

'That's horrific,' said Liz. 'You sound like you know a lot about them.'

'I do,' Harry said, a short answer with a lot of weight.

Everyone stared at him, mouths open now.

'Sorry,' Liz said, 'I didn't mean ...'

'It wasn't a Claymore that did this to me,' Harry said. 'If it had been, I wouldn't have a head. I was caught out by an IED, which is a little different. Improvised explosive device. That meant I was on the receiving end of anything the bomb-maker could put their grubby hands on at the time: scrap metal, nails, anything. But I've seen what a Claymore can do, up close.'

Harry didn't want to say any more. Speaking about his time in theatre, well, it just wasn't something he did. His memories were bad enough. The last thing he wanted to do was go painting horrors in the minds of others.

'And you think one of those is what caused the explosion?'

'I'm sure of it,' Harry said. 'The report from Bomb Disposal will only confirm it.'

'But that's a piece of military kit you're talking about,' Jim said. 'How would anyone get their hands on something like that?'

'Surprisingly easily,' Harry said. 'Not just smuggled in either. You ever thought about how big the Ministry of Defence is? Things go missing all the time. That's just a fact of life. But this links with another detail.'

'The boyfriend,' Jim said.

'Exactly,' said Harry. 'We've now got a clear lead here. Two, actually. One is the search for a possible soldier boyfriend, who may have been seen by Jadyn outside the house. Add in the Claymore, and there's definitely a military line here. And we've got the name and address from the diary.'

Harry looked at the board. Jen was busy scribbling stuff down.

'We still don't have the full name of the victim, do we?'

'No,' Liz said. 'People saw her around, knew her enough to say hello, but that was about it. I got the impression that she didn't really mix. Not that she wasn't friendly, more that she was just keeping herself out of the way of everything, I guess.'

'Like she didn't want to be remembered,' Harry said.

'Maybe.'

'What about the grab-bag?' Matt said.

'What's that, then?' Jim asked. 'You mentioned a bag of clothes or something yesterday.'

'You mind getting it for us?' Harry asked, looking at Matt.

The detective sergeant left the room and returned a moment later with the rucksack Harry had pulled from the car.

'This,' he said, 'is a grab-bag.'

He opened it and spread out the contents on a table for everyone to see.

'As you can see, everything is sealed in plastic bags—clothes, food, first aid, money, a sleeping bag, waterproofs, underwear.' He picked up a bag containing a phone. 'This is probably a burner, a throwaway pay-as-you-go phone. Untraceable.'

'But why would the victim have all of that in her car?' Liz asked.

'It's only for use in an emergency,' Matt said. 'If you have to run, you know you've got enough to help you get by, at least for a few days.'

'Exactly,' Harry said. 'Which tells us what about our victim?'

Jim said, 'That she was looking over her shoulder a lot.'

'Nicely put,' said Harry.

'But you have one as well,' Matt said. 'And you're not looking over your shoulder, are you?'

'No, I'm not. Mine is more force of habit from my time in the Paras. I got used to having everything in a bag so that I could just go at a minute's notice, no fuss, no drama.'

'But you're not leaving, are you?' Jim asked.

'No, of course I'm not,' Harry said, almost too quickly he thought. Then he saw a flicker of relief in the young PCSO's eyes. In the back of his mind was the job offer, the chat with Kett in Norfolk. But he didn't have time to be thinking about that right now, so he locked it all away again.

A knock at the office door caught everyone's attention. Matt answered it, opening the door to find a man pale as milk staring at them. He was small, Harry noticed, and soft-looking, like the closest he had ever got to doing exercise in his life, was opening a pot noodle. In many ways, he reminded Harry of the Pillsbury Doughboy, only in an ill-fitting suit.

'I'm looking for a Detective Chief Inspector Grimm,' the man said.

'And you've found him,' said Harry.

The man walked into the room and reached out his hand for Harry to shake. Harry did exactly that, only to find that the hand he was shaking was soft and clammy. He removed his own from its embrace a little too quickly.

'Ian Bennett,' the man said. 'Pathologist. Here to replace Ms Sowerby.'

Harry didn't like the finality of the man's words, as though he wasn't just stepping in at the last minute, but was turning up to take over for good.

'Temporarily,' Harry said.

'We'll just have to see, won't we?' Bennett said. 'My team's outside.'

'Shouldn't you all be in Reeth?' Harry asked. 'That's where the crime scene is.'

'Never been this way before. Thought we'd just drive through, have a look, and introduce ourselves.'

'Have a look?' Matt said. 'You make it sound like you're on midweek break.'

'Well, most of the time we're in towns and cities,' said Bennett. 'This makes a nice change.'

A nice change? Really? Sowerby was under the knife, two of the SOC team were dead, and here was this clown out playing tourist.

'I'm assuming you have the report from the other team for me,' Harry said.

'No, I don't,' Bennett replied. 'Not my responsibility.'

'But you've replaced Sowerby. And under normal circumstances, we'd have something by now.'

'These aren't normal circumstances.'

'No, they're not,' Harry said, barely containing himself. 'Which is why, as I'm sure you understand, having that report is even more vital.'

'Well, I'll make sure to pass your message on when I get back. Best we get on. Good to put a face to the name.'

Bennett turned for the door. Harry stared at his back in disbelief and caught the same look on the faces of the rest of his team.

'So, that's it then?' Harry asked.

Bennett turned back.

'Actually, no,' he said. 'I've been told there's a really good bakery in Hawes and I would very much like to—'

Harry exploded.

'Bakery? What do you think this is, the bloody tourist information centre?'

'No, I ...' the man mumbled, but Harry wasn't listening.

'Tell you what, while you're here, why don't I show you through our fantastic range of novelty postcards and amusing souvenir fridge magnets! I mean, we've got all the time in the world, haven't we? Sowerby's only gone back into surgery and it's not like we're dealing with three murders, grieving families, cocaine, and illegal weapons, is it? Actually, no, wait a minute, that's exactly what we're dealing with! But you go ahead, mate. You head off into town and grab yourself some cake and fudge and God knows what else! I mean, bloody hell!'

Harry sucked in air through his nose, breathed out through clenched teeth.

Bennett stared.

'Look, I think we've got off on the wrong foot here,' he said.

'Really?' Harry exclaimed. 'And just what exactly gave you that impression, beyond everything you've said since you walked in through that door?'

'Maybe we should get over to Reeth right away.'

'Yes, maybe you bloody well should,' said Harry, his voice quieter now, but no less threatening. 'Probably for the best.

Don't want you waiting around here for another crime scene to appear now, do we?'

Bennett said nothing more and left.

For a moment no one spoke. When they did, it was Jim who broke the silence.

'Nice one, Boss,' he said. 'Couldn't have said it better myself.'

CHAPTER NINETEEN

'HERE YOU GO,' MATT SAID, HANDING HARRY A FRESH mug of tea. 'This'll calm you down.'

'No it won't,' Harry said, who was sitting on a chair stroking Smudge, her head resting against his knee, 'but it's worth a try.' Smudge was staring up at him as though he was the centre of her universe.

'No, you're probably right, it won't,' Matt said, and handed the mug over.

Harry grabbed it, took a gulp.

'So, what's the plan?' Matt asked.

'I wish I knew,' Harry replied.

'Now, don't you be like that just because some wassack comes in here acting like the world's most tactless man.'

Harry sipped his tea. It scalded his mouth. He didn't care and took another sip.

'This is a complete bloody mess,' he said.

'Murder usually is,' said Matt. 'And what's happened here has taken it to an entirely new and unexpected level, that's for sure.'

'You're not wrong there,' Harry said. He shook his head and stared at the board. Jen had done a good job in getting information down and the details they had were all there to be seen, nice and clear. It was just that all the details added up to nothing other than a world of confusion. And it was his job to try and make some sense of it. And soon.

'What did Anna want?' Matt asked.

Harry was impressed at the DS's deft change of subject.

'She's offering her services as a sort of listener, I think,' Harry said. 'To the team.'

'Like confession, you mean?'

'No, not like confession. Though that's exactly what I said.'

'Thank God for that.'

Harry agreed.

'I wouldn't know where to begin or where to stop,' he said.

He then explained what Anna had suggested.

'Sounds like a good idea to me,' said Matt. 'She's easy to talk to. Likeable, too. And confidential.'

'I've said we'll get back to her about it,' Harry said. 'She's going to go check up on Jadyn as well. Only thing she won't be able to do is do the same for Gordy.'

'Conflict of interest?'

'Something like that, isn't it?'

'Popping round to visit Jadyn is a great idea for sure though,' Matt said. 'I was going to do that myself later on, once I'd called him, and go and have a look around the barracks in Catterick, try and spot the car we're looking for, have a word with some of the officers over there as well, see if they know anything.'

'We'll leave Jadyn to Anna,' said Harry. 'She's neutral and she might be able to get the lad talking a bit.'

'Not something he's usually got a problem with.'

'Some things are harder to talk about than others,' Harry said.

'I'll check up on those counselling sessions in a bit as well,' suggested Matt. 'Just so's we know, like.'

'Do that and once you're done over in Catterick, then I want you over to Reeth. Finding that car is a priority though. It's probably nothing, but until we know for sure, we need to find it. It's a long shot, but that's what our job seems to be filled with, doesn't it?'

'I'll go now,' Matt said, standing. 'And I'll keep you informed about what's going on at the crime scene, let you know if they find anything important. I'll go have another chat with folk as well.'

'Good,' said Harry. 'After that explosion, the fire, there won't be much left that's any use for Forensics so we need to prod folk a bit maybe, see if anything rattles loose.'

Matt turned and headed for the door, stopped, and looked back over at Harry.

'He really asked about a bakery, didn't he?' he asked. 'I wasn't making that bit up, hearing things, maybe? Just want to be sure on that.'

'No, he said it alright,' Harry confirmed. 'Those actual words came out of his mouth. On purpose, would you believe?'

Shaking his head, Matt left the office.

Harry pushed himself up onto his feet and walked over to the board. Jen, Liz, and Jim joined him.

'So, what do you want us to do?' Jim asked.

'For a start,' Harry said, 'I need someone to follow up on

that Claymore. It'll be a dead-end, no doubt, because it's not like the MOD are going to openly admit to losing something like that. But you never know and it's a link to whoever this military individual is we're looking for. And check on HOLMES as well, see if there's anything about those kinds of weapons being seized or found anywhere else.'

'HOLMES, though,' Jim said and Harry heard the fear in his voice already. 'Jadyn's the one who's all techy. I'm hopeless. You'll be better having Fly do it with his massive, clumsy paws hammering the keys at random.'

'I know my way around it,' Liz said. 'And if we both get lost inside it we can help each other find our way back out again.'

'Good idea,' Harry said. 'And while you're at it, chase up the photos and the pathologist report. And by chase up, I mean demand.'

Jen said, 'Gordy's just sent a message through. She's heading over in a bit.'

'Then she can help you,' he said looking at Liz and Jim. 'She'll be more than happy to take on the MOD. And there must be more information out there about our victim. Someone somewhere must know her full name, where she's from. You don't just move to the Dales and have no one know who you are.'

Jen laughed. 'Sounds like you're suggesting we're nosy buggers.'

'That's exactly what I'm suggesting,' said Harry. 'Within a few days of turning up here, I'm fairly sure the whole population of Hawes knew more about me than I did. Now, you ready for that trip to the Lakes, or have you got something else to be doing?'

'I didn't think you wanted me along,' said Jen.

'I don't,' Harry said. 'But someone needs to keep an eye on Smudge, don't they?'

Jen did a very good impression of someone looking hurt by what Harry had said. He ignored it.

'Best we get on then,' he said. 'Everyone keep in touch. Jim, can you put a call through to whichever team over in the Lakes covers where we're going so they know we're there? Don't want to be stepping on toes. Not unless I have to. Whatever any of this is, I want to get to the bottom of it sharpish. What we're dealing with, it's just not normal. And I know murder isn't normal, but this is something worse. If that's at all possible.'

'You sound worried,' said Jim, who was crouching on the floor now, Fly at his side. Smudge was creeping over to join in and get in on the action.

'I'm always worried,' Harry said. 'Part of the job description. You ready, Jen?'

'Never anything else,' Jen replied.

'Good,' said Harry. 'Because you're driving.'

Liz and Jim looked at each other, eyes wide.

'You sure about that?' Liz asked. 'I mean, you do know how Jen drives, right?'

'Like a lunatic,' said Jim. 'Every road is a rally stage.'

'I do indeed,' Harry said. 'And being so close to death for the next hour or two will help keep me focused. And also awake.'

Outside, Harry strolled over to Jen's vehicle, Smudge to heel, the detective constable heading round to the driver's side. She smiled.

'You ready for this?'

'No,' Harry said, opening the rear passenger door.

'And Smudge will be okay?'

Harry pulled something out of his pocket.

'Restraining belt,' he said, holding up a strap. 'And she can lie on this.'

He took off his jacket and placed it on the back seat.

'You're a bit of a softy at heart, aren't you?' Jen said.

Harry said nothing, just lifted Smudge into the car, clipped her in, then slid himself into the front of the car as Jen did the same.

'It'll take us about an hour and a quarter,' Jen said, flicking the engine into life.

'It's not a race though, remember that,' said Harry. 'Whatever the satnav says, it's not a target for you to beat. Those things have caused more accidents than you'd believe.'

As Jen eased the car forward, Harry's phone buzzed.

'Grimm.'

'It's Jim,' came the reply.

'Something can't have gone wrong already,' Harry said. 'We've not even left the marketplace!'

'The pathologist's report has just come through,' Jim said. 'I'm forwarding it to you now.'

'Photographs?'

'Chasing those,' Jim said.

Farewells said, Harry opened the file on his phone and told Jen.

'Maybe being shouted at was just what Mr Bennett needed,' she said.

Harry didn't answer. He was scrolling through the report, skimming it quickly.

'You've gone quiet,' Jen said, after a few minutes of nothing from her boss. 'And that's never anything other than unnerving.'

'The powder is confirmed as cocaine,' Harry said. 'And more of those balls from the Claymore were found.'

'But that's not all, is it?' Jen said. 'I can tell. The tone of your voice, if at all possible, is even more ominous than usual.'

Harry let his phone rest on his lap and stared out of the window.

'The victim,' he said. 'There's evidence of torture.'

'Evidence?'

'Her ear, her fingers,' Harry said. 'They were cut off.'

CHAPTER TWENTY

Having spoken with DCI Grimm, Anna decided that perhaps the best thing to do was to get over to see Jadyn right away. No time like the present and all that. The day ahead was as busy as any other, but she could move a few things round easily enough. In fact, her everyday life had to be flexible for reasons just such as this.

Hers was a pastoral calling. She'd never been big on the whole evangelism thing, heading out into the wilds to convert people. Goodness no. Her role was to serve the community, to show the love of God through her actions first and foremost. Hammering someone across the head with a Bible only ever gave them a headache.

The address was over in Catterick so it was a little out of her way, but not by much. A good part of her life was spent visiting people all over the Dales; the infirm, the elderly, the ill. The upside was that she got to know people well and they came to see her as someone they could turn to and trust to be there for them.

The downside was all of the cake and biscuits. Anna had

decided early on that she'd need to say no more often than yes to the kind hospitality of Dales' folk, otherwise she'd soon be the size of a prize bull. The tea and coffee also had to be kept an eye on; too much caffeine and her blood pressure would suffer, something that in her line of work she had to keep an eye on.

Heading from Hawes, Anna took herself through to her home in Askrigg, stopping off to pick up her purse. As yet, she hadn't moved to using the whole tapping thing with her phone to pay for things. It still struck her as just too futuristic and weird to do that, and anyway, she preferred to pay with cash. In Redmire she made another detour, this time to the village shop. Turning up at someone's house empty-handed, particularly if it was the first visit, always struck her as rude. She wasn't quite sure what would be best to take to a young, male police officer, but did her best with what was available. At the checkout she piled up a selection of chocolates, biscuits, a motoring magazine, a book of puzzles, and to her own bemusement two tins of beans and sausages and a loaf of bread. Back in her car, she headed on out of the village, under a bridge, and up a rise until a left turn took her onto another road and on towards Catterick.

As roads went, this one was a cut above the rest, Anna thought, as she rolled calmly along. The Dales was a place rich in lovely lanes to explore, but this one gave such a grand view to her right of the vast sweep of the place that she had to pull over just to stare at it.

Far off, rising out of the tapestry of meadows below her, Pen Hill stood tall, its flat summit a place she'd trod many times, not just for fun, or to clear her head, but on Easter morning, with a few of the hardier members of the congregations from the various churches in the Dale. And snow had never put them off either.

She breathed deep then, not only aware of the sweetness of the air, but that this place had something special she'd not really found anywhere else. History rested itself on this landscape with quiet pride, the lives of generations etched into a view she could stare at for hours. The people here didn't live here simply because it was a lovely place to be. For many, living here was not easy and yet they stayed. Indeed, many left only to return later in life, pulled back by some magic of the place which constantly stirred in them, calling them home.

Onwards Anna drove, the road growing wider as it ploughed its way through the ranges used by the Army, able now to accommodate tanks and other armoured military vehicles. She saw the red flag was up, so live firing was taking place, and with her window down caught the distant rattling crack of weapons fire.

Catterick itself wasn't anywhere to write home about and Anna found herself outside Officer Okri's address with little memory of the last few minutes of her journey.

Pulling herself out of her car, she grabbed the bag of items she had collected from Redmire and walked along the street to the address DCI Grimm had given her. The house was a terrace Victorian, plain, but it looked neat enough outside.

Anna lifted a hand and gave the front door a good knock.

No answer.

She tried again, the knock louder this time, and she leaned into the door to see if she could hear anyone stirring within.

Nothing. Just the ominous emptiness beyond.

It was at this point that Anna realised she should have called ahead, just to make sure the constable was at home. But her assumption that he was made sense as he had called in sick. Perhaps he'd nipped out for a walk?

Anna stood back to stare at the house. She could see no lights on. The curtains upstairs were pulled back and the house was dark.

'You alright there?'

Anna turned to the voice to see a man's head poking out of the neighbouring house. Bleary eyes stared at her from an old face.

'Oh, I'm sorry,' Anna said. 'I didn't mean to disturb you.'

'You're a vicar then,' the man said.

'The dog collar is a bit of a giveaway, isn't it?' Anna said with a smile.

'Well, you're either that or a stripper,' the man said. 'But to my mind, it's a bit early for a stripper, so I went with vicar.'

Anna had nothing to say to that.

'The lad who lives there. Police officer, isn't he?'

'He is,' Anna said.

'He's not in. Saw him leave about an hour ago. Not sure where he was heading on foot. It's not like there's much to see around here, not unless you get in your car and go for a drive, like.'

Anna wondered whether she should just sit and wait for Jadyn to return. But for all she knew he could be out for hours. That he was out at all wasn't a good sign, not after what Grimm had told her.

'Here,' she said, pulling a card out from a pocket. 'This is my number. Would you mind giving me a call when he returns?'

'Is he in trouble then?' the old man asked.

'No,' Anna said. 'Not in trouble. I'm just a friend, that's all.'

'Well, I'll try and remember,' said the old man.

He gave a farewell nod then closed the door.

Anna returned to her car and climbed in, checking her watch. Well, there was no rush back, so she had a choice— either sit around and wait or go looking. Decision made, she started the engine and rolled off down the street. The odds on finding Jadyn weren't exactly great, she thought, but that wasn't going to stop her from trying.

CHAPTER TWENTY-ONE

HARRY WOKE WITH A JOLT TO THE SOUND OF A DOG barking in his ear, and then a dull and worrying rumble from the front of the car.

'Sorry about that,' said Jen.

'About what, exactly?' asked Harry, sitting up, his bleary eyes refusing to focus on the road ahead.

'Pothole in the road. Couldn't avoid it. I'm pulling over.'

'Why?'

'Puncture,' Jen said. 'Hold on...'

Jen pulled the car off the road and onto a patch of grass large enough to take the whole car out of danger from traffic.

'Where are we?'

'Other side of Kendal. Once we get the tyre changed, it'll be about half an hour to Ambleside.'

Harry climbed out of the car and looked at the wheel. The tyre wasn't just flat, but ripped, and the metal rim of the wheel had a large dent in it.

'Bloody hell, Jen! Did you accidentally drive over a brick?'

'It was a big pothole,' said Jen.

'Masterful understatement there, I think,' Harry said. 'I'll get the jack and the spare.'

A bark from Smudge caught his attention. Harry opened the door and attached a lead to her collar before letting her out.

'I'm guessing you could do with a leg stretch and a toilet break,' he said.

Smudge jumped out of the car, bounced for a few seconds, then got to work sniffing the ground. When she eventually found just the right spot, she relieved herself.

'Imagine if we were that particular about where we needed to go,' Harry said. 'We'd never get anything done.'

'It would be worse if we went around introducing ourselves with a quick thrust of our nose at each other's arses,' Jen pointed out.

'I've met a few people in my time who'd relish it,' said Harry.

While they worked together on changing the wheel, Harry noticed he was starting to get hungry. The sleep had done him good, if only to take his mind off what he'd read in the pathologist's report, because what it had contained wasn't just information on a murder. There were echoes of a past he'd had nothing to do with for years and for the life of him he just couldn't see how the two could be linked.

'We'll need a bite to eat sooner rather than later,' he said, having a stretch to get the blood circulating again.

'If you can wait till we get to Ambleside, we'll go for a decent breakfast at a café there,' Jen said. 'Trust me, once you've finished it, you'll not need to eat for the rest of the day.'

'That's a high bar you're setting,' Harry said. 'Go there often then, do you?'

'I get over when I can,' Jen said. 'The Lakes are beautiful and the trails are amazing to run. Sometimes I'll head out with a tent and just camp solo for a night out on Scarfell or somewhere.' She looked up at Harry then, an eyebrow raised just a little. 'How's your running, then? Or shouldn't I ask?'

'Kind of a love-hate thing going on with it,' Harry said. 'I love to hate it and hate to love it, if you know what I mean.'

'Sort of.'

'Sometimes I'm really into it,' Harry said. 'Then life gets in the way or I just haven't the energy or urge to go out in the cold and the wet and thump around the lanes.'

'That's running,' said Jen. 'Sometimes, you just have to head out and do a couple of kilometres. It's not all about the distance. Just moving does you good.'

Harry shrugged. It was a conversation he really didn't want to have.

'Maybe you should train for something?' Jen suggested. 'Having a target might give you a bit of motivation.'

Harry laughed then, the sound big and loud and gruff.

'Me, do an ultra?' he said. 'Don't be daft.'

'Not really what I was suggesting,' said Jen. 'Just a five-kilometre race or something.'

'Race?'

Harry's mind was filled with images of him huffing and puffing on a run while being lapped by hundreds of considerably fitter, younger people.

'It's not about trying to win. It's about taking part. You'd love it.'

'Hmm,' Harry said, with little else to add, the horror of

the idea not one he wanted to become central to the day ahead.

'What do you do about Steve when you're away, then?' Harry asked, changing the subject just enough to move the focus away from himself.

'He's fine on his own for a couple of days,' Jen said. 'He misses me, obviously, but who can blame him? And he's not as needy as Smudge.'

Harry looked down at his dog who was leaning against his leg, her eyes half-closed.

'She's not needy, she's just affectionate.'

Smudge, as though she was aware she was being talked about, looked up at Harry, jumped up onto her hind legs, and nuzzled his hand.

'No, she's not needy at all, is she?' said Jen.

Wheel done, Harry climbed back into the car and Jen took them carefully back out into traffic.

'If you're into pubs, then Ambleside has a few crackers,' Jen said.

The road was busy, Harry noticed, a constant stream of vehicles flowing into and out of the Lakes, working like an artery, supplying it with people and produce and everything else the region needed to live and breathe.

'Well, we won't have time to explore them,' said Harry.

'It's a really trendy, popular place,' said Jen. 'The traffic is horrendous, but it's pretty, loads of shops, cafés and coffee shops every few steps. But most of the pubs seem to refuse to follow what's happening around them.'

'And that's a good thing?'

'I think so,' Jen said. 'Nothing worse than a pub that's had its heart and soul ripped out.'

For the next few miles neither Harry nor Jen spoke, and

he watched as the countryside grew gradually more dramatic. He was hoping that Jen had moved on from the suggestion of him doing a race, but he very much doubted it. On the back seat, Smudge was lying on her back, legs in the air, not a care in the world.

Staring out through the window, Harry noticed the landscape change. When they'd had the puncture, the hills around them had been low and rolling, but now he could see stern shadows rising ahead, the sharp, jagged lines of their ridges cutting into the sky above like stencils. It was a view that looked almost too dramatic to be real, as though they were driving into some artist's dream. Then the pathologist's report pushed through to the front of his mind again and turned the brightly coloured day dark.

Eventually, they rolled on down towards Windermere, from where Jen then threaded the car along the road as it grew more twisty. Then Windermere Lake drew close to the road and Harry stared out across the rippling surface as boats, large and small, navigated their way along it.

'You've gone quiet again,' Jen said.

'Thinking,' Harry said.

'It's the pathologist's report, isn't it?' Jen asked. 'You read that, told me about the ear, the fingers, then you went silent and fell asleep.'

Harry wasn't sure what to say exactly.

'Might help to talk it through,' Jen suggested.

Harry said, 'It's the fingers.'

'Yeah, that's horrendous,' Jen said. 'Doesn't bear thinking about, does it?'

'It's not that exactly,' Harry said. 'Though you're right, it doesn't.'

'What is it, then?'

Again Harry went quiet for a moment. What he was doing now, well, he was trawling through days long-gone, reaching into his memories to pull out stuff he'd filed safely away to never be looked at again. It was safer that way.

'A few years ago, I was working on a case,' Harry began. 'Crack cocaine was rife in Bristol. We had crack houses all over the place, fortified buildings you just couldn't get into.'

'Fortified?' Jen said. 'What, you mean like a castle or a prison or something?'

'Pretty much,' said Harry, remembering all too well what he and his team had been up against. 'Windows nailed shut, mesh and iron bars covering them. Any door into the building would be secured with a New York latch.'

'A New York what?'

'The gangs would have a metal bar slotted into a plate behind the centre of the door,' Harry explained. 'Getting through something like that took more than an enforcer.'

'You mean that hand-held battering ram thing?' Jen asked. 'Never used one myself. So, how did you manage to get in?'

'Specialist teams, usually,' Harry said. 'Made up of civilians who, for whatever reason, are very good at getting into buildings most people would never want to even try to enter. They use all kinds of kit to break in. Hydraulic door jammers usually, which will rip a door out of its frame, or oxy-acetylene torches strapped to their backs. They end up looking like Ghostbusters. Sometimes we'd have to call in the firearms unit to smash a door in with shotguns loaded with Hatton rounds. They'll disintegrate anything they hammer, including hinges.'

'Sounds exciting,' Jen said.

'That's one way to describe it. Then once you're in, the

only way to actually arrest someone is to find them in possession. So we had to go in hard and fast before they had a chance to ditch whatever they were handling. And there was usually a few bargain-basement hitmen in our way, too, happy to slot you for a couple hundred quid and a rock of crack.'

'I take back what I said about it being exciting,' Jen said. 'It sounds bloody terrifying. But what's this got to do with our victim? I know she was covered in cocaine, but you're talking gang stuff, aren't you?'

'There was one gang leader in particular,' Harry said. 'Called himself Hollywood, though his actual name was Daniel Radcliffe.'

That bought out a bark of a laugh from Jen.

'What? As in Harry Potter? You're kidding!'

'That they shared the same name wasn't the only reason he gave himself the nickname,' Harry said. 'Also had a bit of a thing for theatrics. Got into it because of his dad who had been the director of a local amateur dramatics group or something.'

'Really?' Jen said. 'Doesn't exactly sound like the background story to a major drug dealer.'

'Takes all sorts to make a world,' Harry said. 'Though sometimes I wish it didn't.'

'So, he what, did am-dram with his dad?'

Harry shook his head.

'Liked to dabble in a little bit of acting, for sure, but not am-dram as such and not with his dad,' Harry said.

'How's that, then?'

'For a start, his dad lost it from what I remember. Had a mental breakdown and ended up in a psychiatric hospital. A small, private one, though, courtesy of his son's misbegotten gains. As for the acting? It was never on stage. But we found files of him acting out scenes from his favourite movies.'

'That's weird.'

'It was more than weird,' Harry said, 'it was horrific. The scenes were most often real-life murders of anyone who got in his way. He'd do the whole thing in character, carry out the murder, then send the file to relatives, business partners as a warning. Cutting off the fingers was his little call sign. Sometimes he'd send them to relatives for fun. The ear, though, that's a new one on me.'

Jen was quiet, a stark look of horror now in her eyes.

'So, what happened to him?' she eventually asked.

'We had him cornered in a crack house,' Harry said. 'The place was surrounded, helicopter with a searchlight on the place, firearms unit; he wasn't going anywhere.'

'And he still got away?'

'No,' said Harry. 'While he and a good many of his supposed employees were still inside, the place burned to the ground.'

CHAPTER TWENTY-TWO

HARRY WATCHED TRAFFIC LIGHTS DRIFT PAST AND TO their left the watery edge of the lake came into view. Small boats and larger tourist vessels were shuffling themselves between wooden jetties.

'We'll park in town,' said Jen. 'Unless you fancy a cruise on the lake.'

'Not today,' Harry said, closing the file, relieved to take his eyes and mind away from what had taken place back in Reeth. Though a cruise would be very pleasant, he thought. Certainly more pleasant than what they were dealing with.

'This is a rare thing, you know,' Jen said, as they headed along a twisty road with parkland on the left leading down to the water. 'A sunny day in the Lake District. It's the only place I've ever known to be wetter than the Dales.'

Harry pointed to dark clouds ahead. He could see their edges were ripped and torn and tossed by the wind to whip down on the far-off summits, drenching them with rain.

'I think you spoke too soon.'

Out of the blue, Jen asked, 'You ever seen Swallows and Amazons?'

'No,' said Harry.

Jen gasped.

'You're kidding, right? I don't mean the recent one, either. I'm talking about the one from the seventies.'

'Again, no,' said Harry.

'But everyone's seen it! It's like an essential part of childhood.'

'Not mine.'

Jen rolled her eyes.

'Well, that was filmed here,' she said. 'In the Lakes. Some of it was done on Windermere, one of the large islands mainly, but most of it was up on Coniston. I was going to ask if you'd read the book, but I don't think I'll bother.'

'It was based on a book, then?'

'You're having a laugh, aren't you?'

Harry said, 'I'm not a complete cultural dinosaur, you know. Even I've heard of Arthur Random.'

'Ransome,' Jen said. 'His name was Arthur Ransome.'

'That's what I said.'

A few minutes later, the traffic slowed to little more than a crawl.

'Welcome to Ambleside,' Jen said. 'We're about two miles away still, but remember what I said about the traffic? Well, here it is. And we're in it.'

'Imagine having to put up with this if you lived here,' said Harry. 'I've seen the Dales get busy but this would send me crazy.'

'Nowt we can do but be patient,' said Jen.

'Not a trait I'm best known for possessing,' Harry grumbled.

As they crawled forwards, Harry had another look through the forensics report. It didn't make for a pleasant read. The observations were all from what the scene of crime team and Sowerby had found at the house so there was a clear and understandable lack of detail, what with the explosion ripping the body to pieces, the two other deaths, the injuries. But what detail there was, well, it was plenty, Harry thought. Anymore would, in many ways, have been too much.

The victim had been beaten, tortured, had her fingers taken, her ear sawn off, and again he was reminded of Radcliffe, or Hollywood as he preferred, but then there was everything else. Not just the fact she had been forced to overdose on a lethal quantity of cocaine and then, as her mind had undoubtedly spun off into a drug-fuelled coma, been shot in the head. It was the kind of murder he'd only ever seen before when drug gangs went to war.

This killing was a warning, he thought. She was made to suffer so that whoever this message was for understood either to back off or that they were next. The removal of the fingers he'd seen before, so why had the killer done that? But there was another detail, one he'd kept from his chat with Jen, because it wasn't just worse than the finger snipping, it took gruesome and cruel to another level entirely.

The saving grace—if it could be called such—was that according to the report, the victim, though not dead, would have been drugged up to high heaven thanks to the cocaine. It was a dark blessing, Harry thought, but a blessing nonetheless, because to be fully alert and awake as someone removed your tongue? That just didn't bear thinking about.

Then, on top of all this, was the mysterious soldier. Who was he and how did his existence tie in with all of this?

Maybe it didn't, Harry thought, but then again, there was the whole Claymore thing, wasn't there? God, his head hurt just from thinking about it all.

Once they were parked up, Jen led Harry into town. The streets were busy, crowds crawling around the place like ants. Smudge seemed to enjoy herself as she did her level best to say hello to everyone they passed.

'Still hungry?' Jen asked.

'I am,' Harry said, 'but we've not got time for a sit-down slap-up feast. Need to eat on the go. We'll have to grab something on the way.'

'What's the address?'

Harry opened the notebook that Matt had found in the victim's car for Jen to read.

'Mr John Smith? Really?'

'I'm going to assume that's not his real name,' said Harry.

'Well, whoever he is,' Jen said, 'to get to that address we need to walk to the top of this road, follow it to the left, past the House on the Bridge, then take a right at the mini roundabout,' said Jen. 'Just down from The Golden Rule.'

'You really do know this place, don't you?' said Harry.

'There are plenty of cafés on the way,' Jen said. 'We'll pop in and grab something.'

HARRY WAS JUST FINISHING a bacon roll when they came to the address. The cottage was small and tucked away on the right, the road rising steeply into the hills above. A silver Audi sports car was parked outside, the kind usually only ever seen either on the cover of a car magazine or overtaking you on the motorway, Harry thought.

He had a quick look around, saw nothing out of place.

The neighbouring properties were all of a type that were equally pretty and inviting. The kind of place Harry could easily imagine bolting to. Over the road, he saw security cameras fixed to a wall overlooking the small row of terraces of which their property was one. The cameras had the gleam of newness about them. It was nice to see that at least some people were taking home security seriously, he thought.

'Quaint,' Harry said.

'Nice if you can afford it,' said Jen and she made her way past the car and went up to the door to knock.

She hesitated.

'Well go on, then,' Harry said. 'Let them know we're here.'

'The door, it's open,' Jen said.

Harry went over to stand with Jen.

'Now, that's odd,' he said, glancing back at the car, then at the door. 'The kind of person who owns that is going to be someone who gives more than a little thought to security, aren't they?'

Harry handed Smudge's lead to Jen.

'Hold this daft thing for a moment, would you?' he asked and eased the door open with his foot.

The room on the other side, a small lounge, was quiet. Beyond it, through a low doorway, Harry saw two further rooms, the furthest being a galley kitchen.

'Stay here,' Harry said, looking back at Jen. Smudge was sitting at her side, staring at him, her tail wagging expectantly.

'You sure?'

'I'll give a shout if I need you. Might be best to tie Smudge to something just in case I do.'

Harry stepped inside.

The room was simply but expensively furnished. A wood-burning stove sat in the fireplace. A flatscreen television was attached to the wall. A thick rug lay on the floor. Two small and comfortable-looking sofas finished the room off, tucked up against the wall immediately to his left and in front of him, to the left of the low doorway.

'Mr Smith, this is the police!' Harry called out, making his presence known. 'Your door was open so I've let myself in.'

Harry's voice disappeared into the rooms beyond, no echo returning them, just emptiness. He stepped further into the house. The place was cold, he noticed, a chill in the air from a room that had been open to the elements and a breeze for a good while. The air, he noticed, carried only the scent of the day outside rather than that of a house occupied by a living soul.

'Mr Smith,' Harry called again. 'This is Detective Chief Inspector Grimm. If you can hear me, please make a sound.'

The house remained resolutely quiet, the only response to Harry's call being a breeze gusting past him from deeper in the house.

As he walked on in, making his way from the lounge into a small dining area, Harry saw narrow steps heading upstairs to his left. They seemed to lean into the wall as though tired and in need of a good lie down. The kitchen lay ahead and Harry made his way into it. The surfaces were clean, no pans, plates, or cutlery on the draining board. No glasses. He opened the fridge.

Harry saw food, but none of it was in a fit state to eat. The salad in the bottom drawer was leaking and with the door open green fluid dribbled onto the floor. A half-finished bottle of wine sat in the door. On the shelves, Harry saw food outside of its best-before date. And the smell was less than pleasant.

Warning bells started to ring in Harry's head. If someone had been here, they were long gone. But then, why leave the car? What kind of desperate hurry must they have been in to take off on foot?

Shutting the door, Harry called out once more before making his way up the stairs. They were narrow and he found himself almost sideways as he made his way up them.

The landing at the top of the stairs led to three doors. The first two were open, leading to a bedroom with a double bed and another with two singles. Both rooms were empty, the double showing some signs of occupancy, with a ruffled duvet and a suitcase. The window was open, which explained the draught. The third door was up two more steps to his left and Harry made his way over to it and knocked.

No answer.

Harry knocked again then leaned his ear against the door. A faint, thick buzzing sound answered him and behind it the sound of water.

Harry took a breath to steel himself for what was on the other side, took a pot from his pocket to dab vapour rub under his nose, then opened the door.

The bathroom window was hidden behind a blind drawn down. And that was perhaps a good thing, Harry thought, because what was before him was not the kind of thing anyone would want to see.

The walls, the floor, indeed every surface was covered in blood. Great sprays of it painted the space, giant brushstrokes of red swept across at all angles. The toilet seat had been yanked off and lay broken to one side. On the sink, Harry saw blood on the taps, one of which was running, the water swirling a clean path through caked-on blood. But it was the contents of the bath which stopped Harry in his tracks, not just because of the smell, but what he saw before him, half-covered in a bloody, ripped shower curtain that had been yanked from its rail.

The body was bloated and unrecognisable, reminding Harry more of a seal lying on a beach than something which had, until recently, been a living, breathing human being. The electric shower over the bath was spraying hot water and the heat of it had only accelerated the whole awful process of decomposition.

Harry could see wounds and bruises, some of which he knew were marks from the body's own well-advanced decomposition. The rest were stab wounds, dozens of them, not that he was counting. The colour of it was a mix of greens and reds, the water the body lay in a foul, stinking slurry of fluids, trapped by the body's heel jammed in the plug hole. He noticed that the hands, or what was left of them, were swollen, the fingers all missing. Flies buzzed around and Harry saw maggots crawling on and in the flesh, the wounds the body had received at someone else's hands rich with life that feasted on death.

Harry stepped back out of the room, closed the door, then made his way back through the house to Jen and Smudge outside.

'We need Forensics here immediately,' he said before Jen was given a chance to say anything. 'We need to find out about this car, the owner, any details we can, who owns this cottage. Give the office a ring and get Jim and Liz on that. And after what happened over in Reeth, I want Bomb Disposal out here now as well.'

'There's a bomb?'

'I've no idea if there is or not,' Harry said, his hand now being nuzzled by Smudge's wet nose, 'but I'm not taking any chances.'

Harry, taking Smudge's lead from Jen, took a few steps away from the detective constable as she got on her phone. The smell from that bathroom was still with him, clinging to his skin, his clothes. He wanted to shower, to rinse off the awfulness of it, but there was no chance of that. He breathed in deep through his mouth, let the breath out slowly, made his way back over to Jen.

'You okay?'

'No,' Harry said.

'Bad, then?'

'Very.'

'Mr Smith?'

'Whoever he is, he's very dead,' said Harry. 'Assuming of course, that the body I just found in the bathroom is the Mr Smith we're looking for. Which is why we need details on the car and the house.'

A few minutes later a siren blasted into the moment and a police car shot around the mini roundabout at the bottom of the hill then skidded to a halt across the back end of the Audi sports car. Two police officers climbed out, a man and a woman. As they approached, Harry noticed the male officer staring at him, his eyes flicking occasionally down to Smudge.

'That was quick,' Harry said.

'We were in town,' the female officer said. 'I'm Detective Sergeant Mehta and this is Constable Wilson.'

'DCI Grimm,' said Harry. 'And this is DC Blades.'

'You've got a dog,' said Wilson.

'Nothing gets past you, does it?' Harry said.

'So, what have we got?' asked the DS.

'A body,' Harry said. 'Upstairs, in the bathroom. By the looks of things, it's been there for a good while. A week or so at least, I reckon.'

'Who is it?' Constable Wilson asked, still staring.

Harry didn't want to have to say anything, but he would if this continued.

'The only name we have is a Mr Smith,' Harry said. 'Mr John Smith, actually. Though I'm putting my money on that not being his actual name.'

'Why?'

'We got this address and the victim's phone number from a notebook linked to the victim of another murder we're investigating,' Harry said.

'Doesn't mean he's using an alias,' said Wilson.

'We have reason to believe that the other victim was an escort and had visited here a week before she was herself murdered.'

'A client, then?'

'Possibly.'

'And we got the message that you've called for Bomb Disposal,' Wilson said, making his way over to the front door of the cottage. 'You sure about that?'

Harry wasn't taking to Wilson or his questions. And the man was still staring at him, harder if that was at all possible.

'Well, I didn't ask for them to visit just to catch up on old times, did I?' Harry said. 'And you do know it's rude to stare, don't you?'

Wilson blushed.

'I wasn't staring,' he said. 'I mean, I didn't think I was, it's just... Look, I'm sorry.'

Harry ignored the apology.

'While the scene of crime team were going over the other

crime scene an explosive device was detonated. It destroyed the body of the victim, killed two members of the SOC team, and seriously injured the pathologist.'

Wilson had stopped just outside the door.

'So, it's a bad idea to go in here, then.'

'Unless you have a desperate urge to risk ending up looking like this,' Harry said, pointing at his own face, 'then yes, it bloody well is!'

CHAPTER TWENTY-THREE

HARRY STOOD AWAY FROM THE COTTAGE ON THE OTHER side of the cordon tape. Constable Wilson had certainly gone to town with the stuff, turning the front of the place into something resembling a cat's cradle. He'd then stretched numerous strands of it up and down the street to cut off the road. Harry wondered if the tape should've been placed a bit further away, but for now, it would do. Smudge had also somehow managed to get a hold of some and was now lying on her back, twisted up in it, and biting at a length that was wrapped around one of her paws.

Another police vehicle had then arrived with two more officers and Harry and Jen had let them get on with explaining the situation to the locals and clearing out anyone in the nearby buildings. The road was also closed, which was already causing issues. Horns were beeping, windows were being wound down to allow the swearing to escape, and Harry was very happy indeed to just watch and let the local police deal with it all.

'You seen the time?' Jen asked.

Harry checked his watch.

'Mid-afternoon already,' he said. 'Wondered why I was getting hungry again.'

'I can grab you something if you want?'

Harry noticed the eagerness in the young officer's eyes.

'You do remember what I said about this not being a jolly, don't you?' he asked.

'Of course,' Jen said. 'But if I just so happen to pass that running shop I mentioned then I'd only pop in, I promise.'

'Make the sandwich worth the wait, then,' Harry said.

'What about Smudge?'

'She's fine,' Harry said.

'She doesn't look fine,' said Jen.

'Don't let those puppy-dog eyes fool you.'

Jen bounded off.

Harry's phone buzzed. Jim was on the other end.

'Two things,' Jim said. 'One, we've got the report in from Bomb Disposal.'

'Army efficiency right there,' Harry said. 'Which is a rare thing, in my experience. What does it say?'

'I've not read through it in detail,' said Jim, 'but you're right about the Claymore. I'll forward it to you now.'

'And what's the other thing?' Harry asked.

'We've heard back on the car,' Jim said. 'We've got the victim's name and address. I'm forwarding that to you now, too.'

'Great,' Harry said.

'Just one thing though,' said Jim. 'Her name.'

'What about it?'

'It wasn't Melissa,' Jim said.

'How's that, then?' Harry asked. 'That's what her neighbour called her, what everyone we've spoken to in Reeth knew her as.'

'But it's not the name on the driving licence, though,' Jim said. 'According to what we've received, her actual name is Helen, surname Morgan.'

'So, she was going by another name around town then,' Harry said.

'Looks that way, yes,' agreed Jim. 'Why, though?'

'For all we know she had numerous names,' Harry said. 'If she was an escort, there's a very good chance that each of her clients knew her as something else.'

'But Helen will be her real name, won't it?' said Jim.

'Not necessarily,' Harry said. 'Could have changed it easily enough by deed poll, for a start. Any news on Jadyn?'

'Only that he's not at home,' said Jim, before adding, 'I'm not sure I was supposed to tell you that.'

'What do you mean he's not at home?' Harry said. 'Where the hell is he then? What's he bloody well playing at?'

'We had a call from Anna,' Jim said, tripping over his words in a rush to explain. 'She spoke with his neighbour who said he'd gone out. She's looking for him now. Gordy's joined her.'

'What about the photos, then?' Harry asked. 'We must have those by now, surely? Or did stuff only ever get done on time because Sowerby was there to yell at people?'

'That, I think,' said Jim. 'No photos yet. But we're due them within the hour.'

'If they don't arrive, you have my permission to find that photographer and use whatever force necessary to get them from him.'

'I'm just a PCSO,' said Jim. 'It's not like I can threaten to arrest him.'

'I'm sure you can use your imagination. Anything on the Claymore?' Harry asked. 'And don't worry; I'm expecting your answer to be no.'

'Gordy's checking in with some contacts, while she's over finding Jadyn,' Jim said.

'On that,' Harry said, 'if Swift happens to be in touch about anything, probably best we don't mention Jadyn.'

'Understood,' Jim answered. 'And we've not come up with anything on HOLMES about military weapons being used by criminal gangs either. Actually, that's not entirely accurate. There's plenty about military-type weapons being smuggled in or used or seized, but there's nowt about MOD stuff turning up.'

'Well, just keep looking,' Harry said. 'What about Matt?'

'He's still away to Catterick,' Jim replied. 'Not heard anything yet.'

Conversation over, he was then surprised to see Jen return at the same time as the arrival of the SOC team.

'I saw them coming through town,' Jen said, a little out of breath, 'so I sprinted back.' She handed Harry a paper bag. 'Here you go.'

Harry removed a large roll filled with chicken and salad from the bag.

'Nice and healthy,' Jen said.

'Too healthy by the looks of things,' Harry grumbled, but took a bite anyway. 'No shop visit, then?'

'Oh, I had time for that,' Jen said. 'I've asked them to hold onto what I bought so that I can pick it up at the end of the day.'

A shadow cast itself across Jen and Harry.

'Excuse me, I'm looking for the OIC?'

'Officer in Charge?' Harry said. 'That'll be me, for now, anyway.'

The man talking to them was tall, mid-fifties Harry guessed, with slouched shoulders and hair that looked like it simply couldn't be bothered anymore. Behind him, a young man stood, armed with a camera and a large shoulder bag.

'For now? How do you mean?'

'All depends on what we've got,' Harry said. 'But I'll likely hand everything over to someone local so I can head back home.'

'And what have we got?' the man asked. 'The name's Stanley, by the way. William Stanley.'

'Grimm,' Harry said and told him what he had found inside the cottage.

'Did you touch anything?'

'No.'

'Sure?'

Harry decided against answering.

'What about the dog?'

'What about it?'

'Has it been in the house?'

'And why would it have been?' Harry asked.

'Well, you know what dogs are like,' said Stanley.

'I do indeed,' Harry said. 'Terrible reputation for breaking and entering and trampling all over crime scenes. Particularly so if there's been a murder.'

Stanley's lips went thin and he breathed sharply through his nose.

'So, you think there's a bomb?' he asked, clearly deciding to change the subject, Harry thought.

'Possibly,' Harry said.

'Well, that makes it all a bit more exciting, doesn't it?' Stanley said.

'Whatever floats your boat,' Harry said.

'So, when can we go in?' asked the photographer.

'Not until the bomb disposal team have been through the place,' said Harry.

'But I need to take photos.'

'We all need to do something,' Harry said, 'but sometimes we just need to be a little patient now, don't we?'

'Yes, but I've a gig on later and I don't want to miss it.'

Harry did a double-take.

'A gig?'

'Yes,' the photographer answered. 'My diary's pretty full for obvious reasons.'

'You're a musician, then?' Harry asked.

'No,' the photographer said. 'Why would you think that?'

'You said you had a gig to go to.'

'So?'

'So a gig is something with music, isn't it? Where bands play, that kind of thing.'

'I mean, I do play an instrument as it happens,' the photographer said.

'Of course you do,' said Harry.

'Bongos.'

'What?'

'Bongos,' the photographer repeated. 'You know, like drums you play with your hands?' He then proceeded to mime playing some invisible bongos in mid-air.

'No, I heard you the first time,' Harry said. 'It's just that I thought you said you played a musical instrument. My mistake. At least you didn't say it was the ukulele though, so that's something, isn't it?'

Stanley then asked, 'Do you know when the bomb disposal team will be here?'

'I don't,' Harry said. 'But the sooner the better for everyone's sake. You need to get in there and we need to know the house is safe. We've had to clear all the buildings around the place so people aren't exactly having a good day of it so far.'

A barked shout from the end of the road caught Harry's attention. He glanced over to catch a wave from a police officer, then another van came around the corner.

'Looks like they're here,' Jen said.

'Then how's about you and me take five once they're on with what they're doing?' Harry asked. 'You mentioned something about a pub?'

'We're on duty.'

'Well, I won't tell if you won't. And just because we're in one doesn't mean we have to be downing pints, now, does it?'

With the bomb disposal team instructed on what Harry's team had dealt with over in Reeth, but also what he had found in the house in front of them, he left them to it and allowed Jen to lead him to the pub just up the road, Smudge at his side.

'So, why is it called Golden Rule?' Harry asked as they entered.

'Haven't the faintest idea,' said Jen.

Inside, Harry found himself in a room that had very clearly remained unchanged in decades. The bar was directly in front, displaying a good array of beers. To his right was a small fireplace, a fire burning in the grate despite the warmth of the weather outside. A small number of tables and chairs stood around, along with plush benches attached to the walls and seating in the windows. Doors led off to other rooms. Harry heard no music, no sound of a games machine, just the quiet chatter of people having a drink together.

'So, what do you want, then?' Harry asked.

'Just a lemonade,' said Jen. 'And a packet of cheese and onion crisps.'

Harry ordered the same, the sensible side of his brain holding sway over the part that wanted to have a pint, sit down, and then perhaps have a couple more. Not because he necessarily wanted them, just because this was clearly a pub designed to relax you and let you unwind. It was, in every way, absolutely bloody perfect.

They sat down round the fire. A dog belonging either to the pub or another customer came over to say hello, sniffing Harry's hand. Smudge, who had plonked herself down close enough to the fire to almost be in it, stood up and sniffed the dog's rear end. Clearly the aroma wasn't to her liking and she sat back down again, curling herself up on the floor.

'So, you're enjoying being a dog owner, then?' Jen asked.

'Well, I'd pick it over owning something like that dragon you've got lazing about at home,' Harry said.

'Steve's lovely.'

'I'm sure he is. For a lizard.'

Harry leaned back into his seat and stared at the fire. From the back of his mind the whole thing with the job down south bubbled up again. Smudge was up and sitting between his legs, her head resting in his lap.

'You're frowning,' Jen said.

'No, that's just my face.'

'I know your face well enough and I know when you're frowning.'

Harry attempted to relax.

192 DAVID J. GATWARD

'Now you look like you need the loo,' Jen said. 'Why don't you tell me what's on your mind?'

'It's just the case, that's all,' Harry said. 'And for someone who's probably half my age, you don't half sometimes talk as though you're considerably older.'

'Wise beyond my years,' Jen said.

'Anyway, it's just the case, that's all.'

'Is it, now?'

'Yes, it is.'

Harry thought for a moment. Would it really hurt to chat to Jen? She was hardly going to go blabbing to anyone, was she?

'It's about Bristol,' Harry said.

'You think you have to go back, don't you?' Jen said.

Harry was surprised by this reply.

'How did you guess?'

'Well, it's obvious, isn't it?' Jen said.

'Is it?' Harry said.

He was pretty sure that it wasn't obvious at all. He'd heard about the job thanks to an email and then a brief chat with his old DSup. The only other person who knew anything about it was Kett. And that man knew well enough that if he told anyone at all, Harry would probably cut his balls off.

'Of course it is,' Jen said. 'If what we've found here in Ambleside is linked to what happened in Reeth, and it's pretty clear that it is, then you'll have to go, won't you? After what you said about that Hollywood bloke, anyway. And my guess is that you probably don't want to.'

'Don't I?'

'Can't see why you would,' Jen said. 'It's never easy going back to a place when you've made somewhere else your home, is it? Plus you'll be heaving your way through old investigations to see if there's a link somewhere because of those fingers being cut off. It's hardly going to be fun.'

Harry was relieved that he and Jen had been talking at cross purposes. He was also impressed with Jen's thinking on it all. And she had a point.

'You know, you're bang on,' Harry said.

'Thought I might be,' said Jen.

'We could do with Matt coming back with something on that soldier though. That's just too much of a coincidence to be nothing.'

The door to the pub opened and in walked a police officer.

'DCI Grimm?'

'Yes?' said Harry.

'I've been told to let you know that the bomb disposal team will—'

The officer's sentence was cut in half as an explosion shattered the pub windows and covered everyone inside with glass.

CHAPTER TWENTY-FOUR

His ears still ringing, Harry was on his feet.

'Jen! You okay?'

The detective constable looked up at him and he saw a few bloody nicks from the glass on her face.

'Yes,' she nodded. 'I'm fine.'

She was clearly shaken, that much was obvious from her voice alone, but Harry saw a stern look in her eye. Smudge was cowering under a seat.

'Stay here,' he said, handing her Smudge's lead. 'Check everyone in here first before you both come and join me. Understood?'

Harry didn't wait for an answer and was out through the door into a world of chaos.

Running down the hill, Harry saw smoke pouring from the cottage. The windows were shattered, glass covering the street. The perimeter had been enough to keep folk away from the danger, but only just. A police officer stumbled towards him, blood pouring down her face.

'DS Mehta?'

'There was no warning,' the DS said. 'One minute we were being told that the bomb disposal team would be out in a few minutes, and the next...'

'You mean there were people still in there when it went off?'

The DS nodded, her face scored with pain.

Harry saw another police officer stumbling towards him. It was Wilson. He looked okay, just dazed.

'Wilson! Call emergency services! Now!'

The man pulled out his phone, leant against a wall, clearly dazed, and tapped in a number.

Just down the hill, Harry saw the scene of crime team spilling out of their van. The pathologist, Stanley, was in front.

'I think there's been an explosion,' the man said, as he reached Harry.

'The evidence certainly suggests that, yes,' Harry replied. 'Ambulance should be on its way soon.'

As if in support of what he'd just said, Harry heard sirens, which were then cut off by a pained yell from the cottage behind him. He turned to see a man stumble out of the door, holding what was left of his arm.

Harry raced over, Stanley behind him.

'I'm a trained medic,' Stanley said.

'Makes two of us,' Harry said. 'Though I'm a bit rusty and more used to dealing with bullet wounds.'

They arrived just in time to catch the man as he fell, his legs giving way beneath him.

'It just went off,' he said, his voice a whimper. 'We checked it, checked all around for decoys, did everything right. But it still went off.'

Harry helped the man sit down on a bench just outside

the cottage as Stanley did what he could to deal with the dreadful injuries he'd sustained.

'Where were you?' Harry asked. 'In the bathroom? How many others are still inside?'

'Two,' the man said, his voice barely audible, blood on his lips. 'The body, the bomb, that was easy. Really simple to deal with.'

'Who else is in there?' Harry asked again. 'How dangerous is it?'

A screech of tyres announced the arrival of an ambulance.

'It just went off,' the man said again, his voice fading as he slipped in and out of consciousness. 'It ... it just went ... off.'

Harry looked at Stanley.

'Stay with him,' he said, then before anyone could stop him he disappeared into the cottage, Stanley's shout of *don't be a bloody idiot* was soon shut out by the all-out attack on his senses of what had happened inside.

The lounge was a place of dust and ash and dirt. Furniture had been upturned, the ceiling was cracked and great chunks of it had broken off and shattered on the floor. The glass from the stove had blown out. And the television wouldn't be reaching out for any new releases from Netflix ever again, that was for sure.

Harry moved into the dining room. Again, the place was all dust and dirt. The kitchen beyond it was undamaged, but here the dining table and chairs looked as if they'd all just returned from a night out on the beers, all tipped over and on top of each other.

Harry looked up the stairs, or what was left of them. Some of the railings holding up the wooden bannister were snapped, and the stairs seemed to have pulled away from the wall. Stepping onto them, they wobbled, but Harry knew that at the top of them were people in need of help. He pushed on, taking each step as gingerly as he could. Halfway up, the staircase shuddered and Harry fell back. He caught himself on the bannister, swore, then pushed on.

At the top of the stairs, the rooms he remembered were no longer there. The adjoining walls, clearly little more than pinboard, were smashed to pieces, great slabs of them thrown across the beds, which themselves were smouldering, broken things ruined by the blast. The door to the bathroom was gone, the room inside covered in plaster and blood.

Harry saw two bodies, one in each of the bedrooms, or what was left of them, the furniture shattered and smoulder-ing, torn apart by the blast. Neither were moving. As he approached them, he couldn't pull his eyes away from the ceiling, because where it had been, it now wasn't, replaced instead by a vast hole and above it a broken roof open to the sky.

Harry looked into the bathroom where he'd found the victim in the bath. The room was, like the bedrooms, a ruin, the ceiling gone, the bath full of debris, the sink and toilet in pieces.

Harry heard footsteps behind him and turned to find clear, grey eyes staring at him from the youthful face of a female paramedic.

'Sir, we need you to leave,' she said.

'I've not had time to check them,' Harry said. 'They're not moving. I think the explosion was—'

'Please, sir,' said the paramedic, and gestured towards the rickety stairs. 'We've got this. Let us do our job.'

Harry stood up, made his way carefully back through the

house and outside. Jen was waiting for him, Smudge at her side. Stanley and the injured man he had been dealing with were nowhere to be seen.

'You okay?' Jen asked.

Harry nodded a yes as he brushed himself down. He knelt to check on Smudge who then insisted that no, a head ruffle wasn't enough, and that really, the best place for her right now was in his arms.

'The bomb, I think it was set in the loft,' Harry said, standing up, his dog sitting in his arms. 'The blast damage is all from a hole in the top of the house. It's blown through the roof. And ...'

'And what?' Jen said. 'Are they hurt?'

Harry said nothing and that was more than enough.

'How many?' Jen asked.

'Two,' Harry said.

'But how did the bomb disposal team miss it?' Jen asked. 'Another bomb? It doesn't seem possible.'

'You can't check everything,' Harry said. 'They'd been fed information from what happened over in Reeth, hadn't they? So they investigated this in light of that.'

'They didn't check the loft, because they didn't think they needed to,' Jen said.

'Something like that,' said Harry, putting Smudge back down on the ground. 'Whoever did this here, and back in Reeth, they're after high numbers. Collateral damage is as important as the initial victims. More so maybe. But why?'

'That doesn't explain why it went off though,' Jen said. 'What triggered it if it was in the loft? Bomb Disposal would've spotted any booby traps, wouldn't they? I mean, I'm not sure how these things work, but tripwires or whatever, that's what they check for, isn't it?'

Harry didn't answer. He was looking beyond the cottage, into the traffic, windows in buildings in full view of where they now were. And there were so many. Any one of them would have been perfect.

'What is it?' asked Jen.

'Like you said, they'd have spotted booby traps,' said Harry.

'Maybe not all of them,' said Jen. 'Could they have missed something?'

'Maybe,' Harry said. 'Or perhaps there weren't any booby traps at all.'

'Not sure I understand.'

'Maybe the bomb was detonated remotely.'

'You mean someone saw what was happening and blew the place with people inside on purpose?'

'It's possible,' Harry said, looking out once again at all the windows which stared back at him from other buildings.

'But they would have had to have known we were coming today, wouldn't they?' Jen said. 'Otherwise, they would've had to just sit there, staring at this place for days on end, hoping someone would turn up eventually.'

'Maybe they weren't looking at us through a window,' Harry said.

'Then how?' Jen said.

Harry pointed at the wall on the other side of the road.

'Those cameras,' he said. 'Is it me, or do they look a bit new?'

CHAPTER TWENTY-FIVE

GORDY, STILL FEELING A LITTLE WORSE FOR WEAR AFTER
what had happened in Reeth, was first to spot Jadyn. She'd
decided to join Anna in the search for the missing police
constable just to get out and feel useful as much as anything.
She'd got off lightly, to say the least from what had happened,
true, but she still had a bit of a headache. Not that she'd told
Anna that. She was a wonderful woman for sure, but sometimes she was a little too caring, if that was at all possible.
Very good for her vocation, but Gordy wasn't one for being
fussed over, nice as it was now and again.

Gordy pulled out her phone and called Anna.

'I've found him.'

'Thank God! Where?'

'He's in a little café,' Gordy said. 'And I use that description loosely. I'm sure it serves food, but it's hard to tell.'

'Not sure I understand.'

'For whatever reason, the place is called The Mad
Hatter's,' Gordy explained. 'I'm assuming it's a reference to a
certain tea party. And believe it or not, from what I can see,

there's definitely a hat theme going on. The window is full of them, and there's dozens hanging from the ceiling.'

'Send me the location and I'll meet you there.'

Gordy hung up and then headed over to it, pushing through the door to the sound of a tiny bell.

Inside, the café was doing a brisk trade. The majority of the customers were men and women in combat fatigues, all of them tucking into variations on things you can fry. The café was rich with the aroma of bacon and fried bread, and behind that baked beans. Steam billowed out from behind the counter, not just from the kitchen, but from a huge stainless steel water boiler. A man behind the counter was currently adding to the billowing clouds as he filled up a kettle.

'Just grab a seat, decide what you want, and order here,' he called over. 'Specials are on the wall.'

Gordy saw that Jadyn hadn't yet noticed her arrival. In front of him was a mug, empty by the looks of things. No food though.

She walked up to the counter and perused the menu. It had clearly been put together on a home computer by someone who had obviously wanted to use all of the fonts available. The word 'Menu' was done in some kind of horrifying design more suited to black and white movies about vampires and zombies. The titles of the various sections were then in a round, bubble-like script which Gordy thought would work well for children's television but not all that great when deciding on whether to have the breakfast omelette (bacon, beans, hash browns, mushrooms, sausages, black pudding, fried bread), the full English (same ingredients, just not inside an omelette), or the Mad Hatter's Monster Maker, the ingredients of which comprised an entire paragraph and so many exclamation marks Gordy wondered if perhaps a law against their use should be implemented.

'So, what do you fancy, then?' the man at the counter asked.

'What's with the hats?' Gordy asked. 'Is it Alice in Wonderland? You a fan?'

The man looked confused.

'Alice who now?' he said. 'Everyone loves hats, don't they?'

'Do they?'

'Of course! Now, do you want the full English? I also do bacon hash—bit of a speciality—and you can have chips with anything. Even have chips with chips if you want.'

Gordy asked for a mug of tea and a bacon sandwich for herself and ordered the same for Anna. 'And I'll have one full English as well,' she added, for Jadyn.

'Tea?'

'Of course.'

'It'll be about five minutes,' the man said. 'Pay when you're done.'

Gordy went over to Jadyn's table.

'Well,' she said, 'fancy meeting you here.'

Jadyn looked up and Gordy saw confusion then worry then deep concern write themselves across his face.

'I'm ... I'm ill,' he said. 'I, well, I just needed some fresh air, that's all. That's why I'm not home. But I will be in a bit. After the air.'

Gordy sat down.

'I've ordered us something to eat.'

'I'm not hungry.'

'Now that I very much doubt.'

The café door opened, and Anna stepped in. She waved and headed over to join them. Gordy told her what was ordered, and she sat down.

'I'm in trouble, aren't I?' Jadyn said.

Gordy thought for a moment about the best way to answer this.

'Yes and no,' she said.

'Harry's going to kill me.'

'That's not what I meant.'

'This will go on my report, won't it? I just couldn't come into work though. I didn't do it on purpose. I'm not making it up. I'm not!'

Gordy saw the panic in Jadyn's eyes and found herself reaching out to grab his hands.

'First of all, you need to calm down,' she said.

'And no one's going to be killing you or putting this on your report either,' Anna added. 'Everyone's worried about you. That's why we're here.'

'How did you find me?'

'I'm a Detective Inspector!' Gordy said with just enough indignation to bring a smile to Jadyn's face.

The man from the counter turned up carrying a huge tray. He set it down on the table then served the food.

'Enjoy!' he said, then added, 'and are you sure that none of you want chips?'

Gordy considered the vast quantities of food now in front of them and wondered about the table's ability to cope with the weight of it all.

'No, I think we'll be fine,' she said.

Jadyn, she noticed, was already eating.

'Thought you weren't hungry,' she said.

'Fried bread though,' Jadyn said. 'Bit of a treat to have that. Couldn't see it go to waste.'

Gordy and Anna allowed Jadyn a little bit of time to get stuck in. Then Anna asked, 'How are you feeling then?'

'Better for this,' Jadyn answered, stuffing a forkful into his mouth.

'Well, that's something anyway,' said Gordy.

Jadyn sat back for a rest from demolishing the fried feast. He folded his arms, looked down at the table, then started to fiddle with his cutlery.

'I ... I just don't understand what happened,' he said. 'I was fine and then I wasn't.'

'How do you mean?' Anna asked. 'Was this in Reeth?'

'No, after,' Jadyn said. 'When I got home.'

'I was there, remember,' Gordy said. 'What happened, what we had to deal with, it was a high-stress situation.'

'I get that,' Jadyn said. 'But when I got home, I couldn't sit still. And I wasn't even thinking about what had happened, either. I just couldn't relax. And then my brain just went all weird, like it was full of wasps, my thoughts just buzzing around the place.'

'What thoughts?' Anna asked.

'Not about what happened in Reeth,' Jadyn said. 'But before. You know, when—' Jadyn's voice broke and he leaned his head back then rubbed his eyes with his hands.

'You mean the barn,' Gordy asked.

Jadyn replied with the faintest of nods.

'How has the counselling been going?'

'So-so.' Jadyn shrugged. 'I went to all the sessions to begin with, but I've missed a few these past few weeks.'

'Why?'

A shrug.

'You know that's not an answer, don't you?' said Gordy.

'Didn't feel like I was getting anywhere,' Jadyn said, stabbing a piece of sausage with his fork and stuffing it into his mouth.

'This kind of thing takes time,' Anna said. 'And by that, I don't mean a month or two. It can be years.'

'Years?' Jadyn said. 'How can I live with whatever this is for years? I know it's PTSD but just what the hell does that mean anyway? There's something wrong with me, isn't there? It's embarrassing! I don't want to talk to anyone about it. What can I tell my parents? That I've lost the plot completely? That I can't hack the job?'

Gordy leaned forward.

'There's something you're going to do,' she said. 'You're not going to want to, I know, but right now I think it may be the best thing for you.'

'I can't take time off,' Jadyn said, jumping in. 'I can't. I'll go nuts sitting at home on my own. And I can't go back to Bradford, not like this. Please...'

'Jadyn,' Anna said, 'you need to let Gordy speak, okay? She knows what she's talking about.'

Jadyn's eyes flickered between the two women and Gordy wondered if he was looking for an opportunity to do a runner.

'You're going to speak to Harry,' Gordy said.

'What? Are you insane?'

'No, I'm not. In fact, this is one of the most sensible things I've ever said.'

'I'd agree with that,' Anna said with a smile and nudge.

'You're going to have the rest of the day to yourself, that's fine. But tomorrow, you'll come into work and you'll speak with Harry.'

206 DAVID J. GATWARD

'I can't ...'

'You can and you will,' Gordy said, her voice firm. 'He's not just your boss and he's not just a DCI either. If there's anyone who can help you make sense of how you're feeling, of what it's like to deal with PTSD, it's him.'

'The scars you mean?'

'I do,' Gordy said. 'Look, I know he's a gruff old bugger, but I've worked with few if any who care about their team quite like he does. I'll admit, he sometimes has a funny way of showing it, and that grump he wears like a badge can be a little wearing at times, but he only wants the best for everyone. For you.'

Jadyn sat quietly, pushing a solitary baked bean around his plate with a knife.

'She's right,' Anna said. 'Harry is exactly the person you need to talk to.'

'Okay then,' Jadyn said. 'I'll do it.'

'Good,' said Gordy. 'Now finish up and get yourself back home.'

'I will, I promise,' Jadyn said.

'I'll be keeping you to that,' Gordy said, standing up, Anna doing the same. 'Because if you don't, I'm pretty sure I won't be wanting to get in the way of Harry as he drives over here to find you.'

CHAPTER TWENTY-SIX

Matt was growing frustrated. When he'd first headed over to Catterick earlier in the day he'd been all motivated with the idea that he was on the search for something important, a lead, a link to what had happened in Reeth, maybe even a suspect. Now, though, all he was motivated by was the urge to sod off back to Wensleydale and give up a ghost chase.

Following a bit of research, he had discovered there were nearly a dozen specific garrisons that he would have to drive around. Catterick Garrison was spread wide and far, reaching its fingers over into the historic town of Richmond. The idea that he'd somehow stumble on a specific car while driving around was madness, he realised, but then sometimes most police work felt like that.

The job could be tedious and most of the good stuff didn't come from barging through doors or following blood trails, not that drama shows would have you think otherwise. No, most cases were solved by officers being out and about, following up the thinnest of leads, and never giving up till they found something.

Matt had taken it upon himself to have a word with military staff in the buildings with well-armed security on the gates and brought up a bucket of dust from a bone-dry well.

The first car park had borne no fruit at all, either, thanks to it being nearly empty. So, that had been crossed off the list. The second address had been much the same, just with considerably more vehicles, most of them in various shades of either green or sand. So, no blue Subaru, then. The third and fourth barracks had served only to cement in Matt's mind that his decision to never even consider the army as a career had been a good one, perhaps the best, thanks in the main to the state of the soldiers he'd seen in the former, and the soldiers on the gates of the latter.

At the third barracks, and having been allowed on site after a full security check, which had taken far too long, he'd been met with trucks of soldiers spilling out into daylight they'd clearly not seen in a while. It was, Matt had thought, like watching meat being pushed from a mincer, the way they seemed to just flop out of the vehicles and onto the ground, their hefty backpacks hoofed out to them to then drag back to their accommodation. Matt had seen weariness before, people so tired they looked like the best thing for them was a coma. But the exhaustion he had witnessed here was something else entirely. They were grubby, filthy even, and moved as though they had little control over their limbs. For some, just staying upright was an effort, but they still managed to lift their backpacks and move, helped no doubt by the power of a sergeant or officer's voice chasing them as they went.

The fourth barracks had been something else entirely.

Having arrived at the gate to check about heading in, the soldiers guarding it had been less than accommodating when it came to letting him through.

'ID?'

'I've just given it to you.'

The soldier had held up Matt's warrant card.

'I'll have to call this through.'

'I'm happy to wait.'

The soldier had directed Matt to a parking bay then left him there for half an hour. When the soldier had returned, he'd had questions.

'What's the purpose of your visit?'

'I'm following a line of enquiry in relation to a murder,' Matt had said, deciding to go straight for the gut with why he was there.

'Do you have any other documents to prove this?'

'Of course I don't,' said Matt.

'Then I'm afraid I can't let you go any further.'

'Yes, you can.'

Matt was very aware at this point of the weapon the soldier was carrying, an SA80, at least that's what he guessed. Military stuff wasn't really his thing, but this was a rifle everyone knew, not least because no other force in the world used it as far as he was aware.

'I'm sorry, what was that?'

'I'm Detective Sergeant Dinsdale,' Matt said. 'You've seen my ID. I need to be allowed on site.'

'Not happening today, chum.'

'Chum?'

'We can't spare the staff to accompany you.'

'I don't need accompanying.'

'That's for us to decide, not you.'

Eventually, Matt had given up and driven away, deciding that he'd try again the following day if he found nothing.

Barracks number five had sent him on a wild goose chase after a soldier had told him that he'd seen a car matching Matt's description. Following the directions given to him, Matt had found himself running around the site only to end up where he'd started, much to the amusement of the soldier who had directed him.

'Not funny,' Matt said.

'Piss funny, mate,' the soldier had laughed.

Now, rolling into the seventh address on his list, Matt was close to just jacking it all in and heading back. He knew that he wouldn't, because doing so wasn't in his nature, but he wasn't far off. At the security gate, he went through the same conversation he'd had half a dozen times already, except for once this went smoothly and politely and after the relevant checks he was allowed through.

So he drove around and along and down numerous roads, looking and searching but not finding. Hunger was pestering him now, too, so that wasn't helping. He gave it another twenty minutes, found nothing, and rolled on back to the security gate, lowering his window to offer his thanks.

The soldier leaned in.

'A blue Impreza, wasn't it?' he asked.

'It was, yes,' said Matt, waiting for the soldier to then say something about what great cars they were.

'One just pulled in.'

'What?'

'Not five minutes ago. I remembered what you'd said so I took the reg as well.'

The soldier handed over a scrap of paper.

'Where did they go?'

'That I don't know, but they've not come back.'

'And it was a male driver?'

'Yes,' nodded the soldier.

Matt turned his car around and headed back in.

Eyes peeled, he kept his window down hoping that the cool air would help keep him alert. And then he saw the car he was looking for.

Matt parked up, climbed out, and walked over to find that the driver had vacated his vehicle.

'Looking for something?'

Matt turned to find himself face-to-face with a smartly dressed man in combats. No squaddie though, he thought, judging by the plums in his voice. An officer.

'The owner of this vehicle,' Matt said, showing his ID.

'In a bit of bother, is he?'

'I just need to speak to him, that's all,' Matt said. 'Do you know who he is?'

'Corporal Ollie Shelton?' the officer said. 'There he is now.'

The officer pointed and Matt turned to see a soldier not ten feet away staring at them.

'I'm Detective Sergeant Dinsdale,' Matt said. 'Just wondered if we could have a little chat, if that's okay?'

Shelton looked, stared, then ran.

CHAPTER TWENTY-SEVEN

HARRY WAS STANDING BENEATH THE SECURITY CAMERAS he'd spotted and had just pulled on some disposable rubber gloves when he heard his name being called. He turned around to find himself in the presence of someone who, for a change, was bigger than he was. Not that Harry was himself a huge giant of a man, but this was someone who had clearly really enjoyed growing and decided to never stop.

'DCI Grimm?'

The man held out a hand. Harry shook it.

'Well, that's me identified,' Harry said. 'And you are?'

'Detective Superintendent Webb, Cumbria Constabulary. Nice dog, by the way. Labrador?'

'Yes,' Harry said.

'Do you shoot?'

'Pardon?'

'Do you shoot?' Webb asked. 'Labradors are great gun dogs. Unstoppable if you train them right. They'll eat you out of house and home, quite literally in some cases. I had one who had a damned good try at chomping his way through an entire sofa. A Chesterfield would you believe.'

'I don't shoot, no,' said Harry, 'but my partner, she's a gamekeeper.'

'That's good,' said Webb. 'Be a shame to see a dog like that wasted.'

Harry wasn't quite sure what the man meant.

'Sorry about this,' he said, and gestured towards the destroyed building.

'Hardly your fault, is it? I've been updated on everything so far, why you were here in the first place, so I know what's been going on.'

'We weren't expecting this, though, I have to say,' said Harry.

'I don't think anyone was.'

'The two caught in the blast?' Harry asked.

'We're already in touch with their families,' said Webb.

Harry forced himself to not spend time dwelling on what they would be going through right now.

'I hear you went into the house after the explosion and before the emergency services?'

'I did,' Harry replied. 'Someone had to. And I was first on the scene.'

'And now you're looking at security cameras,' Webb said.

'They're pointing at the house,' said Harry.

'Do we have any details on the owner of the property?'

'Not yet. Waiting on my team for that.'

Harry reached up and grabbed hold of one of the cameras.

'Interesting,' he said, then gave the camera a sharp tug.

'Jen?'

'Yes?'

'Grab an evidence bag, would you?'

Harry brought his hand back down, the camera held fast in his thick fingers.

'Perhaps you can explain why you just did that?' asked Webb. 'Or was the destroyed house not enough?'

'Look,' Harry said, turning the camera over in his hand. 'This is battery operated, right?'

'I don't see what that has to do with you damaging what is clearly someone's property,' said Webb.

'My point is, if this is a security camera,' Harry explained, 'then why would it be running off a battery? It wouldn't, would it? Something like this, it would be mains powered. And just look at it; have you ever seen a security camera like this? Doesn't exactly look permanent, does it? And it's pretty small.'

'What are you getting at?'

'I think,' Harry said, 'that this was put here very recently. I also think that whoever put it here not only had something to do with the murder of the victim inside, but also the explosion.'

'They were watching, you mean?'

'I do,' Harry said.

'Just what the hell are we dealing with here?' Webb asked.

'Something that's going to need all of us on it, I think,' Harry said. 'Your forensics team are here and I need to get back to my own team. My suggestion is that I leave this crime scene in your capable hands while I follow things up elsewhere.'

'Not sure that fits with accepted procedure,' said Webb.

'Well—and this is just my own professional opinion,'

Harry said, 'but right now, and in light of what's happened, accepted procedure can bugger off.'

'I beg your pardon?'

Harry held up a hand to calm Webb.

'That wasn't directed at you,' he said. 'I just think that my suggestion is the best way of getting the job done.'

'I see.'

'Agreed?'

Webb rubbed his chin.

'Yes,' he said. 'I do. And between you and me, sometimes I find myself feeling exactly the same way about procedure. Though, perhaps I don't express it in quite the same way.'

'We're all different,' Harry said.

'Probably a good thing.'

'You should give it a go sometime, though,' Harry added. 'Does me the world of good.' He handed the camera over to Jen. 'I'm going to take this with me and head straight back. Any information we find on the owner of the car, the house, we'll share. And I expect your team to do the same. If you need me, just call.'

'Understood.'

'Good,' said Harry, and shook Webb's hand again. 'Speak soon no doubt.'

A few minutes later and back in the car, Jen having popped in to pick up what she'd bought from the shop in town, Harry was looking at the camera, now secured inside an evidence bag on his lap.

'You're quiet,' Jen said, as they headed out of Ambleside, the afternoon now early evening.

Smudge was asleep on the back seat.

'I'm thinking,' Harry said.

'There's plenty to think about with six dead at two crime scenes.'

'There is that,' Harry said with a sigh. He placed the camera on the back seat.

'And what are those thoughts so far?'

'That I've not a sodding clue what's going on and that none of this makes any sense whatsoever, that's what.'

Harry leaned his head back, closed his eyes.

'We've got six dead, two bombs, two crime scenes, a good number of casualties, drugs, torture, and right now we seem to be getting nowhere other than digging ourselves deeper into a bigger pile of shite with every hour that passes.'

'Nicely put,' said Jen.

'It doesn't add up, though, does it?' Harry said. 'Why would someone kill a young woman in Reeth and whoever that was back in Ambleside? And why the bombs, the deliberate collateral damage? There are vendettas and revenge and giving a warning, but which is it? And why? What's any of it about?'

'Maybe we'll know more when we get details on who we found at the house,' Jen said.

'Here's hoping,' Harry said.

With little more to say, and with a headache threatening to ruin the evening, Harry checked his phone to find a message from Grace. He opened it to find a photograph of her and Smudge looking at him. He couldn't help but smile. He had no idea when she had taken the photograph but he was more than a little pleased that she had.

He sent a quick text back, not with a photo, because he was pretty sure no one wanted his face to turn up in a message, but just a few words to say when they'd be back and to eat without him if they couldn't wait.

Grace replied immediately: *We'll wait. Shepherd's pie in oven. Wine breathing. Xxx*

Harry's smile grew.

'That's a look we don't see very often,' Jen said.

'What is?'

'You looking happy.'

'I'll have you know I'm a very happy person,' said Harry. 'Just because I don't spend every hour of the day smiling like a loon doesn't mean I'm unhappy.'

'Things are good with Grace, then?'

'They are.'

'And how's Smudge doing?'

'You can see for yourself easily enough,' Harry said. 'I think she's settling into her new life quite well, don't you?'

'How was your break?' Jen asked.

'Short and broken,' Harry replied.

'You don't take leave much.'

'Never have,' said Harry. 'Never really known what to do with it.'

A while later, and with the Lake District a long way behind them, Harry stared out of the window to see the Dales now laid out before them. The rain he'd seen on the mountains earlier had decided in the end to bypass the Lakes completely and swing round to land on Wensleydale. The sky was a thick grey, the clouds low, and the rain was cutting across the fells like drifting, wind-caught bedsheets. He could smell it, too, wafting into the car through the air vents, cool and rich and alive.

Harry was weary from the day and thinking about what they were dealing with only made it worse. Jen was right, he would have to take a trip south. Tomorrow, probably. The link to Hollywood was tenuous, but the drugs, the thing with the fingers, those were bits of this case that he needed to follow up on. And talking face-to-face with some of the other officers who were involved would be better than a phone call or email.

He could think of two in particular who would be useful, both of whom had worked closely with him as they'd closed in on Hollywood. He couldn't remember the last time he'd seen either of them, their team had been broken up soon after what happened at the crack house he'd told Jen about, their funding pulled and reassigned elsewhere. And perhaps going south again would help him clear up what he was or wasn't thinking about with that job offer.

'How far now?' Harry asked, breaking the silence.

They'd reached the rain and it was smashing down on the car, the windscreen giving Harry the impression that they were driving underwater.

'We're not far off now,' Jen said. 'Fifteen minutes maybe.'

'Nice to be welcomed home by the rain.'

'Wouldn't have it any other way,' Jen said.

CHAPTER TWENTY-EIGHT

MATT QUICKLY REALISED THAT THE ADVANTAGE Shelton had over him wasn't just the head start but his considerably higher level of fitness. He was already well ahead, and Matt had only been chasing for about ten seconds.

'Stop!' Matt shouted. 'Police! Stop!'

But Corporal Shelton clearly had other ideas and somehow seemed to accelerate. Matt wasn't about to give up, though. What Shelton had in fitness Matt had in stubbornness, so he forced his mind to override the pain he was already feeling and kept on.

Not even a couple of minutes later, however, Matt was beginning to realise that being stubborn wasn't all that useful. Athletes didn't win 100-metre sprints because they were stubborn, but because they were fast. And Matt wasn't. Shelton was well away now and there was no way of catching him. Still, at least he knew who the bloke was, so that was something. Shelton could run, yes, but Matt had his name, his car, everything really to find him. And he would.

Matt came to a lumbering, breathless stop, his feet slapping down hard on the ground. He rested his hands on his hips as he tried to suck in more air.

'Detective Sergeant?'

Matt recognised the voice as that of the officer who had spoken to him briefly at Shelton's car. He turned to face him, still barely able to breathe. The officer was standing with Shelton and the soldier's arm clasped firmly in his hands.

'I saw you pelt off there,' the officer said, 'like a dog after the hare, I have to say. And as it was clearly rather important that you have your little word with Corporal Shelton I decided to take a different route.'

Shelton didn't even try to pull away from the officer's grip.

'You went one way, I went the other. Sort of a pincer movement, don't you see?'

Matt walked over, at last able to speak again.

'Thank you,' he said.

'Do you need to take him back with you?' the officer asked. 'Or would you like a little room here to have a chat? I can provide one, I'm sure. Can't have our soldiers running away from the police now, can we? Doesn't look good, if you know what I mean.'

Shelton, Matt noticed, was staring at the ground.

'Well, he's not under arrest or anything,' Matt said. 'So, a room would be good, I think. Thank you.'

A few minutes later, Matt was sitting opposite Corporal Shelton. They had been provided with water, good coffee, and some biscuits.

'If you need anything, just ask,' the officer said and left Matt and Shelton alone.

Matt poured them both water and coffee.

'Biscuit?'

'No,' Shelton said.

Matt grabbed one. A Hobnob by the looks of things, he thought. Yum.

He then went through the usual official stuff of stating who he was and asking Shelton to do the same, taking down his contact details.

'Now then,' he continued, 'perhaps we'd best start with what just happened, that being, your reason for running away from me.'

Shelton shrugged.

'There must be a reason,' said Matt. 'I know I'm not much to look at, no Michelangelo's David or anything, but people don't usually run from me on sight.'

'I wasn't thinking,' Shelton said. 'I just ran, that's all.'

'You know, I reckon you were thinking,' Matt said. 'I reckon you saw me and panicked.'

'No, I just ran. It was a mistake.'

'Have you ever been over to Reeth?'

'What?'

'Reeth,' Matt asked. 'It's a place. A village. Lovely spot. Good pubs. Not too far away at all really.'

'Why would I go there?'

'Car like yours must be fun to drive,' Matt said. 'Some smashing little roads over that way, aren't there?'

'Yes,' Shelton said.

'Ah, so you have been, then?'

'No, I mean I've heard that the roads are good.'

'So Reeth and Swaledale are a common subject of conversation in the mess hall, are they?'

'No, of course not.'

'But you've heard the roads are good? Who from?'

'People?'

'What people?'

'People-people.'

'Where were you the night before last?'

'What?'

'Two nights ago. Where were you?'

'I don't know,' Shelton said.

'Forgotten?'

'No, I just don't know.'

'You got a phone on you?'

'Yes, why?'

'Can I see it please?'

'You need a warrant for that.'

'Not to ask you if you have one I don't,' said Matt.

Shelton gave a nod. 'Yeah, I've got a phone—iPhone Max Pro.'

'Expensive.'

'So? I'm not giving it to you.'

Matt leaned back in his chair and stared at Shelton.

'Are you aware that I can, under certain circumstances, take your phone and have you give me the passwords? Though that might not be necessary if you've got facial recognition. These certain circumstances could, for example, be suspicion of terrorism offences.'

Shelton's eyes went wide.

'What? I'm not a bloody terrorist!'

'Something else as well,' Matt said, 'and this is something I learned a while ago myself. Quite shocked I was, too. Have you heard of something called Significant Locations?'

'No, why would I have?'

'Well,' said Matt, leaning forward again, 'there's a feature in the settings of that posh phone of yours. Not easy to find if you don't know where it is, but a lot of things are like that, aren't they? Anyway, if you've got this particular feature switched on—and it will be, if you've not switched if off, which I doubt you have, seeing as you don't even know what it is—then anyone looking at your phone can easily see where you've been. And I don't just mean the last few hours either. I'm talking weeks and months.'

Matt saw the colour drain from Shelton's face.

'But you can only do that if you suspect me of terrorism,' he said. 'And I haven't. I've not done anything. I had nothing to do with it!'

'With what?' Matt asked.

'What?'

'What did you have nothing to do with?'

For a moment, Shelton's mouth just sort of opened and closed like a fish.

'Okay, so I was there,' Shelton said. 'I saw it, but I'd already left, hadn't I?'

'You're going to need to start from the beginning,' Matt said.

'I saw the explosion,' Shelton said. 'The house. In Reeth.'

'So, you have been there.'

'Yes, I have. Of course I have. She lived there, didn't she?'

'Who did?'

'Melissa!'

'And who's that, then?'

'My girlfriend,' Shelton said. 'Well, she was, anyway, until I found out.'

'Found out what?'

'About what she did. As a job. I couldn't put up with that. No one could! But she expected me to, didn't she? How could I?'

'You'll have to give me a few more details,' Matt said, his notebook filling up quickly now.

'She was ... she was a ...'

'A what?'

'A prostitute,' Shelton said, spitting the word out like he'd just taken a bite of rotten meat. 'She tried to disguise it, called herself an escort, like that makes any difference just because she charges more! Can you imagine? Sharing someone like that? I'd never live it down, would I? What would the lads say, everyone here?'

Matt was going off Shelton by the second.

'So, this was about you, was it?' he asked. 'Why you went over to see her. Did you argue, is that it?'

'What, we argued and then I blew up her house? Are you mental?'

'I didn't say anyone blew up anything.'

'I saw the explosion,' said Shelton. 'I saw the police.'

'And so you ran,' said Matt. 'Didn't cross your mind to head back and see if this Melissa was okay? To help?'

Shelton fell quiet again.

'I was angry, that's all. Is she okay? What happened? I panicked and just drove off, you see. I went over to apologise, but I saw the police and I thought...'

'What did you think?'

'That she'd called them,' Shelton said.

'And why would she do that?'

'We'd argued.'

'People don't call the police about an argument.'

'We'd been away,' Shelton said. 'Sort of a romantic break thing. When she told me everything, I lost it. I lashed out.'

'How do you mean?'

'I ...'

Shelton raised his left hand, pulled it back, let it drop back onto the table.

'Are you trying to tell me that you struck her?'

'I was angry.'

'Angry enough to strike her and then take that anger back to her house?'

'I had nothing to do with any of that!'

'Not how it looks from here,' Matt said.

Shelton's face was a thing riven with panic, then it cleared.

'Here,' he said, and he pulled his phone out, unlocking it, then sliding it across the table to Matt. 'Find that locations thing.'

Matt picked up the phone.

'Why?'

'Because,' Shelton said, 'if it does what you've said, then it'll show that yes, I was at Mel's house, but it'll also show that I drove straight there from the cottage we'd rented in Northumberland and that I didn't even stop. I drove there, to see her, to apologise, and I left. Just drove past. I wasn't there. I had nothing to do with it. Nothing.'

Matt stared at the phone.

CHAPTER TWENTY-NINE

HARRY WOKE TO SEE GRACE STARING AT HIM FROM THE end of the bed. She was all dressed, wax jacket on, and by her side Smudge was sitting and wagging her tail enthusiastically.

'I've a question for you,' Grace asked.

'If this question involves a ring, then I'll be honest, it seems like you're rushing things.'

Grace frowned and threw a slipper at Harry's head. It missed, but only by a whisker.

'You don't have to joke about everything, you know,' she said. 'And I missed you on purpose.'

'I know,' said Harry. 'Go on then, what's the question.'

'It's about Smudge.'

On hearing her name, the dog's tail thumped loudly.

'What's she done now?' Harry asked.

'Nothing,' Grace said, 'but I'm starting to wonder about what she's capable of.'

'How do you mean?'

Grace sat down on the bed.

'How would you feel about me training her a little? Not too much to begin with, just enough to see how she goes on with it, like.'

'Train her? But she sits and she comes to heel, and even more surprising, she'll come back when I call her.'

'I'm a gamekeeper, remember?' Grace said. 'Smudge might have it in her to be a decent working dog. I wouldn't mind finding out.'

Hearing her name three times was clearly too much for Smudge, who leapt on the bed and attacked Grace then Harry with her tongue.

'But she's an idiot,' Harry said, pushing the dog away. 'I mean, just look at her!'

Smudge was on her back, chewing her front paws gleefully.

'She's bright,' Grace said. 'And playful. If I can channel it, she might be a useful little thing to have around.'

Harry pushed himself up.

'You really think you can do something with her?'

'Worth a try, isn't it?' Grace said. 'I'll start today. Take her out with me, do some simple retrieving stuff, see how she does with the sound of the gun, then move on from there.'

'Might make more sense than her being with me,' he said, thinking of the day ahead.

'Busy?'

'Like I said last night, I might have to head to Bristol to check up on a few things.'

'You'll be away this evening then.'

'Possibly.'

'Brilliant!' Grace grinned. 'Even more time for me to spend with this soft lump!'

With all of that sorted, Grace headed off. Ben had

already gone to work, so Harry made himself a lonely breakfast of coffee and toast, threw himself into the shower, then
headed out into the day.

Hawes was already busy, Harry noticed, traffic trundling
past, people milling about. And he wouldn't have half-
minded joining the pack, getting lost for a while in just
mooching about, heading to a café, going for a walk, but it
wasn't to be. Work called and he would answer, as he
always did.

Jadyn greeted him at the door.

'Police Constable Jadyn Okri,' Harry said.

'Morning, Boss,' Jadyn said. 'Tea? I've made a pot, like, so
I can pour you one.'

'That would be much appreciated,' Harry said. 'Why
don't you bring it through to the interview room with you?'

'The interview room?'

Harry saw fear in the young officer's eyes.

'We need to have a little chat, don't we?'

'Yes,' Jadyn replied. 'Yes, we do. Look, I'm sorry
about—'

'We'll talk in private,' Harry said, cutting Jadyn off, then
he marched down the hall.

Harry was attempting to make himself comfortable,
which was next to impossible on the plastic chairs they used,
when Jadyn entered with two mugs of tea, closing the door
behind him.

'I stopped off on the way for these,' he said, placing a
paper bag on the table beside the mugs. 'Cheese and bacon
something-or-others.'

Harry opened the bag and was fairly sure he heard his
heart scream in horror.

'And these are for breakfast, are they?'

'For any time of the day, I think,' said Jadyn. 'They're still warm. Try one.'

Harry reached in, pinched one of the greasy things between his fingers, and took a bite. It was both the best and worst thing he'd tasted in a while.

'What do you think?' Jadyn asked.

'I think,' Harry said, 'that we all need to find healthier things to eat.'

Jadyn sat down.

'So, then,' Harry said, 'how are you doing?'

But Jadyn wasn't listening and instead just started talking.

'About yesterday,' he said, panic and worry curling the edges of his voice. 'I'm sorry. I should've come into work, I know that, but I couldn't. I wanted to, but my mind was all over the place and I hadn't slept and I kept getting these flashbacks, not to what happened in Reeth but the barn, and then I just needed some time, to think, to get my head together, but I wasn't bunking off or taking the piss, I really wasn't, and I don't want to be fired, please don't fire me, please, I...'

Harry raised a hand and Jadyn stopped talking.

'Right then,' Harry said, 'why don't you take a breath, stop rambling, and then we'll have a proper chat. How does that sound?'

'Please don't fire me,' Jadyn said again. 'Please.'

'For a start, I can't fire you,' Harry said. 'I'm not Alan Sugar and this isn't an episode of The Apprentice! And I don't know about you, but I for one am grateful for that. Terrible programme. Don't see the attraction of it myself. Last thing I want to do is hang around with the kind of people who seem to have dedicated themselves from a very young age to getting to the top by making sure they kick everyone else all the way down to the bottom.'

'Not a fan?'

'No, I bloody well am not,' Harry said. 'So, why don't we track back a bit and cover a few things first, okay?'

'Yes, okay,' Jadyn said.

'First, you're suffering from PTSD. You know this. We all know this. And you can't go pretending you're not. You've done well, but putting a brave face on it all, thinking you can just ignore it by working hard, well, trust me, that doesn't work.'

'I know,' Jadyn said. 'But the counselling, I'm not sure it's doing me any good.'

'It's not some magic spell, Jadyn,' Harry said firmly, unable to hold in his frustration. 'You can't just have a few chats and abracadabra everything's okay again. That's not how it works.'

'It's taking too long.'

'And it'll take a lot longer,' Harry said. 'I know that patience isn't something you're blessed with, but you need to stick with it. And stop expecting too much too soon.'

'Understood.'

'Is it, though?' Harry asked. 'I tell you now that what you went through, that was hell. The kind of hell that would turn the minds of most people to mush. Yet here you are, sitting in a room with me, and talking it through. You've got strength, Jadyn, but that doesn't come from pretending something isn't impacting your life. Sometimes—most of the time actually—strength comes from admitting when you're failing, telling someone, and not only asking for help but accepting it when it's offered.'

'You're pretty wise, you know?' Jadyn said.

'Yes, but I was young and stupid first,' said Harry. 'Like you.'

Harry watched as Jadyn's expression wasn't quite sure what to do with itself, whether to laugh or to look serious.

'Now then,' Harry said, 'what have you got planned for the rest of the day?'

'Planned?' Jadyn said. 'Noting that I know of. Not yet, anyway. I wasn't sure if I'd still have a job, to be honest.'

'Well, we've moved on from that, haven't we?' Harry said. 'Perhaps a trip would do you good, then?'

'A trip? What, take a holiday, you mean?'

'No, that's not what I mean, at all,' Harry said. 'I'm going to be heading south later this morning. And I was wondering if you'd like to come along?'

Jadyn hesitated.

Harry leaned forward.

'Just so you know,' he said, his voice quiet and conspiratorial, 'I may have phrased that as a request, but I think you should take it more like an order.'

'Gotcha,' Jadyn said with a nod. Then added through a smile, 'I'd love to come along, Boss. Sounds great. Really great, actually. Exciting even.'

Harry stood up.

'Head home, pick up whatever you need for an overnight stay, then get back here as quickly as possible. And, if you can, leave all that excitable bollocks at home. There's a good lad.'

Jadyn was out of his chair like it had suddenly burst into flames.

'I'll grab us some food for the trip,' he said.

'You do that,' said Harry. 'How long will you be?'

'Two hours max,' said Jadyn.

Harry stood back and let the constable pass.

As Jadyn opened the door to the community centre, he stopped and looked back at Harry.

'Thanks,' he said. 'For, well, you know.'

'I do,' Harry said. 'Now bugger off.'

And Jadyn was gone.

CHAPTER THIRTY

BACK IN THE OFFICE, THE REST OF THE TEAM HAD arrived. And for once, Matt wasn't handing around bacon sandwiches. Instead, he was over by the kettle not actually making a mug of tea, or even pulling open a tin to help himself to whatever was inside. He was checking his phone, putting it away for a few seconds, then pulling it out again. And that had Harry worried enough to go over and investigate.

'Detective Sergeant Dinsdale?'

Matt turned, smiled, waved, then strolled over, all casual. Harry saw through it, though. Probably because the walk Matt had adopted, rather than giving him the air of someone who was relaxed, instead made him look like he was swaggering onto the set of a Western.

'Everything okay, is it?'

'Of course. Why?'

'Call it a hunch,' Harry said. 'I've known you all a good while now. I pick up on things.'

'Like what?'

'That would be giving away my secrets now, wouldn't it? How's Joan?'

Matt didn't answer, instead, he reached into his pocket for his phone, checked it, and put it away again.

'Matt?'

'Yes?'

'Joan? How is she?'

'Oh, she's fine, just fine, yes. Really good, you know?'

Worry lines danced on the detective sergeant's face like ribbons on a maypole.

'Messaged you, has she?'

'No, why?'

'Your phone,' Harry said. 'You've checked it a dozen times at least. So, you're either expecting a message any time now, or updating your social media profiles. I'm happy to put a lot of money on it not being the latter. You don't strike me as the TikTok type, and I don't even know what TikTok is, thank God.'

For a moment, Matt looked like he was chewing something not entirely pleasant.

'Due date was yesterday,' he said. 'Which means it's any time now, doesn't it? And if it goes on too long, she'll be induced.'

'Constantly checking your phone won't hurry things along, you know that, don't you?'

'A watched kettle, right?'

'Right,' Harry said. 'However, now we've got Gordy back, I want you to have that phone of yours on loud and proud, you hear? As soon as you get word from Joan, you sod off sharpish. Just send me a message and get to her; that's where you belong.'

'Understood.'

'It had better be,' Harry said. 'Work's important, family more so.'

'Thanks,' said Matt.

Harry rested a hand briefly on Matt's shoulder then turned his attention to the room.

`Right then, if you're all suitably armed with tea and whatever snack you think is vital for your ongoing survival at this time of the morning, then how's about we get shifting.'

He didn't wait for an answer and walked over to the board. And it was beginning to look very busy indeed.

'Where's Jadyn?' asked Jen.

'I'll cover that in a bit,' Harry said. 'So you're on pen duty again.'

'The responsibility is almost too much.'

'I'm sure it is.'

Jen stood to the other side of the board.

'Detective Sergeant Dinsdale,' Harry said, 'if you could run us through what we have that would be useful. Just the key points.'

'Top of the list we have six victims,' Matt said. 'Two deliberately targeted by our murderer—'

'Or murderers,' Harry said, interrupting. 'We don't know how many we're actually dealing with here, not yet, anyway.'

'The other four,' Matt said, 'were killed by bomb blasts at each crime scene. Victim one we currently know as Helen Morgan, though she was known in Reeth as Melissa. No surname has come to light as yet for Melissa. This, and various other factors, has us wondering if Helen Morgan isn't actually her real name either. I had another walk around, chatted to the shopkeeper, bar staff at the pubs, just in case anyone's memory had been jogged at all, but nothing.'

'And the neighbour?' Harry asked.

'I knocked, but there was no answer. I'll head over and try again if I get a chance.'

'What about photos?' Harry asked. 'Do we not know what she looks like yet?'

'Well, we've got no idea if she had social media accounts or not, though judging by what we've found so far, we doubt it.'

'No,' Harry said. 'She's not going to be living under two names and then splash her face all over the place, is she? What about a driving licence? Passport?'

'Nothing relevant has come up under Helen Morgan,' said Liz. 'We were on that yesterday. Nothing that fits anyway. There are plenty of Helen Morgans, but none of them fit the description we have of the deceased.'

'Definitely not her real name, then,' Harry said.

'And we can't do a search for her anywhere until we have her actual name,' said Liz.

'What about those other numbers in her diary?'

'I was on that,' Jim said. 'Called them all. Most of them went nowhere, no answer or just dead numbers that didn't connect.'

'Another sign pointing towards the life of an escort,' Harry said. 'Her clients use burner phones so that their nearest and dearest never find out. And you said most of them. You mean that some went through?'

'Two, actually,' said Jim.

'And?'

'The first is a stockbroker called Michael Weatherford who lives in York. The second, James Cooper, is an airline pilot from Manchester.'

'Not exactly average earners then,' Harry said. 'What about their whereabouts for the past two weeks? Alibis?'

'Bombproof,' said Jim, then he went a little red at the description. 'I mean ... Oh, God, sorry. Anyway, Mr Weatherford has been laid up at home after breaking both legs kite surfing in the Bahamas.'

'Of course he has.' Harry sighed. 'And Mr Cooper?'

'On holiday,' said Jim. 'Came back two days ago. And it all checks out I'm afraid.'

'Well done for following it up,' said Harry, then he turned to Matt. 'Best you tell us about yesterday, Detective Sergeant.'

Matt proceeded to outline what had happened as he'd toured the barracks looking for the blue Impreza, and his interview with Corporal Shelton.

'Nothing to charge him on then,' Harry said.

'No,' Matt said. 'But I still think we should keep an eye on him.'

'Why?'

'He admitted to striking our first victim,' Matt said. 'And he's military, so that fits with the evidence from the explosions.'

'Motive?'

'His reaction when he found out about what she did,' Matt said. 'He's clearly got anger issues. Maybe he went over there to watch it happen? Maybe what you found over in the Lakes was all part of his revenge or something?'

Harry shook his head.

'I don't like it,' he said. 'There's stretching it and then there's that. Any further and it'll snap. The timings don't sit right, either. Unless this was very premeditated and he's not telling us something. See if you can dig up anything else on him. You never know.' He looked now at Jim. 'Please tell me you got the photos from the crime scene.'

'I did,' Jim said. 'I've printed them all out. They're in a folder behind you.'

Harry turned. Picking it up, he quickly flicked through the pictures until he came to the ones of the woman they knew as both Melissa and Helen.

'I think we all need to see this,' Harry said. 'But I'm warning you, it's not pretty.'

He stuck the photo to the board.

A silence slipped into the room then, a quietness borne of a horror that words just could not touch. And if they did, they would shrink away into the dark.

'Someone did this,' Harry said, pointing at the photograph. 'On purpose. Every bit of it. Tied her to the chair. Beat her. Cut off her ear, her fingers, covered her in cocaine, forced it into her mouth, then put a bullet in her brain. And it takes a certain kind of someone to go to these lengths, to be this cruel. She was living in Reeth under a different name, had a grab-bag in her car, so my gut tells me that whoever did this is the person or persons she was hiding from. Something in her past caught up with her.'

'What about the bomb?' asked Liz. 'Why do that?'

'Right now, I've not a bloody clue,' Harry said. 'And to do it not just in Reeth, but over in Ambleside as well? This isn't just about the two victims. It's bigger.'

'Could it be drugs?' Jen asked. 'Gangs fighting over territory or something?'

Harry folded his arms, shook his head.

'My thinking is that the drugs thing is specific to our first victim, that's all. But the killings are linked, that much is obvious. Although we're waiting on the forensics and photos from the crime scene over in Ambleside, we know that the victim died from numerous stab wounds. A vicious attack to say the least. A hands-on killing. Frenzied.'

'What about the bomb?' Matt asked.

'Waiting to hear from Bomb Disposal on that,' Harry said. 'If someone could sensitively chase it today, that would be good.'

'I've nothing from the MOD,' Gordy said. 'They're very closed-mouthed on whether or not weapons have gone missing. Well, I say that, but they're actually very adamant that nothing goes missing ever.'

'But that's not accurate, is it?' said Harry.

'No, it's not,' said Gordy. 'A couple of years ago, a number of items were stolen from army bases.'

'A number of items?' Jen said. 'I'm assuming you mean weapons and not mess tins and uniforms.'

'Rifles, ammunition, explosive munitions,' Gordy said.

'Explosive munitions?' said Matt. 'How many sins does that cover, then?'

'A lot,' said Harry. 'All of them deadly. As to the identity of the body found in the Lakes, have we got anywhere yet?'

'No,' said Jim, 'but we know that the cottage is a holiday home. It was booked out for two weeks by a Mr Smith, and I'm going to guess that's probably not his real name.'

'Two weeks?' said Harry. 'Why would he book it for that long?'

'Though you may not believe it,' said Gordy, 'people do go away on holiday for longer than a couple of days.'

'Two weeks though,' said Harry. 'On his own? You don't think that's odd?'

No one answered.

'Just me then.'

Harry saw everyone return a nod.

240 DAVID J. GATWARD

'So, we're waiting on photos, a forensics report, and we need to find a name to go with the victim in this photo and the body in Ambleside,' Harry said. 'Looks like we're going to be busy.'

'What about Jadyn?' Jen asked. 'Is he okay? You said you'd say something about it.'

'He's fine,' Harry said. 'And he's not here because I sent him home to pack a few things.'

'Why?'

'Because he's coming away with me for a couple of days,' said Harry. 'To Bristol.'

CHAPTER THIRTY-ONE

HAVING PUNCHED IN A QUICK CALL TO GRACE AND BEN to let them know he was going to be away for a couple of days, Harry was outside in time to watch Jadyn run over to his vehicle.

'There's no rush,' Harry said, catching Jadyn up, but refusing to jog. If seconds needed to be saved in the day, then he wasn't going to be doing it with the jog of a middle-aged man caught short.

Jadyn climbed in behind the wheel. 'You sure you're okay with me driving?' he asked as Harry climbed in beside him.

'I didn't get all the way to detective chief inspector so that I'd have to drive myself everywhere,' Harry said.

'How far is it, anyway?' Jadyn asked.

'To Bristol? Five hours easily,' Harry said. 'And that's assuming the roads are clear.'

Jadyn laughed.

'What's so funny?'

'Five hours?' said Jadyn. 'Like it's actually that far.'

'You do know where Bristol is, don't you?'

'Near Birmingham?' Jadyn said.

'Have you ever been to Birmingham?'

'No.'

Harry pointed at the satnav.

'Just type in Bristol,' he said. 'And I'll direct us when we get there. Near Birmingham? Perhaps I should drive after all.'

Jadyn went to unclip his seatbelt.

'I was kidding,' said Harry. 'You stay where you are. I've some sleep to catch up on.'

A couple of hours had passed when Harry woke up. He hadn't actually meant to go to sleep, but there was something soporific about being in a passenger seat, the soft thrum of the road under the wheels, the light of the day sweeping by, and he'd given into it without even realising. The sweeping vistas gifted by every corner in the Dales roads had been replaced by the monotonous grey of the M6.

'Where are we?'

'You're awake, then?'

'Either that or I'm speaking to you in my sleep.'

'I talk in my sleep,' Jadyn said. 'Used to anyway. I don't know if I do now because obviously I don't hear myself when I'm asleep. I could record myself I suppose, couldn't I? Maybe I should?'

'Why?' Harry asked before he had a chance to stop himself from encouraging the conversation.

'Might be interesting,' said Jadyn. 'What if I'm actually talking to someone, you know? Or some 'thing' if you know what I mean.'

'Well, I don't,' said Harry, 'and before you go on to explain it all for me, I think I'd best tell you that I'm very happy to remain blissfully ignorant. Now, back to my original question.'

'We've just passed Manchester,' Jadyn said. 'I've not been to Birmingham, but I've definitely been there.'

'You don't sound too sure.'

'I'm not.'

'You don't remember it, then?'

'Not sure.'

'Sometimes, Constable,' Harry said, searching his pockets for his phone, 'conversation is very much not your strong point. Now, I need to make a phone call. Probably best I let people know we're turning up, don't you think?'

'You mean you haven't?'

'Didn't have time,' said Harry, phone at his ear. 'Sorted us a hotel room each, so I got the important stuff done.'

A man's voice barked down the phone into Harry's ear.

'Police and Fire Headquarters, how can I help?'

'I'm looking to speak with Detective Superintendent Alice Firbank,' Harry said.

'Can I ask who's calling?'

'DCI Harry Grimm.'

The voice on the end of the line seemed to falter for a moment.

'Is there a problem?' Harry asked.

'No, no problem.'

'Is she there?'

'Let me just check.'

The voice was replaced with music loud enough to burst an eardrum.

'Mr Grimm?'

'Yes?'

'I'm afraid she's unavailable today.'

Harry laughed.

'Of course she is,' he said. 'Did she tell you that herself?'

'Yes, I mean no, I mean ... She's just unavailable. Perhaps you could call back tomorrow?'

'I might just do that,' Harry said and hung up.

'So, everything's sorted, is it?' Jadyn asked.

'They can't wait to see us,' said Harry.

'Who's they?'

Harry looked at Jadyn out of the corner of his eye.

'My old boss,' he said.

WHEN THEY ARRIVED at the Police and Fire Headquarters in Portishead, Harry was struck immediately by how he hadn't missed the place at all. The building was functional in style in a way only a building designed in the early nineties could be. It looked like the kind of building that could quite easily house any kind of faceless, corporate business with ease. A building that would accept numerous rubber plants, a sandwich van at lunchtime, and provide the kind of open-plan design that had once been all the rage but should never have been allowed in the first place. It was all clean lines and practicality and utterly devoid of soul.

'You used to work here?' Jadyn said as they parked up.

'Not here, as such,' Harry said. 'I'd visit occasionally, but only if I had to.'

'It's a bit, well, dull, isn't it?'

Harry pulled himself out of the car and Jadyn followed.

'Not everywhere can be Wensleydale,' Harry said, marching off towards the building as Jadyn caught up.

Inside, Harry walked up to the reception desk to find himself face-to-face with a young man clearly only just out of university. He looked shiny, Harry thought, like his face had been buffed before he'd headed out to work that morning.

'I'm here to see Detective Superintendent Firbank.'

'Do you have an appointment?'

'Could you just tell her that DCI Grimm is here to see her, please?'

Harry showed his ID.

'I'll need to check a few things first.'

'You go ahead and do that,' Harry said. 'And we'll just head up.'

'No, you can't—'

The young man with the buffed face attempted to get out of his chair, but Harry was already through into another part of the building and heading up the stairs, Jadyn hurrying to catch up.

'I think he wants us to wait,' he said.

'I'm sure he does,' Harry replied, 'but I don't want to.'

'Excuse me! Please, you need to stop! You can't just walk into this building!'

Harry ignored the voice and kept walking.

At the top of the stairs, he pushed through a door into an open-plan office humming and buzzing with people, along one side of which were various offices behind floor-to-ceiling glass walls. Except for one, which was at the far end.

As they walked through the office, Harry noticed people were staring. At first, it was just one or two, but the further they walked, the more faces turned their way. Harry was tempted to throw them a wave.

He stopped at a door and looked at Jadyn.

'Ready?'

'For what?'

Harry opened the door.

CHAPTER THIRTY-TWO

JADYN HALF STUMBLED IN AS THE DETECTIVE CHIEF inspector pushed through the door. It swiftly swooshed shut behind them, closing itself with an ominously soft, and strangely well-rehearsed, click. They were now in a large office, a room which comprised mainly filing cabinets, a small table around which were four chairs, and a large desk. A window behind the desk afforded the room a floor-to-ceiling view of the car park and Jadyn found himself wondering if it was really worth the effort and expense. The other walls were mostly bare except for several official photographs of people in police uniforms, and the kind of art only ever found in charity shops. Jadyn also noticed that the room was occupied. A woman was sitting behind the desk, two men in front of it. They were now all staring at Grimm, which for the two men involved meant twisting painfully around in their chairs.

'Hello!' said Harry. 'And how are we all today?'

The woman behind the desk, whose face, Jadyn noticed, seemed to be stuck in a look that mixed both horror and surprise, rose to her feet. He assumed that this was the very same Detective Superintendent Alice Firbank they had come to see.

'DCI Grimm,' she said. 'I'm assuming you have an explanation at hand for appearing out of the blue?'

Jadyn noticed the two men look at each other, at Harry, then back up at Firbank. They nodded to each other and started to get up.

'You're not going anywhere,' Firbank said. 'He is. Aren't you, Harry?'

'But I've only just arrived,' said Harry. 'And we've come such a long way, too, haven't we, Police Constable Okri?'

Jadyn, dragged into the conversation without warning, just gave a sort of non-committal nod and hoped that would do.

'You can't just turn up on our doorstep and barge your way in,' said Firbank. 'You just can't! That's not how it works or how it ever worked!'

'I know,' Harry said, 'but this is important.'

'And a phone call wouldn't have sufficed?'

'I tried that but was told you weren't available, so thought I'd come and see for myself, just in case.'

'Yes, but you clearly phoned while you were on your way.'

The two men made to get up once again.

'Don't move!' Firbank said, her voice knife-sharp and clear.

Harry looked at them and said, 'You know what, why don't you head along now. This shouldn't take long, I'm sure, should it, Detective Superintendent?'

The office door burst open and in stumbled the young man from reception.

'It's alright, I'm handling it,' said Firbank.

'I'm sorry,' the young man replied. 'They just, well, you know, and here they are.'

Firbank leaned forward and rested her hands on her desk.

'You're not going to go, are you?' she said, looking at Grimm.

'No,' Harry replied. 'I'm not.'

'Then I'm going to need coffee.'

A few minutes later, when the detective superintendent had finally allowed the two men to vacate the room, Jadyn found himself sitting at a table with two considerably more superior officers than himself, a large mug of average but strong coffee, and a pastry just on the cusp of going stale.

'Leftovers,' Firbank said. 'Some kind of team-building thing earlier.'

'And how did that go?' Harry asked.

'No idea because I didn't attend,' Firbank replied. 'Spending my time doing role-play activities, yoga, and problem-solving is not my idea of fun.'

'What is your idea of fun?'

'You'll never find out.'

Jadyn bit into the pastry. At least the coffee was there to wash it down.

Firbank leaned back in her chair.

'So, as you've not actually said yet why you're here, am I right to assume this is about the initiative we discussed last week?'

'No,' said Harry, and Jadyn noticed how his boss glanced at him briefly. 'And I'd prefer it if we didn't talk about that right now.'

'The position will only be open for so long,' Firbank said.

'And there are plenty of others interested. I only mentioned it, because I thought that perhaps you may be looking to come back?'

Jadyn saw Harry's jaw clench.

'We can discuss that at another time,' he said, his voice firm. 'We're here about something else entirely.'

'What?'

'Hollywood,' Harry said.

'Radcliffe?' Firbank said. 'He's dead.'

'I know,' Harry said, 'but I need to look at the files again.'

'Why? That was two years ago. The team was disbanded, you've all moved on. You did a good job under tough circumstances.'

'You mean we had sod-all funding, no staff, no resources, and were then chucked out with the rubbish.'

'That's unfair.'

'Is it?'

Firbank was quiet. Jadyn, though, was thinking about what they had mentioned, or not, a couple of minutes ago. What position was the DSup talking about? Was it a job? He didn't like the sound of that at all. And who the hell was Hollywood?

'So, then,' Firbank said, 'you're here because you want to go digging around in your past, is that it? You know that's not healthy. It's got you into trouble before.'

'Sometimes you've got no choice,' Harry said. 'There's been a murder.'

'I've said it before and I'll say it again,' Firbank said, leaning back in her chair. 'People are bastards.'

'We've had two hands-on murders, at two different crime scenes,' Harry said. 'A further four were killed while those were being examined. I need to look at those files today. No ifs, no buts.'

'Six dead?'

'The two clear and obvious targets we haven't been able to identify yet,' Harry said. 'The others... Two were from a SOC team, the other from Bomb Disposal.'

'What? You can't be serious?'

'You know me, ma'am,' Harry said. 'I'm rarely anything else.'

Jadyn was taken aback by the change of tone in his boss's voice. This was someone he respected.

'When did this happen?'

'The first was two days ago,' said Harry. 'The second was yesterday. Two kills, signs of torture, fingers removed, bombs laid at each site to cause maximum damage. Claymores.'

'Dear God.'

For a moment no one spoke. To Jadyn's surprise, it was he who broke the silence.

'I was there, ma'am,' he said, picking up how Harry had referred to his old boss. 'At the first. I found her, saw the explosion. If Harry, I mean if DCI Grimm thinks we need to see those files, then we need to see those files, no question about it.'

Jadyn noticed then that Harry was staring at him, his face expressionless.

'You know it can't be Radcliffe though,' Firbank said. 'It can't be him or any of his gang. They're all dead.'

'All of them?' said Jadyn. 'And who are they, anyway? Who's Hollywood?'

'It was some kind of mad drug-and-money-fuelled suicide pact,' Firbank said. 'They'd all sworn to never be taken alive, alone or together. The drugs, the money, the power, it can do stuff to your mind. It twisted theirs up beyond all recognition.'

'And seeing as we were about to grab them when they were all together,' Harry said, 'they went through with it.'

'Everyone thought it was just macho bullshit,' said Firbank. 'Anything to make them stand out, to keep other gangs on the back foot, keep them scared.'

'You'd have thought the murders would've been enough,' said Harry, 'but that was Radcliffe; theatrical to the end.'

'They really blew themselves up?'

Harry mimed an explosion with his hands. 'Boom!' he said, his voice sombre, quiet. 'And that was that.'

'Until now,' said Firbank.

'Until now.'

'Then we need to get a bloody shift on!' Jadyn said, then added, 'ma'am,' as if that would excuse using such language in front of a superior officer.

Firbank smiled.

'I like him,' she said, pointing a finger at Jadyn.

Harry looked at Jadyn, an eyebrow raised.

'He's an acquired taste.'

'He's keen,' said Firbank. 'And he's not afraid to speak his mind in front of someone like me.'

'He's been around me too long,' said Harry. 'So, we can go ahead?'

'Of course, you can go ahead,' Firbank replied, standing up. 'You know where everything is.'

'What about the team?'

'You want to speak with them?'

'Want is a strong word,' said Harry. 'I prefer need. Where are they?'

'Well, Dan died last year.'

'What?'

Jadyn saw a flicker of shock rip its way across Harry's face.

'Cancer. Went through him like a hot lance.'

'But how? He was fit and healthy compared to the rest of us.'

'Went to the doctor's complaining of some stomach pains, next thing he's being told he had two months to live. Didn't even make it to four weeks. I'm sorry, I assumed someone had told you.'

Harry shook his head. Jadyn saw a sadness in the man's eyes he'd never seen before.

'And the others, Jack and Ed?'

'Ellis is retired,' said Firbank. 'Little place in the middle of nowhere. I'll give you the address.'

'And Ed?'

'Edward Walsh? Well, your guess is as good as mine,' Firbank said. 'You'll have to talk to Mitch about that.'

'Still working undercover, then?'

'It takes a certain type.'

'It does.'

'And he always was one.'

'In too many ways,' said Harry.

'Bit of an acquired taste,' said Firbank. 'Good at his job, though, that's for sure.'

Harry pushed himself to his feet. Jadyn thought then how the movement was slow, as though the news he'd been given was a new weight for the man to carry now.

'I'm sorry to have barged in like this,' Harry said. 'But I need to close this down sharpish. I can't have what happened here turning up elsewhere.'

'You really think that's possible?'

'Right now I don't know what to think,' Harry said. 'But I'm not about to take any chances.'

Firbank laughed.

'Taking chances is all you've ever done,' she said. 'But if you need anything, either of you, just give me a call and I'll huff and puff and get you what you need.'

As Jadyn left the office with Harry, he saw Firbank hold Harry back with a hand on his arm.

'Just a moment, if you wouldn't mind?' she said.

Harry gave Jadyn a nod.

'You go on,' he said. 'I won't be a minute.'

'No worries,' said Jadyn.

Then he watched as Harry disappeared behind the door.

IN FIRBANK'S office and alone now, Harry was under the stern glare of his old boss. She would never mellow with age, he thought, and he respected that. Liked it even.

'If this is a bollocking,' he began, but Firbank held up a hand.

'It's not,' she said. 'Because with you it would serve no purpose at all, now, would it?'

'Then, what?'

'The job,' she said. 'You've thought about it, yes?'

'I have,' Harry said.

'And?'

'And no decision has been made as yet.'

'It would be good for your career.'

Harry smiled.

'But would it be good for me?' he said. 'That's what I've got to consider, isn't it?'

Firbank, Harry noticed, looked a little confused.

'When you were sent north, you treated it like you'd been exiled to Siberia.'

'That's how it felt,' said Harry. 'But things change, don't they?'

'They do. And so do we. Even you, it seems.'

'Hard to believe, isn't it?'

'No, it isn't,' Firbank said. 'That hard, gruff exterior is a good wall to hide behind. But you can't spend your whole life maintaining it, can you?'

Harry held up a hand.

'That's way too deep,' he said.

'You're still human, Harry,' Firbank said, pointedly using his first name for a change. 'You're allowed to fit in somewhere, you know? You've just got to be self-aware enough that when you find it, you don't walk away from it.'

JADYN WAS WAITING at the top of the stairs at the other end of the offices when Harry pushed through the door and came over to stand with him. He was impossible to read so whatever they'd talked about, there was no way to tell if it had gone well or not.

Perhaps it was to do with what Firbank had mentioned when they'd arrived, he thought. Harry had shut that conversation down then, but maybe she'd wanted to discuss it further. Not that he was going to ask. Not his place. Or maybe it was that Hollywood they'd mentioned, whoever that was. Cool name though, he thought.

'So, where are we going now, Boss?' he asked.

'My old station,' Harry said. 'Well done, by the way.'

'What for?'

'What you said in there. You impressed her. And me.'

'I did?'

'Yes,' Harry said. 'Now wipe that grin off your face and move it. We've got work to do.'

Jadyn followed Harry back out into the day. The smile on his face wasn't going anywhere.

CHAPTER THIRTY-THREE

Back up in Wensleydale, with the afternoon rolling on to its misty, grey conclusion, PCSO Jim Metcalf was sitting in the office with Detective Constable Jenny Blades.

Liz had been called out to deal with a traffic incident over in Langstrothdale, which was a rare thing indeed, Jim thought. That was a dale few had heard of and fewer still ventured through. That enough traffic had been passing through it to have a collision was the kind of thing that would end up being talked about for years after.

Gordy had headed home, the aches from what had happened over in Reeth giving her cause to cut the day short. But she'd made it absolutely clear to everyone that she would be in for the full day tomorrow.

And Matt was in the toilet again, though Jim was beginning to think it wasn't just down to the amount of tea the man had been nervously drinking all day. He was on edge, his mind clearly on Joan and the imminent arrival of the baby, and everyone hoped that it would all get moving sooner rather than later, if only to save the carpet from being worn away by his pacing.

'He's not supposed to do that, you know,' Jim said, gesturing to Fly who was now sitting on Jen's lap.

Jen scratched Fly under his chin and the dog slumped even deeper into her embrace.

'Don't be so mean,' Jen said. 'Look at him, lovely little bugger that he is, aren't you, Fly?'

Fly's tail wagged and his eyes drooped just a little further. Soon, the daft animal would be asleep, Jim thought.

'I'm serious,' Jim said. 'He's a working dog, Jen. And that doesn't involve much of whatever that is you and him are doing right now.'

'I'm just letting him know that he's loved.'

'Oh, I think he knows that alright,' Jim said. 'Spoiled would be more accurate, though.'

Matt burst through the door and Fly, startled by the abrupt interruption to the fuss he was getting, jumped off Jen's lap and barked.

'Give over, lad!' Jim said. 'It's only Matt! You're an idiot!'

Jim turned his attention to Matt. The DS was standing in the doorway, staring at his phone.

'Everything okay?' said Jen.

'It's Joan,' Matt said. 'She just rang. On the phone, like.'

'That's how people usually do it,' said Jen. 'Amazing invention.'

'I ... it's ...'

'What is?' asked Jim.

'It's coming,' said Matt. 'The baby. Her water just broke. It's coming. The baby's coming. Oh, bloody hell it's on its way! The baby!'

'Then what the hell are you standing there talking to us

for?' Jim said. 'Go on! Sod off! You've other things to be on with now.'

'But I needed to check up on a few things,' said Matt. 'I was going to go and try having a word with Mr Whaley again, for a start, see if he—'

'Dear God, man, you're going to have a baby!' Jen said. 'You're going to be a dad! So bugger off and get on with being one, would you? And it's too late to be heading over to Reeth. We can get that done tomorrow.'

Matt looked at Jen then Jim, his eyes nervous.

'You'll let Harry know, won't you?' he said. 'He said for me to tell him if something happened, and it's happening now so we need to tell him. That it's happening. The baby.'

'Get out!' Jen shouted. 'Before I hoof you out myself! Go on!'

Matt turned for the door.

'And send our love to Joan,' Jen added, then he was gone.

Jim sat there in silence for a moment, staring at the space where Matt had just been dithering.

'Matt, a parent,' he said eventually. 'I can't imagine it.'

'Can you not?' said Jen. 'I can. He'll be amazing. They both will.'

'Oh, I know that,' Jim nodded. 'Of course, he will. But it'll be funny seeing him with a wee one, won't it?'

'He'll probably try and feed it a pie.' Jen laughed.

Jim looked up at the clock. Time was racing on.

'So, what were these things he said he had to check, then?' he asked, looking at Jen. 'Not like there's much of the day left to be doing it in. Anyway, we've chased the forensics report and photos from Ambleside, and DCI Webb said he was going to give Harry a call as soon as he could.'

'Did he say anything about what they'd found?' Jen asked.

'No,' Jim said. 'he said he thought it would be best if he spoke with our DCI first. Which is fair enough.'

'Ominous, though, don't you think?' Jen said. 'Doesn't make me think that what he's going to tell Harry is anything good.'

Jim thought about that for a moment. Jen was right. He was almost pleased he wasn't with Harry when Webb gave him the call. Poor Jadyn ... He noticed then that something warm and furry was leaning on his leg and looking up at him through bright, I-love-you eyes.

'I think someone wants to go home,' Jen said, looking at Fly as the dog tried to climb up onto Jim's lap, only to be pushed back down again.

Jim stood up.

'Liz is on duty tonight, right?'

'The first half, yes,' said Jen. 'Then I'm on early. So I'm going to head back now as well. Get my head down.'

'Cuddle up with Steve?'

'Probably.'

'You mean, it's possible to do that? To cuddle a lizard?'

'Steve certainly seems to think so.'

Jim stared at Jen, a smile just about showing.

'You know, you're a bit weird, Jen.'

'Weird is good,' said Jen. 'Who wants to be normal?'

Outside the community centre, Jim sucked in a breath sweet with the nectar of the day. There was life in it, green and good, the kind of air that seemed somehow nourishing.

'Well, I'll be seeing you tomorrow, then,' he said, as they walked down into the marketplace.

'We might have a new member on the team by then,' Jen said.

'What? Who?'

'Matt's baby,' she said.

Jim laughed, then looked down at Fly.

'Time to go home, is it, lad?'

Fly's tail thwacked against the ground.

A call came in on Jen's radio. Whatever she was being told had her staring at Jim, eyes wide.

'What?' he asked.

'Another body,' she said.

'What? Where?'

'In Reeth.'

BACK IN BRISTOL, Harry wasn't having the best of times. And by the moans, groans, and grumbles coming from Jadyn, he wasn't either. He'd explained enough about who and what Hollywood had been, and what had happened, that Jadyn had a clear idea of what they were looking for. Not that it was much help.

After checking in at a hotel near the centre of town, they'd been looking through files now for a couple of hours and all they'd really managed to do was move lots of boxes from one place to another—one place being where they were stored, the other place the floor.

And what had they found? Nothing of use, that's what, Harry thought. Though he wasn't really sure what he'd been expecting. He knew the facts because he'd been part of the small team who had headed up the original investigation. He hadn't been in charge, because that joy had been Jack Ellis' alone and he wouldn't have had it any other way. He'd left a message on the number he'd been given for Jack, but there'd been no returned call, yet. Getting in touch with Ed was going to be more difficult, particularly if he was currently on an operation. But he'd work on that specific problem tomorrow.

Remembering his old teammates, Harry thought then how they had all worked more like equals than with any specific hierarchy, all taking it in turns to throw in an idea, get it chewed up and spat back at them, that kind of thing. The work had been tough, high-pressured, stressful, dangerous.

Harry had lost count of the number of blood tests he'd had to take after arrests and smashing their way through crack dens. It wasn't just bullets and blades people were armed with, but needles, fingernails, teeth, spit. It had been hell, but it had been worth it. Or so he'd thought. Because now his past had come back to haunt him, hadn't it? But in a way that just didn't make any sense. If everyone was dead, then what the hell was going on? And why? Or was it just a coincidence? It could be, obviously, but that just seemed like too much of a reach. This wasn't confirmation bias, he was sure of it. So, he shook his head to clear it, then opened the next file.

'Boss?'

Jadyn's weary voice stumbled across the room to Harry.

'What?'

'Just wondering how long we're going to be doing this for?'

'As long as it takes,' Harry said.

'And how long will that be, exactly?'

Harry went to reply but thought better of it.

'You hungry?' he asked and heard movement immediately after.

Turning, Harry saw Jadyn standing up and staring at him.

'Food, Boss? Yeah, I could eat.'

Harry looked around them, at the disarray of boxes strewn about like flotsam from a wrecked ship.

'Then let's make this place look a little less like a tornado just came through here, and we'll go and grab something. My shout.'

The grin on Jadyn's face was bright enough to lighten the darkest days, Harry thought.

Files tidied, they were outside and in the car.

'So, what do you fancy?' Harry asked.

'Food,' Jadyn replied.

'Can you be more specific?'

'Delicious food?' Jadyn said. 'I don't know. You used to live here, right? So, you must know a few places.'

'I do,' Harry said. 'There's a microbrewery you'd like. Good pizza.'

'I'm sold,' Jadyn said.

They drove back to the hotel, dropped off the car, and headed straight into town. And judging by the look on Jadyn's face when Harry took him into the place they'd be eating, he'd made a good choice.

With a beer in front of them and pizza on its way, Harry was about to allow himself a moment to relax, when his phone rang.

He answered it without even thinking.

'Grimm,' he said, and even he could hear the weariness in his voice.

'My apologies for the late call,' said the voice on the other end. 'This is DCI Webb, Cumbria Constabulary.'

'DCI Webb,' Harry said. 'You're right, it is late. And we're just sitting down to a bit of food. Any chance I can call you back later? Tomorrow maybe?'

'I think you'll want to hear this,' said Webb.

A stone sunk to the bottom of Harry's stomach and a chill zigzagged through him quick and sharp enough to make him shiver.

'Why? What have you got?'

Harry saw Jadyn lean forward, concern in his eyes.

'I've got the forensic report in front of me,' Webb said. 'And I've heard from the bomb squad.'

'Really?' said Harry. 'I wasn't expecting to hear from them so soon, not after, well, you know.'

'Same here,' said Webb. 'But here we are. Anyway, you're sitting down, I trust?'

'Why, do I need to be?'

'Yes.'

'Shit...'

'Something like that, I'd say,' said Webb.

Harry took a deep, calming breath then exhaled.

'Go ahead,' he said. 'I'm listening.'

'First of all, that lovely car parked outside the property. It's a rental.'

Harry was a little taken aback.

'You can rent cars like that?'

He knew that you could, he just hadn't been expecting it, and the question came out before he had time to stop it.

'If you have the money you can pretty much rent anything,' said Webb. 'So, yes.'

'Which means it didn't belong to the deceased,' said Harry.

'Exactly.'

'Actually, this is good, isn't it?' said Harry. 'If the car was a rental then he would have had to use ID of some kind to rent it, credit card, anything really. A lot of places want a photocopy of a passport nowadays.'

'They do indeed,' said Webb. 'However, our victim paid with cash.'

'I don't see why that matters,' said Harry. 'Like I said, he'd still need to leave some form of ID. And a driving licence, obviously.'

'Which is a fake.'

The stone in Harry's stomach disappeared and was replaced with a punch that winded him.

'What?'

'The driving licence. It's a fake. A bloody good one, I have to say, but it's a fake.'

'How do you know?'

'Because it looked enough like the real thing for the rental company to not even bat an eyelid at it. And before you ask, no they don't check every licence as they should, because they just haven't got the time.'

'You mean they can't be arsed.'

'Anyway, we checked it against the licensing agency details and they don't come up. Basically, it looks good enough to the eye, but that's as far as it will go.'

'Is this where you tell me it only gets worse?' Harry asked. 'Because right now I'm not sure how it can.'

'I'm afraid it is, yes,' said Webb.

'Great,' said Harry. 'Go on ...'

'Well, the ID is fake, but we were able to get prints from

off the car quite easily and we found a match.'

At this, Harry dared to allow a little glimmer of hope to break through the gathering darkness clouding his mind.

'So, he had a criminal record, then?'

'No,' said Webb.

'But you just said he had a fake ID and you matched his prints. That doesn't make sense.'

'Oh, he has a record alright,' said Webb. 'A police one.'

Harry almost choked.

'What?'

'A police record,' said Webb. 'Our victim is or was a serving officer with a good number of years under his belt, too. Proper career person, he was, by the looks of things. So how he ended up like this, I haven't the faintest idea.'

'How do you mean?'

'Judging by what he's done, I would say he is or was the kind of person who would jump at any chance to get stuck in, if you know what I mean? Some officers, they want to race up the ladder, don't they? But only by using desk jobs as step-ping-stones. And I know that's mixing my metaphors, but I'm quite sure you know what I mean.'

'I do,' said Harry.

'Not afraid to get his hands dirty, basically,' Webb contin-ued. 'Looking through his records it was obvious that he liked to be at the sharp end of things, taking on the tough cases, working undercover, that kind of thing. Never seen the attraction myself. Takes a certain kind of person of which I'm not one, if that makes sense.'

In that moment, for Harry, nothing made sense. An undercover police officer? How could that even be? What the hell could he have been investigating that would have had him driving a sportscar, meeting up with an escort, and

266 DAVID J. GATWARD

ending up getting stabbed to death in a shower in a holiday cottage in the Lake District? It explained the false ID, or at least the ease with which it was used, but nothing else at all.

'You still there, Grimm?'

'Sorry,' Harry said. 'Just caught up in my thoughts for a moment there.'

'Can't say I blame you,' said Webb. 'All a bit of a bloody mess, isn't it?'

'So was he working undercover?' Harry asked. 'Have we stumbled into something we shouldn't have?'

'No,' Webb said. 'We haven't. There's no record anywhere of whatever the hell it was he was doing.'

'Could've been off the books?' Harry suggested, empty hope crowding the words.

'To be honest, I think this was so far off the books as to be floating around in the middle of the Atlantic,' Webb said.

'This officer, then,' Harry said. 'He has a name, I'm assuming, right? A real one. You've got that, yes? You must have, seeing as you've found his police records.'

'His name was Walsh,' Webb said. 'Edward Walsh.'

CHAPTER THIRTY-FOUR

JEN AND JIM WERE OVER IN REETH BARELY THIRTY minutes after the call had come in. They'd punched a call in to Gordy and Liz, but were currently the first officers at the scene. And it was an unpleasant one. Standing with them, a good distance away from the now cordoned-off area, was a young man in running gear. Jim had found a spare jacket in their vehicle to keep him warm. He was now guarding the crime scene while Jen questioned the witness.

'So you found the body, when exactly?' she asked.

The runner looked at his watch, a huge thing clearly designed for sports, Jim thought.

'An hour ago max,' the runner said. 'I was just doing this little route I do now and again, if I want something easy, like. It takes me down to Marrick, across the fields a bit, you know? Don't usually see anyone, but I saw the clothes, the red jacket, and I thought they'd fallen over or something.'

'So, you went to check?'

'Of course I did,' the runner said. 'People fall, trip. I wasn't going to just leave them there.'

'What did you do, exactly?'

'Called out first,' the runner said. 'Just to see if they were okay or needed help. But there was no answer. So, I went closer, to see what the matter was, if I needed to call an ambulance or something, and that's when I saw the blood in her hair.'

'You could see that it was a woman?'

The runner nodded.

'Long blonde hair and the side of her face.'

'And then you called us?'

'Immediately,' the runner said. 'I've always got my phone on me anyway. I listen to audiobooks when I'm running, you see?'

'Did you notice anything else?' Jen asked.

'Like what?'

'Anything out of the ordinary.'

'A dead body stuffed under a bush near a footpath is a little out of the ordinary,' the runner said. 'But no, I didn't notice anything else.'

'How are you doing?' Jen asked.

'Fine, I think,' the runner said. 'Thanks for the jacket by the way. I was getting cold, but I didn't think I should leave the body until someone else arrived.'

'You did the right thing. Nice shoes by the way.'

The runner glanced down at his feet.

'They're just trainers,' he said.

'I'm a runner myself,' said Jen. 'There's no such thing as "just trainers."'

The runner laughed.

'You're right there.'

A siren screamed into the moment.

'What do you think happened?'

'I'm afraid I wouldn't be able to say even if I knew,' Jen said.

'Looked like she'd been hit on the back of the head,' the runner said. 'Don't really see how she could've done that if she just tripped.'

Jen said nothing. She didn't want him spreading rumours about what had or hadn't happened.

'I've got your details,' she said. 'If we need to contact you, we'll be in touch.'

The runner headed off and Jen walked over to join Jim.

'Here we go again,' she said.

A couple of hours later and the crime scene was a hive of activity. The scene of crime team had arrived and so had the bomb disposal team. However, they'd found nothing and now the SOC team was getting on with the job. Bennett was leading them and they'd mostly kept their distance. They'd experienced his charms once already and that was already one time too many. For Gordy, however, keeping her distance wasn't an option. She'd arrived just before Liz and taken charge. Unfortunately, that had meant dealing with the man herself. She hadn't been there the first time around but she was already realising that what had been said about the man simply didn't do him justice.

Standing away from the crime scene, Gordy waited for the pathologist to walk by before she called him over. He approached her in his full PPE, lowering his face mask to reveal a smile as insipid as a weak cup of herbal tea. And by God, did that stuff make her gag.

'Do you have anything yet?' she asked.

'Oh, yes, lots,' said Bennett. 'All very interesting, too.'

'How so?'

'Do you know that before this week I'd never actually

been here before?' Bennett said then. 'To Reeth, I mean. And here we are, twice in just a few days. What are the odds of that?'

'I have no idea at all,' Gordy said.

'There are worse places to be though, aren't there?' Bennett continued. 'It looks very historic, with the village green and the cobbles. And you know I've found myself wondering how often it's been on telly.'

'Can't say that I know or care, really,' Gordy said.

'There will be some Herriot thing, I'm sure,' Bennett said. 'But there must be others, don't you think?'

Gordy couldn't believe it. The man clearly had a mind that wandered everywhere, absolutely distracted by everything around him, instead of focusing on his actual job.

'What about the body?' Gordy prodded.

'What? Oh, yes, that,' Bennett said. 'A sharp blow to the back of head.' He mimed striking something with his hand. 'And she's not been dead long. Just a few hours.'

'Any idea what it was she was struck with?'

'A metal bar of some kind, I would think. Death would've been instantaneous. Probably.'

'Probably? How can you tell?'

'I'll have to confirm it back at the lab,' Bennett said, 'but the strike caved her skull in with quite a lot of violence. Good at my job, you see. All about the details.'

'Anything else? Any information that might help us start looking for who did this?'

'Paint,' said Bennett.

'Paint? How do you mean? There's paint on her? What is it?'

'It's not household paint, that's for sure,' Bennett said.

'It's a waxy material. There are marks of it on her clothes and skin.'

'Waxy paint? From what?'

'At a guess, it's from whoever killed her. The paint itself is sort of brown and sort of green. Hard to tell right now in this light, but I'll do a full analysis later and let you know. It probably rubbed off when they moved the body.'

'What? So this didn't happen here, then?'

'No,' Bennett said. 'My view is that it was done somewhere else and then the body was dumped here. There's no blood spatter from the wound, and there would be after a blow like that. Unavoidable.'

'But this is a footpath,' Gordy said. 'Getting a body here wouldn't be easy.'

'And there are no drag marks either,' said Bennett. 'So it was carried.'

Gordy looked around. There was a track nearby. Someone could've driven down that and carried the body here perhaps. But even so, there was still the lifting and carrying to be doing and that wouldn't be easy, not if you were on your own at any rate.

Do you know if any of the pubs serve food?'

Gordy did a double-take, the question catching her off guard.

'Pardon?'

'Food,' Bennett said. 'Once we're done here, I might go for a quick bite. Can you recommend somewhere? You see, I had something prepared for this evening but with being called out here, well, my plans were all thrown askew, weren't they?'

Gordy stared at the man in front of her. She just couldn't

find the words. And in the end, she shook her head and walked back to the rest of the team.

'So, what have we got?' Jen asked.

Behind her, the body was being moved to the ambulance.

'Blow to the back of the head,' Gordy said. 'And it didn't happen here. The body was brought here from who knows where. Can't be far, though, because she's not been dead long enough to have travelled far. As for who she is, we'll have to wait for that delightful man to get back to us with his report. Hopefully sooner rather than later.'

'And that's it?'

'No, they found some paint,' Gordy added. 'Waxy stuff, apparently. Brown and green.'

'You mean like camo-paint?'

'What?'

'Camo-paint,' Jen said. 'Soldiers wear it, don't they? I was seeing a soldier for a while. That stuff gets everywhere. Waterproof, too, so it's a real bugger to get off.'

A chill raced down Gordy's spine and she saw realisation dawn on Jen's face as well.

'The soldier Matt interviewed,' she said. 'We've got his details, right?'

'Of course,' said Jen. 'He's at one of the barracks over in Richmond.'

'Then it looks like we need to bring him in for questioning,' said Gordy.

'But why do this?' Jen asked. 'Seems a bit random to me.'

'Random or not, that camo-paint clearly links this to someone in the military,' Gordy said. 'We need to bring him in. We'll head over together now. Advantage in numbers.'

Leaving the footpath, Gordy, with Jen at her side, headed

back to the centre of Reeth when a voice called out. She turned to see a man running towards them.

'Excuse me,' he said. 'Please, can you wait? I need to speak to you.'

Gordy could see that he was flustered. Worry was in his eyes and he was sweating like he'd been out for a run.

'Can we help?' Gordy asked.

'My wife,' the man said. 'Have you seen her? She went out a while back now. Egg delivery, you see? We've a few hens out the back of the house. It started as a bit of a laugh, but we've got about a dozen now and they keep laying, so we give some to friends.'

'Slow down,' said Gordy. 'What's happened?'

'That's what I'm trying to tell you! She's been out too long. Three, four hours now. I've been running around trying to find her. I don't know where she's got to. She's not answering her phone. I need to find her! She might have tripped and hurt herself or something. I don't know what to do. She's got blonde hair and she's wearing this bloody awful red duffel jacket. You can't miss her. I don't understand where she could've got to.'

Gordy, though, knew all too well.

CHAPTER THIRTY-FIVE

Harry hadn't slept a wink and dawn would soon be breaking. Well, that wasn't entirely true. He'd passed out at points for sure, but in between those rare moments of unconsciousness, he had laid in bed staring into the inky darkness trying to make sense of what they had so far.

He was making no progress. Every time he found something or learned a new detail, it would just sit there in front of him daring him to try and make sense of it, to put it in a place that meant the rest would then all come together—a confused and messed-up pile of jigsaw pieces finally presenting a clear picture.

Six dead. Six! And now, not only a police officer among them, but an old colleague to boot. It was a link. A terrible and confusing one to add to the whole thing with the long-and-very-dead Hollywood, and Harry knew that today he would have to find out more somehow. And the only way to do that was to speak with anyone who had been working with Ed over the past month, to try and find out what was going on.

His family, too, Harry thought. He had a wife, a daughter at university. But talking to them when they were dealing with this news wasn't going to be easy. And there was old Jack Ellis, too. Perhaps he would know more? And on top of all that there was the sad news about Dan.

Unable to even attempt another quick nap before the day began, Harry rolled out of bed. A shower would do him some good, so he stumbled from bed to bathroom, stubbing his toes on the way and swearing blue murder at the corner of the desk that had got in the way. It was all he could do to not grab it and throw it across the room, if only in a futile attempt to get rid of some of the frustration he was feeling. The only good thing he could hold on to was that Jadyn was doing well. He'd bravely spoken up in front of Firbank yesterday and for Harry, that was sign enough that he would be fine. They just needed to keep an eye on him, that was all.

The soft rumble of the waking city outside was soon washed away to nothing by the water jets pummelling his body. He was weary and the shower was surprisingly power-ful. Hot as well, and the burning sensation was just the right side of painful for him to endure.

A few minutes later, and down at breakfast, Harry spotted Jadyn. He was over at the self-service food counter, helping himself to food. When Harry came to stand beside him, his jaw fell open.

'Hungry, then, Constable?'

Jadyn had tongs in hand and was reaching for a fourth sausage. Where it was going to go on his plate, Harry wasn't sure, what with the eggs, bacon, beans, and whatever else was hiding under the three slices of fried bread he had on there already.

'It's free, Boss!' Jadyn said, glee in his voice. 'You can have as much as you want.'

'You do know how hotels work, don't you?' Harry asked.

'I might come back for seconds.'

Harry knew then that the answer to his question was that no, he clearly didn't.

'So, what are we on with today?' Jadyn asked as they sat down together, Harry with considerably less to munch through.

Harry said, 'I need to speak with Ed's wife. Not something I want to do under the circumstances, but she'll understand. And I want you to see if you can get something on anything else he was working on.'

'You don't mean looking in files again, do you?'

Harry shook his head.

'Firbank will help,' he said. 'She'll be able to put you in touch with someone who knows something I'm sure. It's her job, not to necessarily know everything that's going on, but to keep an eye on all those who do.'

'That's confusing,' Jadyn said. 'But I think I know what you mean.'

'And I want you to get in touch with Jack Ellis as well. Arrange for us to go and have a chat with him. Again, Firbank will have his details. You going to be okay with that?'

Jadyn was on his feet.

'Yes, Boss, no problem,' he said.

'Where are you going then?'

The constable tipped his plate up to show Harry.

'Empty,' he said. 'I fancy seconds,' and he headed off back to the buffet.

. . .

HAVING DROPPED Jadyn off at the station, Harry had then driven over to Ed's place. It may have been over two years since he'd been there, but he still knew the way.

He'd spoken with Firbank before heading over. She had sounded as shocked about the news of Ed's death as Harry had when Webb had told him the night before. He had then spoken with the family liaison officer who, in turn, had checked in with Ed's wife, Diane. And, despite the awful circumstances, she had agreed to speak to Harry.

'Actually, she was pretty adamant about doing so,' the officer had said.

'How do you mean?'

'I think her exact words were, "*I want that gruff bastard getting whoever did this to my Ed.*"'

Harry pulled up outside the house as a call came through. He answered immediately.

'Harry, it's DI Haig.'

'You sound very official,' Harry said. 'Which doesn't give me confidence that this will be happy news you're about to share.'

'It isn't,' Gordy said. 'We've another victim.'

'What? Where?'

'Reeth again,' Gordy explained. 'I'll send you more details as we get them, obviously. But so far what we have is a woman, mid-thirties. Someone was out running and found her.'

'Do we know who she is?'

'Waiting on the official confirmation, but yes, we do,' Gordy said. 'We were leaving the crime scene when we were approached by a man looking for his wife. She'd been gone for nearly four hours, delivering eggs, apparently.'

'Eggs? What the hell has any of this got to do with eggs? How was she killed?'

'Blow to the back of the head it looks like.'

'Bloody hell, Gordy, what's going on?'

'I wish I knew. We've got a possible lead on who was responsible though.'

'What? Really?'

'Camo-paint found at the scene,' Gordy explained.

'A soldier?' Harry said. 'You think this was the one Jadyn saw and Matt had a chat with?'

'We won't know until we speak to him,' Gordy said. 'We've been over but he's not at his address.'

'On exercise?'

'We're checking on that now. If he's not, then we'll have to put out a call for officers to be on the lookout for him and bring him in as soon as possible. I'll keep you posted.'

Harry paused for a moment, deep in thought, another piece of the puzzle that didn't fit with any picture he could think of right then.

'You still there?'

'I am,' he said.

'How's things progressing down south?'

'Slowly,' Harry answered. 'I'm following something up now, Jadyn's on with something else, and we're aiming to head back today as soon as we can.'

Goodbyes said, Harry put his phone away along with any space in his mind to think about what Gordy had just told him and approached Ed and Diane's house.

When the door opened, Diane stared up at him from behind eyes bloodshot to hell. She'd yet to get changed out of her dressing gown and Harry wondered if she'd been to bed at all. Probably not.

'Harry,' she said.

'Hello, Diane.'

'Been a long time.'

'It has, that.'

Diane stepped back and gestured for him to enter.

Inside, Harry followed Diane as she shuffled along the hall and into a small, neat lounge.

Nothing had changed, Harry noticed. The walls were filled with photos of good and happy times, Ed smiling out through the years, his wife with him, and his daughter.

'Ellie is on her way,' Diane said, sitting down in an armchair and wiping her nose. 'First year at university, you know. What a way to end it though. She finished a few weeks back. Was staying on to work in a café. But she's on her way back now.'

'Hard to believe she's that old,' Harry said, noticing then two empty bottles of wine by the fire.

'Tea?'

Harry shook his head.

'Diane, I'm so sorry.'

'Don't,' Diane said, her lips thin, tight, her voice hissing through clenched teeth. 'Just... just don't, okay? You don't have to. And I don't want you to. I don't need you to, either. That's not why I said I'd have you over, not by a long shot.'

'I only found out myself last night.'

'And yet here you are, right smack bang in the middle and mixed up in it all,' Diane said. 'Strange that, wouldn't you say? Uncanny.'

Harry noticed her tone. She'd not warmed to him when Ed had been alive. There was little chance of that ever happening now. But he wasn't here to make friends.

'What do you know?' he asked.

'Enough,' Diane said. 'Not the full details because no one will tell me. Don't want to "prejudice the investigation" were the words they used, I think. A right load of old bollocks that, if you ask me. I'm his sodding wife! I deserve to know!'

Harry understood.

'Yes, you do,' he said.

'So, you're here to tell me, are you? Is that it?' She laughed then, the sound cold and harsh, hacking its way out of a throat raw from crying. 'You, of all people, Harry. I always knew that if my Ed ended up in trouble, you'd be right in the middle of it. You knew that, didn't you? I always said it. Told you to your face a few times as well, I'm sure. Almost like wherever there's a big pile of shite, you're somewhere close by. Still, I can't think of anyone better to be out there looking for those responsible, can you?'

'I'll take that as a compliment.'

'Take it however you want, it's just a fact, that's all.'

Harry let the silence sit between them for a moment.

'Do you have any idea what Ed was working on?' he then asked.

'Like you, he was good with his secrets,' Diane said. 'All part of the undercover officer police set, isn't it?'

Harry leaned forward.

'And you were good at getting them out of him, if I remember correctly,' Harry said. 'Don't think I didn't know that.'

'I couldn't live in the dark, could I?' said Diane. 'What kind of life is that for anyone?'

'So, you did know something, then?'

More silence, this time because it was Diane's choice.

'It all started a couple of months ago I think,' she said

eventually. 'Maybe it was three months? I'm not exactly sure.'

'What all started, Diane? A new job?'

'That's what I thought to begin with. It was the usual stuff, you know? Away for days on end, nothing said, coming back smelling ... strange.'

'How do you mean?'

'Jobs, they always smell different,' Diane explained. 'You wouldn't notice it, I guess because you were always in the thick of it and wore the stink like a badge of honour. But I did. A whiff of cigarette smoke here, a scent of perfume there, none of those were things that had anything to do with Ed's normal life or the everyday office stuff. They were like secrets coming in with him for me alone. I even got to know the smell of a gun on him. Can you imagine what that's like?'

Harry could and did.

'Go on...'

'It was the perfume with this one, that's for sure,' Diane said. 'And his aftershave. I knew he showered before he came home, always did, but it never washed off completely.'

Harry guessed those were scents from his meeting with the escort.

'This time, though, Ed was different.'

'How do you mean?'

'Usually, he'd be pretty good at leaving the job at the door,' Diane said. 'He didn't want to bring it home with him. Always respected that. But this time? No, the job came home with him like a monkey on his back.'

'He spoke about it, then?'

Diane shook her head.

'He was scared,' she said.

'Ed?'

Harry couldn't disguise his disbelief.

'Exactly! He didn't scare easily. Never had. Not that he was brave or heroic. And he wasn't like you, either, thank God.'

'How do you mean?'

Diane rolled her eyes.

'You're a fighter, Harry, that's why I never liked you. Good at your job, that's true, but sometimes it seemed like you were just out there looking to crack skulls. And you're reckless. No thought given to the destruction you cause as you do whatever it is you think you have to do.'

'Do you know why he was scared?' Harry asked, keen to move the conversation away from Diane's thoughts on his own inner demons.

'No, I don't,' Diane said. 'But I could tell. He kept telling me that he loved me. He always had, that's not what I'm saying, just that he said it more, all the time almost. And he'd bring me presents. At first I thought it was guilt, you know? Like he was playing away? But that wasn't Ed. And it wasn't what was happening either. I know my husband. Something was wrong. And now he's dead and that's that. He's gone, Harry. Gone forever. Never coming back. One moment he was here and now it's never again, isn't it?'

A sob broke out of her then, but Diane cut it short, refusing to let it control her.

'Is there anything else?'

'I'd hear him crying sometimes,' Diane said. 'He never knew, but I did. What makes a man like that cry, Harry? What?'

'When was the last time you saw him?'

'Couple of weeks ago, I think. And no, I didn't know where he was going. Not that day, anyway.'

Harry leaned back, stared at the ceiling, wondering what she meant by that.

'You know what?' Diane said, knocking Harry's thoughts off-kilter for a moment. 'I don't think it's a coincidence that you're here now.'

Harry lowered his head to look at her.

'How do you mean?'

'Whatever Ed was caught up in, you're involved in it, aren't you?'

'I'm investigating a murder,' said Harry. 'That's all.'

'You moved to bloody Yorkshire!' Diane snapped back. 'Why the hell would you be down here within hours of me hearing about my Ed if you weren't caught up in it, eh? You wouldn't be, would you? And yet, here you are, and sitting in Ed's chair, too, I might add.'

Harry stood up.

'Like that'll make a difference.'

'I don't know what Ed was caught up in. All I know is that something I was investigating in the Dales led me to... well, to Ed. I was as surprised as anyone, Diane.'

'Surprised?' Diane was on her feet. 'That's the best you can do, surprised? I need you to be more than that, Harry, do you hear?' She jabbed him hard in the ribs with a finger. 'I need you to be absolutely bloody raging, Harry, that's what I need! For Ed and me, for us both, goddammit! What fucking use are you to me if you're not that, eh? I need you so fucking livid you'll tear down every fucking house and home to find whoever did this to Ed! I want them dead, Harry, you hear? I want them fucking dead!'

Harry stepped back.

'I'm doing everything I can to find out what happened, I promise.'

'Are you though, Harry? Really? Because it doesn't sound like it to me. And it certainly doesn't look like it, either.'

Diane shoved Harry then, hard enough to make him take a step back.

'Diane ...'

'I followed him once, you know? Not that last time, but this one time before. A couple of weeks ago, I think. I never told him. My secret. I watched him leave then got in my car and followed him. I thought he'd spot me, but he didn't. Or, if he did, he never said.'

'Do you have any idea how dangerous that was? What were you thinking?'

'Do you have any idea how much of a shit I could give? I followed him. My husband. Because I knew something was wrong. Something was off. And I needed to know.'

'What happened?'

'I saw him,' Diane said. 'I parked just a way down the road from him. Rough place it was, properly dodgy. And there he was, striding along like he knew it well.'

'Where, Diane?'

'I kept far enough behind so he wouldn't see me and if he turned around I could duck out of sight. Then he crossed over the road and pushed his way through this fence or whatever it was. All corrugated iron. Couldn't for the life of me work out why he was there. And I knew I should've turned back, but I didn't.'

'What happened?'

'I went through the fence as well,' Diane said. 'And there he was, scrabbling around in the dirt. Looking for something or burying something, I couldn't really tell. Then he left.'

Diane stepped back.

'And you went home?'

Diane shook her head.

'Of course I didn't! I had to see, didn't I? After all that time, I had to see, to find out what he'd been doing. Otherwise, what was the point? And he'd buried something. A little tin it was, one of those cheap money boxes you use if you're running a tombola stall or something. It wasn't locked or anything, just hidden under a slab. I shifted it, had a look. Like I said, I had to know.'

'So, what did you find?' Harry asked. 'What was in the tin?'

'Two things,' Diane said. 'Two photos. One was of a woman, the other a man. Though, I say woman, but she was younger for sure. Looked older though, but her eyes were youthful.'

'Did you recognise them?'

'I can show you if you want,' Diane said, in answer to Harry's question. 'Had my phone with me, didn't I?'

She turned then from Harry and went over to where she'd been sitting and picked up her phone from the floor.

'Here you go,' she said, and turned the screen for Harry to see. 'Like I said, it's no coincidence that you're here at all, is it, Harry? No coincidence at all.'

Harry stared at the two photos on the screen. The first, the woman, was someone he recognised from two years ago. Someone who'd helped him, so he, in turn, had helped her.

The other was a photo of him.

CHAPTER THIRTY-SIX

'WHERE ARE WE GOING?' JADYN ASKED.

'Back in time,' Harry said, staring hard through the windscreen as Jadyn pushed through traffic lights and took a right soon after.

'I mean seriously, where are we going?' Jadyn repeated.

Harry didn't want to say. Not yet. Not until he saw their destination with his own two eyes.

'How did you get on? Find anything of use about what Ed was doing?'

'Not really, no,' Jadyn said. 'Even those who worked closely with him on other jobs didn't know anything about what he was up to.'

'Nothing at all?'

'No,' Jadyn said. 'They said Ed had told them that due to the sensitive nature of what he was on with, he had to keep the specifics to himself.'

'And despite that being a huge pile of bollocks, they trusted him because of his reputation.'

'Seems that way, yes.'

Harry recognised the street they were on, the area, but didn't say anything, not yet.

'And I've left a message on Mr Ellis' phone. A few messages actually. He's probably sick of the sound of my voice.'

'You have his address?'

'In my notebook,' Jadyn said, fishing it out of his pocket. 'Here.'

Harry opened the book and found the address.

'Know it?'

'Not the address as such, but the area, yes,' he said. 'It's over on the Mendips.'

'Much there?'

'No, not really,' said Harry. 'Fields mainly.'

Jadyn took a left.

'Looks like we're here,' he said. 'Satnav says the destination's just ahead.'

Harry felt himself grow heavier as Jadyn drove them on, almost as though the weight of the memory of where they were was growing heavier the closer they drove.

Jadyn pulled the car over on the left, yanked on the handbrake, turned off the engine. He leaned forward to stare out through the windscreen.

'Not really sure what to say, Boss,' he said. 'What is this place?'

The road featured a collection of boarded-up buildings, most of them shops that had died over the years and never reopened, not even as charity shops or off-licences. And that, thought Harry, was as sure a sign as any that where they were was a forgotten place, even in a place as alive and happening as Bristol.

Harry climbed out of the car and Jadyn followed. Litter

bumbled along the road, the pavement, like drunks rolling home after a night on the lash, stumbling and bumping into overflowing litterbins, getting caught in fences, slipping down drains. This was a dirty place, a forgotten place, somewhere that local councils chose to pretend did not exist. It was a haunt of those who had fallen through society's cracks and been unable to drag themselves back out again, the doorways stuffed with stinking sleeping bags, cardboard boxes, bags of goodness knows what, and beneath it all, lost souls keeping warm between begging, hostels, and hangovers.

'Over there,' Harry said, pointing over the road.

Not waiting for Jadyn, he made his way to a corrugated iron fence.

'Find a gap,' Harry said. 'We need to get over to the other side.'

'We do?'

'Yes.'

'Why?'

'Because I said so,' Harry said. 'That's a good enough reason, isn't it, Constable?'

Jadyn gave a short nod and started looking.

'Here,' he said a moment later and Harry saw Jadyn heaving back a section of the fence. 'Should be able to get through.' He then ducked down for a quick look before glancing back at Harry. 'Can't see why, though. There's nowt there, Boss. Just rubble. A right mess by the looks of things. Watch where you step.'

Harry said nothing, his stare enough to have Jadyn moving. On the other side, Jadyn's description had been acutely accurate. Wherever he looked, all Harry could see was rubble. The shattered remains of a building which had at one time been respected, at another feared.

Here and there jagged sections of broken walls jutted out of the ground, the skeleton of the beast Harry had once known. Because it had been a beast, hadn't it, this place—a great monster chewing people up, devouring lives? And it had been hungry, too, an appetite that was never sated. So it had kept on feeding and feeding and feeding and God, that day, when they'd finally come to put an end to it, and rip its heart out. The flames... the screams...

'Harry? Er, I mean, Boss? Are you okay?'

Harry blinked, pulled himself out of his memories.

'You went quiet,' Jadyn said.

'And you thought that was a good enough reason to use my first name?'

Jadyn said nothing.

'I've been here before,' Harry said. 'Not for a couple of years, but it's hard to forget.'

'Why? What happened?'

'Used to be a building here,' Harry explained, making a sweeping gesture. 'I think it had been an old printing mill or something, back in the day. Properly run down. Not a nice place to be at all.'

'Was it knocked down, then?' Jadyn asked.

'I think it's been knocked down since I was last here. But that's not why it came down, not to begin with.'

'Old buildings do that,' said Jadyn. 'If they're not looked after.'

'This one was solid,' Harry said. 'They'd reinforced it, you see? Called in favours, had the builders in you might say.'

'Someone did it up, then?'

'Not really. It wasn't turned into an executive warehouse apartment or anything like that. Shame really, as it would've been quite spectacular. No, this isn't a place that was ever on the list for gentrification.'

Harry was remembering more and more now, playing the moments over and over in his mind, a movie on fast forward.

'There were only two doors, one in, one out,' Harry said. 'The others had all been bricked up. And the two remaining ones had bars across them on the inside. They were rein-forced, too. The windows were all wired up, had iron bars installed. It was a fortress.'

'What, here?' Jadyn said, looking around. 'In the arse-end of Bristol? Why?'

'Drugs,' Harry said. 'This was a crack house, but not like the others. This was like a citadel. We'd left it alone for a good while, mopping up the smaller ones around it instead. They were easy, you see? They still had those sodding New York locks, but they were smaller, not so well-protected, and we could break into those in seconds, take everyone by surprise, carry out the arrests. Proper shock and awe tactics.'

'Shock and awe?'

'Sometimes we'd have a couple dozen officers with us, volunteering to join in because they knew what we were dealing with, and knew that if we could smash the drug rings apart, we'd be making some progress at least in getting the streets safe again. The locals were losing family and friends, not just to drugs, but to fear. Moving out. No one wants to live in a place where there are crackheads on every corner, needles in every bin, and idiots doing drive-bys and killing each other. Bullets go astray, Jadyn. People die, and usually, they're not the ones that were targeted, either.'

'So, what happened here, then?'

'Everything happened here,' said Harry. 'Everything. This was the end of it all. We'd done all the other dens, like I said, flushed them out, the streets were getting safer. The scrag-ends and the really mean ones, those at the top, we corralled them I suppose, though they didn't realise it, I don't think, not to begin with. They thought they were untouchable here, you see? Thought we wouldn't be crazy enough to even attempt it. They were armed, heavily, too. And a body count doesn't make good press, does it? Bunch of coppers do a drug raid and half of them end up dead? No, they thought we'd stay away. They were wrong.'

Harry realised Jadyn was just listening now, staring at him. He kept talking, the words just falling out of him.

'The night was a dark one. The kind even streetlights can't fight. We had everyone with us, ghosties to deal with the locks, a helicopter with a searchlight, and everyone going in was fully up for it, kitted out in riot gear, the works. It was ending that night for good. We weren't messing around. The adrenaline, you could taste it.'

'Sounds terrifying.'

'Terror and excitement are close bedfellows,' Harry said. 'Only way to do it was hard and fast. So we raced in with the vans, blocked all the roads, any route out of the place, had that searchlight on. The helicopter was low, barely a few metres off the roof, the sound of it thumping down on the place and disorientating everyone inside.

'The first door went down easily and we were in, just piling in there like you wouldn't believe. Screaming and yelling, grabbing anyone we saw, dealing with them hard, three or four to one of theirs, total control. It was chaos, but we were in and we were making headway, dragging people out, filling the vans. The place stank, made your eyes water. Sweat, rotting food, crack, human waste. Anyone who tried to bolt out of the back door was caught in a net, officers just grabbing them as they spilled out.'

'I'm getting the feeling this doesn't end well.'

'The building had three floors,' Harry continued. 'We made it to the second, cracking skulls as we went. They were armed as well, some of them. Knives, glasses, anything they could get a hold of. Guns, too. Some officers were shot, no one fatally, which was just down to luck, I think and the fact that those who were doing the firing were so coked up they could barely see, never mind hit anything. When we got to the third floor, we came to another door. This one wouldn't budge. Nothing would go through it. But we kept trying. We had information on what was behind it thanks to an informant. We needed to break through.'

'What was it?'

'Money, drugs, weapons, everything,' Harry said. 'It was their Fort Knox. And they'd upgraded their security since our informant had been there. Risked a lot, that one did. Everything actually, not that she had much to begin with. But if all you've got left is your life, risking it to get something better takes a desperate kind of bravery, don't you think? Anyway, it was only a few days, but it had been enough since she'd last been there. They'd somehow got wind of what we were planning and made their own plans.'

'Why didn't they move the stuff?'

'Arrogance, stupidity, who knows,' Harry said. 'They didn't think we'd do it. And I think we came sooner than they expected. Caught them by surprise. Then the fire started.'

'Fire?'

'They'd laced the place with accelerants,' Harry said, his nose curling as he remembered the smell. 'We found ourselves in the middle of a fireball.'

'Shit...'

'Yeah, you could say that. We had to get out, empty that building as quick as we could, and we did, but those trapped on the third floor? There was no chance, no chance at all. Some pact or something, that's what we heard. They didn't want to be taken in. The madness of it.'

Harry's face fell and he looked at Jadyn.

'I can still smell it, you know? Right now, two years later, and the stink of it is still on me. The fire, the people inside it. We heard them screaming, couldn't get to them. By the time the fire engines turned up, the place was an inferno. Never seen anything like it. Reminded me of the napalm scene from Apocalypse Now, the flames were that high, that hot. The roads melted. A couple of buildings nearby started burning. Nothing was surviving it. Nothing was meant to.'

For a moment, neither Harry nor Jadyn said a word. They just stood staring at the bleak landscape in front of them, imagining the horror that had taken place on that very spot, as though the ghosts were still there, calling out to them, screaming for help.

'So, what's this got to do with what happened in Reeth?' Jadyn asked. 'Why are we here?'

Harry pulled out his phone and showed Jadyn the screen. On it was the photo of what Diane had found in this very same place.

'Ed's wife saw her husband bury these right here,' Harry said. 'I'm guessing they were for someone else to pick up. A sign that Ed was either doing what was asked of him or had done so.'

Jadyn's eyes widened as he stared at Harry's phone.

'But that's you,' he said.

'All of this is me,' said Harry, putting his phone away

again. 'This place, what happened here, everything that led up to it. It's me. And it's looking like it's followed me north.'

'But I thought Jack was in charge,' Jadyn said.

Harry laughed, shook his head.

'Jack? Good God, no, he was never in charge! Officially, yes, he was the one who'd send the reports up the ladder as it were, kept those at the top off our backs so that we could get on with what we were doing. But Jack wasn't the one who put the team together, spearheaded the whole thing, put the fear of God into every dirty little drug pusher out there ruining lives, destroying families. No, that was all me. Every single bit of it.'

'Sounds like you won, though,' said Jadyn.

'If we'd won, you and I wouldn't be standing here now.'

'So, what do we do?'

'We go to war,' Harry said.

CHAPTER THIRTY-SEVEN

WITH JADYN DRIVING THEM TO JACK'S ADDRESS, HARRY was on the phone, Firbank at the other end.

'We're going over to see Jack now,' Harry said. 'But I need details on Hollywood's father.'

'Radcliffe is dead,' Firbank replied. 'And everyone who worked with him either died in that fire or is behind bars. You know that as well as I.'

'Even so,' Harry said, 'his dad might know something.'

'And what, exactly, do you think that he might know?' Firbank asked, struggling to keep her voice level and calm. 'All he knows is the inside of a private psychiatric unit. And you can't just turn up at one of those without permission either; you're not family, are you?'

'But I am the police.'

'Not the whole of it you're not! You can't just walk in there waving your warrant card around in front of people's faces and interview a man who's in a secure ward!'

'If I need permission then I need you to get it for me,' Harry said.

He heard an audible gasp.

'You do not order me around, Grimm!'

'It was a request,' Harry said. 'That's all. I need to speak to him.'

For a moment all he could hear was his old boss breathing; probably trying to calm down, he thought.

'I'll see what I can do.'

'Thanks,' Harry said.

'Give my best to Jack.'

'I will.'

Conversation over, Harry saw how the view had changed. Bristol was long gone now and they were driving through the countryside, a string of traffic laid out in front of them and behind.

'How far now?' Harry asked.

'Satnav says about forty minutes, but it might be two hours with all the tractors on the roads.'

'You say that like you're not used to seeing them.'

'Yes, but the roads in the Dales aren't rammed like these ones, are they? Where the hell are all these people going?'

'Tractors are never on the road for long,' Harry said. 'They always turn off in a mile or two.'

Harry's phone buzzed. He picked it up to answer but a voice on the other end got in first.

'Harry? It's Matt!'

'Matt? Are you okay? What's wrong? You sound, well, I don't know how you sound, but you don't sound normal. Is this about what's happened over in Reeth?'

'What?'

'Gordy rang,' Harry said. 'I know all about it.'

'That would make sense,' Matt said. 'I mean, I've not told her but Jim and Jen probably have.'

Harry was confused. They were talking at cross purposes.

'This isn't about the other victim, is it?' he said. 'Why've you called me?'

'I'm at the hospital,' said Matt. 'What other victim?'

'Hospital?' Harry said. 'You can't be! What's happened now?'

'Nothing's happened,' Matt said. 'Not yet anyway, but it soon will. I'm so wired right now. Too much coffee. But what else am I supposed to do? I've been in the room, out of the room, pacing up and down, getting coffee. I even had this bloody awful toastie from a vending machine! I mean, how is that even food? And how do they heat it? It was like something out of Star Trek, except I'm pretty sure that the food on the Enterprise would be a hell of a lot tastier, that's for sure! And she keeps insisting on having the window open, and it's so cold in there now and—'

'Matt?'

'What?'

'Stop!'

'Sorry.'

'Start at the beginning,' Harry said. 'You're in hospital, and ...' And then he remembered and nearly punched himself in the face for being such an idiot. 'Is it Joan? Is she okay? Is the baby on its way?'

'Supposedly yes,' Matt said, 'but it's taking its time about it!'

'When did you head in?'

'Yesterday evening,' Matt said. 'Got a call from Joan just as I was finishing work. Came back and grabbed her. We had her suitcase packed and whatnot, the child seat in the car, and we've been here ever since. Honestly, that toastie, Harry. It was awful.'

'This isn't about you, it's about Joan,' Harry said. 'How is she?'

'She was excited to begin with, but as it's gone on I think she's become a bit scared of the whole thing. We both are. Is it always like this?'

'Not sure I'm the right person to be asking anything about childbirth,' Harry said. 'Best advice I can give is to just stay by Joan's side, keep her as comfortable as you can, and leave it to the medical staff. They know what they're doing.'

'I feel a bit of a spare part though,' Matt said. 'I've been mopping her brow with a cold, wet flannel for the last few hours.'

'And she liked that?'

'For a while and then she told me to get the bloody thing away from her and leave her alone!'

Harry laughed.

'It's not funny!'

'Yes, it is,' Harry said. 'Now get yourself back at your wife's side, do whatever she says, stay out of the way and out of trouble, and call us with the good news when the new Dinsdale arrives.'

'Will do,' Matt said. 'You all okay down that way, then? Must be weird going back there, after so long, like.'

'It's been different,' Harry said. 'But I've had Constable Okri here to keep me company.'

'How's he doing?'

'Very well, I think,' Harry said. 'Now you get back to Joan and we'll get on with the case.'

'Speak soon, Harry.'

Matt hung up.

'Baby's on its way then?' Jadyn said.

'By the sound of it, you'd think it was more of a trial for Matt than it is for Joan,' Harry said.

'I helped deliver a baby once, you know,' Jadyn said.

Harry snapped his head round at this.

'You what?'

'Took a while, but we got through it in the end. Still don't know what the hot water and towels were for.'

Harry saw that they were now drawing close to Jack Ellis' address.

'Looks like we're nearly there,' Harry said. 'And I know I'm probably going to regret asking, but whose was it?'

'Whose was what?'

'The baby.'

'Actually it was more than one,' said Jadyn.

'What, twins?'

'I think there were nine of them in the end.'

Harry shook his head, as though trying to dislodge the information Jadyn had just given him.

'Nine babies? Are you sure about that?'

'Oh, that's normal for a litter,' Jadyn said.

'A litter? What are you on about?'

'Rabbits,' Jadyn said.

'You helped give birth to rabbits ...'

'Had to. I was the only one there at the time.'

Harry knew there was nothing he could say to that, so he didn't, and allowed them both enough time to fall into silence.

Fifteen minutes later and they were heading down a rough track that cut across a couple of meadows. The track was white, and Harry guessed there was a lot of chalk in it from a local quarry in amongst the gravel. Rain was sweeping in but Harry needed a breath of fresh air regardless so he wound down the window. Rain sprayed against his skin, refreshing him. He wound the window back up, staring out through the glass to watch the world drink in the storm, the colours changing as the clouds closed in.

The day had started clear but was now a bleak thing, ominous and grey. Around them, a world of mottled green stared back from meadows and trees, and a view that stretched out before them to the horizon, which was now seemingly growing ever closer as the clouds erased it.

He saw villages and towns in it that he knew so well, places he had once lived and worked in. He could come back here again if he wanted to. There was a job to consider. And this was, after all, his home. Or at least it had been until he'd let the Dales and the people who lived there get under his skin.

A hand tapped against his leg.

Harry stared at it, went to say something less than polite to the constable next to him, when he saw that Jadyn was pointing ahead of them, a worried look in his eyes.

'Jadyn? What is it?'

Harry turned to see what had caught his attention.

'That, Boss,' Jadyn said.

Though they were still a good way from Jack's house, they had a clear view of it, despite the rain. A small place, nothing spectacular; a detached cottage with a decent sized garden, partly set to vegetables, a couple of sheds, a summer house, a garage. But it was what was sitting in front of the garage which had Harry and Jadyn staring.

They saw a car, parked in front of it, which in itself wasn't unusual. What was though, was the fact that it was a convertible, the roof down in the rain, and in the front two seats, the slumped shapes of broken bodies.

CHAPTER THIRTY-EIGHT

HARRY WAS OUT OF THE CAR AND RUNNING. THE TRACK was sodden, potholes filling with the rain now coming down harder, and white water splashed up his trousers as he raced on. It was as though the world was doing its best to wash away the horror he was racing towards, but no amount of rain was ever going to do that, and no darkness could ever hide it.

Harry tripped, stumbled, fell to his knees, but Jadyn was with him and heaved him back up again. Hands and knees grazed, but Harry didn't notice any pain, his mind focused only on getting to the car, desperate to be able to do something, anything, though he already knew that hope was long gone.

Skidding to a halt, Harry's mind couldn't process what he was seeing. It was a vision that just didn't belong in such a quiet, peaceful, restful place, and yet there it was in front of him, a hideous scar on something otherwise so beautiful, so perfect.

The car, which Harry could now see was an old Mazda MX5, something Jack had probably bought to enjoy in his retirement, had been shot to hell. The bodywork was riddled with holes, but they weren't small, neat things punched into the metalwork. These were large and nasty and had torn into and through the car like it was nothing more than paper. Harry's first thought was that they were from high-powered rounds. Nothing else could have caused this level of damage to the car, or to the two bodies still inside it.

'Stay back,' Harry said, his hand held out to stop Jadyn from walking any closer.

'I'm okay, Boss,' Jadyn said. 'Really.'

'I know,' Harry said, 'but I need you to call this in. Bomb squad, too.'

As Jadyn got on his phone, Harry turned his focus to the remains of two people he recognised, even in death.

The nearest body was that of Jack's wife, Karen, sitting in the passenger seat. She was dressed well, Harry noticed, like she'd made the effort for a summer's drive with her husband. He saw a hat in the footwell, caked in blood. The rounds from whatever weapon had been used on the car had shown even less regard for her soft body than it had the car. She had been ripped apart by the deadly spray, her nearest arm blown off, the back of her head missing, her torso a mess. And at her side, Jack was no better, but Harry walked around to have a closer look regardless. He owed his old friend that much.

Jack, Harry saw now, had tried to protect his wife, his body leaning over to shield her from their attacker, someone who had come from around the side of the garage, between it and the house, and just opened up on them both. In so doing, his back had taken most of the hits, though some had caught his head and there was little of it left.

Standing back, Harry saw now that there were more rounds in the car than those which had been used to murder

Jack and Karen. Whoever had done this had killed them first but hadn't stopped there. Instead, they must have reloaded and continued with their attack, hammering the car all over with rounds, puncturing it relentlessly in a hail of metal. Harry could see as well that the wounds were all still fairly fresh, the rain making the blood flow like rivers, the water on the ground pooling red as it drained out of the car.

Harry moved away from the car and headed over to Jadyn.

'They're on their way,' Jadyn said, then added, 'You okay, Boss?'

'No, I'm not okay,' Harry said, his voice dark. 'Not by a bloody long shot.'

'You're sure it's Jack?'

'I am,' Harry said just as his phone rang.

'It's Jim,' said the voice as Harry answered.

'Not a good time,' Harry said.

'I've got the photos through,' Jim said. 'Sending them to you now.'

'Send them to Jadyn as well,' Harry said. 'Saves me constantly having to give him my phone.'

'Will do,' Jim said. 'How is everything? When are you heading back?'

'Not sure right now,' said Harry, unable to tear his eyes away from the smashed bodies of Jack and Karen. 'I'll let you know.'

He killed the call.

Harry stuffed his phone back into his pocket.

'Give me a few minutes, will you?' he said, looking at Jadyn. 'Get some cordon tape around the place. Not that there's much need for it, but you may as well. Make it look official, like we know what we're doing. Then get in the car and out of this weather. I can't be having you go down with a cold on top of all this.'

Without a word, Jadyn headed back to the car and Harry went for a walk back down the lane. He needed a moment to deal with what they'd just found and to run through everything that they knew so far.

He roared then, the frustration of the past few days bursting out of him in a tidal wave of rage. It raced through him, burning his blood as it went, smashing his mind to pieces. Everything that had happened was thrown to the wind and Harry closed his eyes, allowing it to all fall down around him.

That was eight bodies now. And all that death was linked back to what had happened in that crack house two years ago, to Hollywood, a man who burned to death in his own castle alongside the worst of his criminal friends. So, who was doing this and why? It didn't make any sense. It couldn't make any sense. Hollywood was dead! That building had been sealed, surrounded, and he'd not come out, they'd made damned sure of that, checking every person they arrested more than once to make sure who and what they had. And the bodies, or what was left of them, found in the still-warm ashes of the fire, they'd used dental records to confirm identities. So who? Was there something they'd missed? And why now? What the hell was going on?

Harry's phone rang again and he snatched it from his pocket sorely tempted to dropkick it into the mire of the muddy fields in front of him.

'What?'

'It's Firbank.'

'Apologies, ma'am,' Harry said. 'Rough morning.'

'What's happened?'

'It's Jack,' Harry said. 'And Karen. Both dead. We're at the property now.'

'What? How? What the hell happened?'

'Shot,' Harry said. 'Something high-powered, an automatic rifle on full-auto, by the way it looks.'

'I'm so sorry,' Firbank said.

'We've called it in.'

'Anything I can do?'

'Telling me why you called might be a start,' Harry said.

'I've been in touch with the hospital,' Firbank replied. 'The one where Radcliffe's dad has been these past few years.'

'And they're happy for me to go visit him?' Harry said. 'I know it's a long shot, but this is all to do with what happened to his son. This makes two of the team that brought him down. He might know something even if he doesn't realise it, if that makes any sense.'

'It does,' Firbank replied, 'but it won't make any difference.'

'What? Why?'

'Radcliffe senior has been in a coma for the past two years,' she said. 'Apparently, they think it was brought on by the shock of the news of his son's death. Whatever he knows, or doesn't, he's not going to be telling anyone any time soon.'

CHAPTER THIRTY-NINE

H ARRY STARED INTO THE RAIN, PHONE STILL IN HIS hand.

'Grimm, are you still there?'

'Yes,' Harry said. 'A coma? You're sure about that?'

'He's been looked after at home for the past year,' Firbank said. 'Private care as there's no other family.'

'He could afford that?'

'You know how it is,' Firbank said.

'Oh yes, I do, very much so,' Harry answered. 'But I'd still like it if you enlightened me.'

'We can seize just about everything from a drug bust, but some of it gets through. Daniel made sure his dad was cared for. Nothing we could do about that, no matter how much we wanted to.'

'What's the address?'

'Were you not listening, Harry? He's in a bloody coma!'

'And I'm standing here in the blood of an old friend on top of an ever-growing body count! I need that bloody address!'

'What the hell do you think you're going to do, head round there and shake him awake or lay hands on him or something? You're not Jesus!'

'That may be, but I'm willing to give anything a try, that's for damned sure!'

'And what then? What information is it that you think he'd be able to give you? He's been in a coma! He doesn't know anything about any of this. He can't!'

'Horseshit!'

'It is not horseshit and I'm going to let that one slide for now under the circumstances,' said Firbank. 'I'll give you the address but for one reason only: so that you can see for yourself this is nothing more than a dead end.'

'I'll be able to speak to whoever's looking after him,' Harry said. 'They might know something.'

'Just don't do anything stupid or reckless. And I know such a request is a tall order, but humour me, will you?'

Conversation over, the address came through a moment later. Harry walked over to the car and climbed in next to Jadyn. The constable was looking at his phone.

'Just having a look through the photos Jim sent,' Jadyn said.

'Spotted anything that'll help?'

Jadyn shook his head.

'Hard to know what I'm looking for.'

'Sometimes we don't know until we see it,' said Harry. 'And you remember what I've told you, yes?'

Jadyn looked up from the screen to Harry.

'Well, right now it's fairly hard to spot something specific that should be there and isn't, or that is there but shouldn't be, when all of these photos seem to be that and nothing else. And saying that out loud made my head hurt.'

Harry heard sirens.

'Here comes the cavalry,' he said. 'Once they've arrived, I need you to stay here and keep an eye on things.'

'What? But I'm just a constable,' Jadyn said.

'You were first on the scene,' said Harry. 'You'll need to tell them what we found when we arrived. They'll set up their own scene guard so you don't need to worry about that. Just let me know if anything comes up.'

'Where are you going?'

'I need to visit an old relative,' Harry said.

The police were the first to arrive, with forensics and the bomb squad on their way, Harry joined Jadyn in giving them a rundown of who they were, what they were doing there, what they'd found. Then Harry jumped in the car and headed off, leaving Jadyn to do his best not to get in the way.

The address for Daniel Radcliffe's dad was a house on the outskirts of the small town of Bradford-on-Avon. A pleasant and pretty little place, the river Avon forming a central feature of the town centre, crossed by a historic bridge and lined with old mills and warehouses and exclusive dwellings. The town also sat alongside a section of the Kennet and Avon Canal, a place Harry had walked along many times in the past to clear his head, and to sometimes enjoy a pint or two at the pubs that sat with their toes dipped in its waters.

Arriving at the house, Harry was faced with an electronic gate of solid wood encased in a metal frame. He leaned out and pressed the intercom button, introduced himself, and watched the gate slowly open. On the other side, a gravel drive led him through lawns and trees to a substantial Georgian property.

Staring up at the place, he knew deep down what had

paid for this, the people who had suffered, and his blood boiled. A car was parked just a little to the left of the front of the house, shaded by the house and the trees clustered about it like fans waiting for an autograph. It was a BMW, top of the range, too, Harry guessed, judging by those idiotic wheels and the cream-leather interior. Grubby white splash marks dotted the paintwork. He leaned his hand on the bonnet and the front door to the house opened.

'Good morning, Detective.'

A small woman with short hair was standing in the doorway.

Harry lifted his hand from the car, stared at it for a moment, then walked over.

'Apologies for dropping in on you like this,' Harry said.

'It's not a problem,' the woman said with a smile, though Harry thought it looked just a little forced, her eyes not party to the whole affair. 'I'm Doctor Sally Walker. I've been responsible for Mr Radcliffe's care for the past two years, both in the hospital and now here, at his home.'

'This is quite a place,' said Harry, rubbing his chin thoughtfully. 'How does he afford it I wonder?'

The doctor invited Harry inside, leaving his question to float off unanswered into the ether.

'This way,' she said.

Harry followed her to find that the house only grew grander, with high ceilings, a chandelier or two, a tiled floor polished to a mirror finish. Recently, too, he thought, spotting a mop and bucket close by. Though there were footprints marring the floor, Harry noticed, which struck him as odd.

'Looks like he did well for himself, doesn't it?' Harry said as they walked on past the kind of sweeping staircase built for dramatic entrances in posh frocks.

'I'm only here in a care capacity,' said the doctor. 'I'm not sure what help I can be.'

'Well, we'll have to see, won't we?' Harry said.

They came through to a large room. Inside, a hospital bed was set in the middle of the floor, draped in crisp, white linen. Harry heard the beeps and wheezes of various bits of medical equipment behind the sound of a television. The walls were covered in paintings and photographs. Fresh flowers were near the bed.

Harry walked over to where Radcliffe's father was laid out, his face half-covered by an oxygen mask.

'We fill his day with as much familiarity as we can,' the doctor said. 'Sounds, smells, touch.'

'Touch?'

'I have to massage him daily, but that's not just a case of pummelling and stretching muscles. I let his fingers touch things; his food, different material, anything that will help pull his mind back into the present.'

Harry saw that a black and white film was playing on the television. He recognised it but couldn't name it.

'Does he get many visitors?'

The doctor shook her head.

'Sadly, no.'

'Can't say I'm all that surprised.'

'How do you mean?'

Harry turned to stare at the doctor.

'Well, if he was anything like his son, then my guess is that Radcliffe senior here was, and probably still is, a proper bastard, if you'll excuse my language.'

Harry had been expecting a response to that, but not the one he got. For the briefest of moments, he saw her eyes widen, not so much in shock, but anger.

'How can you speak like that about someone in a coma?' she asked, gathering herself.

'Easily,' said Harry. 'I know what bought this property, what paid for this care, and it wasn't money earned honestly or by helping sick puppies, that's for sure.'

'Is this why you've come around?' the doctor said. 'To insult a sick man who can't respond?'

'Not at all,' Harry said. 'I just needed to see things for myself, that's all. How often do you visit?'

'What?'

'And who looks after him when you're not here?'

'There's a nurse,' the doctor said, flustered, her words fluttering like scared birds.

'Can I speak with her?'

'She's not here today.'

'I can see that,' Harry said. 'And you were here early this morning, were you?'

'Yes, of course,' the doctor said.

'Are you able to give me a time?'

'Eight o'clock.'

Harry looked at his watch.

'So you've been here for what, coming up to four hours, then, correct?'

'I suppose so, yes.'

Harry walked around the body on the bed.

'What's all of this doing then?' he asked looking at the various bits of equipment around the bed. Wires trailed everywhere like spilled spaghetti.

'Keeping him alive of course,' the doctor said. 'And I don't know where this is going, but I'm quite sure I've had enough of it already. I'm busy as you can see.'

'Where did you train?' Harry asked. 'For your medical degree, I mean.'

'What's that got to do with anything?'

'Humour me,' Harry said. 'I like the details, you see. Comes with the whole detective thing that I've got going on. Details, details, details; that's what we were taught.'

'Imperial College London, if you must know,' said the doctor.

'Those footprints in the hall, for example,' Harry said. 'They're a detail. Probably don't look like much to you or anyone really. But to me? Well, they stand out, you see. There's a bit of white to them, if you look closely. And that's odd, isn't it?'

The doctor did her best to draw herself up to her full height.

'If there's nothing else, I think it best if you leave. I have work to do.'

'Do you indeed,' Harry said. 'Can't see much of it for myself. He's fine just lying there, isn't he? Not exactly going anywhere as far as I can tell.'

The doctor was now standing at the door to the room.

'Like I said, Detective, I have work to do, so, if you wouldn't mind?'

She gestured out of the door and back down the hall.

Harry walked over and drew just a little too close for comfort, making use of his size, casting a shadow.

'You say you arrived here at eight, that's right, isn't it?'

'It is,' the doctor said, stepping back, worry lines furrowing her brow like ripples in the sand.

'And that's your car out front, I assume?'

'Well it's hardly his, is it?' the doctor snapped back.

'No, no it's not, you're right about that,' Harry said. 'That car is definitely not Mr Radcliffe's. But if you arrived here when you say you did, perhaps you can tell me why the engine's still warm?'

The doctor went to respond but wasn't given a chance as the body in the bed sat up, pointed a gun, and fired.

CHAPTER FORTY

Harry had been ready for something from the moment he touched the bonnet of the car in the drive. That it was warm had bothered him, not least because there was no direct sun thanks to the still falling rain and the shadows it had been parked under. Whoever had driven it clearly hadn't been at the house very long at all, and that struck him as odd.

Then those footprints had caught his attention. It hadn't been until he'd been in the room with the hospital bed, and seen all that white linen, that he'd thought back and realised that those footprints had been flecked with white. Like the spots on his trousers, the car parked outside with the bonnet warm from the engine beneath, the rain-sodden track to Ed's place. Then the figure in the bed had sat up, only it wasn't Radcliffe.

The bullet missed Harry and slammed into the doctor instead. She didn't even scream as the round tore into her, driving a hole through her back, exiting her chest in a burst of red mist. She dropped to the floor like a puppet with its strings cut.

Harry didn't have time think who it was shooting at him, or to check whether the doctor was still alive or not, as the figure in the bed fired again, swinging themselves onto their feet and charging.

Diving out of the room, Harry raced back down the corridor towards the front of the house. It was at times like this that he sometimes wished the police were armed, but the last thing he really wanted to do was end up in some last stand courtesy of the now very clearly missing father of a notorious and very dead drug dealer.

Another crack sounded, as his pursuer took a shot on the run. Never a good idea, Harry knew, because it was impossible to shoot accurately at a sprint, but he wasn't going to stay around and test his luck.

With no weapon to hand, and now racing back down the corridor, Harry grabbed the mop he'd spotted earlier, and thundered out onto the gravel drive. He knew that he didn't have time to jump in his own car and race away. His pursuer would be on him any moment, plus there was the gate to deal with. He had to think fast.

With barely seconds to spare, Harry pushed himself up against the wall of the house. The gunman charged out into daylight and Harry swung the mop around with a roar. It smacked into the other man's stomach, the impact doubling him over and sending him tumbling. Harry didn't hesitate and went in hard with his attack.

He saw the man bring his gun around, but Harry was too quick. He swept the mop at the hand holding the pistol. It connected with a sickening crunch. The man roared in pain as the gun span from his hand, taking a finger with it, still hooked around the trigger. Harry didn't give a moment's thought to what he'd just done and dropped his full weight onto the man's chest, slamming him to the ground. The man groaned but was already struggling to buck Harry from him. And that was when Harry saw the glint of a knife in the man's other hand.

This was no normal arrest, Harry knew that for sure, so it was time to forgo any niceties or politeness.

Harry crashed his forehead into the man's nose. The flesh and cartilage exploded, blood shooting out across the man's face. He roared in agony as Harry jumped up, heaved him over onto his stomach and dropped onto his back. Another groan as the wind was punched from his lungs and he dropped the knife. Harry grabbed the man's wrists and without even thinking about it had him cuffed.

'Stay,' Harry said, hissing the word into the man's ear. He quickly searched the man and found car keys in a pocket. Then he raced back into the house, phone to his ear, calling emergency services as he ran.

Call over, he dropped down next to the doctor. She was sprawled across the floor, half in and half out of the room. Harry heard her groan. Blood was oozing from the wound in her back. For the briefest of moments, he was somewhere else, dust everywhere, the sound of weapons fire, people screaming. He shook his head, forced himself back into the present.

He raced into the room with the hospital bed, grabbed the sheets, and headed back to the doctor. Pulling a small knife from a pocket, he quickly cut and tore the sheets into strips. Then he gently lifted the nurse enough to lean her against the wall. He turned some of the strips into thick wads and used the others as bandages to hold them tightly in place, wrapping them around her despite her screams.

'Ambulance is on its way,' Harry said. 'But you have to

focus on me, you hear? My voice. Stay awake. Can you do that?'

The doctor's head slumped.

'No you don't!' Harry roared. 'You listen to me! That's all you have to do and it's all you're going to do. Come on! Don't you dare give up! I won't let you! I'm not letting that bastard win!'

The doctor raised her head, stared at Harry through bloodshot eyes.

'My family,' she said. 'He threatened my family. That's why I did it. I had no choice. You have to believe me.'

'Who threatened you?'

The doctor coughed.

'Radcliffe,' she said, blood on her lips.

'He's dead.'

'He woke up.'

'What? You can't just wake up from being dead!'

Then Harry realised the abject stupidity in what he'd said.

'Walter,' the doctor said. 'Walter Radcliffe. He's the one who woke up.'

'Not Danny,' said Harry, shaking his head. 'His dad.'

The doctor coughed. Harry heard sirens.

'I thought all those visitors at the hospital had been family,' the doctor said. 'None of them were. They were just like him. Criminals.'

'Right, no more talking,' Harry said.

'No, you don't understand! My family! They're in danger! You have to help! Please!'

'What did they do?'

'They know where I live. Showed me photographs, my children at school, even asleep in bed. I had no choice. I had to go along with it, with all of this! What else was I supposed to do?'

The sirens were loud now. They were at the gate.

'There's a button,' the doctor said. 'To the right of the front door, just inside. Please, my family ...'

The doctor's head dipped forward.

'I need your address,' Harry said.

'My phone,' the doctor said. 'Pocket.'

Harry grabbed it. She told him the code.

'Contacts, under *home*,' she said. 'Please, you have to help them.'

'I will,' Harry said, then he rushed along the hallway to let in the paramedics.

When they arrived, Harry was back with the doctor. He told them of the wounds then left them to it. The doctor was fading in and out of consciousness now but she was in the best of hands.

Harry made to head back to the front door when a medic called after him.

'Mate, what about that bloke out front?'

'What about him?'

'He's bleeding. Need me to sort it?'

'No,' said Harry. 'First, we're going to have a nice little chat.'

CHAPTER FORTY-ONE

HARRY HAD HIS PHONE TO HIS EAR AS HE OPENED THE car and had a good look around to see what he could find. And what he did answered at least one question about who had killed Jack and Karen. He then went and stood over the crumpled sack of a man who had attacked him earlier. His face was a mess, the blood mixing with the dirt they'd rolled around in. His finger had clotted just enough but it still oozed. In many ways, Harry thought, he didn't look very happy at all.

'We need police there now, ma'am,' Harry said. 'I don't think I can express quite how urgent this is.'

'I understand,' Firbank said. 'I've a team on their way now. Can you tell me what happened?'

'I'm still working it all out myself, and I need to ask someone a few questions first I think.'

'I'll leave you to it, then.'

Harry slipped his phone back into his pocket then crouched down on his heels, bringing his rubber-gloved hands up in front of his face, the fingers interlocked.

'Hello,' he said. 'My name is Detective Chief Inspector Harry Grimm. So, who are you, then? I'm assuming you've got a name.'

The man spat at Harry. The bloody phlegm landed on Harry's jacket.

'Right then,' Harry said, 'if that's how it's to be ...'

He stood up, grabbed the man by his shoulders and heaved him to his feet.

'In case you're wondering why I'm wearing these gloves,' Harry said, 'there's two reasons. One is so that I can touch any evidence and not leave behind any DNA, you know, contaminate it. That pistol of yours for example. Nice that, I must say. Glock 17. That knife, too. Fancy thing there, for sure. Though that's a fixed blade knife and we both know that's just as illegal as the Glock, don't we? Unless you're able to provide a good reason to be carrying it. And just so we're clear on that, trying to kill me with it is not a good reason. And the second reason is, of course, so that I can touch *you* without leaving behind any of my DNA. Which means that I can do pretty much whatever the hell I want, can't I?'

Harry pressed the button on the keys and opened the car with an overly loud beep.

'Now, why don't you sit down and make yourself comfortable?'

With a shove, the man fell into the backseat of his car.

'Oh, well, I'm sorry about that. Seems you've got blood all over that lovely expensive car interior of yours.'

'You're dead!' the man spat. 'You're fucking dead, you hear?'

Harry thrust himself into the car beside the man, shoving him along the seat.

'I've had a quick look at your car,' he said. 'Taken a few samples here and there. For example, there's all that white dirt on your tyres and splashed down your paintwork. Oh, and would you look at that, there's even some in your footwell. Just a moment.'

Harry climbed out, collected some samples, then got back in next to the man. He lifted a small evidence bag in front of his face.

'You have a problem,' Harry said. 'I'm going to put money on this dirt matching a certain track leading to a certain house. I'm also going to put money on ballistics getting a match between what we've found at a crime scene earlier and that gun of yours.'

The man laughed.

'Something funny?' Harry said. 'Not known for my comedic turns, if I'm honest, so enlighten me, please. By which I mean, let me in on the joke.'

'The gun,' the man said. 'You won't find a match.'

'You sound confident.'

'I'm carrying a pistol, aren't I?'

'So?'

'So, you won't find a match!'

'Oh, I see,' Harry said. 'Just a moment ...'

Harry climbed out of the car, disappeared for a moment, then returned, carrying something in his hands, holding it in front of him like it was something dead and rotting.

'Had a quick look around your car a couple of minutes ago,' Harry explained. 'I found this. Recognise it, do you?'

At the sight of the automatic rifle in Harry's hands, the man's face had fallen so far it nearly fell off.

'Where did you get it, anyway?' Harry asked. 'Not exactly easy to come by. It's a C8 Carbine, if I'm not mistaken. And I'm liking this suppressor, too, by the way. Very sexy.'

Harry was still holding the weapon like it was diseased, but that he knew what it was had clearly confused the cuffed man in the car.

'We both know you murdered two people earlier today,' Harry said. 'Plus there's the fact that you had a fair old try at slotting me, just now, didn't you? So, here's what I want from you.'

'I'm not telling you anything. Fuck off.'

'You see, your problem is you still think you're in control,' Harry said. 'You think that because you've done a little bit of murdering, because a few high-rolling criminals have you on speed dial, that, like this rifle here, for example, you're invincible. Well, I hate to tell you this, but you're not.'

Harry snatched the rifle up into the air, caught it, and stripped it, right in front of the man's eyes.

'Funny, isn't it,' Harry said, holding only the empty magazine in his hand, the rounds spilling out onto the ground through his fingers, 'how something like that can just be taken apart? And you know what? The same's going to happen to you, too. Not by me though. Or the police. And do you know why? Because I'm going to let you go, that's why. Right now actually. But not before I've put word out about this, about what you did, how you failed, how you told me everything, about Radcliffe, what he was up to, where he is. And that word will spread faster than you can run, I promise you that. Then, when they catch you?' Harry glanced down at the pieces of the rifle littering the floor. 'You'll end up like that,' he said. 'In pieces. And with a hell of a lot more screaming.'

His point made, Harry leaned in, thunked the man on

the head with the empty magazine, then turned back to his own car.

'You can't do this!' the man shouted. 'You can't! They'll kill me! They'll fucking kill me!'

Harry kept walking.

'Please! You can't let me go! I'll tell you whatever you want to know! Please!'

Harry stopped, turned around, walked back.

'I want protection,' the man said.

Harry laughed, shook his head, turned back to his car.

'Wait! Please! Just ... just stop!'

Harry turned on his heels.

'What've you got?' he asked.

'I wasn't trying to kill you,' the man said.

'Could've bloody well fooled me!' said Harry.

'No one was to kill you. No one except him. Mr Radcliffe.'

'You mean Walter.'

The man nodded.

'When he woke up from his coma, that's when this all started. At first, he couldn't remember anything about what had happened to his son, to Danny. But when he did, all he wanted was revenge.'

'Bit dramatic, don't you think?' Harry said. 'But that doesn't explain everything, does it? Going after me, the team, that's one thing, but all the collateral damage, the escort up in Yorkshire ...'

'She was key,' the man said. 'I don't know why, he never said, but he obsessed about her more than anything. Said she'd betrayed Danny. You were supposed to find her first because then you'd know.'

'Know what?'

'That it was all your fault,' the man said. 'That what you did back then, it killed her in the end, too.'

Harry clenched his fists, things starting to slot into place. Not everything, but enough.

'I've told you all I know,' the man said. 'I don't know anything else.'

'So, you'll be wanting that protection you asked for then, I suppose, is that right?' Harry asked.

'You have to protect me! They'll kill me. They'll get to me, here or inside. Please!'

As the man spoke, Harry had stepped closer to the car. He leaned in, pushing his face right up close to the man's bleeding nose.

'You killed an old friend of mine and his wife,' he said, 'and you think that this little confession is enough?'

'You said ...'

'Actually, no, I didn't,' said Harry. 'I said nothing, you panicked, you blabbed, and now you're going to have to deal with that, aren't you?'

Fear scratched at the man's eyes.

'What? You can't!'

'Can't, what?' Harry asked.

'Just leave me! That's not fair, that's not how it works! You have to protect me! It's your job! You're the police!'

'Not the whole of it, I'm not,' Harry said, and turned away, leaving the man alone with his nightmares.

A while later, having waited for the police to arrive to deal with the crime scene at the house, and after a quick call to Firbank, Harry had then headed back to pick up Jadyn. He'd also quickly popped into a little shop in Bradford-on-Avon to pick something up to give to Matt when he next saw him. He wasn't sure how appropriate it was, but it seemed like a good idea at the time, so he just went with it. He'd been able to get something for Joan, too. On the way, he'd put a call into the team back in Wensleydale and spoken with DI Haig. They'd managed to find the soldier, a Corporal Shelton, and were in the process of bringing him in for questioning.

'Bloody hell, Boss,' Jadyn said as he climbed into the car. 'You look like you've had a proper shocker.'

'It's not been the best of times, that's for sure,' Harry said. 'How's things here?'

'Grim,' Jadyn said, then his eyes went wide. 'Oh God, sorry, that's not what I ...'

Harry attempted a smile.

'Don't be afraid to use the word just because my face looks like what it describes.'

Jadyn gave a short, sharp nod.

'Bomb squad checked everything,' he said. 'Found a device under the car. Forensics are still busy. So, what now?'

'We go home,' Harry said. 'Someone's hiding up there, waiting for me, and I need to make sure I find him first, wherever the hell he is.'

'Who?'

'Radcliffe,' Harry said, and told an increasingly stunned Jadyn what had happened at the house.

Sometime later, and well over halfway into the journey, Jadyn let out a sigh of such desperation Harry had to ask.

'Something the matter?'

'It doesn't make sense,' Jadyn said. 'Any of it. The woman at the house in Reeth, the bloke at the Lakes, the bombs. It's like it's all connected but also not.'

Harry had been wondering the same thing for a good while, but after speaking to the gunman at the house, a few things had clicked into place, and the truth had rolled over him, slow and deliberate, as though it wanted to cause more pain.

'Her name was Kate,' Harry said, remembering what had happened, hardly able to believe where it had all eventually led. 'The woman you found at the house.'

'You knew her?'

'I didn't realise it at the time, but I think so, yes.'

'Who was she?'

'A kid,' Harry said. 'Younger than you when I first saw her. I'd seen her knocking about, arrested her too many times, but nothing ever stuck, she'd wriggle free somehow. Though it was hardly the kind of freedom most people would want to run back to, that's for sure.'

'This down in Bristol, then?'

'It was,' Harry said. 'Turns out she ended up mixing up with Hollywood. I didn't know that at the time, found out later while we were trying to bring him down. I saw her during one of our raids. She got away. But that's when I knew who she was with.'

'What happened?'

'For a while, nothing,' said Harry. 'I kept an eye out for her, but she'd disappeared. She could do that. Had a real knack for it. She was wraith-thin anyway, but she could just fade into the background. And then a while later, I started to see her again. She was different. Had put some weight on. Not much, but enough to not look like she'd snap if she sneezed. She had new clothes, a haircut, a bit of a strut to her walk as well, like she was suddenly important. She wasn't though. It was just Hollywood, playing his games, looking after her but only so he could use her.'

'Not sure I understand,' Jadyn said.

'It was how he worked,' said Harry. 'He only looked after those he had a use for. He'd take people in, give them things, buy them, twist them to whatever shape he wanted, then throw them away. And that's what had happened when I found her.'

'Where was that?'

'We were on another raid,' Harry said. 'We crashed into this place. Went in fast, as always; it was the only way. Catch them before they flushed their gear down the toilet or threw it out the window or just onto the floor. And there she was, hiding under these filthy sheets in the corner of the room, barely moving, like a starved rat. God, the stink of that place. I can still smell it. Eye-watering.'

'Doesn't sound like it was much fun.'

'It wasn't,' Harry said. 'Hollywood had taken her in and then spat her out again, simple as that. She was a scrag-end, a piece of meat he'd grown tired of. She was hooked on crack, filthy, covered in sores. He'd passed her around between friends. It was hell and she knew nothing else. To be honest, even now, I'm amazed she survived it.'

'What did you do?'

'Helped her,' Harry said. 'Helped everyone we could, though that's not easy if people don't want to be helped. And crack addicts don't. All they want is the next hit, that's what their life is, living from one fix to the next. Nothing else matters. It's horrific. Not a life for anyone.'

'I still don't see how she ended up in Swaledale, though,' said Jadyn.

'No, neither do I,' Harry said. 'But he obviously found her.'

'Why, though? All you did was help her get her life together.'

'There was a bit more to it than that,' Harry said. 'Remember what I said about revenge? She wanted hers, so she gave us information, told us about that last crack house, the big one. She knew it well, drew us plans, told us where the weapons were, money, drugs, who was there, everything.'

'Shit.'

'She served Hollywood and his pals to us on a platter. And at no small risk to herself either. Had to put her through witness protection. Even taught her to put together a grab-bag, just in case, so she at least could make sure she'd have enough with her if she had to run.'

'So, was it Witness Protection that put her up in Reeth, then?'

Harry shook his head.

'No, she did a runner herself before that went through.'

'What?'

'That knack for disappearing I mentioned,' Harry said. 'She made good use of it.'

'So what was the cocaine about? Just making a point?'

'Maybe,' Harry said, and left it at that.

A couple of hours later, when they eventually arrived in Hawes, the day had already drawn itself to a close, the shops shut, the pubs open, and the team had all headed home. Jim was on duty, but he was away to Bainbridge for something.

'You've been good company,' Harry said to Jadyn as they parted ways for the evening. 'One day, you never know, you might even make a decent detective.'

Heading home, the last thing Harry had wanted was to have to answer another call. And yet, as he'd crossed over the threshold into his little flat, his mind already focusing on a beer and a bit of something to eat, that's exactly what he did. And Smudge did not look happy about it at all.

'Grimm,' he said.

'It's Jim, we've had a call in from Reeth.'

'That's not funny,' Harry said.

'No, it isn't,' said Jim. 'It's that old Mr Whaley. I've just spoken to him. Sounds bloody terrified.'

'What? Why?'

'Says he saw someone round at the crime scene next door. Apparently, he told them to bugger off, so they chased him back into his house. He's hiding inside behind locked doors. I'm headed over now, but I thought you might want to join me, you know, seeing as what's been going on, like.'

'That's a very sensible suggestion,' Harry said. 'But I'll head over myself.'

'You sure?'

'I'm sure,' Harry said. 'Not least because I'm a little scarier looking if there is anyone around playing silly sods.'

When Harry arrived in Reeth, the sky was a silvery grey, the horizon still trying to burn with the vanished sun. Lights shone out across the green from pubs and houses, spilling evidence of the lives inside. Parking up, Harry glanced over at the Black Bull pub and its odd upside-down sign. Light spilled out from there, too, but it struggled to get beyond the windows, as though it wanted to stay inside to enjoy the warmth and the company of those enjoying their evening.

Harry made his way over to Mr Whaley's, but first had a quick look around the crime scene next door. It was hard to believe that Kate, someone he'd barely known but had tried to help, had died there just a few days ago. Why she had been here at all he couldn't fathom, though he doubted it was down to luck.

Seeing nothing out of sorts at the house, he gave the place a respectful nod, then headed around to see Mr Whaley. The house, he noticed, was dark. He made his way to the door to find that it was already open.

Harry stopped, hesitated.

'Mr Whaley?'

No reply.

He tried again, projecting his voice further, still nothing.

Harry pulled a small torch from a pocket and clicked it on, sending a bright beam inside.

He called again and stepped closer to the house. Somewhere in the back of his mind a small part of him was telling him to wait, to call for backup. But another part knew that Mr Whaley might be in no fit state to wait.

Harry stepped through the door, tried the light switch. Nothing.

Then his phone buzzed.

CHAPTER FORTY-TWO

Halfway down the hallway, Harry answered his phone. If Mr Whaley was somewhere out there in the dark, then he wanted him to hear him and hopefully call out. It would make it a lot easier to locate him.

'What now?'

'It's Officer Okri,' Jadyn said. 'Sorry, if you're busy I can leave it till tomorrow. No bother. Sorry, Boss.'

'Well, you've bothered me with it now so you may as well finish telling me why you called,' Harry said.

'It's not important though,' Jadyn said. 'It's just I've been thinking.'

'Very dangerous,' Harry said.

'Yeah, you're right, I'll speak to you tomorrow. Sorry.'

'You're not making this any better for yourself,' Harry replied. 'Get to the point.'

'If you're sure.'

'Constable Okri ...'

'I've been looking through the crime scene photos and

I've just spotted something. I should've spotted it earlier. Can't believe I missed it.'

'What?' Harry said. He moved deeper into the house, tried another light switch, still nothing. 'What have you spotted?'

'I know we've not got any photos from what happened today, but I don't think that matters,' Jadyn said. 'But the others, there's a clear link. At least to me there is anyway.'

'Instead of telling me what you think the link is by not actually telling me what it is, why don't you actually tell me what it bloody well is?' Harry said, irritation in his voice mixing with his increasing worry over the whereabouts of Mr Whaley.

'The first crime scene,' Jadyn said. 'Kate, the lass you knew, she'd had her ear cut off.'

'She had,' Harry said, forcing himself to not think about what the girl had gone through in her final moments.

'And the one over in Ambleside, he was stabbed in the shower, wasn't he?'

'Bath or shower, I can't see why it matters.'

'There was a shower, he was in it,' Jadyn said. 'That's what matters.'

Harry smiled. Jadyn's confidence was growing, he thought.

'Go on ...'

'The third crime scene, they were both shot in their car.'

'I don't see what you're getting at,' said Harry.

'Seriously? Not at all?'

'Nope, not a bit of it,' said Harry.

'What I'm getting at is Reservoir Dogs, Psycho, and Bonnie and Clyde. They ring any bells? I've not seen that last one, but the death scene is full-on. Caught that on YouTube a few minutes ago. It's why I called you.'

'Keep going,' Harry said, encouraging Jadyn to explain further.

'You see, Reservoir Dogs, whether you like Tarantino or not, is notorious for this one scene where someone's ear gets cut off. They're tied to a chair, and someone just pulls out a knife and cuts it off. Psycho, you've heard of for sure, with the woman in the shower getting stabbed. And then Bonnie and Clyde—'

'Get shot up in their car,' said Harry. 'I've not seen the film, but everyone knows the story.'

'Exactly,' said Jadyn. 'They're all scenes from classic movies, aren't they? The murders were all staged.'

'I know,' Harry said.

He'd managed to make his way into the kitchen, but still no sign of Mr Whaley.

'What? How? You know?'

Harry could hear just how crestfallen Jadyn sounded, his voice reaching a pitch high enough at one point to crack a wine glass.

'Not in the way you've just explained,' Harry said. 'That's you, and that's some bloody good detecting right there, Constable. But something was off about them all. And that all just links everything together even stronger. Well done.'

'I'm right, then?'

'You are,' Harry said. 'All of this, it's Hollywood. Or his dad, anyway. It's clearly not Daniel. He's nothing but ash now.'

'You mean the one in a coma?'

'Was in a coma,' corrected Harry. 'Remember? Kept it

quiet by threatening the doctor charged with his care. Poor woman had no choice and ended up getting shot for it in the process.'

Harry rubbed his hands then, wondering if he could still see spots of her blood there on his skin. But there was always blood there, sadly. It just wouldn't go away, probably never would.

'So you really think that he planned all this?'

'Revenge is quite the driving force, I assure you,' Harry said. 'Now, will there be any other revelations or can we leave anything else till tomorrow?'

'I don't think so, no,' Jadyn said.

'Then why don't you go grab yourself a good night's sleep?' Harry suggested. 'And leave me to what I'm on with now.'

'You're not at home yourself, then?'

'No, I'm not,' Harry said. 'I'm trying to find Mr Whaley.'

'You are? Why?'

'Apparently, he saw someone messing around the crime scene, and they saw him as well,' Harry explained. 'They chased after him so he locked himself in his house and called the police. Only, I've arrived to find the door open and it doesn't look like Mr Whaley's home.'

Jadyn fell quiet at the same time as the front door slammed shut behind Harry, caught by the wind, he suspected.

'You still there, Constable?'

'I am,' Jadyn said. 'Sorry, it's just that what you said, are you sure that's right? About Mr Whaley?'

'What about it?' Harry asked.

'Mr Whaley calling you from inside the house. That's what you said, isn't it?'

'Yes, that's what I said. Why? What's the problem?'

'The problem,' Jadyn said, 'is that he can't have done.'

'And why the hell not?'

'Because,' said Jadyn, 'he hasn't got a phone, Boss, that's why!'

'What?'

'He used a telephone box to call the police when I went over. He doesn't have a phone!'

Harry turned to look into the gloom of Mr Whaley's house, the phone still in his ear.

'And you're sure about this? You're positive he doesn't have a phone.'

'Very,' Jadyn said. 'He told me himself.'

'Maybe he got his story wrong, that's all,' Harry said. 'Easy to do.'

'No, he was pretty clear about the fact that he didn't have a phone,' Jadyn said.

Harry was running through a trillion and one things in his head all at once and they were all demanding his full attention. He stared into the gloom in front of him as he moved out of the kitchen and back into the heart of the house. Downstairs was empty of life. And that meant he'd have to head up to the bedrooms.

'Constable, I need you to send backup. And yes, I know that sounds like we're in the movies, but I mean it.'

'Why? What's happened?'

'Nothing, yet,' Harry said, now at the bottom of the stairs, 'and perhaps nothing will, but right now, I think something's happened to your Mr Whaley and I don't want to take any chances.'

'I'm on it,' Jadyn said. 'I'll see you as soon as I can.'

Harry hung up.

For the next few moments all he could hear was the sound of his own breathing. He was forcing himself to control it, to stay focused.

Harry knew he had a simple choice, to either head back outside, or venture further in. If Mr Whaley was here, then Harry had a horrible feeling that nothing good had happened to him. But he was alone himself, and for once, sense and reason won out. He made his way back towards the front of the house, gave the handle a twist, then yanked the door.

Nothing.

Harry tried again, but it wouldn't budge.

Locked? Why the hell would Mr Whaley lock him in? And never mind why, what about the how? No one had gone past him since he'd entered so had someone locked him in from outside? What the hell was going on?

Then a voice came to him in the darkness, slipping through the house from somewhere upstairs. It was a voice he didn't recognise, but the accent was familiar enough as he'd carried it with himself his whole life.

'Hello, Harry ...'

CHAPTER FORTY-THREE

'Radcliffe?' Harry called out into the darkness. 'What have you done with Mr Whaley? Where is he?'

The voice laughed, the sound cruel and cold.

'He's got nothing to do with this,' Harry said. 'He's innocent. Let him go. We can talk.'

'You killed my boy.'

'He killed himself,' Harry answered back. 'Nothing to do with me. I didn't lock him in that place. I didn't light the fire.'

'If you hadn't been there, he'd still be alive.'

'I doubt that,' Harry said. 'He'd made more than a few enemies along the way. Sooner or later, one of them was going to have a go at taking him down.'

Something clattered on the ground at Harry's feet. He shone his torch down and saw a phone.

'That was hers,' the voice said. 'The girl who betrayed him. Gave him up. Stole from him, too, you know. Just enough to set herself up elsewhere.'

Harry picked up the phone as a cold laugh danced in the

dark. Another burner. In the contacts was only one number. He recognised it. That number was his.

'Your son, he had it coming,' Harry said, pocketing the phone. 'I'm not saying he deserved what happened, don't get me wrong, but if it hadn't been us, then someone else would've got to him. Just a fact of the life he'd chosen. You know that as well as I.'

'She moved here because of you. You know that, don't you?'

'What?'

'The girl next door. Melissa or Helen or Kate or whatever the hell she was called. Came here because you were nearby. I think she thought you could protect her. She had your number in that phone, after all. Just never got a chance to make the call. She tried, but I managed to get there first.'

Harry remembered a missed call at Kett's, a number he hadn't recognised. Had that been her?

'Where's Mr Whaley?' he asked again, as much to change the subject as to find the old man he'd come out to check up on. Once he was safe, then he could deal with Radcliffe senior.

'You'll find out soon enough.'

'Whatever this is, he's got nothing to do with it,' Harry said. 'Let him go.'

Another laugh came through the dark so harsh and mean that Harry stepped back. Then he heard engines outside, car doors open and shut. That was quick, he thought, thinking back to his chat with Jadyn and his request for support.

'There's nothing you can do,' Harry said. 'You're not going anywhere. And it's not just me now either. I called for backup. They've just arrived.'

'You sure about that, Harry?'

Harry fell quiet. Why was no one trying to break down the door?

'You killed my boy,' Radcliffe called down from somewhere upstairs. 'You destroyed his world and mine. So, I've destroyed yours. The bombs, they were a nice touch, don't you think? Collateral damage, you see, like with the fire. And you weren't expecting it. Surprisingly easy to get a hold of, too, weaponry like that. If you know the right people. And Danny did. And now so do I.'

Harry heard footsteps outside. Whispering.

'You know what they say, don't you, Harry?'

'No, what?'

'One bad turn deserves another.'

The door opened and Harry saw two men charge at him as more laughter floated down from upstairs. At once all his senses went on full alert, adrenaline a hot fire in his veins. He turned to race to the kitchen, but a hand caught his jacket and hooked him back .

Spinning round, Harry brought his torch up into the face of his assailant, blinding him with the light first before shoving him away. Then he was moving again, looking for another door, an exit out through the back of the house. Footsteps chased him down.

In the kitchen Harry found another shadow waiting for him, a large man, his grimace clear in the moonlight spilling into the room through the window. Harry didn't give him a moment to think. He charged into him with his full body weight, hammering his shoulder into the man's solar plexus. The man gasped as Harry drove him backwards into the wall, then he heaved his head up sharply, connecting with the man's chin, breaking it with his skull.

The man dropped to the ground, gurgling and crying.

Harry turned to find the two men from the hall were now with him in the kitchen. Neither was armed, or if they were, their weapons were still holstered and he couldn't see them in the dark. They want me alive, Harry realised. Not good. And not about to happen, either.

The small kitchen table was between him and the two men. They were each taking a side, trying to trap him. They were going careful though, Harry thought, their eyes flickering between him and their broken, bleeding, moaning friend rolling around on the floor.

'We don't have to do this,' Harry said.

'There's two of us, only one of you,' the one on the left said. 'Good odds, I think.'

'Not for you,' Harry said, grabbing the table and heaving it violently to his right, ramming it into the legs of one of the attackers. The man roared as the sharp edge made contact. Ignoring the other man for a moment, Harry took the advantage, grabbed a pan from the stove and slammed it across the man's face. The sound was thick and wet and it dropped him with a moan.

'Two down,' Harry said, staring at the only one left.

'I didn't need them anyway,' the man said.

Harry glanced around for a weapon and saw something down by the stove. He grabbed it and found himself brandishing the poker. He remembered then how Mr Whaley had waved it around and marked his trousers with it when he'd popped round to see him.

The other man laughed as Harry waved the poker around in front of his face.

'That won't protect you,' he said.

'It's a distraction,' Harry replied.

'From what?'

While he'd been waving the poker around, Harry had spotted a few small pots by the side by the stove. He'd grabbed one of them and flicked off the top.

Harry threw the contents of the pot at his attacker. A greyish powder filled the air and flew into the man's face, his eyes.

Harry sneezed. Pepper, he realised.

The man stumbled, fell back, rubbing his eyes, sneezing, roaring in anger as the pepper went to work.

Harry followed him, grabbed his shoulders, then yanked him down violently as he sent his knee up to connect with the man's stomach. He did it a few more times just to make sure, moved on to the man's face, his knee connecting with it thickly. Then he dropped the man to the floor to writhe blindly in pain as he vomited over himself.

Harry walked back out into the hall only to have the lights come on. There in front of him was someone he recognised.

'Mr Whaley? You're okay? Where's Radcliffe? Did he let you go?'

Mr Whaley didn't move, just stared.

Behind the old man, the front door was now open. 'We need to get out of here. Come on.'

Harry made to move Mr Whaley out of the house, but the old man stayed stock-still.

'It's okay,' Harry said. 'Other officers are on their way. They'll be here any moment. We'll be safer outside, trust me.'

Mr Whaley stared at Harry, then he seemed to stand up, like someone was pulling him up from the top of his head, stretching him upwards just enough to straighten his back.

'You still don't know, do you?' Mr Whaley said. 'Haven't realised your little error?'

'Know what?' Harry said, confused now. 'What error? We need to move!'

The gun in Mr Whaley's hand took Harry so by surprise that he laughed, even with it having the hammer pulled back.

'This isn't funny, Harry,' the old man said. 'Not for you, anyway.'

'Radcliffe,' Harry said then. 'Of course.'

The man was now standing tall, the gun in his hand pointing at Harry's head.

'The plan was to take you alive,' Radcliffe said. 'Make you suffer. But not all plans come together, do they? Still, it'll be fun to see the light die in your eyes, so that's something.'

'Where's Mr Whaley?' Harry asked.

'Dead,' said Radcliffe. 'Has been for a good few days now. He wasn't planned, but when I found your Kate and saw who lived next door, I just couldn't resist it, you know? I thought, if I could just be him for long enough, I'd be able to watch your world burn. And I have, Harry. It's been so much fun.'

'You pretended to be him?'

'From the very beginning,' Radcliffe said. 'Your young constable, he was the test. And I passed with flying colours, didn't I?'

Harry said nothing, preferring to just let Radcliffe talk while he did some thinking.

'An uncanny likeness to the old sod, even if I do say so myself,' Radcliffe continued. 'I've still got it, you know? A bit of make-up, a change of the voice, and there you go.'

'She wasn't my Kate,' Harry said. 'She was just a kid who wanted a fresh start.'

'No, maybe not, but you were her Harry, weren't you? The one who saved her, persuaded her to betray my Danny.

That's why I took her tongue. For talking, for ratting on my son.'

Harry's rage was boiling, but he kept a lid on it. Just.

'You say that like it was a bad thing.'

'My only son, Harry, that's what he was. And you took him.'

'So all of this, you did out of revenge?' Harry said. 'Really? That's the best you can do for all of this? You should've stayed in that coma.'

'A coma caused by what you did.'

Harry shook his head.

'You're all the same, people like you, you know that, right? Never able to take any blame for themselves, their family, always looking to put it on someone else. It's pathetic.'

'You really think what I've done is pathetic? It took months to plan. I had to get well again, healthy enough to do all of this.'

'And you've so much to show for it, too,' said Harry. 'All that violence and death. You must be proud.'

'I am.'

'You want applause? Is that it?'

'All the world's a stage,' Radcliffe said.

'Ed was the first, I assume?' Harry asked. 'You got to him, threatened him and his family, had him find Kate. So, he did what he could do better than most, went undercover and found her.'

'They all had to die,' Radcliffe said. 'But you had to find the girl first, you see? It had to be because of her that you'd find everything else. You used her to destroy my son and I used her to destroy you. I left a few clues along the way. Not to help you find me, but just to rub your face in it.'

'Yes, the movie references in the murders,' Harry said. 'Like I said, pathetic.'

'It is not pathetic!'

Harry remembered something then. 'When I came round to chat to Mr Whaley, that was you. The mention of Local Hero, I didn't realise at the time how odd that was. But now?'

Radcliffe shrugged.

'It's a good movie,' he said. 'Pity you'll never get to see it.'

Harry noticed that Radcliffe's hand holding the gun was shaking now.

'My guess, is that Kate never saw you as Mr Whaley, did she?' Harry said. 'Whether he was dead before or after you got to her, it doesn't matter. You killed her then played the part, called it in, had us fooled. Then all you had to do was just keep out of the way of the locals long enough to watch everything come together.'

'I wasn't expecting you to find my house,' Radcliffe said. 'That was a surprise. But it worked out well enough. You still hadn't worked it all out by then, had you? The soldier boyfriend was a help as well. Nice to be able to throw that one in, just to keep you guessing. And he was useful in the end.'

'It was you who killed the local woman?'

Radcliffe shook his head.

'No, I had my lads do that for me. She'd caught me unawares, you might say, something about some eggs. She realised I wasn't Mr Whaley so something had to be done. Did her in with old Mr Whaley's poker. No reason, just a bit of theatre, if I'm honest. A little bit of the old stage makeup on the body and I knew it would give your team something else to think about, point them in the direction of the boyfriend, while I played my final hand.'

'The call about locking yourself inside,' Harry said. 'You tripped up though. You phoned from inside the house. But there's no phone here, is there?'

Radcliffe laughed. 'Yes, old Mr Whaley was clearly a bit of an odd one. Gave me plenty of material to draw on. Had to question him quite a bit. And he took some persuading. But then I can be very persuasive if I want to be and if I've got the right tools to hand. There was so much here I could use to get his character right, right down to those bloody awful pickled eggs. God knows how anyone eats them. But a little bit of local colour adds to the whole act I think.'

'So now what?' Harry said, still staring at the gun. 'You've had your fun, made your speech. Is that it?'

'You know, I think that it is,' Radcliffe said. 'Any last words?'

'The cocaine,' Harry said. 'Was that another clue as well?'

'No,' Radcliffe said. 'That was what she deserved. How do you think she managed to escape in the end, to disappear? Because she was no better than Danny in the end, you see? She stole from him, took a kilo of the stuff for herself. Had it stashed away somewhere. Then, just before she disappeared, she sold it. Your Kate, the girl you saved, she ended up doing what they all did, using the drugs to get ahead. Ironic really, isn't it?'

'Not sure you quite understand what irony is,' said Harry, then he grabbed the pistol with his left hand, pushing it hard to the right, at the same time stepping out of the line of fire.

Radcliffe wasn't quick enough to respond. The gun went

off, the bullet smashing into the wall, but Harry was out of the line of fire. He didn't wait for another and now rammed the pistol forward into Radcliffe's gut at the same time sending his right elbow into the man's face. Radcliffe cried out in pain as his nose exploded. He fell back, bleeding and dazed, so Harry sent in another elbow strike for good measure. Then he reached down with his right hand and with both hands together on the pistol gave the weapon a violent twist, breaking it from the old man's grip along with one or two fingers if the accompanying scream was anything to go by.

Harry turned to see one of the other attackers stumble out of the kitchen. He raised the pistol.

'I'd stop right there if I were you,' he said.

Outside, lights and sirens broke the night.

CHAPTER FORTY-FOUR

Harry was sitting in his flat, Grace beside him, Smudge at his feet. There was still plenty to be getting on with about the case, but there were enough people involved now to allow him to step back for a moment or two.

A week had passed and the local community, not just in Reeth, but all across the Dales, were slowly coming to terms with what had happened, even if they didn't know all the details. People had died and that pain would be felt long and deep, but those wounds would heal eventually.

Radcliffe and his gang of thugs were behind bars. Not only that, what had happened had led to further arrests down south, with Detective Superintendent Firbank very much enjoying pulling apart a small corner of the criminal underworld. The soldier, Ollie Shelton, was in the hands of the Military Police. Not for anything to do with Kate, but for a bar fight that had put a few civilians in hospital. Clearly, he was someone with anger issues. Sowerby was out of hospital and staying with her mum while she recovered. Apparently, they had both argued hotly about this, but eventually

Margaret had won. And no broken leg was going to get in the way of her looking after her daughter.

Harry was looking forward to a long weekend of doing very little. His Saturday morning had already started well with a good lie-in and a large breakfast. And now he and Grace were doing nothing more than reading the paper, listening to the radio, and trying to not fall asleep. Unlike Smudge, who was asleep on the floor, her head resting on his feet.

Harry reached down to stroke the dog's head as a knock rattled the front door.

'I'll get it,' Grace said, pushing herself forward, Smudge making chase.

Harry wasn't going to argue and allowed the sofa to suck him in just a little deeper. He was about to close his eyes when he heard his name.

'Harry?'

Opening his eyes, Harry looked up to see that Grace had been joined by two other people.

'Detective Sergeant Dinsdale,' he said, leaning forward and pushing himself up onto his feet. 'If this is about Hawes Gala and that animal made of vegetables thing Jim mentioned ...'

Harry then saw that Matt wasn't alone.

'I see you've brought the whole family with you,' he said.

Matt was all smiles, Harry noticed. Joan, well, she was smiling too, but she didn't half look tired. They both did.

'Well, you've not met the wee one yet, have you?' Matt said. 'So, we thought it was about time that you did.'

Harry stared at the bundle in Matt's arms, all wrapped in a thick white blanket. He moved closer and there it was, the tiny, squashed face of a new life.

'This is Mary,' Matt said. 'Mary-Anne, actually.'

'Named her after my mum,' Joan said. 'She'd have loved to have been here to see her.'

Harry reached out a finger to brush the baby's cheek. 'Welcome to the world, Mary-Anne,' he said. 'And I think we can all be thankful that you've clearly taken after your mum rather than your dad in the looks department.'

'Do you want to hold her?' Matt asked.

Harry shook his head.

'No, I'm good, thank you,' he said. 'Not one for babies, if I'm honest.'

But even as he protested, Matt held out little Mary and there was nothing Harry could do.

Mary-Anne lay in his arms, her wide eyes staring up at him from her soft, fresh face.

'There you go,' Matt said. 'You're a natural.'

'Am I now?' Harry said, feeling hot, like holding the baby was a trigger to his internal heating system.

'We've got something for you,' Grace said, and held out a small basket for Joan. 'Just some nice stuff for yourself, really, for when you feel like you can handle a relaxing bath or shower, plus some hand and face creams and other things. Thought you might appreciate it.'

'And chocolate,' Harry added.

'Nothing for me, then?' Matt asked.

Harry handed the baby back to the DS.

'Yes,' he said. 'These.'

He reached over to a small table at the side of the sofa and picked up two metal tubes about six inches in length and at least an inch thick.

'Cigars,' Harry grinned. 'Grabbed these from a little shop in Bradford-on-Avon, along with the chocolate. Thought we could share them at some point, once things have settled down for you.'

Matt laughed and held up the cigars.

'I look forward to throwing up with you, then,' he said.

Later that day, having taken a walk around Hawes, Harry was alone on the footpath over to Gayle. Grace had headed off to get a few things in for the evening and he'd taken the opportunity to just be on his own for a while, to let his mind wander.

Down by the river, Harry breathed in the Dales, the air rich and bright. There was a message on his phone that he had to answer and he'd been trying to find the best way to say what he wanted to. But that wasn't easy, because as soon as he said it, then that would be it, wouldn't it? And this decision? Well, it would change everything.

With a deep breath, Harry pulled out his phone and flicked through to his messages. He saw two waiting for him, one from Firbank, another from Kett. In the fields opposite, sheep grazed in the sun, their bleats soft as they called to each other. Behind them, Wether Fell stood proud against a pastel-blue sky. A bird call mewed from above and Harry looked up to see two birds of prey circling in the thermals. He heard the gentle thrum of a tractor somewhere out in the fields.

Harry opened the message to Firbank and with a smile on his face, he started to type.

Thrilled by One Bad Turn? Then hold on tight for Blood Trail, the next nail-biting Harry Grimm crime thriller!

JOIN THE VIP CLUB!

WANT to find out where it all began, and how Harry decided to join the police? <u>Sign up to my newsletter today</u> to get your exclusive copy of the short origin story, 'Homecoming', and to join the DCI Harry Grimm VIP Club. You'll receive regular updates on the series, plus VIP access to a photo gallery of locations from the books, and the chance to win amazing free stuff in some fantastic competitions.

You can also connect with other fans of DCI Grimm and his team by joining The Official DCI Harry Grimm Reader Group on Facebook.

Enjoyed this book? Then please tell others!

The best thing about reviews is they help people like you: other readers. So, if you can spare a few seconds and leave a review, that would be fantastic. I love hearing what readers think about my books, so you can also email me the link to your review at dave@davidjgatward.com.

AUTHOR'S NOTE

I take my research seriously, having had a go at everything from skydiving to full-contact fighting in the quest to get the story right. When it came to the drugs side of things in *One Bad Turn*, I read *Crack House*, by Detective Sergeant Harry Keeble, and freelance investigative journalist, author and ghost-writer, Kris Hollington. This true story, of the man – Harry Keeble – who took on London's crack gangs and won, is eye-opening to say the least. I cannot recommend it enough and any mistakes you read in this tale are my own.

I would like to take this opportunity to thank Keeble and his team for the work they did, and continue to do, as police officers. When we hear so much negative press about the police, to read something like *Crack House* really does show you how there are still good people out there, working crazy hours, doing things most of us would run from, and bringing criminals to justice. We all owe them more than we will ever know. Thank you.

ABOUT DAVID J. GATWARD

David had his first book published when he was 18 and has written extensively for children and young adults. *One Bad Turn* is his ninth crime novel.

Visit David's website to find out more about him and the DCI Harry Grimm books.

facebook.com/davidjgatwardauthor

ALSO BY DAVID J. GATWARD

THE DCI HARRY GRIMM SERIES

Welcome to Yorkshire. Where the beer is warm, the scenery
beautiful, and the locals have murder on their minds.